The Prince's Boy

by
Cecilia Tan

To Stacie —
Thanks for coming
on this quest with
me!
Cecilia

MISTI-CON
'17

Circlet Press, Inc.
Cambridge MA

The Prince's Boy
Copyright © 2011 by Cecilia Tan

Cover illustration by Scarlet B.

Published by Clasp Editions, the erotic romance imprint of
Circlet Press
39 Hurlbut Street
Cambridge, MA 02138

All Rights Reserved.

ISBN 978-1-61390-009-3

First Paperback Edition April 2011

Originally published as a web serial beginning on July 29, 2009 at www.cir-clet.com.

Introduction

I must give you a warning, dear reader, before you begin. No, not the warning about the intensity of the bondage and sadomasochism scenes herein, not about the dubious consent, eroticized violence, or situations of sexual jeopardy in these pages (though they are assuredly there). I must warn you that what you are about to read is a serial.

A serial? "How is that different from a novel?" you might well ask. It *looks* like a novel. It has chapters. It has an overarching fantasy plot that pits good versus evil. It is even a Romance with a capital R. Why isn't it a novel?

Well, common wisdom says a novel wouldn't have a sex scene in every chapter. That would be Too Much Sex for the reader, who would fall into fatigue—or worse, boredom. Sex should not be tedious! But *The Prince's Boy* was not written as a novel, with the sexy bits paced out here and there, but as a serial intended to be read one chapter per week. The serial began running on the Circlet Press website in July 2009 and wraps up in June 2011. My goal was to deliver a delicious meal each week to the hungry reader who had waited so patiently for it. I tried to get a sex scene into each chapter, or at the very least a torture or fight scene (and indeed, these all these types of scenes somewhat blur together in this book).

Common wisdom says that trying to barrel headlong through such a work would be as unpleasant as overeating. Common wisdom, however, may not take into account readers who have built up their constitutions reading fan fiction serials and WIPs. I know I am not the only person who has stayed up all night reading a fanfic serial, chapter after chapter after chapter... and I know from comments on *The Prince's Boy* on circlet.com that many readers did just that with the online version.

So, if you have the legs for it, feel free to run the marathon that is *The Prince's Boy!* The rest of you, please pace yourselves for maximum enjoyment of the pleasures herein.

Cecilia Tan
Cambridge, MA

One: Kenet

I have a memory that I know I cannot have. And yet it persists in my mind as clearly as any other memory. I remember her screaming. I remember my father holding her in his arms as she died. I remember him crying. You must understand, my father never cries. I cannot imagine him doing it. So it must be a memory, since I would never be able to conjure up such an image on my own. I remember them covering her face with a cloth, and bearing the body away. And then I remember my father collapsing into someone else's arms. A soldier dressed all in black.

Jorin says it can't be a memory, because no one can remember when they were born. No one can remember that moment or the minutes afterward. But I remember my mother dying while bearing me.

So I'm either deluded, or different.

Jorin would say I'm both.

My next earliest memory is of Jorin himself. We were probably three or four years old at the time? Far enough back it's more likely closer to three. I could walk and talk and always understood more of what adults were saying to me than they seemed to think I gleaned. And I had gotten the knack of knowing when they were trying not to tell me something.

Which was how I knew when we went to the orphanage we were going there so I could pick out a boy of my very own. Oh, I know now how it was supposed to happen. I was supposed to play and socialize and eat with the children until my father or someone else decided on the child who would be my ladra'an and I was supposed to be none the wiser. But someone had let it slip, spoken of it where I could overhear, or maybe a maid even told me—that part I don't remember. I do remember swaggering out into the play yard where a couple dozen boys were running about on the hard-packed dirt. I didn't like how they were kicking up so much dust. I hadn't been allowed near many other children before, and they seemed brutish and noisy. One of these was supposed to be mine?

"That one," I said, though my handlers as usual were not paying attention to anything I said. I pointed to a dark-eyed, dark-haired boy, sitting by himself in the shadow of the stone building that was the orphanage, hugging his own knees.

I ran over to him and hugged him myself. "This one."

Much hullaballoo ensued, in which they tried to detach me from him, several adults trying to physically pry us apart and telling me no-no-no, it wasn't done like that. To them I shouted, "Mine!" and to him I whispered, "If you hang onto me, you'll come to live in the castle with me."

He didn't answer, but clung to me as tightly as I did to him.

I held onto him all the way home in the carriage, as if he were a doll. They tried to separate us again at the castle, telling me he had to be cleaned up, but I suspected that if I let go then, I'd never see him again. I wasn't stupid. I knew a guard wouldn't be who would take him for a bath! Only a maid would do that. I pointed out I was just as dirty, now, too. My father finally relented when someone pointed out in a wry voice that if we were going to live inseparably, as a prince and ladra'an should, then they may as well leave us be and let the maids scrub us both.

I held his hand in the bath, because he was scared of everything. I could tell. He hadn't said anything yet, but it was obvious that everything was strange and new to him. "It's all right," I kept telling him. "I'm a prince and I'll protect you."

They cleaned us up and presented us that night at banquet. I was just about falling asleep in a throne so large I could actually curl up sideways in it to sleep, when my father called for my attention. And for Jorin's.

I hadn't actually heard his name yet until my father bade him stand on his chair and speak it. Perhaps I thought I was going to name him, like a pet. That's highly likely, though I'm not certain what was going through my child mind.

Now my father spoke to me in a stern voice. "You need to learn that you cannot just seize things you want, nor can you bite your guard because you disagree with him, nor is it seemly to shout at anyone, especially me, in public. That is three infractions."

I didn't know the word "infractions," but it sounded dire and dangerous. A moment later a guard had seized Jorin, flipping him over one knee and pulling down his breeches where everyone in the room could see. I was horrified. What were they going to do?

"It's also not seemly to strike the royal flesh," my father said, coming to stand beside us, a stick in his hand. "So instead of striking you, Kenet, I will administer the punishment to your ladra'an."

"No!" I was on the verge of tears.

He raised the stick and I shrank back, despite what he'd just said about not hitting me. "Do not make it worse. Three infractions." And he proceeded to whip Jorin three times. Jorin bit his lip and made a horrible face, but he made no sound.

It was me who cried. I seized him the second the guard let him down, bawling my eyes out, terrified that now he'd hate me. I swore I'd never let them do that to him again. I refused to let go again, and Bear had to carry us both together to bed, and stuck us in it still in our clothes, and I cried until I fell asleep in Jorin's arms. He was the one who took the punishment, not me, so why was I the one who was crying?

I suppose maybe that's why having a ladra'an persists as a tradition. I learned my lesson, didn't I?

And I suppose now you know everything you need to know about me and Jorin.

Two: Kenet

It took me a long time to realize that being whipped in front of all assembled on his first day in the castle was no less a cruelty than Jorin expected. He hadn't known exactly that his fate was to be my whipping boy, but he hadn't expected life to be kind. The orphanage was not a kind place. The castle, at least, would be a step up. He told me this later, much later. Back then, he didn't tell me anything, because he hardly ever spoke.

That did not bother me in the slightest as apparently I talked enough for us both. I have only the vaguest memory of that time. He slept in my bed with me and went everywhere with me, except for the meetings with my father, twice a week, the only times my father and I were ever alone, unattended.

Jorin started to speak more than just the occasional word to me after we began formal schooling. Reading, writing, mathematics, ancient tongues, and fencing. Until then I think most of the household believed him mute. But he had to speak when our tutor asked him for answers. He still almost never spoke to anyone but me. And why should he? What did he have to say to guards or maids or attendants?

We spoke the most at night. In whispers.

Some things have not changed, now that we are of age.

Jorin's breath was sweet from chewing on sechal bark, and warm against my neck as he spoke. "Sergetten says he won't teach me anymore," he said.

"That's ridiculous." I was holding him close, our limbs entangled as usual. After banquet we'd sat on the stone edge of the balcony, just the two of us, chewing sechal and watching the stars fall until we'd gotten cold. And then we'd gotten in bed like we have done for more years than I can count, and wrapped around each other until sometimes I couldn't tell which hand was mine. "He can't teach me without teaching you."

"I'm not so sure about that. He said I'm to start training with the heavy weapons, broadsword and axe. I'll do that while you study political theory or something else that I won't need to know." His breath was warm and his lips brushed against my skin as he spoke.

Something sparked in my belly. "Jorin..."

He took his name as a cue to move subtly against me, lips now tracing a vein in my neck, no longer making a pretense of speaking. My blood surged and I knew he felt the hardness growing against his thigh. Was he hard, too? I couldn't quite tell as we were, and I shifted in his arms. He rolled easily under me and I slid my cock, swathed in silk pajamas, against his. Yes, just as hard as I was. I shed my silk and pulled his down and then rubbed against him bare skin to bare skin, my back chilled by the night air but I didn't care. Jorin was heat beneath me and I rutted against him for a while, until he pushed me to my side, slicked his hand with spit, and took both of our lengths in his grip.

I have no idea why his spit was always so much slicker than mine. Royal blood was supposed to be thicker than others', wasn't it? Was thin spit the trade-off? Or did he just have a knack I didn't? I was grateful, though, as Jorin stroked us.

"Faster," I rasped.

"No," he said, a gleam in his eye. "You'll spill too soon."

"But..."

"Hush and let me."

I fell silent in acquiescence. He kept his strokes long and even, his thumb drawing a circle around the slick tips at the top of each stroke, mixing our dew together and keeping his grip slippery. Every now and then he would lick his palm to make sure, but his touch never felt rough or dry to me. "Jorin...!" I whispered with some urgency.

"Yes, Kenet, my prince?"

"I want... I want to come..."

"You will. Have I ever left you unfinished?"

"Well, no..."

"Seriously, Kenet, is it that you like to beg? Or do you actually think if you don't, I might forget to finish you off?"

"You can't talk to me that way!" I hissed. "I'm the Prince of Maldevar!" But it was a jest, and we both knew it, because in the night, in our bed, he whispered that sort of thing to me all the time.

"Yes, my prince," he said, with infinite patience. "Of course, my prince." He had added a twist to his stroke that robbed me of my ability to answer temporarily.

But once I could speak again, I couldn't help myself. "Make me spill Jorin, and then you can finish yourself using my milk to make it slick."

"Tempting," he breathed. "But maybe it should be the other way around. Maybe I should spill all over your cock and then stroke you so hard you nearly go blind when you finish."

"I... that... that would be acceptable, too."

At that he just laughed and slowed his stroke even more.

Three: Kenet

I have nightmares sometimes.

Some of them recur, some of them are unique. Just a few nights ago this was what I dreamed. I had been for a ride with my father, just the two of us, through the woods to the north, several hours riding along the ridges, gone all day... and when I returned to my room I found Jorin.

He had been tied by thick leather cords around his wrists to one post of the bed, stripped naked, and whipped three times across his back. When I rush into the room in the dream, he is unconscious, hanging by his arms, the weight of his body making his hands purple and swollen, the welts also purple and raised. I run my fingers down them as if I could read somehow there who had done this and why. It's clear to me Jorin struggled to get free, leaving useless tooth marks in the leather, and after falling unconscious pissed himself.

And yet he is not dead. Not yet. I hurry to cut him down, and he falls into my arms, his weight bearing me down with him to the floor. His eyes flutter open as I brush his hair back from his forehead.

"Who did this to you?" I demand.

And he answers, "You did."

Four: Kenet

I arrived for my audience with my father just after lunch, taking the Snake Ladder from my chambers to his instead of walking through the whole castle as I properly should have done. But I was nearly late, and though I am full grown by every measure, when I am hoping to cheer him up sometimes cannot help but be the playful boy I was. So I hopped and hurried down the clandestine stairs and narrow passages that took me to him, pausing just behind the tapestry that hid the final doorway.

I could hear raised voices.

Sergetten's first. "When will you get it through your thick skull that Night Magic is no more dangerous than Daylight?"

"You are the one always telling me to heed the danger of the Frangi Night Mages!" my father roared back.

"The Mages, yes, but not the power itself! If anything you should be giving me leave to learn more, to do more, so that if they should attack, we can be better protected! We should not rely on Lord Seroi alone. This won't be like the last time I brought a boy to the castle—"

"No!" I heard the sound of something falling and breaking, and the pain in my father's voice. "Sergetten..."

Silence for a few moments. Then I had to strain to hear Sergetten's quiet answer. "Very well. I shall not sully myself any more than you deem necessary, my king." I could easily imagine the bitterness on his face. Sergetten and bitterness went together like salt and fish.

I heard another crash of something breaking. Probably my father heaving a piece of crockery after him as he took his leave, and hitting the stone archway.

I could not go into the room now. It would be far too obvious

I had eavesdropped on matters I was supposed to know nothing of. I crept back up the stairs and made my way down in proper fashion, although this made me late, but I knew, too, it would give the servants time to clean up the mess.

I presented myself at his front parlor, then, and was shown into the study, where he was sitting with his back to me, hunched near to the hearth, a mug of something in his hand.

"Here I am, father," I said, trying to sound chipper and ignorant.

He turned and his eyes burned with anger. "You're late."

I drew back in dismay. "I... but..." I could not tell him I'd given him some extra time on purpose, could I? No. "I was reading and lost track of the time," I stammered, instead.

He rang a bell and one of his guards hurried in from the outer chamber, short, crimson cloak swinging from his shoulders. "Bring Jorin to me. Immediately."

My mouth fell open in shock. "You're not serious..."

"You are late and deserve to be punished. My schedule is very pressing, Kenet, and it is time you learned that." He stood and went to pull an instrument of punishment from the wooden chest in the corner.

I had not yet learned to keep my mouth shut, even after all those years. "But it's been years since you..."

I broke off as the sound of a short whip cracked the air. "I know. Not since before you came of age," he said, his voice cold. "But if Jorin is still here in this castle, then by the sky above he will perform his function, or leave."

Jorin himself spoke then and I looked up in surprise he had come that quickly. "Do you mean that, your highness? That if I will no longer accept lashes on the prince's behalf, you'll turn me out?"

But my father was too angry to put up with banter or argument. He seized Jorin by the collar and pushed his face against the wall. "Kenet. Strip him."

I had never seen him so angry over so little, and never before had he asked me to assist in such a way. I dared not protest, though. I hurried to untuck Jorin's shirt, to pull the breeches down to expose the globes of his arse, lines of slightly darker skin than the rest of him showing the evidence of old whippings. My father let go, and Jorin stood still while I removed his vest and shirt, too, neither of us fool enough to do anything but follow every order as literally as we could.

"Hands on the mantelpiece," my father said, his knuckles white where he gripped the handle of the whip.

Jorin was the picture of placid as he did as he was told. I stood back, not wanting to make it worse, but... "How many?" I blurted, unable to completely contain myself.

My father checked the timepiece above the hearth. "It is now twenty minutes beyond when we should have met..."

"But I was only ten minutes late!"

He went on as if I hadn't spoken. "So it shall be twenty strokes."

"Twenty!" I had seen a man die under twenty strokes once, a man accused of spying for the Night Mages. Of course, that had been twenty strokes with the bullwhip, not the mere two feet of leather my father held in his hand now, but the number still struck me as unjustly large and dangerous.

"Hush, Kenet," Jorin said, closing his eyes and bowing his head.

The first stroke came across the back of his thighs, making him buckle and nearly fall. The next tore squarely across his arsecheeks, leaving an instant welt of painful red. The third slashed down his back, where the skin was sparsely crossed with the marks of old thrashings, some whiter, some darker, and he grunted.

He didn't start to cry out until after ten lashes, by which time my own cheeks were wet with tears, but I kept silent. Jorin's knees gave out at fifteen and he received the last five across his back prostrate in front of my father like a supplicant begging for mercy. Maybe he was. I could barely watch, only forcing myself to do so because if I didn't, any stroke I missed would be applied again.

My father let the whip fall after the last stroke and strode from the room, only my voice stopping him at the doorway.

"Why?" I demanded.

"Be on time for our next audience and perhaps that is a lesson you will learn," he growled before he left.

I gathered Jorin up and helped him dress, careful not to stick his shirt to the places on his back where the lash had split the welts into bleeding. Once his breeches were back on, I helped him to our rooms.

Bear said nothing when he saw us, just shook his head, handed me a small jar of some kind of salve, and left us alone.

Five: Jorin

The salve put me to sleep. It has some kind of herb in it that makes me sleep without dreams. But the moment it wears off, I am wide awake.

I woke to the sound of wind rushing outside, to Kenet frantically pushing at the north-facing window to get it shut. Wait, no, the south-facing window. I was disoriented, unaccustomed to waking up in my own bed instead of his.

He managed get the latch closed, and then the sound of his breath was louder in the room than the storm that was coming.

"Kenet." My throat was dry; I could barely speak.

He hurried to me, nearly spilling the water in the pitcher in his haste to pour some into a goblet. I sat up too quickly, trying to snatch the cup from his hand before he could drop it, and felt a welt tear open across my shoulder. I could not hold back the hiss.

Kenet knelt gently on the bed next to me and I sipped slowly, until the tightness in my throat eased. Then I set the goblet aside.

"I'm worried," he said, his face wan and his eyes puffy from crying. I had never been able to convince him not to cry for me. Not after all these years.

"I'm afraid they're going to take you away from me," he said then.

"Ah." I let my eyes fall closed. When the king had ceased beating me a year or two earlier, I had wondered then why I was allowed to remain at Kenet's side, if he had outgrown the need for a whipping boy. "Why now? If anything I'm finally old enough to take what your father really wants to dish out." The joke fell flat even in my own ears, though. The beating I'd just received was by far the most brutal in my memory. No, wait. I reminded myself that the most recent always seemed like the worst. No reason to...

Kenet gasped as he saw the fresh blood seeping. All right. Perhaps lying to myself about how bad it was wouldn't help us through this after all. "Will you tell me what you did to make him so angry?" I asked.

"It wasn't even my fault!" he began, but then related to me a tale of wanting to surprise his father, only to overhear a conversation he shouldn't have. Surprise his father. Kenet may be a man in reckoned years, but he is a child in so many ways. This, I assumed, was why they kept treating him like one, continuing his schooling at a time when his ancestors would have been normally bound into marriage pacts and expected to produce heirs, and allowing him to keep me. Had he been a second or a third son he might have already been rising through the ranks of the army.

But he was the sole prince, the sole heir, and had never been treated by his father or his retainers like anything but a precious treasure. Even Seroi, the Lord High Mage, would make condescending bows to Kenet when he was a boy and then give him a wide berth.

I was afraid Kenet was right. I was only still here by the indulgence that the prince was still a child at heart somehow.

I took his hand. "Your father can beat me bloody every day, if it means I can stay with you," I said.

"No!" He squeezed my fingers hard enough to hurt. "I mean, no, I won't let him, not no, I don't want... I can't live without you, Jorin. They... they can't..."

"Shhh." I pulled him closer, both of us ignoring the blood. The seepage was slowing down anyway. I pulled Kenet's head into my lap and stroked his hair, shining golden like the treasure he was in the light of a single lamp. "You know that someday they are going to marry you off..."

He clucked his tongue. "To some ice princess for political reasons, who will want to keep her own chambers and no doubt a secret lover on the side."

I fell silent. Sometimes I wondered if Kenet was even really aware of how lax the rules around us had been. Every night I made sure to muss my bedclothes, so that the maids would not gossip about how the two of us always shared a bed. Even if it had been entirely innocent—which it was when we were children and which it most certainly was not now—the rumors alone could have been enough to bring ruin on us. Or on me, at least.

Every night I closed the door behind us, and set a block of wood against it such that if anyone unlocked the door and pushed it open, I would have the warning of the sound of the block hitting the stone. I could be halfway across the room before the intruder could make it from the entryway to our inner archway. Maids no longer attended us anyway, now that we were older. Servants cleaned and set things to rights while we were gone each day, but Kenet's guard Bear was the only one who regularly entered the rooms these days while we were in them.

His face lit up suddenly. "That's why they've insisted you increase your weapons training. When Bear gets too old and slow, you're going to be my new guard. You see, you'll always be with me, Jorin." He reached up into my hair, scooping it behind my ear. "You're mine. I won't let them take you away from me."

I bent to kiss him then, ignoring the burning in my back where I stressed the flesh by doing so. Neither blood nor pain had ever kept me from my prince before, and would not this night either.

Six: Kenet

"What do you mean, Sergetten isn't here?" That my father's advisor and my tutor should not be present when expected stunned me.

"I mean," said the scholar who kept the archives in order, "I have not seen him yet today, my prince. Normally he arrives long before you."

"You're sure he's not in there somewhere?" I waved a vague hand at the entrance to the archives themselves. I rarely ventured there myself and the keepers preferred it that way, usually only allowing Sergetten and some other high ranking scholars to enter the repository. Others had to petition to have materials brought to them and it was in the reading room where they would wait that Sergetten and I usually had lessons.

"No, my prince, he is definitely not here. As I said." The man was short and his hair was shot through with gray. Velred was his name, and he had been head archivist since before I was born. "He left no instructions and sent no messages."

"And can you verify that I am on time?" I pondered how long I should wait, if at all.

"Yes, my lord, you are most definitely on time. And this is most definitely unusual for him to be absent." He nodded sagely. "If he arrives, where shall I tell him to seek you out?"

Well, that decided it. "The afternoon's too nice to waste indoors anyway," I said. The last of winter had left the mountains and spring was in full bloom. "I shall be in the garden, or perhaps the terrace. Yes, the terrace. I may as well read the histories out there."

Velred cringed a bit, probably at the thought of me taking one of my ancestor's diaries out of doors, but the books were mine in truth, not his. And it is not as if I would have sat out in the rain reading.

So I went out to the terrace, but I did not get much reading done. Not when I heard the clang of metal on metal from the terrace level below me. I looked over the hedge-topped wall to see Jorin on his back, his sword on the ground next to him, and Bear looking down at him and laughing.

"That was hardly fair!" Jorin said, taking the proffered hand and getting back to his feet, then picking up the sword again.

"Fair. They won't fight fair if they're trying to kill you, cub." Bear took a step back and raised his sword in an offensive stance.

Bear was only a name, of course. He was a man, but a large one, with a dark-brown beard. They say I am the one who first called him Bear when I was too small to remember.

Jorin raised his weapon and I held my breath. Jorin had been learning arms for two years now, but I had never seen him practice. We used to have fencing practice against each other when we were younger, but no longer. Jorin seemed impossibly small compared to Bear, half his size or less, and even his sword was smaller. Would he end up on the ground again?

But then there was a flurry of movement, sword clashing against sword, and Jorin was suddenly behind Bear, who turned too slowly, and received a slap on the back of the shoulder with the flat of Jorin's blade.

I suppressed the urge to applaud. They had no idea I was watching.

I had no idea Jorin could move like that. And with crusted welts still on his back from yesterday, too. I wondered if he would let me salve them again tonight or if he would insist on shrugging me off. He and Bear were laughing about something now, and taking up their positions again.

"It is almost like a dance, isn't it?" said a voice behind me.

I turned to see not Sergetten but the Lord High Mage himself, Seroi. I gave him a nod of my head as befitted his rank, though I wasn't compelled to use his honorific. "Yes, rather," I agreed, returning my gaze to the combatants below, trying to pretend I wasn't unnerved by Seroi's presence.

I had not spent much time with him in my life, mostly seeing him at banquet dinners and in the occasional council session with my father. There was one diplomatic trip to the northern border we took, my father's retinue and I, that he accompanied a few years ago. The plain truth was that there were times when I felt he could see straight down into my soul. He knew depths of magic that even my father and Sergetten could never hope to fathom and I always wondered what truth he saw when he looked at me.

There was one night in particular when our encampment and that of a traveling band of tinkers shared a fire pit. Jorin and I and some of the tinker lads had played a game, tossing a braided ring of willow back and forth with sticks, until the fire had burned low. I had left Jorin talking and joking with the lads while I stole off to the creek to rinse myself.

I still remember the moon that night, because of how brightly it burned, but also because as I stood in the stream, washing myself, I felt very strongly that someone was watching me. It was as if the moon itself were a great eye taking in the sight of my naked flesh. I dressed hurriedly once I got out of the water, trying to shake the feeling. It was only after I returned to the camp, and saw Seroi returning shortly after, that I began to suspect perhaps he had been the one watching me.

But he had never approached me, never touched me, never did anything that could be considered wrong. In fact, we had barely exchanged enough conversations to count on one hand, so I could hardly consider him much of a threat to me.

"I understand your tutor has abandoned you, at least for the time being," he said, dragging my attention back to him from the swordplay below. He was strange to look at, as if his face were too smooth sometimes, his hair too perfect, slick and black. The only hint of his age was a few silver streaks in among the black. In the sunlight the effect that he was not quite real was heightened.

"Yes," I said, not wanting to speak ill of Sergetten—not to this man, anyway.

His smile showed even, white teeth. "Well. Perhaps it's time I took an interest in your education, my prince?"

Seven: Jorin

I raised my sword again and charged. A moment later I was on my face in the grass, the rich scent of earth in my nose, just a vague impression of the touch of a heavy hand on my shoulder still in my skin. I pushed myself to my knees.

"Again, cub."

"Bear, I've had enough."

"Again. The only way you'll grow into that sword is if I keep making you lift it." He laughed. Making comments about how I needed more meat on my bones was a usual tack for him.

I got to my feet. The sword was heavier than the one I had been using the past few weeks and my shoulders and arms ached. I was tired and sweat was stinging my eyes. "I was better with the smaller sword," I pointed out.

"Soon you'll be just as good with this one," Bear said with an indulgent smile. "Once you put some meat on your bones."

I attacked him, but the sword made me too slow again, and took too much effort to wield. He had me on my back before I could even bring it all the way around and it fell with a heavy thud a moment after I did. I groaned. "You're just angry that with the lighter one I could beat you all the time," I said, looking up at the clouds with a grin.

Bear's bearded face and his own toothy grin came into view as he looked down on me. "Ah, you've figured me out. But not how to beat me with the heavy sword."

I growled in answer, launching myself at him unarmed, and tumbling him over. I knew I couldn't hope to beat him in a wrestling match, but I held my own atop him for longer than you might think. Eventually I lay pinned under him, both of us panting.

He barked out another laugh. "Now here's a heavy sword." He

smacked the erection that had blossomed in my breeches with the flat of his hand, making me see stars. He got to his feet and waited until I had, too, before he spoke more seriously, looking left and right before he went on in a low voice. "Now I know you aren't the least bit thinking of bedding me, cub. A man your age needs to take care of that kind of thing, regular and often."

I was probably blushing furiously as I tried to stammer something, anything, in my defense.

"Now, now, don't take this hard. I know our prince dotes on you, can't bear to be parted from you. But I'd advise you to spend some nights with the milkmaids, cub." He reached out his hand to help me up.

"But Kenet won't..."

Bear pulled me closer with my hand in his. "Listen to me. You don't want people thinking you and he are doing anything... funny, you know?"

I made a scandalized face, opening my mouth to protest.

"Hush, cub," he said, now his voice not above a whisper. "I've watched you two since you were both small. I don't know exactly what you do in his bedchamber, but above all right now you need to act as if you don't. I've no idea why the king's left you together for so long, but if you want to stay, you'd best give him no reason to suspect you've become his son's bed toy."

Or the other way around. I nodded, trying to blank my face of all emotion, but his last words had chilled me. Maybe Bear didn't know what went on in our rooms at night, but the fact was that if anyone was anyone's bed toy, it was Kenet who was mine.

This thought did nothing to help my erection subside. I wanted his lithe, nimble fingers playing up and down my shaft like a flute. I wanted to lie beside him and pull at each other to see who would spill first. Hm, no, I wanted to make it a contest to see who could last longest, and name some penalty for the loser.

But that would have to wait until tonight, until after banquet, wouldn't it? "Well, here's your proof there's nothing 'funny' going on between us because if there was, I wouldn't be so desperate, would I?" That got an appreciative chuckle out of him. "Hm. I can't go down to the baths like this."

"Not unless there's a maid sweet on you who would eat that ripe fruit," Bear said with another laugh.

Eat? "Perhaps you should be teaching me to flirt instead of weapons," I said, even as my mind went quite suddenly to an image so strong it made my cock ache with each beat of my heart. Kenet, one hand cupping my balls like ripe plums, his mouth devouring my cock. Was it clean? Would his teeth cut me? I didn't know; we'd never used our mouths for anything but kissing. I knew how his mouth felt to my lips and tongue, though, and could imagine the soft wetness against the hard, heated flesh that needed soothing.

I must have blushed more suddenly.

"Have you never had a maid taste your plums?"

I shook my head.

"Cub. I love the prince with all my heart. But you need to spend some time for yourself." He took up my sword and his own, slinging both across his back with straps and then leading the way back through the gardens toward the castle entrance. "He's at the age when he ought to be experimenting some, too. As long as there's no bastards, I don't see why..." He broke off suddenly as we heard a movement in a bush off to one side. He went to its left, I went to the right...

But there was no enemy of Maldevar hiding there. A frit burst out in a flurry of wings, cheeping in alarm as it took to the sky. That was the end of the conversation, though. Even the thought of the beasts of the kingdom overhearing us talking about sex was enough to make me button my lip.

"Not the baths," Bear said, his voice low and serious, then. He nudged me on the shoulder and held up a finger tinged with blood where I had split a welt open again. I followed him silently knowing that more of the salve awaited me, as well as a long nap.

Eight: Kenet

I followed Seroi into a tower I had not been in before, in a section of the castle I had only passed through briefly a few times in all the years I'd lived there. For some reason I decided this time would not be when I would gawk at the tapestries on the corridor walls, and instead I focused on the spot in the center of Seroi's back, trying to act like I had walked these stones a thousand times. Why, I do not know, since surely he knew full well I did not frequent this area.

Was this where he lived? I had no idea. My father had always said very little about the Lord High Mage. I assumed he lived somewhere in the sprawl of walls and towers that was the castle, but had never thought about exactly where. I'd truly never given Seroi too much thought at all.

Now the man was leading me up a set of spiral stairs, barely lit by the slits of windows, and it seemed almost as if we were descending into darkness instead of ascending into a tower, and he seemed the most solid thing in my reality.

No, it wasn't just the dimness, the air was heavy with a cloying mist and the scent of something heady and exotic. I blinked, but a moment later, a door opened above us, and he led me through. It closed behind us with a heavy thump, the air suddenly clear and bright again. I coughed.

"Forgive the guardian incense, my prince, but it is necessary to ensure that only those who are purified enter this place." He gestured around him at a sparse, round room, the walls bare stone, the center of the floor scored with symbols, a small table and two chairs facing each other off to one side. He pulled out one of the chairs for me and I sat. He sat across from me.

His eyes were disconcerting if only because very few in the

kingdom had either the rank or the familiarity with me to look
me straight in the eye as he did, and other than my own father, no
one had ever given me such a measuring, appraising look. Not
even Sergetten at his most schoolmasterish. I felt myself swallow.

"Your father and I agreed after your birth," he began, "that we
needed to take certain measures to ensure your..."

I hung on his pause, trying to guess what word he was searching for. My future? My education?

He licked his lips. "Purity," he finally said, his gaze only sharp-
ening.

"Purity?" I asked, uncomprehending.

"I assure you, my prince, the full explanation is in the offing,
if you will be patient. With your mother gone and no hope of sib-
lings for you, we took measures to protect the integrity of your
bloodline and your seed." He folded his hands on the table's top,
while I sat stock still, trying to pretend this was not a deeply mortifying topic to me. "A male of your age and status would normally
have... pursued certain activities and desires that you have not. Neither your father nor I will ask your forgiveness in this matter of
course, should you feel cheated of pleasures that would have been
your due, but as sole heir you are expected to make certain
sacrifices."

"But I have no interest in women," I blurted out.

"Yes, I know." He took a deep breath and let it out slowly, as if
preparing himself for a difficult fight, though his expression remained placid. "Your suppressed libido is our doing and has left
you innocent of sexual matters that a male of your age and status
would normally have experienced by now. It falls to me to rectify
the situation. Once you are betrothed you will be expected to perform not only adequately, but with royal ability... well, to put it
baldly, you must be trained."

I could not hide my recoil. "Trained?"

One corner of his mouth twitched as if he were hiding a
broader smile. "Forgive my choice of words, my prince. Rather
than seek your own experience in this matter, you shall be guided
through the process with care. Please understand, this is not an

issue of morality or scandal, but of the inherent potency in your blood that we cannot afford to squander. If your firstborn were to be a bastard—or worse, killed by the mother, perhaps leaving you unaware—it would spell disaster for you and your bloodline, which carries a magical heritage."

I hoped my face looked suitably serious and not bewildered, but my apprehension was rising. "I understand. Or perhaps you will enlighten me if I don't. You and father have been suppressing my... natural desire for sex?"

"Yes," he said, an indulgent smile breaking onto his face. "Magically. Since your birth. Naturally, we cannot let the restrictions go all at once, for that would be both traumatic and emotionally disturbing for you. At the same time, my prince, there are magical legacies you are heir to that it is time you learned of, legacies which you cannot grasp until after you have reached a certain level of... sexual maturity and experience. I apologize again for the scrutiny that your private life must bear. Most men..."

"I am not most men," I said suddenly, irked by the entire conversation, yet intrigued to know that there would be some magical training in my future.

"Of course, of course," he said, waving his hands in conciliatory motions. "It is merely that I know some of what I will suggest will be distasteful to you at first, given that your desires are still suppressed."

"I assure you I will tolerate no questioning of my manhood," I replied, sounding entirely like my father in my ears as I got to my feet and planted my fists on the table. "Whatever you ask of me, I will perform. I assure you of that."

He looked up at me, unperturbed by my outburst. I suppose I should not have been surprised by this, given that he surely withstood my father's own tirades on a regular basis? What was I but a kitten trying out its claws to him, when he was used to a lion? "Excellent," he said. "Your enthusiasm will go a long way toward cracking the shells that bind you. But please, sit, and let me give you a thorough explanation. It would not do for us to have a misunderstanding at this juncture."

I felt sullen now, and sat, at a loss for what else to do other than obey.

"First, only three of us know of the spells on you. You now, your father, and I. It must remain that way, of course." Seroi opened the palm of his hand and I stared as a squat round candle flew from a small chest near the wall into his grip. He lit it with a snap of his fingers and set it on the table between us. "Second, lifting the spells will require you and I to perform some acts that would, to your normal citizen, seem morally questionable or at the very least quite odd. I will require your promise that you shall never speak of the things we do here to anyone, ever. Not even to your father or later to your wife."

"Why would I..."

"Your promise," he demanded, eyes glittering with the pin-point lights of the candle in his eyes. "You may decide your own reputation is your own business, but I have my own status to think of, my prince. A loose word of this nature could be disastrous to Trest's reputation among her enemies."

Indeed. I knew that Seroi's strength as a mage was one reason few weaker enemies of ours dared to attack. If they thought him weakened or distracted, even if it were not true, could only spell trouble for us. "I promise I shall never speak of the things we do here to anyone, ever," I said, using his words to be sure I was getting it right. The candle between us flared bright as I spoke and I felt a tug on my heart, making it skip a beat. My eyes widened.

"Your promises, as a royal male who has come of age, are magically binding," he said with a serene smile. I could feel the heat from the candle. "Now show me your cock."

"I... what?" My heart began to leap wildly in my chest, quite sure of what he had said even if my ears weren't.

"Stand up," he said. "Open your trousers. And I assure you I am quite serious and that getting a look at you is only the beginning. Please, my prince, these steps are quite necessary."

I pushed back my chair as I stood, but found my hands shaking too much to do as he said. I took a deep breath, trying to calm myself.

"It's all right," he said, voice soothingly low. "I will not be betraying your confidence either, you know. And I think you will enjoy the results of today's lesson, my prince. Even if it does seem exceedingly strange now."

I turned my back to him to undo my trousers and bare myself to the air. My cheeks were hot and the air was cool on my exposed privates, which were shriveled against the gold of my curls.

"Turn around," he said, a simple and direct command.

I obeyed, unable to meet his eyes.

"Very good," he said, his voice suddenly closer than I expected. When had he gotten up from his chair, when had he stepped so close? As his fingers curled around my limp cock, the gray cloth of his robe brushed my tunic.

My cock responded to his hand as quickly as the candle had, soon at full hardness in his grip. He stroked me slowly and I squeezed my eyes shut as I thought about all the nights Jorin had touched me like this. Would Seroi make me spill? He quickened his stroke.

"Have you ever done this to yourself?" he asked, his breath moving my hair as he pressed close.

"Never," I said, which was more or less the truth. I never stroked myself more than once or twice before Jorin, even if he was already asleep (or pretending to be), would take over.

"Have you ever had issue during the night? Wet dreams?"

All pretense of using my title or the word "please" seemed to be gone from his voice, but perhaps that would have been too strange, using formal titles while his hand was on my cock? I decided to hedge my bets. "Yes. Not often, though. A few times."

"Ah, a shame this will not be your first issue, then," he said, hand moving more quickly now on my shaft. "Still, I shall bottle it to use on the binding spells."

"Would the first have been more potent?" My breath caught as he dragged a sharp fingernail slowly across the head of my cock, the sensation not one I would have guessed would be pleasurable, yet it made my cock throb in his hand like an urgent heart beating.

"Something like that," he said. "One lesson at a time. Tell me,

Kenet, what did you dream of when you would soil your bedsheets?"

"I..." What was the answer he sought? I was afraid to be caught in a lie and have my whole deception unravel. He thought my flesh innocent of a sexual touch, even from my own hand. I could not betray Jorin to him. "I have no memory of those dreams," I said.

"None? No dreams of a fair face or the scent of perfume?"

"None, my lord." I was drawing close and speaking was a struggle.

"In a few moments you will experience paroxysm," he said gently. "Do not be alarmed by the way your body may react. I will guide you through. Concentrate on the feeling of my hand on your flesh and the sound of my voice. Close your eyes, Kenet."

"Y-yes, m-my lord." I was barely aware of my hands clutching at his robes, of standing in the bare stone room. I felt indeed like I should have come already, but his hand and rhythm were unfamiliar, so different from Jorin's. Jorin would only ever keep me on edge like this to sweeten the release when it came. He would do it by lightening his stroke when I begged for harder, slowing it just when my hips were urging him to go faster.

I do not know what force was holding me back. I could barely breathe. Seroi's hand moved in a blur between our bodies, then suddenly stopped, gripping me tight but giving no more, and I cried out in plain dismay.

"Now, Kenet, come now," he commanded, voice soft in my ear but no less a command. And on the second "now" I felt the sharp point of his thumbnail pierce the tenderest spot, just at the cleft of the head, and I screamed as my traitorous cock released a torrent of white seed, fountaining up from that tiny mouth. I had looked at the moment of pain and saw the brightest crimson thread of blood swirl in the white, and then my vision went black.

Nine: Kenet

When I came to, I was in my own bed. The horns were blowing, heralding the return of the hunters from the day's hunt. Banquet was still a few hours away then. I sat up slowly. I was clothed in my silk sleeping clothes and I had to wonder if Seroi had dressed me, or if a maid had, or if Bear...?

Seroi. He wouldn't have handed me over to Bear, not and kept his word of silence. He had to have brought me here himself. I slipped down my pants and inspected my cock for a wound, but I found nothing. Had I imagined that prick, the drop of blood? I pulled back my foreskin, stroking myself gently to better inspect the full length.

"Tsk. Are you that eager to see me, my prince?" Jorin stood in the doorway to the bed chamber, a grin on his face.

I looked up at him and could not help but notice he was in a similar state. "Looks like you're the one who cannot wait."

"Indeed." He tossed his jerkin aside and stripped his tunic off as he approached my bed. He shed the breeches last, just a moment before he crawled atop me and flattened me against my pillows with insistent kisses. "Kenet."

"Jorin." The need for secrecy between us had never been higher or more evident. But now was not the time to articulate that. "Make me spill? Please?" I sounded desperate even to myself.

"What's gotten into you?"

"Please," I begged, unable to explain. "Please please, Jorin." I wanted him to erase the feeling of Seroi's hand on my cock, to take away the sharpness of the memory of coming at Seroi's command. "I need you."

"I know," he whispered, as he held himself above me, rubbing his cock up and down my length. "Hush now. We've plenty of time. I'll make you come just like this. My cock on your cock."

I jerked in surprise but could see the appeal of the idea. What made him think of that? He'd always used his hand to finish me before. "Yes, please. Oh, that would be perfect."

"I know," he said with a chuckle. "Now don't writhe, you need to stay still for this." He pressed my hands against the bed, pinning me in place. "You know I'm not letting you up until I come, too."

That brought a whimper out of my throat.

"Yes, Kenet, once your stomach is slick with your milk, how good it will feel to rub my cock against you then..."

I whimpered again, my entire body taut with need now. Despite his admonition to stay still, I bucked under him. I struggled to free my hands, wanting to grab onto his arsecheeks and pull him against me harder, faster. But he held me fast.

"Please, Jorin," I begged. "I need..."

He was silent as he rutted against me, then again his breath was hot in my ear. "Don't hold back, my prince."

"I'm not!" There was an edge of panic in my voice. What had Seroi done to me? Did I need his magic to reach release now, even though I hadn't needed it before? We both panted and worked, trying to push me over the edge. I found Jorin's eyes boring into mine, searching for something.

"Tell me to spill," I urged him.

"What?"

It was worth a try. "If you're... you're really going to dictate what I do, then do it."

He chuckled and nipped at my neck with his teeth. "You're a twisted little thing, you know that?"

"This is news? Jorin—!"

His voice was hard, a growl I hadn't heard before. "Come then, come before I change my mind and leave you hard all through banquet, come before I punish you for failing me..."

I came. For the second time that afternoon, I jerked in orgasm, this time the pleasure flowing all the way to my toes. And quite suddenly I found Jorin's mouth on mine, kissing me with a hungry desperation. His tongue claimed my mouth, leaving me subdued and gasping as he drove his own cock against my stomach until he threw back his head and shuddered, his own release joining mine on my skin.

He collapsed against me after that and we lay there panting for a long time before he asked, "So what happened to you this afternoon?"

"Tell you later," I said. "Sleep. Nap. Now."

"Yes, my prince."

I was asleep, his weight still halfway atop me, before either of us could say another word.

Ten: Kenet

Jorin was as quiet as always during banquet. His eyes roamed the room as they always did, while I made small talk with the baron seated to my right and his wife, visitors from the western coast. Jorin truly would make a good guard, I thought, regardless what fancy I held in my head.

The baron and his lady got up to join one of the courtly dances and I remained in my seat, wondering what I was going to tell Jorin about my mysterious lesson with Seroi. I was magically bound by the promise not to speak of it. Presumably the tug I felt on my heart each time I tried to imagine the words in my mouth was a warning that if I broke the promise, I would die.

This only made me the more curious as to what exactly I could say. And what story would I tell in its place? Was I allowed to say the Lord High Mage was teaching me in place of Sergetten? Or did even that fact have to remain secret? Sergetten was not at banquet either, some high-born lady sitting in his customary seat at my father's table. Where was he?

I decided the person who would know would be Bear, so I made my way toward him, sitting near the door, his eyes scanning the room, too. "What are you looking for?" I asked, as I placed myself in front of him, my arms crossed.

"Trouble," he said, but he smiled a wide smile. "And how are you this evening, my prince? I would have thought you'd join the dancing." At this he laughed. I never danced, and he knew it. I wondered if the reason I never wanted to was that Seroi's magic had been suppressing my normal desire for girls all this time? The court dances often seemed to me to be an excuse to touch them.

"Do you know where Sergetten has gone?" I took a seat next to him then, the music for the dance getting louder as it sped up.

"He was supposed to tut—"

"Hush about that now, cub." Bear's face still had a smile on it, but I knew the smile wasn't for me, but for anyone who might be watching us talk.

"Trouble?" I asked.

He just nodded and clapped me on the shoulder. "We'll speak more about it later, eh?"

I returned to my seat. Jorin watched the baron and his wife. He leaned over to murmur in my ear. "His doublet parts when they spin... see? Thunder's roll, he looks built like a stallion, doesn't he? I bet you they don't stay through dessert. He wants too much to plough her on one of the castle's fine beds."

I tried to hide a laugh as I saw what Jorin meant. There were certain moves in the dance that inadvertently revealed the size of the sausage he was hiding under the rather tight cloth of his leggings, worn in the coastal style.

"I won't take that bet," I murmured back. Indeed, at the end of the dance the two of them returned to our table only to say their goodbyes to me. They then went to make their goodbyes to my father, and were soon gone.

"Do you know what room they are in?" I asked, as the musicians struck up another dancing tune.

"I heard him say the South Wing," Jorin said. "But I don't know which room."

I tugged his sleeve to mean "let us go," and then bowed to my father. It was one of the games we had played when we were much younger, of course, sneaking out of bed to spy on my father's guests. They rarely did anything of note, sometimes playing cards, or drinking too much brandy. The ambassador from Rykik sang badly. But I found myself with the burning urge to see what these guests would do.

Not every room was suitable for spying on, but we knew the back passages, the niches and spaces, and if we were lucky we might even find them in a room we could see into. Some of the back passages were made for the passing of servants, but the best for spying only I could open the secret doors to.

My heart quickened its pace as we made our way up the dark, winding stairwell from the laundry to see a sliver of light from a room ahead. A warm light from fire and lamp.

Perfect. They were in a bedroom that was nearly round, the bed directly across from the door we now hid behind, two gaps between the heavy wooden boards allowing us both the ability to see.

"Get on your knees, you wanton harlot," he was saying. His legs were bare, but he still wore the doublet and some of his other clothing, unstrung and hanging from his shoulders.

She was laughing as she turned around so that he could undo her dress for her. "Yes, my lord. A baroness in public, your own personal whore in private, is that what you want?"

"Yes, lightning strike me if I lie, yes, you know me too well." He undid something and the dress fell open at the back. I found my mouth fell open as he rubbed the ruddy length of his cock against the white globe of her arsecheek. He bent her over the bed then, and the next thing I saw was his cock disappearing into her body.

Jorin's hand found my breeches with unerring accuracy, and I felt him free my cock while I kept my eyes on the scene in the bedroom. But then I gasped as I felt something that was most definitely not his hand move wetly up my shaft. I looked down to see him looking up at me, his face striped by the lamplight through the cracks, and then he did it again, licking me from root to tip.

I pressed myself against the stone of the passage as he grinned at me, following on his knees and gripping my balls with one hand, not too tightly, just enough that I couldn't pull away—though why would I want to? I wanted him to do it again. I couldn't speak for fear the baron and his wife might hear us, so I asked for more by thrusting my hips up, resulting in a tug on my balls.

But he knew what I meant, and did it again, his eyes finally moving from mine to examine my cock as if it were a particularly delicious treat. And then licking it as if it were.

I wanted to ask what it tasted like, but I couldn't. Now he moved to short licks all around the top and I had to put my hand over my mouth to keep from crying out, it felt so good.

Quite suddenly he was doing up my breeches, but my pang of disappointment was short-lived. He led me back to our room as quickly as we could go, then knocked me flat upon my bed, divesting me of my clothes from the waist down and then kissing his way up my bare thigh until he reached my cock again.

"Jorin..."

"Hah?" He couldn't really speak with his tongue now licking my balls. Why did I interrupt him to make him speak? I don't know.

"What... what made you think of this?"

He shrugged as he worked his way up the shaft again, then tickled the most sensitive spot on my cock with the tip of his tongue. I nearly came from that, bucking suddenly, but he pulled back and looked at me, taking my balls in a loose grip again. "I know how good your tongue feels against mine," he said. "I thought it might feel nice other places, too."

"It does f—" I broke off then, though, as his mouth engulfed my prick, and I spilled quite suddenly. He coughed, caught by surprise, and spat out what was in his mouth, only to look curiously at the softer, later spurts now oozing from the tiny slit at the tip of my cock. He licked at it carefully, probing the slit with the tip of his tongue and causing a few stronger twitches to pump out even more.

"What does it taste like?" I asked.

He laughed and ran a finger through my issue and then pushed it into my mouth. I suckled his finger and found it bitter and salty, and in my mouth I tickled his fingertip with my tongue. I let go of it then, to say "Your turn."

"Yes, my prince." He shed his clothes and lay back, his cock jutting out gracefully from his body and curving back toward his stomach. I wiped myself clean of my own issue with my shirt and then threw it into the laundry before crawling over to him.

I licked a stripe from the root to the tip like he had done and was pleased when his eyes rolled back into his head. His flesh tasted quite salty, just like the palm of his hand, which I had kissed and tasted from time to time, and soon I found the slippery, clear fluid that leaked from him next was as salty as tears.

I carefully fitted my mouth over the head of his prick, but he did not shoot off as I had. I was vaguely disappointed by this, and wondered if I were doing it wrong. I sucked, then, drawing as much of him in as deep as I could, and the groan that came from him was pure pleasure all the way to my core. I felt my own cock begin to stir to life again.

"Kenet," he rasped. "You don't have to..."

I stroked him with my hand while I talked. "You made me spill with your mouth. Don't you want me to do the same?"

He closed his eyes a moment. "I'm not sure it's clean."

I snorted. "You licked mine up eagerly enough."

"Yes, but I'm a dirt-eating bastard child," he said. "You're..."

"A prince, I know. Well, royalty usually get their way, don't they? I want you to spill in my mouth so I can taste it, too." I held his cock and licked at the head like a treat. "All right?"

He laughed. "All right, but only if you can make me come." He folded his arms over his chest.

"Oh, a challenge, is it? Fear not, I am up to the task." I stroked him a few more times, then bent my head to suckle him like a calf at a milk cow's teat. I eventually resorted to suckling on the head while my fingers pumped up and down his shaft the way they normally did. He bellowed as he began to squirt into my mouth.

I coughed, too, and lost much of what I might have taken otherwise, swallowing only a little. It burned on the way down, but something about the muskiness of the scent of it made me want to lick up a little more, and rut against the bed as I did it.

Jorin noticed this after a while, rising out of his post-orgasmic stupor to swat me lightly on the leg. "Are you hard again already?" He reached for me with his hand. "Have you ever wondered what's the most times you could spill in one night?"

"I can't say that I have," I answered, pumping my cock into his fist. Was that because of Seroi's magic? Did other people wonder these things? "You?"

"Someday, we'll find out," he said, running his thumb over the head of my cock, spreading the slickness. "But not tonight. I bet you won't be awake for even a full minute after I make you come the second time."

"Hah! I bet I will."

"Hm, will you? What will you give me if you lose?"

"What do you want?"

He grinned. "I want you to suckle my prick again. This time in the back corridor while I watch the baron and baroness do what they do."

In the end it wouldn't matter that I fell asleep as predicted, though. I hardly needed to be convinced to do what he wanted. We had a new game to play, and I was happy, even if it meant something new to hide from Seroi.

Eleven: Jorin

Once Bear decided I was ready, he took me down to the guard barracks to train. There were several men already leaning on the split wood of the pen, watching two of their fellows striking at each other with sticks. As we drew closer I saw they were not merely sticks, but wooden practice swords. Each man dipped his weapon into a pot of ground powder before they began, and afterward each examined the streaks left on his uniform where various blows and cuts had landed.

One of the men called out to Bear and the two combatants stopped to watch us approach.

"This one is Jorin," Bear said, pushing me forward toward a tall, thin man with a scar under his eye.

"I'm Captain Jaiks," the man said, looking me up and down. I knew who he was, of course, but we'd never before been introduced. The palace guard all knew who I was, as well. "He's a bit skinny for a fighter, isn't he?"

"Bet he can take a blow to the back, though..." said one of the soldiers, provoking laughs from the other men.

"Only one way to shut them up," Bear grumbled in my ear, pulling a wooden sword from the barrel standing nearby and handing it to me. "You won't find him easy meat!" he called to the others, then again just to me: "Don't prove me wrong now, cub."

One of the men vaulted over the fence and the one who remained twirled his sword by the handle. I copied the move to get into the ring and landed on sand. The footing was tricky to get used to, but at least if I fell, I wouldn't break anything. I dipped several inches of the wooden blade into the powder.

He came at me before I could quite set myself but I didn't care. The moment he swung at me I charged inside his guard and hit him in the sternum with my shoulder. He fell back on his rear end in the sand with an indignant grunt. I stepped back to wait for him to gain his feet again.

"No points for knockdowns," Captain Jaiks said, stripping a bit of bark off a sechal cutting and chewing it. "Only for clear blows."

"You're saying I should have struck him while he was down?" I called, which brought out a few chuckles from the others.

"Thunder, yes!" Jaiks cried. "One right on the sword arm would have been perfect. Then take him for questioning or kill him at your leisure. On the battlefield, though, just go for the decapitation and then go after the next milksucking whorefucker you see."

The man charged again and I slipped aside and struck him on the back as he went by. It was the last clear blow for a while, though, as he changed to subtler tactics after that, finally accepting he had to fight me like an equal. We circled and feinted, exchanging blocks and blows, until I finally landed a lucky one that clipped him on the chin. He grunted as he wiped the powder from his face, trying to look tough, but the sneeze that followed somewhat ruined that image.

"Enough, Bolan, let someone fresh have a try," Jaiks said then. My opponent gave me a quick salute and hopped out of the ring.

Another took his place, and we traded back and forth for several minutes. The sun was rising high in the sky, and he shed his uniform coat and shirt, stripping to the waist. I did the same without thinking, then heard the tone of the commentary behind me shift. The evidence of the king's last beating must have still been visible. I hadn't paid it much mind myself, since the bleeding had stopped.

My opponent couldn't see what they were muttering about, but he was distracted nonetheless. I came in awhirl, ducking his blow, and striking him in the gut with the handle. He stumbled back and fell, and I laid the tip of my sword against his bare breastbone.

"Well?" Bear said to Jaiks.

"All right, you've proved your point. Jorin!" The captain tossed the stick in his hand aside and motioned for me to approach him. He stood with one boot on the lower rail of the fence. "You've proved you won't get killed practicing with us. I run a group of men here every other day, sword, hand to hand, axe. Can you ride a horse?"

"Yes," I answered. "Captain."

"Might work on that, too, sometimes, just for fun. Not much need for cavalry skills inside the castle, after all." He whistled and the men came to attention. "Time to eat. You two heading back up, or will you join us?"

Bear grunted. "Join you, Captain."

"Inside." Jaiks turned on his heel and made for the doorway to the barracks, where I presumed their midday meal was served. The others followed him briskly.

I put my shirt back on and with one hand on the top of the fence, swung my legs over.

"Hurry up, cub. Rations are a bit short right now," Bear said.

"Are they?" I hadn't noticed any shortage at the king's nightly banquet, but then, I supposed, the king would be the one man not to cut back.

"That grain blight in the south has put bread in short supply, gruel and meal, too." He cuffed me on the head. "Up there you won't notice, where they just pile up more meat and fruit, but the meat will start to run short soon, too, if they can't feed the animals." He shook his head. "Got to hope the heat of summer brings on a good northern harvest to make up for it."

We entered a low, dark building that smelled of charcoal and woodsmoke. At one end I could see the cooking fires and ovens, long tables laid out lengthwise. We joined the line toward the cooks.

I barely paid attention to what I ate, though. Some kind of meal-cake soaked in gravy, with a few strips of slow-cooked meat across the top, but my attention was on the chatter of the men around me. I took a seat and Bear left me then, hurrying to catch someone he wanted to talk to. Inside the castle, the guards rarely spoke, almost as if they'd taken a vow of silence. But out here, among their fellows, I got quite an earful. Grain blight, bad fishing on the coast all winter, poisoned wells to the east, all were being blamed on the Night Riders, though I couldn't see how a roving band of rebels could have ruined the fishing. And how could they have been in the east and the south at once? Everyone knew they were working with the Parvanians and the Frangit to destabilize us, but... Well, what did I know of fishing? Nothing. And the reason the Night Riders evoked such fear was they supposedly had evil magic at their disposal. A band of bogeymen to scare children into being good, I sometimes thought. If they were truly evil mages, why didn't they just attack the castle directly? I suppose Seroi was the answer there, and they weren't strong enough to challenge him.

"Have you ever actually seen a Night Rider?" I asked the man next to me, who had finished his meal and was cutting a strip of sechal bark with his boot knife.

He handed the first strip to me and I accepted it with a sign of thanks. "Not around here," he said. "They keep to the fringes, you know. But before I joined the castle garrison I was stationed at Tiger's Mouth."

"Where is that?" I asked, truly curious. Geography had been in Kenet's lessons, so I had learned some, but not to the detail he had.

"Where the two rivers come together, where the Getten meets the Serde, they call it Tiger's Mouth," he said, pocketing the twig again and just chewing on the sliver he held in his fingers. "I'm here now because that entire garrison was destroyed in one night by the Night Riders."

I stared at him. "How?"

"How not?" he answered, with a slap on my back. "Flaming balls of fire from the sky, dark beasts tearing down the walls... we were forced to flee into the forest and in the morning all that was left standing were a few piles of rubble and charred stumps. The army won't rebuild there until they can send a suitable force, and with the Parvanian raiding parties stepping up their activity now they the mountain passes are free of snow again? I don't know that suitable force exists."

I frowned. "I thought General Roichal had ten thousand men."

"Total, yes. Not all in once place. They won't send less than a thousand to purge the area of Tiger's Mouth, though. We were almost two hundred fifty and they routed us."

"How many of them are there?" I asked.

He shook his head. "No one knows."

A heavy hand landed on my shoulder. "Come on, cub. Time to head back."

As we made our way up the hill, through the inner guard wall, I could not help but ask. "What use is training with axes and swords if the Night Riders can throw fire?"

He cuffed me on the head. "Most of the enemies you could meet, can't. Learn to fight men first, cub. Then ghosts."

"The Night Riders are ghosts?"

"Of course not!" he scoffed. "But they appear and disappear like them, and you might as well concern yourself with them about as much."

We reached the quarters I shared with Kenet and I frowned to see the door open. Bear motioned me aside, checking carefully, but just on the opposite side was a maid on a step stool, cleaning the soot stains from the stone above the door. She rushed off, back through the servant's door at the other end. There was no sign of Kenet.

"He's at his lessons, still," I said with a shrug. "Though I seriously wonder what he's learning, given that Sergetten seems to be gone. He said he just reads the histories down at the archive. Will Sergetten be back soon, you think?"

Bear grunted. "Don't know. I..." But then he turned suddenly at some sound from the hall.

There stood Kenet, looking pale and drawn. His eyes met mine and widened. "Jorin," he said, like he suddenly recognized me.

"What's wrong?" Bear demanded, but Kenet threw his arms around my neck, trembling. "What's happened to you, princeling?"

He shook his head, though, refusing to speak.

"Have you been bitten by something poisonous? Fall from a

horse? Eat something bad?" I asked. He shook his head again and again. "Do you need to lie down?" This time a nod.

"I've got him," I said to Bear. "Give me an hour with him and then send up some soup if I don't call for help sooner."

Bear folded his arms. "Be careful with him."

I glared at him, but without much malice. He knew Kenet was the most precious thing to me in the kingdom. I guided him to his bed and heard Bear shut the door firmly behind him. I set my usual alarms on that door and bolted the maid's entrance.

I brushed my dry palm over his forehead. He was a bit sweaty. "Can you tell me what's wrong?"

"I can't," he whispered. "Just... just hold me, Jorin. I'll be all right in a little while."

I started to slip from my trousers and breeches, but his high-pitched "No!" spoke of panic. "No, just, right now. Hold me... as you are."

I curled against him, my clothes, his, and a blanket between us, making him a warm, solid bulk under my arm. He was quickly asleep and I was left wondering what could possibly have happened to him during his lessons to leave him this way.

Twelve: Kenet

I saw Seroi almost every day, except a few times when he merely sent me to the archives to read certain ancestral accounts. Each time I saw him, he milked some seed from me before I left. It took less and less time for him to bring me to the point of spilling, and it seemed to me his touch grew lighter and lighter each time as well, as if he moved from pulling the seed out of me to coaxing my cock to give it to him like an obedient animal.

This impression was never higher than the day he began, rather than ended, our lesson with the milking. I climbed to his tower as always, the incense making me dizzy but my head clearing once I reached his side. He looked up from the ledger he was writing in and a smile broke slowly across his smooth cheeks. "Kenet," he said, as affectionately as one might to a pet dog that has just fetched your shoes.

"Seroi," I answered, one eyebrow raised.

"I'm pleased to say we can move to the next stage of your training," he continued, still beaming at me. "Strip out of your clothes and kneel in the center of the markings there." He gestured to the space on the floor that was ringed with symbols.

This was not unusual and I began to remove my clothing immediately, balking only when I saw that he was beginning to do the same.

I had never seen Seroi's bare legs before. I had seen a sliver of his torso through his robes from time to time, depending on what he was wearing, but I found myself openly staring as he folded his outer robe over the back of the chair he had been sitting in, then the under robe, and so on, my breath catching as he revealed his legs.

And his cock. It was at that point I looked away and

remembered I was supposed to be kneeling where he told me. Most of him looked the way I expected from his face. Smooth and hairless and far too young for his actual age. He looked like he might be about the same age or younger than my father, with gently curving muscle and a flat belly, yet I knew he had been Lord High Mage even in my grandfather's day.

But his cock was long and thick and so heavily veined it reminded me of an old tree. The head was blunt like a branch stump as well, looking just as gnarled. It hung between his legs, longer than mine as well as with greater girth, and this was him flaccid.

I jumped when he touched me, for I had closed my eyes, as if examining the image of that cock behind my eyelids in secret. He knelt in place behind me, reaching around my chest with one arm, grasping my cock with the other hand, and stroking me quickly to hardness with just a ring made of his thumb and forefinger. I looked down to watch it, wondering at how it could respond like that when in my gut I was feeling repulsed.

Repulsed, but also aroused, I realized, by the sight of that massive, grotesque prick. I told myself the only reason I felt aroused while seeing it was that I knew my own release was coming soon.

With the hand that was not stroking me, he pinched my nipples and I jerked indignantly in his embrace. "That hurts!"

"Yes, but you must bear it," he said, no apology in his voice at all. "Even if you do not enjoy it. This is not about your enjoyment, my prince, but about ensuring the magical changes necessary for you to carry on your royal duty."

"I know," I said, jerking again as he pinched the other.

"Take hold of your own cock for a moment," he said, in his tutoring voice. I did as he asked. Then he pinched me again, hard. "What did you feel?"

I could not lie, for surely that is what he had felt himself. "My blood... surges. When you pinch."

"That is correct." He took hold of me again, his mouth close to my ear when he held me that way. "Pain and pleasure are two sides of the same coin."

"Does that mean I like pain? Or... or is it necessary for breaking through the spell you put on me?"

"Oh, very good, my prince," he purred. "You begin to understand. Yes, the pain is quite necessary to free you from the chains we had put on you. But, in fact, you should experience it as pain. Your cock's response is perhaps related to the surge in desire you experience as the spell is gradually lifted. Now, on all fours."

He pushed me forward and placed a goblet under me, just tall enough that the rim touched the head of my cock. Now he stroked me with just two fingers, his thumb down the underside and his index finger on the opposite. Not even ringing the shaft. He guided the loose skin up and down, up and down. I began to tremble and shake from the teasing.

"Kenet," he said, lying down beside me, and resting his chin in his other hand while he continued the torturously light pressure.

"S-Ser—"

"Spill for me now," he whispered, his voice no less a command than ever, even in a whisper.

I cried out as I spilled, as my cock began to burn with each spurt, my body surging through release but with only a hollow feeling of nausea sweeping through me rather than pleasure. I retched once, but then his hand made a circle on my back and the feeling instantly eased. Then he was gone, putting away the goblet, and he returned with another container.

"During the next step you must be protected from the effects of certain humours that will try to invade your body," he said, as he began to spread something cool across my back. "I will cover every inch of you with this. Even your eyelids, and anoint your head." He encouraged me to lie on my back while he worked it through my scalp, my face and lips, then massaged it into my chest. My nipples were still sore from the pinching and stood up hard and defiant under his palms. He worked down my arms, then down my legs, doing my cock and balls last. They were sore to the touch and I hissed as he made quite thorough work of coating them, including holding the head in one hand and daubing into the slit with his smallest finger. Then he moved me back to all fours and worked down my back and over my arsecheeks.

I sucked in a breath as his moist fingers brushed over my arse-hole. "Every inch," he said, as if reminding me. "Anything that might be exposed, and that includes here." I could not help it, though. The touch in such a private place made me clench tightly. Not even Jorin had ever touched me on that side.

"Kenet," he said, voice soft with warning. "Rest your head on the floor, and reach back with your hands to spread yourself for me."

I hesitated only a moment, then did as he asked, spreading the cheeks wide.

"Very good," he said, his finger slathering the unguent up and down over the puckered hole, and then just the tip of his finger pressed into me.

I squeaked like a mouse. Not only because of the cold, slick intrusion, but because my cock sprang to life as he did it.

He chuckled. "Very good," he said again. "My apologies if the previous paroxysm was not pleasurable for you, my prince. It is important that you realize that this is not love-making you are experiencing now, of course. But I assure you it is not my intent to make every moment unpleasant. You are allowed to experience some pleasure. Would you like a more pleasurable release before you leave here, today?"

"Yes," I said, through gritted teeth. My cock was throbbing then as if I hadn't just spilled at all, but had been teased mercilessly all along.

"Will you do everything I say?"

I hesitated. "Don't I already do everything you say?"

"Kenet. There are protocols to be followed in ritual magic." He moved his finger in a circle then, making nerves spark all around my hole and all through my body. "Will you do everything I say?" he repeated. "If you do, I will reward you with a pleasurable release."

"Yes," I said, still holding myself wide for him. "Yes, I will."

"Very good," he said again, and I began to realize that those words were ritualized, too. "I will not lie to you, my prince," he said. "Freeing you of the necessary spells is not without some risks.

The oil I've coated you in is necessary because what I do must crack your armor, your psychic armor, some of which is your own natural protection, but some of which is what we are working to have you shed. This..." And here he twirled that finger again, "Is one of the chinks in your armor." He withdrew the finger then, and I clenched my hole tight once more.

He pulled me upright against him then, and I could feel that club of a cock against my tailbone. He was hard and it felt like I could feel his heartbeat through his turgid flesh. "Do you know what magehands are?"

"No."

"It is a power some of us develop that allows us to essentially have one or more spirit hands at our disposal. Look down, my prince."

I looked down my torso to see his two hands cupping my chest, his thumbs coming to rest against my nipples, his forefingers tweaking them, rolling them gently without pinching. Then I gasped as I saw the head of my cock disappear into the loose skin around it, as if a hand were stroking up from the base. "Invisible hand..." I whispered in awe.

"Yes, my prince." Now instead of pinching, he continued to tease at my nipples, and to stroke with his spirit hand, which was an even lighter touch than the teasing contact he'd used earlier.

"There is one way for me to ensure that you are truly ready for release," he purred into my ear. "To ensure that this time will not be painful, as the last one was."

"Wh-what is that?" I gasped, feeling the need to come but not yet ready to.

"You will beg when you are truly ready," he whispered. "When you cannot stand it for another moment. When you beg, I shall give you the release you crave, and not a moment sooner."

Seroi was a man of his word.

Thirteen: Jorin

Days passed without Kenet letting me touch him after that. He kept telling me he wasn't feeling well enough, though he'd let me hold him when we were in our nightclothes. He was sleeping fitfully, too, jerking in his sleep, and sometimes moaning and rocking against me. They must have been nightmares, but my deprived body interpreted the sounds as something else. More than once I hurriedly tugged myself to completion while he slept.

That was probably the only thing that kept me from the fate of one of the guards. I had gone with Bear down to practice with the men every morning, and one day the drill involved wrestling one another to the ground. I had already gone through three rounds when one of the others, a bearded man named Dubacki, got a bit too excited while wrestling Jaiks himself.

At first I didn't see what had caused Jaiks to stop the match and force the man to stand at attention while being upbraided, but the reason became clear soon enough. Especially when after several minutes of being lectured about perversity and self-control, his erection still had not subsided. At that point Jaiks tore open his breeches, freeing a cock that would have been hard to hide even when soft.

"Line up!" he called to the men, and Bear nudged me to get in line with the rest of them. They lined up shoulder to shoulder facing the man, who was cringing. "Open hand slap," Jaiks then said.

The first soldier in line then went toward Dubacki, and we followed. He delivered a hard slap downward on the man's cock. So did the next man, and the next, and the next, as we filed past him. I wanted to say I was sorry, but I didn't dare do anything differently from the others. He was whimpering but still very hard when I gave him his smack, and I was last in the line, following the others back to our places.

Jaiks inspected the offending organ. "If anything, this milk-sucking whorefucker is harder than before," he announced with gritted teeth. "Spread your legs. Wider. Oh, you milksucker, that'll never do. Up on the rail." Dubacki hopped up to sit on the top rail then, spreading his knees as wide as he could and holding on tightly. Now his balls hung low below the jutting penis.

To the rest of us Jaiks said, "Two finger slap. Go."

Now Dubacki cried out as each man put two fingers together and slapped him right on the jewels. "Faster!" Jaiks insisted. By the time I reached him, the man had tears streaking the dirt on his face. But still his little soldier stood proudly at attention.

"Can you believe this whorefucker?" Jaiks said. "On your knees. Now."

Dubacki stumbled as he jumped down off the fence, and crawled to the center of the practice ring.

"Riding whips, belts, or laces," Jaiks said. "On his back until he either softens or spills his milk." He walked around to the front of Dubacki to judge. "Go."

Several of the men had undone their belts already. A few just had leather laces and were braiding them into short lanyards. That's what I did with the drawstring of my breeches. And some had their riding whips in their boots already, the ones who were on cavalry duty, I assumed.

For the first time through the line, Dubacki just took the blows stoically. But as his prick remained bloody red and hard, he finally gave in and started stroking himself furiously. The blows continued to rain down as each of us took a turn, until he was bent over, leaning on one hand while the other moved like a blur, and we closed around him in a circle, the blows raining down on him now not in any particular order. He screamed and gnashed his teeth, pulling on his flesh desperately. He must have been raw and bloodying himself with the grit and dirt, but eventually he did spill, heavy wet blobs falling to the dust under him.

Jaiks whistled to end it, and Dubacki collapsed onto the dirty puddle of his own seed.

I started to pull myself to completion every morning before

meeting Bear after that. I also never saw Dubacki again. I finally got up the nerve to ask Bear what had happened to him.

"Oh, he's fine, cub. He's a tough lad, that kind of treatment wouldn't put him out of commission for very long," Bear said. "But he's been sent off to Tiger's Mouth."

"Where the attack was?"

"Aye. Not an assignment anyone is wanting right now. Nigh unto a suicide mission, some say."

"That's awful, just because he... his..."

"Well, you weren't going to send a milksucker like that to the Frangi border where the boywhores might make him crazy, were you? Clearly he couldn't stay here, though." Bear's voice was low with warning.

"Right. Of course." Kenet, I thought. What was wrong with Kenet? And what was wrong with me? When Kenet touched me, or let me touch him, everything felt right. And now that he was ill, everything had gone wrong.

Fourteen: Kenet

I ascended the stairs into Seroi's tower, passing through the barrier of incense and into the chamber. He no longer had any pretense of being robed when I would enter. For a few days he would tell me the moment I came into his domain to shed my clothes and then kneel on the designated spot. Then one day he no longer told me, but just stared at me, one eyebrow raised, until I did so. Now he did not even look up from what he was writing until after I had been kneeling there for several minutes.

"Very good," he said, without looking up, and I felt the words of praise wash through me like a warm draught. Then I was dashed with cold water: "But you are still not quite ready."

My hand went to my cock and I made myself hard as quickly as I could.

Then he came to me and stroked my hair. "Very good," he said again, and the warmth returned. Standing beside me as he was, the pendulous flesh of his cock was very close to my face. "Part of this training, my prince," he said, "is to teach you to sense the ebb and flow of desire, which has been denied you for so long. After all, I will not be in your marriage bed with you to direct your movements."

"I think I can figure out what to do in the marriage bed," I said with a frown, then was startled as he slapped my cheek.

"Have you not learned by now that the magical threads we are weaving are delicate? Rebel against me and there could be dire consequences! I allowed you some small disobediences early in your lessons because of your ignorance! But you cannot claim ignorance now."

I bowed my head. He sounded like my father when he would chastise me for something.

"Your feelings are awakening and I know they can be... difficult at times to understand or to accept," he went on in a gentler voice. "You must trust me, that although they may seem odd or wrong, you must give in to them to break the spells. Tell me, Kenet, tell me what your instincts are telling you to do."

My eyes were closed. "I should... apologize."

"And how will you do that?"

"I will ask you to forgive me, my lord." His title rolled easily off my tongue whenever I was in trouble.

"And if asking is not enough?"

I hesitated, trying to divine what answer he wanted. "Then... then what can I do to make it up to you, my lord?" After all, my whipping boy was not here to take my punishment for me. But punishment was not the only way to clear the air after a mistake, was it?

"Listen to your instincts, Kenet," he said. "There is a way to mollify me and make things right between us again."

I don't know what compelled me to try this, but without opening my eyes, I turned my head, and brushed my lips along the gnarled head of his cock.

"Oh, very good," he whispered, voice dropping. "You are definitely making progress."

I let my tongue out to taste what I expected to be salty, because Jorin's was, only to find his flesh bitter like the rind of a green fruit. I gagged, but a moment later his fingers sank into my hair, pulling my head forward until my mouth engulfed the whole head of his cock.

"Good boy," he said. "Yes, very good..."

I wondered if the incense were leaking through the door, because I felt dizzy and light-headed. And quite suddenly, the more he praised me, the more enthusiastically I tried to swallow his flesh.

And then, just as suddenly, I felt the spasm of that muscular bulk in my mouth, and my tongue was suddenly flooded with his acrid, almost burnt-tasting seed. I coughed and spat, and earned a slap, and then he thrust deep into my throat, ensuring I was forced to swallow. But then his hand was stroking my cheek, and he was apologizing. "I'm sorry, my prince, but your tooth... it was purely a reflex. I know you did not mean to bite me."

I bit him? I did not recall biting down at all, but I did feel dizzy. I licked him as he softened, trying to soothe any hurt I had made.

"Ah, that's good. Very good. You make up in enthusiasm what you lack in technique. I am very pleased with you today."

I was suddenly exhausted and my eyelids felt heavy. Indeed, they were closed.

"Not yet, my prince," came his voice. "I must milk you, still."

"Oh..."

"I will make it pleasurable for you, now that you are starting to glean some enjoyment from our practice, at last," he said.

"Thank you, my lord," I said, slumping to the floor. I felt his body against mine and he pulled me close, my back to his chest, the way Jorin so often held me. It felt distinctly odd to be held by anyone else that way, and I could feel the bones of him poking me in places that Jorin's didn't.

And one bone in particular, against the base of my spine. Could he be erect, still, after spilling in my mouth? Or again, so quickly? But all he did with it was press it against my tailbone while he stroked me.

"Do you remember what you must do, my prince?" he whispered in my ear, "If you would like your release to bring you pleasure instead of pain?"

I remembered. "Beg," I said, already jerking my hips toward his fist. He held his hand still and I did the work, pushing forward into his grip and pushing back against his cock. "I will beg for release, my lord."

"Very good, my prince." Somehow now when he said "my prince" it no longer sounded like it used to. It was no longer a title of respect and had become almost something obscene for him to whisper to me in these unspeakable moments. "Soon, soon," he crooned, and I thought he meant I would come soon, but I could feel the rising of anticipation in him. Would he climax again, when I did?

No, he did not, but he made me beg for quite a while before

he allowed me release. I slept some after that, waking up with my
hair over my eyes and my own milk crusted to my belly. He was
nowhere to be seen. I cleaned up as best I could, then decided I
had best stop at the baths before going back to my room. Jorin
would see it, would smell it, most likely, unless I bathed. I felt a
pang in my heart as if my promise to keep silent were reminding
me of the consequences of breaking that promise.

I was about to descend from the tower when I noticed a folded
piece of parchment with my name on it.

> *Tomorrow is your meeting with your*
> *father. You will see him instead of me*
> *tomorrow, but return to me on the day*
> *after to resume your progress.*

The letter was not signed. I knew I should get rid of it, but I
didn't know what lighting a fire in his sacred space might do. I
folded it three times over and slipped it into my pocket to get rid
of later.

Once in the bath I began to doubt what had just happened. It
seemed too unreal. It must have been the hallucinatory effect of
the incense smoke, combined with the lifting of the restrictions
on my sexual urges. My imagination was going wild. That had to
be it.

Fifteen: Jorin

Two weeks. Two more weeks passed without Kenet touching me or inviting me to touch him. I began to rack my brain incessantly for a clue to why he would have withdrawn like this. Had I pushed him too far, too fast? Perhaps I never should have suggested we go beyond touching with our hands. I had told him it wouldn't be clean to take me in his mouth. Was he afraid that was what I wanted him to do every time? Or had something else put the fear in him? Had he seen something like what I had seen with Dubacki's chastisement?

Had the king said something? Did he suspect something?

But no. If that were the case, then I have no doubt the king would have separated us. I would have been long gone from the castle.

I continued to give myself release quickly before each practice down at the barracks. It was brutish and unsatisfying, but necessary.

Then one night I woke to find Kenet buried deep under the coverlet, his mouth on my cock like wet velvet, suckling eagerly. There was nothing I could say or ask—he couldn't hear me under the heavy covers anyway—and I was not even sure he was aware he was doing it.

That didn't stop me from sinking into the pleasure. His fingers played with my balls, tugging them gently, and I wondered what could have given him that idea. Wet, so wet, and then a teasing finger brushed back and forth on the crinkle that was my hole. I came with a muffled shout, burying myself under a pillow, while he continued to suck and lap until I was completely soft and sated.

Only then did he emerge to kiss me deeply, filling my mouth with the musky taste of my own milk.

When he pulled back, he pressed a finger to my lips, asking me for silence. Then he settled himself in my arms and was fast asleep in mere moments.

So I asked the questions in my head. Kenet, dear Kenet, what's happened to you? What is happening to you? Will everything be all right now? Don't you need release, too?

I had no answers.

The next night I decided I would give him what he had given me. I woke when the first frits began to sing, even though the sky was still night black, and he was deeply asleep. I slipped slowly under the covers, moving oh so slowly so as not to wake him. Getting his cock free of his sleeping clothes was easy, though, as he was flaccid.

Though not for long. I took him into my mouth and was gratified by the sensation of him growing firm between my lips.

I hadn't meant to slip a finger inside him. I had meant just to tease at his hole as he had at mine. But the slick tip of my finger entered him, and it was like his body drew me in the rest of the way. I pulled that finger back once and pushed it in again and he spilled without warning into my mouth. I nearly gagged, as the fluid that came forth was far more bitter than I remembered. But it sweetened as his spurts went on, and I licked him clean before I surfaced again.

He appeared to have slept through the whole thing, his lips only barely responsive to mine as I kissed him, wondering what he was dreaming of.

Sixteen: Kenet

My father and I went riding together, over West Hill, the next time we met. His moods had not improved lately, yet he still insisted we spend this time together, as designated, every week. The air was warming nicely now, the frits nesting and full summer not long off.

"I hear that there is a grain shortage," I said to him.

"Where did you hear that?" He rode with one hand holding the reins, the other on the pommel of his sword. The path the horses climbed was too narrow here for us to go side by side, so he went first.

"Here and there." Jorin had told me he had heard it from the guards. "Is it true?"

"It is true," my father allowed. "But the greater threat is the Night Riders and the infiltration from Frangit and Pellon. They might have spread the blight to make it difficult for us to feed the army, weakening us. It is too dangerous for us to contemplate a tour for you."

"Tour?" He had never spoken to me of a tour before.

"We should begin planning the ceremony to celebrate your coming of age. I know it's happened some time since, but the Lord High Mage tells me you are nearing readiness for the actual ceremony."

My throat closed for a moment. Did Father know? No, he couldn't. And even if he did, he probably was sworn not to speak of what Seroi and I were doing almost daily in that tower.

My father went on, ignorant of my distress. "He will choose an auspicious time for the ceremony, and we will mint a coin in your likeness, but taking you on an actual tour of the territories is out of the question. It is far too dangerous at this time." He sighed.

"I myself did not go on a tour at the time of my own coming of age, because of the plague that had struck. Your grandfather thought it wise, and he was quite right, for us to stay here. I waited until your mother and I were married, and then we went together."

I had not heard this story before, but it explained one of the tapestries that hung in one of the large halls downstairs, that depicted my mother and father on horses, leading a grand parade of some sort. "Where did you go?"

"Everywhere. We went all the way around the border, from city to city, from military post to military post. Father stayed here of course, as it took a full year for us to return, and then he abdicated the throne to me once we returned." He had reached the crest of the hill, and I brought my horse alongside his. "Your mother and I reigned side by side for nearly seven years."

Nearly seven years until I came along and killed her, that is. If you asked him, he would tell you he didn't blame me for her death. He would say she knew her duty to the bloodline was more important than her own life. But in his heart, I think he blamed me. It was never more plain that at a time like this, when his emotions were raw to begin with.

I began to wonder if he agreed to Seroi's plan to keep me away from women for reasons of his own. Would seeing me courting some young, beautiful noblewoman bring back memories too painful to bear? Or mere envy? I stayed mum on the subject.

He turned and looked at me then. I was his height in the saddle now, though I had not the muscular girth he did. If the image in the tapestry was to be believed, I was as reedy as my mother had been. "Seroi will find a time for the ceremony. Perhaps at high summer."

"All right." I met his gaze calmly, wondering what else he would say.

We were silent for a long time, while he thought about something and I waited to hear what he was thinking. I could see his expression changing subtly, as he studied me, and came to some decision.

"You may keep your boy so long as I am king," he announced. "So long as I hold the authority, you will still need a ladra'an. But neither of you will be treated as boys once your ceremony is complete. You will have duties to perform at court and in the cabinet. Jorin will... do something useful."

"Bear is training him to be a guard," I said. "Didn't you know that?" I had thought it was my father's idea in the first place to make Jorin train with weapons while I went to my other lessons. Maybe it had been Sergetten's idea, though, and he only presented it as if it were my father's idea. Which was exactly the sort of maddening thing Sergetten would do. I missed having him around to be angry at.

Father's horse started and whickered at something in the grass. He calmed her with a hand on her withers. "I did not realize that, but Bear is wise. He knows you may need someone in the future. Someone other than Bear himself."

"Bear is not that old..." I began.

"He is old enough," Father said. "He is slowing down. He is a good man, to take on the training of his own replacement."

We headed back after that, my horse leading the way this time. I imagined we were going through the forest on a grand tour to far-off cities, and any moment we would come out of the trees into the cleared land before a city's gates, and a great cheer would rise up from the people amassed on the city's walls. And they would be chanting my name and tossing flowers to me, because the kingdom would be mine as soon as my father stepped aside, as soon as I completed my grand travels to every corner of the land.

In my visions, though, it was not some queen or noblewoman on the horse beside me, but Jorin. Jorin wearing a crown of falla blossoms and holding my hand.

Seventeen: Jorin

"Tcha. You just need to suck the heat out of it," Bear said, drawing up water from the pump behind the stable and soaking my shirt with it, then pressing the wet, wadded cloth against my eye.

I did not flinch from the pressure or the cold. The chill dulled the pain, and in some way I couldn't explain the feeling of Bear's other hand, holding my head steady, felt as soothing as the cloth itself. I stayed still, then he pressed my own hand against the cloth and went back to pump up more of the water so cold it was nearly ice.

I had taken a boot heel to the temple and all around my eye was swollen. The king's guard were not exactly welcoming of me, but then I hadn't expected them to be. This sort of training was supposed to be difficult. Hand to hand fighting was not supposed to be polite. It was a far cry from the genteel fencing that Kenet had practiced with me a few years ago.

I shivered as a trickle of the chill water ran down my chest when Bear replaced the cloth with another.

"Your face won't be very nice to look at over the banquet table tonight," he said gravely. "It might be best if you beg off."

"Do you think so?" I sat up straighter, as if someone might be evaluating my manners even now. "Kenet will be unhappy without me there."

Bear just sighed heavily.

I had known him too long to let that pass. "Something the matter?"

"He hasn't been too happy of late, has he?" Bear asked.

"No." We had not touched each other again, not in that way, since the night I had sucked him and found his seed to be bitter like poison. "He's not well," I finally said, in a low voice. "I don't know what it is, but he's definitely ill."

Bear just looked at me and gave a small nod.

"I don't know what to do for him. It isn't like a fever." I could take the physical punishments his father wanted to hand down, but I could not take his ailments or injuries, though I wished I could. Was that why his seed had tasted the way it had—illness?

"He doesn't seem to have a pox," Bear agreed. He shook his head. "Something's changed, though." He fixed me with a look then, and opened his mouth to say something, then thought better of it, getting to his feet instead. "Come on. Come up to my quarters and let me put some salve on that."

I followed him silently back to the castle. Neither of us spoke again until he had shut the door firmly behind us and latched it.

His quarters had a small front room with a carved wooden table far more ornate than one would expect to see in a burly guard's room. For all I knew, though, this had once been a lady's maid's room, and Bear had just never changed the furniture. He sat me on the chair and himself on a footstool as he opened the jar of salve.

"I can do it," I offered, holding my hand out for the jar.

"You can't see where the bruise is," he said.

"I can surely feel it. Besides, have you a mirror?"

"Tcha. Suit yourself, cub." He handed me the jar and then opened what I had taken for a cabinet above the table, but turned out to be a mirror behind the doors.

He folded his arms and did not speak again until I was done, and had closed the doors over the mirror again.

"Bear," I said, handing him back the jar, "you're acting strange."

"They say spirits can see from the other sides of mirrors," he said in a low voice.

I frowned. "That's just a superstition."

"Hush up. It isn't ghosts I'm worried about, if you catch my meaning."

I shook my head. "I don't. And you're worrying me."

"And Kenet is worrying me." He put the jar into a small chest of drawers. "Listen. Has something changed between you two? Something... physical?"

I hesitated before answering. Up until now, we'd always left everything unsaid, only hinted at, meaning that Bear could always pretend he didn't know. "Bear..." Telling him meant making him complicit in what we did. "Tell me what you think is wrong with him," I said, instead.

He took a breath, weighing his own words. "Maybe it's my fault, for introducing you to the maids downstairs."

"Oh, Bear..." I slumped a little in the chair. "It's nothing like that. I mean... well, perhaps it is, but..." My cheeks flushed as I tried to think of how to explain without incriminating myself or him.

"Cub," he said in a serious whisper, "if you've been lovers, and you suddenly stopped..."

I shook my head urgently. "We only... we only touch each other. It's not..." Not as if we lay together like a man and a woman.

He seemed to understand. "Have you, then? Lately?"

"Touched?" I dropped my gaze. "Not much. He hasn't wanted to."

Bear shook his head. "You had best try it, then."

"But he..."

"If it's what he's been missing, then that's what he needs," Bear hissed urgently. "You're the only one who can take care of it. For him. I know it's not what you're supposed to..."

"I don't mind," I said quickly. "I'd do anything for him, you know." It wasn't as if I had any pride to lose or could even feel shame, after I'd spent my childhood bare-arsed in front of most of the court on a regular basis. What I couldn't explain to Bear was that Kenet had actually begged me not to undress that time, and we had not bared ourselves to each other since.

"Please try," he urged me. "And tell me how he does. If he doesn't seem obviously better, that is."

I put my palm over my swollen eye. "At least my face isn't what he looks at when we do it," I half-joked.

Bear hissed, scandalized but amused nonetheless.

That night, at Bear's advising, I begged off attending banquet, and was not wholly surprised that Kenet did as well. We had a little light food brought to our room, then sent the dishes away quickly, which I thought boded well for my plans for him that evening.

I couldn't help it when I saw the mirror there, set on the wall by the dressing table. I covered it with a scarf. Bear had made me superstitious.

My heart was hammering in my chest as I contemplated what I was going to do next, though. If he pushed me away or said no, it would be more painful than a boot to the face.

There was no putting it off. I slipped my hands around his waist from behind, my palms finding his flat stomach under the loose tunic he wore. His breath caught, but he said nothing, neither encouraging nor discouraging me.

I ran one hand down the front of his trousers, gently rubbing as I kissed the back of his neck and nibbled on the fine hairs behind his ear. I could feel him swell gradually, finally making a sound of surrender as he came to his full length, the leaking head of his prick pushing up above the edge of his breeches. I continued to rub outside the cloth, until he was rutting into my palm, swiping the thumb of my other hand through the slick issue gathered at the slit.

"It's not healthy for you to go so many days without release," I whispered in his ear.

He froze then, and I could just feel it was not like when he went stiff with desire. I nearly pulled back, stung by the thought that he had been giving himself release when we were not together, but then thinking that was exactly what I had been doing. When had I decided that Kenet's pleasure was mine and mine alone? Just because it had been, or had seemed to be, didn't mean it always would be, did it?

I ran my lips along his ear and then whispered to him. "Oh, I see, been having it off without me, have you?"

"No, no..." he tried to protest, but feebly.

I clucked my tongue. "Don't lie to me, my prince. If you've been getting your regular release, I cannot fathom why your skin looks so grey, your eyes so dull... unless that it's my touch you've been in need of..."

His breath caught. "Oh yes! Please..." He bucked into my palm. "Jorin... oh, Jorin..."

My name on his lips always inflamed me. I felt my own cock throbbing in my trousers. "Bed," I said, rubbing against his hip, and then pushing him toward his bed. Before he had even climbed atop the coverlet, I had shed my clothing and soon climbed after him.

He lay back and loosened his laces but had not disrobed. "Lie still," I told him. "Let me unwrap you like a gift from a faraway court."

He did, letting me undo his clothes and reveal him bit by bit. I kissed what I found as I uncovered it, his collarbone, his shoulder, his nipple. His belly, his hipbone, his cock.

I lay atop him then, rutting gently in the hollow of his hip and thinking of something the baron had said to his wife, and something one of the soldiers had said to taunt the man whose erection had interrupted practice. "Kenet," I asked softly. "Do you like how I touch you?"

He propped himself up on his elbows, as if he couldn't answer that while lying flat on his back. "Jorin, of course. Every... every touch you've made, I've enjoyed. And I've enjoyed doing the same to you."

"Even when it wasn't just our hands, but our mouths?" I pressed.

He nodded, solemn. What was going on in his head? Why had these touches and games between us become something that made him so grave? I thought about how just a few weeks ago there had been a night he'd begged me to touch him with an urgency I hadn't understood. I still didn't.

"Kenet," I whispered. "Do you want more from me?"

"What do you mean?" His eyes were silver in the lamplight.

I crawled up him a bit more to kiss him, forcing him to lie back, and then looked down into his eyes while I continued. "I know it's not easy to speak of. But Kenet, we're not children anymore."

He just swallowed and looked up at me, waiting to hear what I would say.

"Do you want me to..." How could I ask this? "There is a way two men can lie together like a man and a maid," I said, reaching up to stroke the blond silk of his hair. "Do you want me that way, my prince?"

His eyes were wide and for a moment I was certain the word that was forming on his lips was "yes." But what he said was, "We can't."

"That isn't what I asked," I said, my heart trying to kick as hard as the soldier who had left me bruised. "I asked if you wanted to." Just to be clear, I added, "It matters not to me which of us plays the part of the maid."

He stared, jaw moving as if he were trying to say something but I had shocked the words right out of his mouth. "Jorin..."

"You can say no, my prince. Just please... tell me what you want. Have I done something to displease you?"

"What? No! Jorin, of course not..."

"Then why haven't you wanted to touch?" I rutted again against him, then shifted so that my cock ran along his, holding myself up on my arms. "I thought you weren't afraid of us getting caught."

He shook his head suddenly. "It's not that."

"Then what, my prince? You haven't seemed yourself lately. I know I used to make you happy. I can only assume I've been failing to do that lately. Do I make you unhappy?"

"No," he said softly, pulling me down into a kiss. His tongue was as luxurious as the velvet of his robes. I would never tire of tasting it. "No, it's not you at all."

"Someone else then," I teased, and was shocked to see the truth of that pass through his eyes. I stared incredulously. "Someone else?" I repeated.

"I can't explain," he said, almost frantic. "I literally can't."

I was trying to figure out what he could mean by that when he slipped his hands over my buttocks, urging me to rut against him harder. My cock slipped into the hollow of his hip again, and I groaned involuntarily, the image I had in my mind of me bending him over the way the baron had his wife, and pushing my cock into his body, suddenly at the fore as I pushed harder against him.

"I would be the maid," he said, voice trembling. "For you. If you wanted." His hands continued to pull at me, setting me into a rhythm.

I panted softly at his ear. "But you, would you want it, Kenet? I wouldn't try to..."

"I want it," he blurted suddenly. "I do. But I can't." He moaned, his hips rocking, rubbing his own cock against me with every thrust, too.

"Why?" I asked, without really thinking about the question.

Which was why his answer surprised me so very much. "It would make a hole in my psychic armor," he said, quite seriously.

"It would?" I was so shocked I nearly stopped moving, which only made him tug at me with an even hungrier desperation.

"It would," he assured me. "I can't tell you how I know. I can't."

Can't. He had insisted it more than once now. Had he been sworn not to tell me? I wondered if Sergetten had something to do with it. But Sergetten had been gone for weeks. Had he read it in a book while studying in the archives? They said there were some secrets contained in magical tomes that once learnt could not be spoken without the subject being cursed, but like spirits in mirrors I had thought them just old wives' tales.

"I shan't do it, then," I said, "if it would damage you. I would never hurt you, Kenet. You know that."

He nodded, eyes suddenly bright with tears.

"Tell me how you want to come, then," I said. "You do want to come, don't you?"

He nodded.

"In my mouth?" I asked.

He shook his head. "Either... either just like this, or the old way, with your hand."

I slipped to one side of him and circled his shaft with my fingers, but he hissed as if the pressure were too much, so I loosened my grip. He moaned with pleasure at that, and I slid the loose skin there up and down his prick.

"You..." He spoke haltingly, breath catching as he got close. "You come too..."

"I will," I assured him. "But this time you first."

He didn't argue—he didn't have time to. He was spilling in hot spurts into my fingers, then.

And then there was a banging on the door. "Jorin! You're being summoned."

Both of our heads jerked up at that, and then we were in a mad scramble for our clothes. "But Bear...!" Kenet was saying.. "I haven't done anything!"

He pulled open the door once I got my breeches closed over my still quite stiff rod.

Bear's expression was dark. "The King is insisting on you both. I don't know what you did, Kenet, but he's very displeased."

I had a sinking feeling in my gut. "Are we to meet him in his chambers?"

Bear shook his head. "Banquet hall. I'm sorry, cub."

I let out a laugh. "Not like they haven't all seen it before. Well, except for this part." I gestured at the erection still visible through the cloth.

He growled. "Do what you can to get rid of it, eh? It's scandalous enough what he's doing, you both full grown and all."

"Then why's he doing it?" I asked.

"Don't know, cub. But I guarantee it will be considered your fault, not his, if you scandalize the court with that sausage of yours."

"Bear!" Kenet had finally spoken, a shocked exclamation.

Bear put a hand on his shoulder. "It's time you were growing up, my prince," he said. "I think your father's decided now is the time. That's what this is really all about."

"Then I'll have to take it like a man," I said, chuckling again and pretending it was nothing. "You know he always feels better after he exerts himself. Come on, Kenet. Everything will be fine after he's done with me." I smacked my erection a few times to see if it would flag. It didn't. Perhaps it would wilt when I was finally faced with our angry monarch.

Eighteen: Jorin

It took us some time to move through the corridors and across the courtyards to reach the banquet hall. I had never dreaded a beating so much.

No, that is probably not true. But one forgets the dread, in between. My back tingled with the memory of how severely the king had whipped me the last time, though, and I thought about Dubacki and wondered if the king would even hesitate to unman me with the whip if I could not control myself.

That was the thought that caused my balls to shrink, I think. By the time we reached the banquet hall, and by the time I was disrobing upon the dais, all trace of my arousal was gone. Thankfully.

With a gesture the king bade Kenet sit to the right of the throne, beside the Lord High Mage, who watched us with one eyebrow raised, as if he were watching a clever but scholarly play being enacted. The room was silent except for the crackling of the fire and some stifled coughs from the assembled at the tables below the dais. There were probably seventy or eighty pairs of eyes watching me as I stripped down, again at a gesture from the king, who held a riding whip in his hand.

That did not bode well.

It was a thin rod, tipped with a loop of leather, and I had seen the welts and bruises it had raised on Dubacki's back and shoulders when wielded by the guards.

Horses have very thick skin. Comparatively.

He gestured again, a signal that I should present myself for punishment. I placed my hands against the table where so recently he had been eating. I faced the throne, exposing my back to the assembled in the room and spreading my legs without being asked. That sent a bit of a murmur through the room.

The first touch was a trail of the cowhide loop down my back, making me shiver.

And then Kenet spoke. Kenet, oh Kenet, shut up! "What is the infraction?"

The king brought the whip down with his full strength on the table, the sound making me jump and several women in the room gasp in fear. His voice was dangerously low, but I had no doubt he could be heard by all. "Are you questioning my right to mete out the judgements I see fit?"

"No, father, not at all!" Kenet's eyes glittered and I saw his jaw set. Oh, my brave prince. "But you should name the infraction and the punishment before beginning!" I closed my eyes, worrying that his speech was only going to make this worse for me, but knowing what he feared, knowing what he was trying to protect me from. If the king were to fly into a rage and beat me senseless? There were those criminals whose sentence of death was delivered in such a manner. "If this punishment is to aid me in correcting me, in teaching me, then I must know what the infraction is."

"And can you not guess?" Here the king put a fist into my hair and bent my head back, running the tip of the whip up and down my back. "Perhaps I shall beat him until you get it right."

The first blow fell across my buttocks even as Kenet opened his mouth to speak, and then he could not answer because my cry was too loud for him to be heard over. Thunder's roll! It hurt a great deal more than I expected, a sharp, sudden agony that faded very slowly.

"My absence!" Kenet called out. "Did you expect me at your side tonight? I... I did not know you..."

He fell silent as the king spoke and I was grateful for the opportunity to recover from the first blow. "You have forgotten already what we spoke of? That I expect you now to take a more active role in governance?"

Kenet's eyes fell. "I... I didn't realize you meant I should attend every banquet. You... that isn't what you said."

"You are past the age when I should be explaining these things to you. You had Sergetten tutoring you for years in matters of state, did you not? If you have not grasped the subtleties by now, it is because you are not trying hard enough. Perhaps this will motivate you."

I felt his muscles tense as he spoke and knew the blow was coming. Steeling myself for it helped not at all, as the strike hurt even more than the first. I manage to choke off my scream this time, though. Then another, and another, and one more. Five, that was five, I thought to myself. Was that enough?

There was a pause, and I could tell by looking at Kenet that he and his father were staring at each other. The Lord High Mage, meanwhile, only had eyes for Kenet.

Five more blows came, in quick succession, and my knees buckled as I screamed.

"I'm sorry!" Kenet screamed, as well. "Is that what it will take for you to stop? My apology? I'll try harder, father! I will! I am sorry to have disappointed you. I didn't... you're right, I didn't think. I should have sent word! I... I've been feeling ill."

I made a distressed noise as the grip in my hair tightened painfully. "The penalty for lying to me is fifty strokes."

"I'm not lying!" Kenet got up from his seat and looked on the verge of falling to his knees. To my surprise, the Lord High Mage was up just as quickly, and he put a hand on Kenet's shoulder, steadying him.

"Your highness," he said, his voice deep but powerful. "The prince is not lying. I can attest that he is not well. His complexion looked ashen this afternoon and I find it likely he is in need of some fortifying treatment."

I could feel a tremble in the king's arm. "Very well. The penalty is five strokes for your absence, five strokes for challenging my authority, and five strokes for your ignorance and to spur you to be more aware of your duties. You will notify me in the future."

"Yes, father." Kenet remained standing, though I could see he wanted nothing more than to collapse. My brave prince. He straightened his spine as the Lord High Mage steadied him with a hand at his back.

"Jorin." I was surprised to hear the king say my name. He let go my hair. "Step back from the table. Hands atop your head. You will remain upright as I deliver the punishment."

I did as he said, my upraised arms making the stutter in my breath all the more obvious as my chest shuddered when I inhaled. Kenet's gaze met mine.

I could not hold it, though. By the third blow I had clenched shut my eyes, and was doing everything in my power to stay on my feet. It was only five, but they were delivered just quickly enough that I could not recover between them, just slowly enough that staying in that position without moving was a challenge. The fifth one caught me right at the base of my buttocks and sent shooting pain down both legs, at which point I buckled and went to my knees.

But it was over. The king signaled to the musicians to begin a tune, and I found Bear putting a cloak around my shoulders, and I do not even recall the walk back to our rooms.

I do remember Kenet's stoicism shattering once we were in bed together. "Oh, he's awful! Just awful."

"Hush," I said, drowsy and almost intoxicated with the relief of being warm and safe in his bed. "You mustn't speak of the king that way."

"I'll speak of him how I like," Kenet hissed. "After I'm king, he'll no longer be able to touch you."

I chuckled. "No, indeed, then when you make a mistake you will have to whip me yourself."

"Never!" His hand smoothed my hair over and over. "Listen to me, Jorin. I've spoken to him of it. You're to replace Bear after my coming of age ceremony. And after the war with the Frangi is won, I'll go on a grand tour of the kingdom with you at my side, and when we return, I shall be king."

I opened my eyes to look at him. "You've spoken to the king of this?"

"Well, to be more accurate, he's spoken to me of it. But you see? It's exactly as I said. You and I will never be parted." He kissed me then, his mouth on my mouth, as if he were hungry. When he pulled back, he said, "Bear is wise for training his replacement, or so my father says."

I sighed, daring to dream that it might be true. "All I care about is that we are together now," I said. "What did the Lord High Mage mean he saw you this afternoon and you looked ashen?"

Kenet froze, then met my eyes. "I can't tell you," he said. "Can't."

I could hear the emphasis in his voice. "Can't, eh? Just like you can't tell me how you know your psychic armor isn't to be pierced? Kenet, is that what's making you sick? But no. No one has pierced it yet, have they?"

He shook his head.

"If there were someone to ask about your psychic armor, I would think Lord Seroi would be the one," I mused. "Did you go to him to find out why you're sick?"

He shook his head again. But who else but Seroi would speak of something like psychic armor? Then I remembered how he had frozen when I had implied someone else had been touching him besides me.

My breath caught. "Lord Seroi has been... he's the one you've... It's Seroi, isn't it?" I stammered.

He just stared at me, and did not shake his head no this time.

"That's what you can't tell me, isn't it." Again, no denial. "He's cursed you to silence, is that it?" He bit his lip, looking skeptical, but again not denying it. So that wasn't exactly it, but it was close.

He kissed me again then. "I want to lie with you, Jorin. Like a maid does. I don't even know exactly what a maid is supposed to do, other than lie there... but I can't. It's too dangerous. For me."

"Hush, don't speak then, if that's dangerous, too." I licked my hand and shifted position so I could take both of our cocks together in my grip. We were soon both hard. "But if we're never to be parted," I whispered into his ear, "then no matter what you have to do with him or to him, you must promise me this."

"Promise you what?" he whispered back, his voice urgent in the darkness.

"Promise that I shall always have this, my cock and your cock together." I stroked us as I spoke. "Promise that you are my prince, mine always, and you will welcome my touch in the night in our bed."

He swallowed first, but then pressed his mouth close to my ear. "I promise," he breathed, and I felt a surge of something go through him, and through me, and it was like no other time we had come together—indeed, it was so strong and yet so different I was not entirely sure we had come at all until I felt the hot spurts through my fingers.

"My prince," I breathed back, my lips brushing his forehead as he fell into exhausted sleep, my hand still holding our cocks close.

Nineteen: Kenet

I leaned against the stone, first with my hand, then my cheek. I could climb no more. Seroi's tower was not unsurmountable; I knew I had climbed these selfsame stairs many times before. But a leaden fatigue overcame my limbs as I passed into the curtain of incense that hung in the air as always.

I sat down heavily on the stair, my head in my hands, wondering at the sudden tiredness. I wanted to lie down, but I knew Seroi was waiting for me. And I shivered in a kind of instinctive fear of displeasing him, my skin remembering the sensation of his slap on my cheek even if I had convinced myself it had been only a dream.

I turned and put my hands on the stairs, crawling upward. The incense seemed particularly stifling today. Perhaps as spring's heat turned to summer this was how it would be? I shed my clothes as I went.

Thus it was that I crawled, naked, into his chamber, my progress across the room toward him arrested only by an object sticking up from the center of the floor where I usually knelt. I fixed my eyes dizzily upon it. The black thing was perhaps the length of my longest finger, and twice as wide, as smooth as glass and shaped like a small tower, tapered at the top. That was my first thought, that it was a piece from one of the grand siege boards my father and some of the regional governors sometimes used to plan military campaigns.

Before I could move to pick it up, though, Seroi spoke. "You come to me so eager, my prince. I am very pleased."

My nakedness was suddenly mortifying and I blushed, unable to look up and meet his eye.

"But are you truly eager?" He was close by me then, and

tapped upon my shoulder with a rod. "Up. Let me see the state of your cock."

Oh. I straightened up, though I remained on my knees, letting my hands fall to my sides, and looked down. I was expecting to see a flaccid member, but somehow I had arisen fully, a dewdrop glistening at the tip. My breath caught, as I imagined Jorin looking up at me, and licking it away as if it were honey. I closed my eyes.

"Oh yes, my prince, you please me well. You will give much milk to me this time, won't you?"

"Yes, my lord," I said, as I felt the tip of the rod cross my shoulders as if he were drawing a line from one to the other.

"You are no doubt wondering, though, what this is you've encountered upon the floor?"

"Yes, my lord."

"That is for you, my prince. Something to deepen your pleasure when you release."

My breath caught again as the purpose of the object suddenly became clear in my mind. As the destination of it hit me. I clenched my buttocks reflexively.

I felt the rod's tip draw a line down my back and then press into one of my arsecheeks, pushing it aside and exposing my arsehole to the air. I clenched tighter, and the rod disappeared.

I felt his hand, soft on my hair. "There is no need to be afraid," he said, his voice gentle now. "This is for your pleasure, my prince, not pain."

"But... but I thought you said it would breach my psychic armor to...?"

"Hush, hush, you understand little. I have charmed and prepared this object for you, to protect you. You are inevitably opening, my prince, just like a rose that has begun to bloom, and this is a step we must take now." He continued to stroke my hair and I relaxed against his touch, then was surprised to be pulled into his robed arms. He was clothed? I had felt the air move when he stepped close and his robes swished, but I had not taken notice of it at the time.

I was suddenly chilled, rather than overheated, and his robes only emphasized how small and naked I felt. I was nearly Seroi's height, but somehow like this I felt as vulnerable as when I had been a child. In fact, his lips brushed over my forehead.

"I'm not ready to do that," I said, not even sure why now I was resisting him, why the thought of taking the object into me made me cringe, despite his assurances it would not hurt.

"My prince, my darling prince, what I have not told you or your father yet is that I have chosen the day for your coming of age ritual," he said, his fingers finding my cock, which was still as eager as ever. He stroked me lightly, so lightly, and I felt magehands then too, circling each of my nipples, an invisible finger stroking along my lips. I was starting to whimper. "I have chosen a date just a few weeks hence near midsummer. We must have the old magic cleared from your body completely by then."

His hands moved again, one into my hair, the other tugging at one nipple, then pinching it sharply when I tried to twist away. The magehands were stroking between my buttocks then, and they felt slick, teasing over my hole and pulling on my cock with an oily surety. They could not be escaped no matter how I moved.

"You will do as I say," he hissed into my ear. "I know you only fight me because your body, mind, and spirit are still not completely awakened to lust as they should be. I know you want to come, Kenet. I know you do." The magical stroking did not stop or even slow. "Isn't that why you are never late to our appointments? Isn't that why you come to me now with your cock already hard and glistening with dew?"

"Yes," I hissed back, barely able to answer, my body was so taut with need. He somehow knew just how much stroking to give me to keep me on edge yet not give me release. I knew from experience now that he would keep me on that edge until I broke down and begged, sometimes with tears, for him to let me come.

It was as if he knew what I was thinking. "There shall be no begging this time, my prince. Or, at least, I assure you your pleas will fall on deaf ears. Begging shall do you no good. I will not allow you release until you crawl over to that spike and impale yourself on it."

I spasmed in his arms, something like bursting into tears except there were no actual tears. He pushed me away then, gently, until I was on all fours and he had stepped back, out of my reach.

"Please, my lord, not this time. Next time. I promise I will take it next time. I will give you so much milk, remember?" I reached for my own cock, but only stroked it once before the rod caught me on the knuckles and I yelped in pain, letting go and shaking my hand. "Please, my lord..."

But he merely remained silent, and let me abase myself even further before I finally believed he was serious about what he had said.

It took me a long time to call up the courage to approach the thing again. "Must I... sit upon it?" I finally said meekly. "Or may I spread my legs and take it in hand?"

He knelt beside me. "Had you asked earlier, before your defiance and refusal, I might have considered your preference," he said, his voice quiet, but no less commanding than if he'd spoken louder. "Now I will be satisfied with nothing less than perfect obedience."

I was shaking. "And if I refuse?"

"You do not dare refuse," he said simply. "Would you risk being unmanned? That is what will happen if we do not complete the cycle we have begun to free you of the spells before your coming of age ceremony."

"Unmanned?"

"Well, you will not lose your cock completely," he said, "if that is what you are thinking. But it will cease to rise. You will no longer derive pleasure from it and you will be unable to use it for its intended purpose of planting the royal seed in some noblewoman's furrow."

I had no argument for that. I stalled one last time. "It will not hurt?"

"I promised you it would not, so it will not," he said, in that same, soft, commanding voice. "Though I am sorely tempted, if you test my patience any longer, to punish you for your disobedience in some other way."

I crawled to the thing, touching it with my fingertip. It was affixed at the center of the ritual circle, but how I could not tell. I could feel my cheek burning as if he had just slapped me anew, though he had not. "I thought... I thought it was... wrong for anyone, even you, to raise a hand to royal flesh," I said.

"My prince," he purred, suddenly quite close, "have we done anything in this tower that makes you believe the usual rules of right and wrong apply here?" I felt his arms, now bare of robes, go around my chest, and the hard, hot press of his cock against the back of my thigh. "Did I not warn you in the very beginning of how it would seem, yet how necessary it would be?"

"You did," I choked, as the magehands began stroking me all over again, my cock especially. I crawled out of his embrace and positioned myself over the thing, my shins against the stone, lowering myself until I felt it just touch my hole.

I could hear a slick sound as I wavered there, slick and rhythmic but not from the invisible hands touching me. Seroi was tugging on his own cock behind me.

Two magehands spread my cheeks, whether to make the way easier for me, or the sight more enticing for him, I do not know.

I lowered myself still more, my haunches shaking slightly, as the tapered tip breached me. The magehand wrapped around my cock slowed, then squeezed tight, as if it would not resume stroking until I had completed the task.

I sucked in a breath. The thing was smooth as glass, and as cold as ice. Should it warm to my body? I slid further down it then, all too aware of how chill it felt, each inch of it as it pushed into me. And yet Seroi had promised pleasure, and there was that too, in the odd but intensely likable sensation I could only liken to having my cock stroked... but from the inside. I pushed myself down faster to finish and that was what it felt like, a stroke from the inside. I dared to rise up and push myself down again to see if it would feel that way again, and it did.

Far from angry at my disobedience, Seroi was pleased. "Ah, my prince, you begin to see. Do you like the way that feels?"

"Yes," I admitted.

"You may ride the spike if you enjoy it," he said, and I could hear the slick rhythm of his hand on his own cock speed up.

I rocked forward and back, impaling myself several more times on it, pulling completely free and then down onto it again.

"Very good," he praised. "You should know that with the threat of punishment always comes the possibility of reward. You have pleased me now, my prince. I already promised you would spill pleasurably. Is there anything else you would like to request as a reward for pleasing me?"

I shook my head. "No, my lord. I... just please let me finish."

"Tsk. My prince. Is there some particular way you might enjoy your release, then?"

An idea struck me then, that I would enjoy looking down and seeing him servicing me the way I had him. "Your mouth, my lord. I would... I would like to come on your tongue."

He laughed, full of mirth. "Oh, an excellent choice, my prince."

He knelt in front of me and placed his hands on my thighs, widening the space between my knees. I was no longer moving on the spike, but it felt almost as if its coldness were pulsing inside me. I looked down on the back of Seroi's head as he took my prick into his mouth. The wet suction was heavenly after the ghostly touch of the magehands, but then I cried out in surprise as I felt him lick his way up. His tongue was rough like a cat's, and soon he was stroking the shaft while he concentrated on licking only the too-sensitive head. It wasn't pain exactly, but it made me scream as he dragged it slowly, so slowly up the cleft of the head, and I wondered if I were being scraped raw enough to bleed. And yet, it was the most arousing sensation I had ever felt.

He paused and looked up. "I will lick three times more, and you will come on the third one," he said.

As usual, he was correct. Milk was fountaining up from me nearly the moment that third lick began, and then he caught it all in his mouth.

My shoulders slumped as the tension drained from me on release, but he held me upright a bit longer, and suddenly I had his slick cock in my own mouth. I could not tell if it was his real hands or magehands that held my head steady as he drove over the slickness of my tongue with short, quick jerks of his hips. The ashenbitter flood he released made me choke and cough, but there was no escape from the iron grip or the flesh pushing into my throat.

I must have blacked out for a while. When I came to, he was fully robed again. My head was in his lap and he was stroking my hair.

"Are you well, my prince?" he asked, and I felt a tender fingertip trace one of my eyebrows.

"Am I?" I asked.

He chuckled. "You are not injured. You are not bleeding or bruised. And your psychic armor is undamaged. But are you well?"

"I suppose," I said, wondering about the leaden limbs which had returned. "Do you need me to spill again? I... I didn't think how my choice of reward would deprive you of my milk for working the spell."

He chuckled again. "My prince, you are a treasure. Your milk is best direct from the source. I have been consuming it as part of a potion, but there will be no more need for that."

For some reason I felt even more leaden and heavy as he revealed that he had been drinking my seed all along. I stayed silent.

"You may go," he whispered, "if you wish, or you may stay and sleep just as you are."

I shook my head. "I... I should go. Don't... don't want to rouse suspicion of any kind."

"Ah, my prince grows wise," he said, fondness making his voice rich. "Fear not, sweet prince. We have a few weeks yet to indulge these pursuits."

I clung to his robes then, remembering what he'd said. "But... but you said you were going to... p-punish me next time."

"Hush, hush." He calmed my trembling with a hand, his real hand, stroking my bare shoulder. "That was only if you disobeyed. But you did not. You were perfect, my prince."

And quite suddenly I felt my chin tilt upward and then the slick warmth of his lips against mine, so completely unlike Jorin's that at first I jerked in surprise. But my body responded, my bare skin rubbing against his robes, and as his cat-rough tongue pushed into my mouth I felt his hand wrap around my reborn erection. "Looks like you will be giving me some more milk today after all, my prince," he said, as he began to stroke.

Twenty: Jorin

I woke as Bear was carrying me across the courtyard, cradled in his arms.

"Lie still," he said.

"I have little other choice," I replied, "given how you are holding onto me. What happened?"

"You'll remember in a little while. Or maybe you won't. Had a bit of Footsoldier's Ease and it can make you loopy."

"You didn't answer my question." I tensed now, starting to worry. "Am I lame? Have I lost a limb?"

"Hush. Do you remember anything about horses?" He shouldered open an inner door and took me toward the wing of the castle that contained our rooms.

"Ah, yes." We had been practicing dueling on horseback, fighting with wooden swords which were, I soon learned, used more often to try to knock one's opponent from the saddle than to strike a blow with. "Did I fall?"

Bear chuckled, and held close to his chest as I was, I could feel it rumble. "Not so much as leap from your saddle to your opponent's, which worked like a charm until his horse decided to unseat you and attack you himself."

"Oh." I had no memory of that at all. "Well, no one told me the horse was allowed to fight, too..."

He laughed again. "Kicked you in the face a mite harder than that soldier a couple of weeks ago, and then stepped on your ankle. It's only your boot that saved it from being crushed completely. As it is, you won't be walking on it for a while, I don't think. They have a good bonesetter down there, and he gave me a decoction for you to take. If you're lucky, you'll be walking again in a few days. If you're not... well, let's just not think about that."

"All right," I said, solemnified by his words. The torches flickering caught my attention. I hadn't even realized it was nightfall. Kenet would have gone to banquet without me. I hoped he had done nothing to incur his father's wrath tonight, for I would be unable to stand in front of all assembled if he bade me to.

Bear took me to his own room first, and lay me back on the bed. "Are you sleepy? Hungry? You should be sleepy, but it will be some time before you want food in your stomach again."

I shook my head. "I am not sleepy. I was asleep long enough under the potion's powers," I said. Then I jerked my chin toward the mirror. Bear nodded and closed the cabinet doors over it. Then he sat very close by the bed so that we didn't have to raise our voices. "Someone has put a spell on him that prevents him from telling me certain things," I said.

"Someone," Bear repeated with a significant glance toward the mirror. There was only one someone with that kind of power, now that Sergetten was gone.

I nodded in agreement. "I think... I think Kenet and he..." I could not say it either, but not because of any spell on me. A wave of dizziness seemed to rise up from my stomach and I put a hand over my mouth.

Bear put a hand on my stomach, steadying me. "You'll feel the aftereffects of the decoction for a while." And then in the same breath, "Is he a threat?"

"I don't know. Since he can't speak of it, what can I do but guess?"

Bear gritted his teeth. "They say there are secrets only mages and royalty know..." His face was wrinkled with skepticism. "I overheard the king say that Prince Kenet was practicing for his coming of age ceremony with the Lord High Mage."

I pondered that. Kenet had all but told me that Seroi touched him and gave him release... could I be wrong about the threat? Was this just some kind of royal manhood rite I was meant to be ignorant of? Surely if it were the case, it would have to be a closely guarded secret. The people, as a matter of course, would not accept a ruler who was a milksucking Frangi-lover. Perhaps that was why the secret was guarded with a spell?

"I don't know," I admitted. "You may be right and that is all it is, a bound secret for royalty and mages alone, but I think that is the source of his sickness. The practice. Or the magic itself. I don't know." I felt great enmity toward Seroi then, but I did not know if it were that I truly worried he was hurting Kenet, or just that I now saw him as a rival for Kenet's body, Kenet's affections.

No, I thought. Surely Kenet was not affectionate with him at all. Surely if they performed some perverse but necessary rite, it meant nothing...

Another wave of dizziness hit me from the decoction. This time I closed my eyes and went off into a dream and did not wake up again until I heard the frits singing. I opened them to find it still dark, and Kenet clinging to me under the coverlet.

I was half undressed, as if that was as much as Bear could stand to do. I could feel Kenet's bare flesh touching me everywhere, though.

"Sky above," he swore softly as I stirred. "I was worried you'd never wake."

I grunted and turned onto my side, pulling him against me. I was still wearing breeches, but my hand slid down his bare leg and then cupped his buttock. "Did Bear tell you a horse attacked me?"

"Yes." His lips found mine and I kissed him deeply, pulling back suddenly in the dark. "What's wrong?"

"You taste bitter," I said, reaching up to cup his face. There was a little light from a single candle above the bed. Would this hair, fair enough to almost mark him a Frangi, turn dark like his father's after his coming of age ceremony? I didn't care what color his hair was, but I was worried about the taste of his tongue. "Is this more of Seroi's doing? Just stay silent if the answer is yes."

He was perfectly silent, making not a sound.

I tried to move my foot and found I still could not feel it. It was immobilized with bandages; I had seen them, but I could not feel them.

A thought came to me then.

"Pinch me if by your silence you mean yes." My heart leapt as he squeezed my arm gently. "So. You cannot speak of your secrets, but you would tell me if you could." Another squeeze. "And apparently you can pinch me, but not say the words." A more emphatic squeeze.

"Have you been practicing something secret related to your coming of age?" Yes. "Something that is secret because it involves... this?" I slid my hand over his skin until I reached his prick, and was gratified to feel it come to life quickly in my grip. Yes.

I was dying to ask what Seroi did, but I couldn't even fathom what ritual magic might require. I knew he touched him like this, that he milked Kenet, and I also knew he didn't penetrate him, not in the way the men in the barracks said the Frangi did their boy-whores. I didn't know what else to ask.

Instead, as I felt the head of his cock grow slippery with his eagerness, I turned the questions to other things. "Do you like it when I touch you like this, Kenet?"

A more emphatic squeeze yes.

"Do you like it slow?"

Yes.

"But..." I teased, tugging quickly and lightly with a ring of my fingers just under the cleft of the head, something I did to myself when I wanted to reach release quickly before going to train with the guard. "You like it fast, too."

Yes.

"Hm. I want to kiss you as you come," I said, "but you taste too bitter. Would you suck my milk, Kenet?"

Yes!

"Be careful of the bandages..." I let go his cock and he dove under the blanket, finding the opening of my breeches in the dark and pulling them off me. A few moments later, the wet bliss of his mouth found its target.

The decoction was still running through my system, and I know it was supposed to make me feel everything less. But with his mouth on me I felt all the more. I pulled the covers up, over my own head, hiding us both in the dark.

Now he could not speak because his mouth was full of my flesh. No reason not to keep talking to him though, now that he had a way to answer. "Squeeze twice for no," I said.

He squeezed once to acknowledge.

"Do you like the taste of my milk, my prince?" One squeeze, yes.

"I like the taste of yours usually, too, but lately it has been bitter. Did you know that?"

No, he didn't.

"I wonder if it will run sweet again after your coming of age ceremony? Do you think it will?" No answer. He didn't know what to think, then.

"But you know, my prince, if you wanted me to suckle your prick, I would, no matter what poison might run through your veins," I said, my voice low. He squeezed my thighs emphatically then, and I thrust into his mouth, reminding him to pay attention. "I would," I repeated. "You need only ask."

He started to lift his head and I don't know what came over me, but I put my hand on the back of his head and kept him there, my prick driving between his lips. "If you asked it, I would give it to you," I continued. "Any desire of the flesh, Kenet, no matter how..." I broke off then, unable to even say that what we shared might be wrong. It didn't feel wrong when we were in bed together. It all felt right. "Any desire you have," I repeated. "I would do anything for you, Kenet. Anything at all. And I have a feeling you would do the same for me."

Another emphatic yes, but again I did not let him lift his mouth free to speak it. Instead I tightened my grip in his hair and thrust up harder into his mouth, spilling directly into him. He made satisfied sounds as he swallowed, then licked as I softened. When I let go, he surged up and kissed me, and I tasted the tang of my own milk as we emerged from the covers.

"Your turn," I said.

Now he spoke, at last. "Just use your hand, Jorin, if it tastes like poison. I... I worry it could be harmful to you."

"Harmful?"

"I worry," he repeated.

I reached down and stroked him. "Are you sure..." I whispered in his ear, "that you do not want me to take your prick into me like a Frangi boywhore would?"

Just the idea was enough to send him over the edge, spilling into my fingers. I held up my hand then for him to lick clean, and in the wan light I could see the face he made. "Bitter like ash," he said with a frown.

I rubbed my dry thumb along his cheek. "Your skin has had an ashen look of late, too."

He hugged me tightly then. "I hope it will end with the ceremony."

"Me, too, my prince. Me, too."

21: Kenet

I was on time for my meeting with my father, as I had been every time since the winter. We met on his private terrace, high up the side of the castle. Sometimes the castle itself seems like a mountain, as if it formed there by the forces of nature rather than by the work of human hands. From the terrace I could look down one side and over the gardens where I had seen Bear and Jorin practice in the spring.

Father's gaze was for the horizon, so close to us on this side thanks to the mountains. I had often heard it said that no army would find a way to us over those mountains and through those trees, and I remarked on it.

"That is why they attack us by other means," he replied.

"I have heard about the blight in the south," I said, trying to sound more like one of his advisors than like the boy I had so recently been. "Although there is still talk about a battle that took place on the Serde? At Tiger's Mouth?"

My father hissed as if in pain. "If you want stories of battle and glory, go down to the guard barracks and listen to them. But the tale of Tiger's Mouth is not one of glory."

"What happened there?"

"So few survived, we are still not sure," he said, leaning heavily upon the stone wall with both hands. "I suspect that the Night Riders took advantage of some freak occurrence of nature. Even a mage like Seroi could not single-handedly wipe out a garrison of five hundred men."

"What is the Night Riders' most dangerous weapon?" I asked, wondering if there was some spell or fighting technique they used.

"Lies," he said, surprising me. "They are masters of deception and when they infiltrate a town, they spread deceit and distrust.

They create rumors against the crown, undermine the local governors and lords, set the people against each other... which weakens an area such that when they attack, the resistance crumbles."

But surely a garrison of soldiers would not be deceived by lies and political propaganda? I opened my mouth to say so, but he had turned toward the doorway and led me into his quarters. There he poured us each a glass of chilled nectar and bade me sit at the ornate table in the parlor. His bedroom was beyond another door; this room was furnished in rich style, with a table that could be set for four or replaced with a larger one, accompanied by a chest of serving things topped with a gilt-edged mirror. A maid had once told me that my father had brought the furniture back from Pellon. Now I wondered if he had acquired it during the tour he and my mother had taken.

I sat gingerly on the edge of the cushioned chair and sipped from the glass. Falla nectar and honey and the deep chilled water from under the mountain.

"How are preparations for your coming of age ceremony progressing?" he asked. "Seroi has kept me in the dark on the details."

I looked up in surprise. "Did you not have such a ceremony?"

"I did, but mine was different from yours. I had different magics worked on me as a youth than you."

"Oh." I felt the heat starting to come to my cheeks as I tried not to think about what Seroi was doing to me to undo the suppressive spells that had kept my sexual urges in check. If not for this meeting with my father, I would have been in his tower today, this minute, doing who knows what to abase myself for the privilege of release. "To tell you the truth, he hasn't told me much about the ceremony either, but we do prepare magically. I believe when the time comes he'll tell me what to say and what to do."

My father nodded, and I could see the indentation in his forehead that the crown he normally wore had left like a dueling scar. "He certainly did for me. He will not give you the chance to fail." At that he chuckled. "I will tell you this much, if he has not. The actual ceremony will be performed in the woods, with just him, me, you, and perhaps two or three others present."

I sat up straighter suddenly, not because this news dismayed me, but because I felt the distinct sensation of a hand coming to rest on my crotch. I glanced down, wondering if I were going mad and had forgotten where my hands were. But no, one was around my glass, the other on the arm of the chair.

"Bear and Captain Jaiks, perhaps, to ensure we are not ambushed," my father went on, oblivious to my distress. The hand began to move, stroking me through my leggings. "After we return to the castle, there will be an official sort of ceremony in front of all assembled, but it is just a formality for the court. The true ceremony will have already been performed."

"I-I understand," I said. The sensation intensified, and then there was a sudden pinch right at the cleft of my cock head! I yelped, sloshing some of my drink into my lap a moment later to cover why. I leapt up, setting the glass down, rubbed at my leggings with my tunic. I tried to brush the sensations away, but they continued. "Clumsy! An insect bit me and now look what I've done."

My father chuckled indulgently. "You will need a steadier hand for dinners with other heads of state," he said.

I sat back down quickly, now trying to use the table to hide my groin from view. I hunched over. "Yes, definitely," I agreed. "Sergetten didn't teach me that part of manners. Will he return soon, you think?"

"I do not know," my father said, his face suddenly grave. "You should not speak of his absence if you can help it. I wish as little attention be paid to it as possible. If anyone should ask you where he has gone, you must say he went to research one of his arcane interests, and then tell me who it was that asked."

"Y-yes, Father..." The sensation of the hand—wrapped around my cock now and stroking me with quick tugs—made it difficult to speak.

"Are you well, my son?" he asked, brow furrowing with concern.

I clutched my stomach, a lie rolling easily off my tongue. "I think perhaps something I ate at midday was not good."

"Go to your rooms and I will send a nurse there to meet you," he said, rising and pulling a bell cord near the door. "You look flushed. Is it the return of the fever you suffered so recently?"

"Doesn't... doesn't feel like it..." I got up hurriedly as a maid opened the door in answer to the summons. "Sometimes... the spells that Seroi casts..."

My father did not hesitate. "Take him to Seroi," he barked at the maid. "I will see you at banquet, Kenet, if you are feeling better."

"Yes, father." I hurried out, ahead of the woman who trailed after me, flustered. She closed the door behind us and then chased me into the corridor. I slipped onto a settle there as the hand that stroked me continued, hidden from her view by my tunic and my hunched position. "I will... I can make my own way there..."

She fanned me with her apron and pressed one cool hand to my cheek. "If it's the Lord High Mage you're needing, I can fetch him here for you, Prince Kenet."

I shook my head. "My father jumps to conclusions. It's merely something I ate. I'll go to my own room."

"If you're sure, my prince."

"Yes, yes, I'm sure." I got to my feet and hurried down the corridor and then once I was around the corner, slipped into one of the secret passages behind a tapestry that hung to the floor. My goal was not a shortcut to Seroi's tower, but merely to get out of sight.

I freed my cock from my breeches, moaning as the sensation increased all the more. Magehands. This had to be Seroi's doing! I groaned again, as the sorcerous touch kept me on the edge of coming without actually being enough to take me over. I tried to take hold of my flesh myself only to find the way blocked by the invisible hands.

I do not know how long I lay there, my back against the tunnel's wall, before I realized that only Seroi would be able to give me relief. I began to crawl in the direction of his tower, knowing this back passage would at least bring me out near the courtyard of the Tour Tapestry.

Jorin wouldn't be able to find me here, I realized. Only I had the touch that would open the doors to the secret passages. I hadn't realized that at first, but Bear had told me once I'd asked him why I could and Jorin couldn't, that it was a matter of royal blood. There were spells one could put on locks and doors and boxes and things such that they would only open for us. The Rose Gate, he said, was the largest of them all.

I passed through a part of the tunnel that was completely dark, but I pressed on, getting to my feet and hurrying, then hugging the wall at the bend, trying helplessly to rut against the stone itself, but to no avail.

I was lying at the bottom of a few stairs, desperately but vainly trying to rub my cock against the floor, when the secret door there opened and Seroi scooped me up in his arms. His real hand took hold of my cock then as he kissed me, his tongue darting into my mouth to coax more hungry moans from me.

"My prince, my prince," he said, his voice soothing in the dark, "there is no need for you to suffer so. I am here."

"Seroi." My voice was rough and dry. "Please. I need release."

"I know, my prince. I know. You must have missed me to be in such a state."

I was thrusting into his hand, which was wonderfully slick, his grip firm. "Was this not your doing? Were you not... touching me magically?"

"While you met with your father?" He gave a scandalized hiss. "No, my prince. This magic is your own doing. This is your need calling to me."

I whimpered, needing to come more than ever and fearing now that I would not be able to, even with him stroking me as he was.

"Your magic runs deep, my prince," he crooned. "Your needs, deeper. Else you would not have opened the door here for me."

Oh. I was the one who opened the door? Just by wishing? That didn't feel right but what did I know of magic? "Please, Seroi, I need to come. Please make me spill."

"Indeed, my prince, I am surprised you have not yet. But perhaps all your body's cravings have not yet been met." He lay me back on his robe then, and knelt between my knees, licking the head of my cock and then suckling in earnest while his fingers scratched at my hole, stabbing me suddenly and prying me open. I cried out with the sharp pain but also the sudden rush of ecstasy as my orgasm broke loose. Release at last! He sucked up every drop with not a complaint about its flavor and I counted myself curious enough to pull him up to kiss me, his mouth on my mouth. But I tasted mostly the sweat from my own upper lip.

When he pulled back it was to stroke my hair tenderly. "I will teach you the proper way to ask for a kiss later," he murmured. "For now, it pleases me that you desired one. Expressing your desires is very important for you right now, my prince. You must not hide them from me."

"No, my lord," I said, weak from the sudden release after being held on edge for so long.

"You are beautiful," he said, as he picked me up in his arms. I was surely too large for that, but he must have had some magical strength to carry me thus. He carried me through the passages and somewhere in the darkness I fell into a deep sleep.

22: Jorin

I was stretching my muscles with the other guards that morning when Captain Jaiks strode into our midst, whistling merrily. He was without his usual jacket and insignias, and I don't think I had ever seen him without a hat before, but the scar under his right eye made him unmistakeable. He began to stretch, too, and the guards began to get nervous.

I kept my grin to myself. So, Jaiks would be in the ring today? I found myself looking forward to the challenge and wondering whether we would be on horse or on foot.

As it turned out, we would be weaponless, with bare hands and feet. Jaiks paired us off, and the man who faced him first looked glum. "You fight until one yields or loses consciousness. No maiming." That brought forth a few nervous chuckles. "You're no good to the crown maimed. Any man who breaks the rules will be sent straight to Tiger's Mouth. Lose to two opponents and you are eliminated. Last one standing gets a bonus of a week's pay, unless it's me, of course." His feral grin showed he expected to be the last man standing.

"What if it's Jorin?" one of the others called out.

Jaiks clapped me on the shoulder. "We'll think of a prize for him if he makes it that far."

Thus began an enjoyable morning. I liked these kinds of competitions, probably because the more I trained, the better I became at them.

A barehanded fight, Bear explained to me, goes through five stages. He called them circle-distance, when the two opponents are too far apart to touch, foot-distance, when they are close enough to kick, fist-distance, when they are close enough to punch, close-distance, when they are close enough to grab onto, and kiss-distance, a nice way of saying they were close enough to bite. No maiming meant no biting, I had learned early in my training with them, even though I thought it should have been possible to bite someone just hard enough to make them let go, without actually ripping out a chunk of their flesh.

The guards had learned to try to beat me at kick- and fist-distance, because once they grabbed me, I fought with my elbows and knees. I don't really remember having to defend myself that way as a child before Kenet picked me out of the orphanage, but I must have. It was almost instinctual.

But with training I had become deft at the first few stages of the fight, too, waiting for my moment to close the distance. To me it made sense to close the distance and fight that way if I had no weapon, even if my opponent had a sword. Once close enough to them, I was no longer a target for their blade.

My first two opponents went down easily enough. We were all fighting simultaneously, while Jaiks' second in command went around judging the matches. Once it was down to eight men who hadn't yet lost, though, Jaiks among them, they had us fight one pair at a time, while the rest looked on.

Jaiks, despite the limp he tried to hide and the bits of grey in his hair, was as fit as any of his men, and I was surprised by his quickness. He, too, liked to close and force his opponent to yield, the bone of his wrist against their windpipe, for example. Man after man went down before him, usually emerging unbruised compared to their other fights, but just as defeated.

I had my worst trouble with a cavalryman Bear's size, who would crush me if I ended up in his arms. Fortunately he could be taunted into charging, and I could flip him off me, his own weight making him groan as he slammed into the ground.

That trick, I soon learned, did not work on Jaiks himself. I had barely wiped the dust out of my eyes from my last fight before I realized we would be facing each other. He was standing in the center of the packed-dirt ring, arms crossed and a grim smile on his face.

He shook hands before beginning and then his second barked

"Start!" and before I quite knew what was happening, he had borne me to the ground and struck me across the jaw. Hitting the ground knocked the wind out of me worse than the punch, and I got hold of his collar, pulling him in even as I tried to hit him with my elbow. It felt like he had three arms, though, and I could never quite get one of mine free for a shot at him.

But he couldn't quite make me yield, either. His second finally shouted at us to separate and start over. The men were murmuring, then calling out their encouragement and jeers as we circled each other. I kept expecting him to charge, but now he was patient, feinting with little shuffles of his feet and movements of his hands.

I was caught wrong-footed, suddenly committed to lunging at him when I wasn't quite ready, but I got my arms around his middle and bore him down. We twisted and wrestled then, again neither one of us quite reaching the point of making the other yield.

Again we went back to our places, both panting and red-faced, both grinning. "You're still not much of a wrestler," he said, as we started to circle again. "And your face is still too pretty."

That made me laugh. "The court ladies seem to like it."

"Your face, or the wrestling?" shouted one of the onlookers, drawing more laughter.

This time I kicked him in the leg before we went down, and my advantage lasted for perhaps a minute before he finally managed to get an arm around my neck. He could easily choke me to unconsciousness. I tapped him on the back to yield and he let me fall limp to the dirt.

He was looking down into my face, still atop me, when he said, "You would have had me, had you kicked my bad leg instead of the good one."

"I'll remember that next time."

"But next time I won't go so easy on you." Then he was up and giving me a hand up.

It wasn't until much later, as we were heading back up to the castle to get washed up, that I realized how much everything hurt.

23: Kenet

I stood at the base of the tower facing the door that would lead me up into Seroi's realm. It was time, perhaps past time, that I climbed the stairs to meet him. What was he doing up there right now? Was he wondering where I was? How bad would the punishment be if I delayed longer? Would it worsen the longer I waited?

I shivered, unable to imagine what he might do to me, and then shivering all the more as I realized my cock was growing eager. I hissed softly as it grew, thrusting up against my belly between my skin and the waistband of my breeches. Evil thing, my prick, I thought, as if it wanted me to suffer.

Maybe that was Jorin's doing? He used to tease me so mercilessly, perhaps he had conditioned me from the start, before Seroi even began his magical treatments on me?

I leaned my head against the wood. Surely once my coming of age ceremony was complete, I would no longer need these rituals and spells? I could certainly force myself to go through with it just a few more times. It wasn't as if the process was truly painful—in fact, it was usually quite pleasurable—and Seroi himself had assured me it was necessary for my health and my future. I couldn't take the chance that he spoke true that stopping short of completely freeing me of the magical shackles on my libido would result in crippling me for the rest of my life.

I would be brave. Jorin and I would be together forever with no more threats once I was king. The first step in that process was the ceremony. I pulled open the door and began to ascend.

I emerged at the top level of the tower fully clothed this time, but swayingly dizzy from the incense. I put a hand to my forehead, as if I could steady the swimming of my vision. I stumbled forward with my eyes closed, then opened them cautiously.

My breath caught when I saw what awaited me at the center of the magical circle. Another thing like the previous one, only this one was much larger, as thick around as my wrist and as long as Bear's dagger, handle included. It gleamed like wet glass and I saw it was sitting on a dark irregular spot—a small puddle.

I looked up to see Seroi glaring at me, arms folded over his chest. "Are you ill today, my prince?" he asked in a low voice.

I shook my head. "Just... perhaps. I haven't felt... right."

He gave a slow nod. "Your reluctance is the last vestige of the magics you are shedding. Haven't I explained that?"

Oh. "Yes. You have. It just... it feels like the feelings are my own."

"Of course it does," he said, sounding more indulgent now. "That is how insidious the restrictions are. I suppose I should be proud of myself for having woven such a strong web. But I will tell you, Kenet, I am growing concerned with how little time we have left before the ceremony."

I merely nodded, wringing my hands and waiting for him to tell me what to do. But of course he didn't tell me, just stared at me and waited for me to give in. I swallowed once more and began to strip down until I was as naked as the day I had been born. I even took one step closer to the thing sitting on the floor.

And then I surprised myself. "No. I can't."

He didn't move, but I felt magehands caressing my body, from my thighs upwards. "Why is that, my prince?"

I just shook my head. I didn't want that thing inside me, but I couldn't say that to him. I knew it would only draw ridicule and more scolding.

"Are you afraid it will hurt? The previous one did not, you may remember."

I just closed my eyes, silent, mind racing for a way out, even as I could feel my heartbeat in my rampant cock. The invisible fingers stroked up and down my shaft wordlessly promising pleasure.

I shook my head again. "I said no. There must be another way."

A low chuckle set the hairs on the back of my neck rising. "And if there is another way, will you take it, my princeling?"

I nearly said yes, then held my tongue. "What is this other way?"

"I assure you, the easier method is to do as before. If you like, I will even allow you to lie back instead of lowering yourself..."

"What is the other way?" I insisted.

He was suddenly close, moving with magic so that one instant he was standing outside the circle, the next, he was pressed against me, his robes scratchy against my bare skin and one arm behind my back. "The other way is to take something else in its place, namely the prick of the mage who bespelled you to begin with."

I tried to push him away, but he was holding me fast.

"I assure you, Kenet, I have no qualms about doing so if that is what you would prefer," he said, eyes glittering.

"N-no," I stammered. Then abruptly, he was gone, standing a few steps away once more, leaving my knees weak.

"I did not think you would choose that way," he said, smoothing his robes. "It is raw and barbaric, but I would have made it pleasurable for you had you wished it. You are back to my original choice for you, my prince." He indicated the protrusion with a gesture of his hand. "It need not go all the way in, if that worries you, though you will need to take at least half of it for it to be effective."

I shook my head, this time turning away from him and the thing so that I would not need to see either any longer.

There was a long stretch of silence in which I tried not to even breathe.

Then a long sigh came from him. "Kenet. Have I explained to you the consequences of..."

"You have."

"We cannot go back now. We can only go forward. I do not have any more choice about this than you do."

My shoulders slumped. "Please," I said. "Give me until tomorrow. I'll come again at the same time and I'll try to do it tomorrow."

Silence again. I resisted the urge to turn around. Jorin leapt into my thoughts, but I held still and quiet.

"If you cannot manage it," Seroi whispered, "if you cannot

work the ritual phallus into yourself, I will be forced to tie you down and use my own prick to finish the ritual."

Very well. Tonight I would let Jorin be the one to do it. Tomorrow I would come back to Seroi and tell him I didn't need him or his thing because it was already done by my Jorin's cock. "Tomorrow," I repeated. "I'll come back tomorrow and all will be well." I turned suddenly then and threw myself to my knees at his feet, clutching at his robes. "Please, my lord, please. Should I promise...?"

His hand on my hair was so gentle it brought a sudden sob to my throat. "Hush, no. No promise. Oh, Kenet, you have a good heart. You are lovely and pure. The people will love you as king."

My tears soaked his robes as he went on. "I love you, my prince," he said. "You are very dear to me. Return tomorrow and we shall finish this."

"And all will be well," I said, making a promise to myself in my heart that it would be, one way or the other. Would lightning strike me dead if it were not?

I was ready this time when he bent down to kiss me, and instead of ash, the kiss tasted of tears.

24: Jorin

"That was some fine work," Bear said, as he lifted the bucket of warm water over my head. "Even if Jaiks barely admits it."

I grinned, running my hands through my hair as the water cascaded down, splashing at my bare feet on the stone. "I still wouldn't want to be on the wrong end of his dagger," I said. "He didn't get to be captain of the guard by accident. Should I have really gone for his weak leg?"

Bear chuckled and dipped the bucket into the steaming tub before pouring it over me again. The dirt from the practice ring had been ground into my hair and ears, under my fingernails, everywhere. I looked at my hands. Under the dirt, I was finally starting to see the normal color of my skin, tanned from the summer sun.

Our voices echoed from the vaulted ceilings of the baths, but the continual splashing of water also masked what we said. We appeared to be alone at the moment, but I was always careful what we spoke of. "Bear," I asked, "if all this is so that someday I may replace you... there is something I must know."

"Go on, cub," he said, handing me the bucket. I filled it and then stood on a bench to be tall enough to get it over his head.

"I'll ask you later," I teased, "when you don't have water in your ears."

He laughed at that, shaking his head under the water like a dog. He wasn't half so dirty as I had been, having just watched from the side.

I waited until we were seated at banquet that night. As had become usual ever since the night the King had beaten me last, Kenet was seated at his father's side at the high table, between the king and the Lord High Mage. Bear and I sat below the dais, to one side, where we could see the whole room.

While the musicians were playing I leaned over to say in Bear's ear, "So, my question. If we're supposed to be Kenet's guards, you now, me in the future, how are we to protect him if he's up there and we're down here?"

Bear glanced up and I looked away as the Lord High Mage leaned toward the king to say something, placing his hand all too familiarly on Kenet's shoulder.

"Take a drink," Bear said under his breath. I must have looked distressed. I sipped my wine and smiled at him. "Better. And the answer, cub, is I don't know. I liked it better when he used to sit between us here. You might ask, indeed, why he needs a guard at all when he's barely ever left the palace."

I nodded, thinking if the greatest danger to him was the man sitting beside him, then there was nothing to be done with daggers or swords or wrestling prowess anyway. I hid my face behind my goblet again. Then I asked Bear, "How did you become his guard in the first place?"

He cracked a wide smile at that. "Same way you did, cub. When he was too tiny to speak he would grab hold of me and not let go!"

That made me laugh. We took turns watching him after that, but Seroi did nothing out of the ordinary. It wasn't as if we were going to catch him dropping poison into the prince's wine. But neither of us could leave Kenet completely unobserved. I nearly got to my feet as I saw him go to join the dancing, though. Bear held my wrist under the table.

Kenet joined in a ring dance, and I watched jealously as he spun in and out of the arms of the two young noblewomen on either side of him. No, it was better if I did not watch. I concentrated on tearing a piece of bread into tiny pieces, then eating them one by one.

Bear nudged me when the music ended, and Kenet paused to greet some of the other people at one of the lower tables. Bear grunted. "If you're to be his guard, you'll need to learn the names of every person he meets."

I looked. I could name perhaps two of the six people seated there. "Tell me."

"One step at a time, cub. I'll wager Kenet doesn't know their names either, eh?"

"I thought that was the sort of thing Sergetten was supposed to be teaching him, before he disappeared."

"You don't need to learn the lineages and all that. Just who's who. And who's dangerous."

"I already know that," I said darkly.

"Hush. Here he comes."

Kenet came to us next, sitting next to me and taking a swallow out of my wine goblet. "Clouds above, dancing is thirsty work," he said. His skin was damp and I knew if I licked him behind the ear now I would taste salt. I took the wine back and sipped it instead and Kenet looked at me with such intensity that I felt he was trying to read my thoughts through my eyes.

I narrowed mine at him trying to ask him if something was wrong. He just squeezed my thigh once, then spoke. "How was your practice today?"

"Excellent," I said. "I fought Captain Jaiks to a standstill twice."

He grinned, pleased, and I leaned close and whispered, "I will show you how I pinned him once we are in bed together."

He laughed, a high fake laugh, but squeezed my thigh under the table once more, then slipped away for another dance.

Upon the dais, Jaiks was leaning over to hear something the king said into his ear. He nodded and left without another word, then returned quickly but did not speak to the king again, just took up a post standing to one side of the throne. I had never noticed until now that the boot heel on his bad side was taller than the other, helping him to hide his limp. I wondered how old he was.

Would I someday stand in that very spot while Kenet listened to the counsel of his ministers? I could not imagine Kenet taking his father's place, though. I simply could not picture it.

I saw Seroi get to his feet. He was taller than the king, almost as tall as Bear, but didn't look as if he had much fat or bulk under his heavy robes. He motioned to Jaiks and the two of them put their heads close together in conference. I saw Jaiks shake his head, but then his gaze suddenly met mine, and although I looked away quickly, my stomach felt full of stone.

Bear's hand moved to his hilt automatically when he sensed me stiffening like that. "What's wrong?" he said under his breath.

"Hopefully, nothing," I answered. I wanted to get up and leave. But whatever was about to happen, I knew they could summon me back at a moment's notice, and my absence would only make it worse. I was no longer looking at Seroi and Jaiks, but now Bear was.

"What's he want with him? Don't look, cub. They're having a bit of an argument."

I searched for Kenet. He had finished another ring dance and was standing on the side, clapping his hands while some of the others danced. What had he been trying to tell me with that look, that touch? It wasn't like him to do something like that right here in front of everyone, even though I'm sure even Bear could not have seen it. I lifted the wine goblet to my mouth again, my lip touching the place where he had sipped.

The king and Seroi were speaking now, and I felt as if I were sinking when the king signaled for quiet and stood.

"Kenet," he said, and his voice was low and quiet. That worried me more than when he was simply angry and shouting.

"Yes, father." Kenet hurried to the foot of the dais. "What is wrong?"

"Your tutor tells me you failed to obey his instructions today while practicing for your coming of age ceremony."

I saw Kenet falter where he stood, as if he might sink to his knees on the spot. "But... but I..."

"Do you deny this?" The King's face was impassive, almost as if he were tired of the proceedings already.

Kenet hung his head. "I cannot. It is true. I asked... to be allowed to try again tomorrow."

Try what? I wondered. The nobles assembled probably thought Kenet had refused to memorize a poem or something. I could not help but wonder about the things Kenet had told me—and not told me—about what Seroi did to him.

"You are too willful in these matters. The Lord High Mage must be obeyed when it comes to issues beyond your ken!" Now the king's voice rose at last, perhaps with a note of panic. What had Kenet done? Had he jeopardized himself somehow with his refusal?

Or was it merely that he had defied a man who exerted more power than any, other than the king himself? I glanced at him and saw Seroi was looking at me with a cruel smile. Because who would pay for Kenet's mistakes?

I would. I broke out in a sweat just sitting there, but I would not move until I was bade to. They exchanged a few more volleys, setting the terms of the infraction and the punishment, its duration and its instrument. I could only hear it with half an ear, as my heartbeat seemed to grow louder and louder.

But one part I did hear that brought my head up sharply and caused Kenet to cry out, "No!" The king had handed a short, coiled whip to the Lord High Mage and told him to do the honors.

"Jorin," Seroi said, gesturing to the empty space in front of him on the dais as if he were inviting me to dance.

I shot to my feet like a soldier coming to attention. I felt every bit as much dread as Kenet did, but I was not going to show it. There was no use shrinking from it. No one but the king himself had ever punished me in public before. Oh, Sergetten had swatted me during lessons when Kenet would miss an answer or his attention would stray, but this...? Coiled leather meting out punishment in front of the entire court would be severe enough, but for the whip to be in non-royal hands...? This could not be good.

I shed my boots and clothes quickly, piling them upon a chair before taking my position in front of Seroi, my back to him and facing the assembled, my legs spread and my hands clasped in front of my stomach, my head bowed. Then from above me I heard a chain rattle. I could not help it. I looked up in surprise. A hook on a long chain swung just above my head.

"Captain Jaiks," the Lord High Mage said, and a moment later, Jaiks was putting my wrists into iron manacles. His eyes held a flicker of sympathy for me, but he could say nothing. The hook lowered a few more feet, took hold of the chain between my wrists, and then up it went.

The king had never chained me like a criminal in order to beat me. It's merely theatrics, I told myself. Just Seroi's way of scaring me. Telling myself that didn't actually make it any less intimidating, though. The hook went up until I was on the tips of my toes, still touching the dais but agonizingly caught between hanging from my arms and holding myself up with my feet. It was difficult to breathe this way. Or maybe the fear was stronger than I thought. I tried to be calm. Surely he hasn't got much muscle, I thought. He can't possibly hit as hard as the king.

I was wrong. Maybe the blow was enhanced by magic, but it felt to me like he sliced open my back with a red hot dagger, and I screamed. Thunder's roll, how many would it be? Ten? Had they said ten? I wasn't certain I could stay conscious past three.

He waited, the bastard, until the pain had completely ebbed away from the first blow, which was a long time to hang there, panting and dripping sweat. I hoped it was just sweat and not blood, anyway. Then he laid on the second.

It tore me from shoulder all the way to hip. This time it took me a little while to stop screaming. When I did, I realized Kenet was shouting at Seroi.

"I didn't do it just to defy you!" he insisted, and I could hear he was on the verge of tears himself.

"But you did defy me," Seroi said, his voice calm and smooth. "Your intent is not at issue here, my prince. Your actions, or lack of them, are. Or can you give me a plausible reason for your reluctance to follow my orders today? Perhaps if you could, it would mitigate the punishment."

I wanted to tell Kenet to shut up, that I would survive this, and not to give in to the wily bastard. But I could not actually say anything at that moment. And I knew to actually voice those thoughts would make it even worse.

"I just... I just wasn't ready!" he cried. "I told you that! You said tomorrow!"

Seroi clucked his tongue. "That is not an explanation, my prince." And with that he struck me again.

I tried not to scream quite so much this time, choking my own cry as much as I could, trying to hear what Kenet might say. Oh my prince, say nothing. Don't give in to him. I had no idea what Seroi's game was, only that it could not be good.

Then I shivered at the sensation of a hand skimming down my welted back and over my backside. Who? I was certain no one was that close to me.

"I suspect, my prince, that your resistance to my orders comes from a source other than your own heart." Seroi's voice carried throughout the hall, even as it also sounded intimate. "I'm afraid this punishment might be more appropriate than you know. Tell me, my prince, has Jorin been feeding you lies about me?"

"What? No! Don't be ridic—"

The next blow cut across my buttocks and I was already beginning to doubt I knew how many that had been. Four? Each blow sent my mind spinning.

Then my breath caught as the distinct sensation of fingers brushing lightly over the shaft of my prick sent a ripple through me. I strained to look down, but there was definitely no one there.

Seroi was addressing the king then. "You see, my king, I suspect the source of the corruption is none other than your son's ladra'an himself. The very boy who spends every night in your son's company."

Kenet was staring, as pale as his white tunic. "That... that isn't... I cannot believe..."

The stammering was getting him nowhere. Meanwhile I fought to hold in a groan as the sensation of a hand working me brought my erection to full length. I heard a female gasp as someone noticed it.

The next blow came then and I tensed, ready for another stripe of agony, but much to my surprise this one—although it sounded just as loud—was much lighter. Almost sensual. My cry had a distinctly different tone to it.

"You may as well confess," Seroi said from behind me. "I glimpsed the truth today while the prince and I were practicing the ritual. You desire him, you sick creature. While he sleeps, you satisfy your lust for him upon his body, do you not?"

My cock was throbbing now, and I could not hold in the groan this time as the invisible hand milked a glistening droplet from me. This had to be some sorcery of Seroi's, but I had no way to stop it. I tried to say "No..." but it came out a whisper.

After all, what he was saying was true. Mostly anyway. I could hear the king's boot heels as he came around in front of me. I opened my eyes just before he smacked my erection with his open palm. "Can you deny it?"

"I would never do anything to hurt Kenet."

"That isn't what I asked you!" He smacked me again, and I had the sudden fear that they were going to unman me with the whip. Kenet must have as well, for he rushed forward as if to stop them, only to be grabbed by the king himself who held him with one arm around his throat from behind, forcing Kenet to face me.

He slashed open the front of Kenet's tunic with his belt knife, exposing Kenet's chest to me just as the wicked hands squeezed my balls and circled the head of my cock with a phantom thumb. He flung Kenet to the floor then. "You do. You desire him. It's written in every line of your body."

I shook my head. "No."

"Prove it to me, then. If you are still like this," he smacked my cock once more, "when I am done beating you, you will never lay eyes on my son again. If you are soft, you will be allowed to remain in training as his guard, but you will pay a price of blood to remain with him."

"But my king..." Seroi said, daring to interrupt.

The king merely snapped his fingers impatiently for the whip. Seroi may have been an evil bastard, but he was not stupid. He handed over the coiled, braided hide and stepped back.

It was me who spoke up. "Price of blood?" I had to know.

"You won't need this." He struck my erection with the handle of the whip and I saw stars. "If you are bound by a blood bond, you will never have a wife or family of your own, anyway. And I will be able to trust you to guard my son again, once your fang has been cut from you."

Kenet's sob echoed off the stone. I dared a glance at him. Bear was holding him. Bear was there.

Bear would be there to protect him if I was not. "How long will you beat me, my king?" If what he truly wanted was to unman me, he could simply go on until my cock eventually would go limp.

His whisper was for me alone, as he gripped me by the back of my head, his fist in my hair. "Until Kenet begs me to stop."

So, it was as it had been that day when I had been plucked from the orphanage, my fate entirely in the hands of those more powerful than me. The king threw the whip aside and signaled for the chain to be released. With his grip never slackening from the back of my head, he struck me across the face with his other hand, a heavy, open-handed blow that made me taste blood.

I cannot honestly say whether the phantom touches continued or ceased. I do know I was as erect as ever as I began to lose consciousness between blows. I wondered how much my mouth and nose were bleeding.

Kenet, my dear Kenet. He stepped in to save me, as I had known he would, but at what cost? I do not think at that moment he was even thinking about what might happen next, only that he could not bear to see me struck one more time.

Jaiks and another guard dragged me away. Bear had to hold Kenet back. The Lord High Mage was assuring the king that with the corruption rooted out, his son would surely progress as planned. I passed out as they dragged me down the steps at the back of the dais.

When I came to, someone was shoving me across the bench of a carriage. Jaiks. My hands were bound behind my back now, and I was in rough clothes of some kind. "Captain?" I asked.

"You stupid fool," he said, sounding weary. "If you weren't such a fighter, I never would have spoken up for you."

"What?"

"Death or banishment? Seroi wanted you killed. Though I may be sending you to your death anyway." In the darkness I could not see his face. "You're off to Tiger's Mouth, son."

He shut the door of the carriage then, and I heard the latch rattle on the outside. There was the sound of a whip cracking and I was thrown to the floor as the horses leapt forward.

I stayed there on the floor, my hands behind my back and my cheek pressed to the wood, without a single thought for myself then, but only of Kenet. Kenet, my prince, I promise I will return to you. Be strong, be wary! I will return. I promise. We shall be reunited.

I let out a scream of pain and this one had nothing to do with my injuries or bruises. It was the pain of my heart being torn from my chest, the agony of knowing that tonight, for the first time in over fifteen years, he would not sleep in the circle of my arms.

25: Kenet

Don't ask me what came over me. As they dragged Jorin away, and another scream was building in my chest, I suddenly became calm somewhere deep inside. I would not let them do this. It was as if in that moment the light shone on me for the very first time and I saw the world around me.

I screamed. And then I fell limp into Bear's arms, feigning a faint, knowing that he would carry me straight to my room. Or at least hoping so. He lifted me into his arms as if I were half my size and carried me from the hall.

We came to a stop in what must have been the corridor just outside the banquet hall. I heard my father's voice. "Is he well?"

"I'll put him to bed, my king," Bear said in a low voice. "Surely it's just too much excitement for one day. It isn't every day the prince sees such brutality."

It was as close to a criticism as I had ever heard Bear make in front of my father. I was tempted to crack open one eye to see the expression on my father's face, but I didn't dare. I heard the rustling of robes as another person joined us.

I felt a cool hand on my brow. Seroi. I gave a great shiver then as if his touch were icy cold.

"Seroi, will he be well? The truth, man. Is this some consequence of the preparations you and he are making?"

"Well, my king, I did try to warn him that not to obey me in magical matters could have severe consequences..."

"Seroi!"

"He is in a very vulnerable state, my lord," Seroi went on. "I have been bringing him gradually to the state of readiness to accept the ritual. I have gone slowly for his sake, but perhaps we have gone too slowly. The... step we were to take today is a major one, and without it... He is vulnerable, my king. Very vulnerable."

"Very well. I do not care what he thinks. Enough babying him. Seroi, do what you must. Tonight."

"But my lord!" That was Bear. "He's ill!"

I shivered again as Seroi's fingers sifted through my hair. "He does not need to be conscious for me to finish the spell, though I would greatly prefer it."

"Your preferences can go hang," my father said. "I do not want him left in this vulnerable state any longer than necessary."

Bear cleared his throat. "My lord and king, if I might. He's been prone to these fits of hysteria before. They never last. He'll sleep a little and then wake up good as new. Then the Lord High Mage may finish whatever magic he needs."

"Indeed," Seroi added, "I would not want to rob him of any important understanding of his coming of age that could result from his participation..."

"Fine, fine! I leave him in your hands, the both of you! But if anything happens to him, I will have both of your milksacks strung from hooks, do you hear me?"

I heard the rustle of Seroi's robes as he bowed and I felt myself dip in Bear's arms as he did the same. My father returned to the banquet hall.

"I'll put him in bed," Bear said. "And send for you when he wakes."

Seroi made a long thoughtful hum. "I would prefer to wait by his bedside."

Bear stumbled. "Begging your pardon, my lord, but I have never allowed anyone to enter that chamber without the prince's permission and I find this a poor time to start."

I silently thanked him for the untruth. He allowed maids into the room all the time. But perhaps in some measure he had my permission for them? It did not matter. He was doing his best to get me away from Seroi even if only for a short while.

"I shall wait outside his door then," Seroi countered.

"Very well."

They walked the rest of the way in silence. Bear carried me into my room, set me on the bed, whispered "hush" into my ear, and then walked away.

I opened one eye to see him covering the mirror with a short cloak of Jorin's. He returned then and put his hand on my forehead as if checking to see if I were ill. He spoke in a strange kind of whisper, such that I barely saw his mouth moving under his mustache. "I know you're feigning it, my prince. I did my best. What do you want to do next?"

I could not imitate what he did. I rolled onto my side and whispered. "Bear." I tried to tell him what Seroi was going to do, that the milksucking bastard was going to come in here and stick his prick in me, and that I didn't care if it killed me, I wasn't going to let him do it. Not after what I'd seen tonight. But just thinking the words made my throat tighten and I knew I wouldn't be able to speak of it. Instead I said, "I'm going to run away."

"Then you'd best hit me over the head with a candle stand, my prince. Can you do that? Where will you go?"

"You're not going to try to stop me?" I asked, surprised.

"Jorin told me the mage has some evil designs on you. I believe him. But I cannot help you flee, my prince. You must knock me on the head or they'll think I have."

"I'll go through the passageways. I'm the only one who knows my way through them, anyway." Well, Jorin knew them almost as well as I did, but not quite as well. Perhaps once upon a time my father had known them, too, but by the time he could be summoned to open the door I would be long gone. That well of calm that had suddenly sprung up as Jorin had disappeared from my sight seemed to fill my chest. "All I have to do is get through the passageway door and shut it behind me. You won't be able to follow."

"True, cub. But make it look good for old Bear, eh?"

"You really want me to hit you?"

"You heard your father. I'm rather attached to my milksacks, you know."

"All right. Let me get a dagger and some things together..."

"I fear he has some magic way of seeing us, my prince."

"The mirror?"

"I don't know."

"I hope not, since if that's the case, then he knows you're onto his spying, no? Go toward the door. I'll... I'll use the candle stand." I held my breath for a moment. Could I do this? I thought of Jorin, his face bloody and bruised, and knew I could.

Bear turned away from me and walked toward the door as if to summon Seroi. I picked up the candle stand in one hand and brought it down hard. I think I hit him on the back of the shoulder mostly, only grazing the side of his head. He fell to his knees, grabbing at the wound and crying out in surprise. I'm sure he hadn't meant to do that. I grabbed the cloak from the mirror and then ran to the doorway across the room. It opened to my touch and as it was closing behind me I heard the main door to my room opening, and Seroi's voice, raised.

I hoped he didn't hurt Bear. I hurried down the dark curve of the passageway. I cursed as I realized in my haste to get through the door I had forgotten to take the dagger from the chest beside the bed.

Then I held my tongue as I heard the door behind me open. And Seroi's voice call after me. "My prince?"

I ran, then. He shouldn't have been able to open that door! Then I remembered he had done it once before, but had said it was me, my wish, that opened it for him. Did I secretly desire him?

No! I ran as quickly as I could in the dark. Could he see me? I could hear him following. He could probably hear me. I stopped for a moment to doff my boots and then ran on doe feet, silent and quick.

I knew these passages. Surely he did not? I came to a branching way. If I went right it would lead me down toward the first guard tower. From there I could climb down to the main road up the mountain.

I stifled a scream as I felt a touch across my stomach. A mage-hand! It pulled at my tunic and I shed the already rent garment easily, leaving it behind and running as fast as I could now, not toward the tower but deeper into the castle. Down toward the baths. Yes, that would be all right, too. There was a way that skirted the kitchen and then led to the place where the wagons came in with supplies.

I pulled the cloak around my shoulders as I ran, expecting at any moment to feel another of those eldritch touches, but none came.

As I made my way down a dark spiral of stone cut within the castle I could feel the air growing close and warm as I neared the baths. The way was dark but I knew these ways like they were a part of me, like the castle itself was a part of me.

I could smell the kitchens shortly after, and then hear the sound of a cook talking to someone as I came to a thin slit in the wall, barely wide enough to be named a window. It was only wide enough for me to see out with one eye.

The two men were sitting on the short wall beside a hitched wagon, piled high with casks. They appeared to be chewing sechal bark and waiting for something.

"The whole castle is in an uproar," one was saying to the other. "It's an ill omen to find evil so close to noble blood."

"Quiet your tongue," the other said. "That boy was exactly that. Just a boy. They should have parted them a long time ago, but there was no evil in him."

"Well, he's the army's problem now," the first one said, and I saw him pitch the ball of chewed bark onto the ground. "Aha. Here's that last one. This'll keep the general and his men in good spirits, eh? Some of the finest from the king's own cellar?"

Another man appeared on the landing then, pushing a barrel. He rolled it right onto the wagon and then two of them wrestled it upright while the third pulled a piece of cloth over the top of the load. Two of them went back inside then, and the third went to check the horses.

I suddenly knew what I must do. I rushed down the rest of the stairs and emerged behind the curtain of vines further down the wall from where they had been sitting. I crept along the hedgerow that skirted the road until I came to a gap in it, and then I waited.

A few moments later I heard the hoofbeats and then in a

moment, the wagon was past me. They had not yet picked up much speed and I ran after them, catching hold of the back of the gate and swinging myself up and over it. It rattled as I did it, but the wagon did not slow; perhaps over the sound of the horses the driver heard nothing. I ducked under the edge of the cloth cover, pulling the cloak around me as much as I could, the hood over my head. The night was warm enough, but I had no tunic and did not want to be visible.

But I could not help but look up at the castle as the wagon made its way down the mountain. Every window seemed to be ablaze, and the torches along the battlements. They must have been looking for me all through the place by now, if Seroi had given up trying to find me. I hoped that Bear would not suffer because of what I did.

All I could think was that some incredible luck must have been with me. This wagon was carrying a load of ale and whiskey to the army's high command. Hadn't the man just said himself that was what they had done with Jorin? Shipped him to the army? I knew they did that with criminals sometimes, to let them redeem themselves and die in the service, instead of killing them for their crimes. It boiled my blood to think they considered Jorin a criminal.

I hid my face in my arms then, the fiery glow of the castle still burnt into my eyelids even as I saw again the way his prick had stood out from his body, ruddy and vigorous in the bright light of the banquet hall, straining toward me as my own father tore open my tunic.

Oh, Jorin. And to think that tonight I was ready for you to...

The calm I had felt, that had carried me and armored me since that moment in the banquet hall, suddenly cracked, and I felt myself starting to weep. I kept silent, trying again and again to swallow the lump in my throat but unable to stem the tears, as I wondered where he was and how much he had suffered. For me.

I made a promise then, to myself, that I would find him. That I would find him and everything would be different when I did. I would no longer be the source of his pain, but his pleasure. I still did not understand what Seroi had started, but only Jorin would finish it. I vowed this in silence to myself and my tears abated. I could not sleep, the wagon jostling me as it made its way through the night, but I rested, the calm returning. I would find him.

Had I known, all those years ago, that the boy I chose that day would suffer in my name... would I have chosen differently? Would I have picked a noisy, unpleasant urchin in whose pain I could delight, instead of one I could love?

I had clung to him tenaciously that day, and I was not about to let go now.

26: Jorin

I was woken once during the night, when the driver stopped to urinate and urged me to do the same. He didn't untie my hands, instead just pulling down the rough trousers I wore and telling me to crouch. Once back in the carriage, I stayed on the floor, afraid of being thrown from the bench if we hit a rough patch of road.

I woke again when the carriage lurched to a stop and I hit my bruised cheek against the floor. Daylight came through the narrow window and I could hear voices. I raised my head only to find my neck so stiff from having slept with my arms tied behind my back that I could barely get myself into a sitting position before the door swung open. I blinked, trying to clear my vision, then realized one of my eyes was swollen shut. The man standing there was wearing a military uniform.

It took me a moment to remember why I was in so much pain. Seroi. The king. The beating.

I flinched as the man reached for my face, but it turned out he was just probing my swollen eye with his thumb. Not a gentle touch, but not a painful one either.

"Get up," he said. "You won't be here long."

I scooted myself to the door and lowered my feet carefully to the packed earth of a rough courtyard inside stone fortifications. The man exchanged a few words with the carriage driver, shut the door on the empty carriage, and we stepped back as the team pulled away. He didn't wait to see them through the gate before he began walking toward a low building against the wall. I followed.

He led me past the building to the pit latrine, then looked me up and down. "You must need to piss," he said.

I just nodded, expecting him to do as the driver had. Instead he opened the door to the privy and let me step inside before he joined me. His hand was warm against my balls as he freed my cock from the trousers. Not a gentle touch. But not a painful one.

For a moment I wasn't sure if I could do what I had to, with him holding me like that. But with no sorcery in the air, just the touch of a real, warm hand on me, my body cooperated and I sighed with relief as I emptied my bladder. He shook me dry, pulled up my trousers again, then motioned for me to keep following him.

He led me to a building deeper in the compound then, sat me on a bench, and then went inside. I tried to stretch my fingers, clenching and unclenching my hands and rolling my shoulders, trying to lessen the tension of being tied that way.

Then he returned, with a boy holding a bowl. He took a cloth from the bowl and wiped my face with it. He was bearded, and now that I could study his face I could see he was older than he'd looked at first glance. Was the boy his son? Neither of them spoke, though he wrung the cloth out twice as he worked dried blood off my skin and from around my nose. My swollen eye opened somewhat.

"You're lucky your nose isn't broken," he finally said. "That must have been some brawl you were in."

Brawl? Then he didn't know who I was or why I was being banished. "Should've seen the other guy," I croaked, my throat raw and dry. The boy smiled then forced a serious look on his face as the older man turned to wet the cloth once more.

Finally he straightened up, satisfied with his examination of my face. "Cut him loose, Braan. This one won't make trouble for us, just the enemy. Am I right? The driver said your name was Crieg. No family name?"

I shook my head. So, Jaiks had sent me off with a clean slate. "Orphaned at a young age."

He nodded like it was a story he often heard while the boy sawed my wrists free with his belt knife. I stifled a cry as my arms came forward, the sudden change of posture painful in itself, but the movement also tore open a welt on my back. They watched me suspiciously for a moment, but when I made no other sound, the boy came forward and unwound the rope from my wrists, then rubbed at the skin with the palms of his hands.

"Thank you for your kindness," I said.

At that the older man laughed bitterly, a short bark of a laugh. "Are we kind to heal you, only to send you to your death? Don't thank us, Soldier Crieg." At that he put a hand on my shoulder. "You're joining the vanguard unit to Tiger's Mouth, you know. Although who knows. If you're half the fighter Jaiks said you are, maybe you'll survive. I don't know. I'm Pashal, the camp healer. This is Braan. I doubt I'll ever see you again."

I merely nodded. "What do I do next?"

"We'll feed you and get you some shoes. They won't give you swords or weapons yet. The transport moves out tomorrow with you and about twenty others."

They led me to another low, smoky building where the soldiers were fed. Both the building and the food were similar to what I knew with the king's guard, only rougher. No one spoke to me except Pashal. Braan brought me a pair of boots that fit. The men here, they were rougher, too. I supposed if they were all picked for this suicide duty, they were all some kind of criminals or troublemakers.

I looked for Dubacki. Hadn't that been the rumor—that he had been sent to Tiger's Mouth? But I did not see him. Perhaps he had long since gone to his demise.

After the meal Pashal examined my face again. He brought a commanding officer to look at me and they spoke in low voices for a bit. The officer left and Pashal returned to me. "You'll spend the night in the infirmary," he said, "instead of the barracks. You'll join the others soon enough."

"All right."

He led me outside and I realized with a start that the light in the sky I had taken for early morning had actually been dusk. How far had I traveled and how long had I been unconscious in the carriage? I had not studied Sergetten's maps as carefully as I should have when he had been teaching Kenet the lay of the land. The summer evening was long but coming to its inevitable end.

Pashal showed me to a low cot in one corner of the building where he had tended to my face. No one else was there, although there were two other cots.

"I have a tincture," he said, as I sat down on it, "that will help you to sleep if the pain keeps you awake. But I will only give it to you if you want it."

I shook my head. "I won't need it."

"Good." He waited until I had lain down and pulled the blanket over myself before he left, shutting the door behind him.

Now, alone in the gathering dark, I allowed myself to think of Kenet. The cot creaked as I shifted carefully, afraid that if blood crusted my shirt to the welt I would re-open it again and again if I moved too much.

Kenet. Where was he and what was he doing now? How had he made it through the night and how would I make it through this one? I wondered if I should have taken the tincture, but I didn't want to have my wits dulled if anything should happen while I was asleep.

So it was that I was wide awake some hours later, but feigning sleep, when the door creaked open. I could not make out the figure but it certainly sounded like it could be Pashal. He came close and knelt next to the cot, the wooden floorboards creaking under him. "Crieg," he whispered.

"Pashal?"

He put a hand on my chest, warm and solid, and just sat with it like that for a long minute. At first I wondered what he was doing. Then I felt the hand begin to move in a slow circle. A kind of caress. My breath caught.

"If my touch is unwanted..." he began.

I put my hand over his to tell him it wasn't. But I did ask. "Why?"

"I could tell when I held your cock for you to piss," he whispered in my ear. "That you might. It's one of the reasons men are sent here."

Ah. And I had no objected in the slightest to how he'd held me in the privy, a clue that I might welcome more. His hand slipped into my trousers then, finding the organ in question and stroking me to full length. My breath caught again. His hand was calloused and clumsy, so unlike Kenet's, and yet it was solid and real and warm, so unlike the sorcerous touch that had provoked me in front of the king.

When I felt his breath moist near my ear, though, I asked again. "Why?"

"Men being sent to their death are also more willing to accept pleasure from a stranger's hand," he answered.

He milked me until I was on the edge of spilling, then stopped and let me rest. He did this three times. On the third time I asked, "May I touch you as well?"

"Only if you want to, Soldier Crieg."

"I want to. And my sense of honor demands it. But I want to."

"Very well." He pulled away for a moment, shedding his trousers, then slipping onto the cot next to me. I wasted no time in wrapping my fingers around him. He was much larger than Kenet, weighty and thick, and I wondered if such a prick would yield more milk.

I came with a gasp, spilling into his fingers and then catching what I could in my own palm and stroking him with the cream, causing him to groan. He spilled almost immediately and I wondered if he had been thinking of this moment ever since he'd touched me in the privy.

Now that we were both spent, neither of us was inclined to speak. He slipped away a few moments later, leaving me wondering how many other men like him were hiding among my countrymen.

He had given me a greater gift than he knew. A bit of pleasure, yes. And spent as I was, I was finally able to sleep. But he had given me hope, too. I couldn't quite explain why, but just knowing he was there, that he existed, emboldened my heart somehow. In the morning I would leave for Tiger's Mouth, though, and I supposed I would need all the courage I could muster.

27: Kenet

I wondered if the wagon would roll all night. Didn't horses need to sleep, too? What about the driver? For myself, I was not sleepy at all. I was thankful for the summer night, as a chill stole over me that surely would have been unbearable had the air been colder. The creaking of the wheels and the sound of the hooves lulled me, but I did not sleep.

I could see little of what we passed. The road down the mountain was lined with trees, then at some point the way became flat. I could see from the stars above that now the mountains were to one side of us. East. We were going east, but I had no idea how far.

I thought about slipping away, leaping off the back of the wagon, before I could be discovered, but then how would I know where to go? How far away was the army? If that was where Jorin had been sent, then surely I needed to get there as quickly as possible. These thoughts battled back and forth like two fencers, until I felt the wagon begin to slow. I could not risk being discovered or I would surely find myself delivered back into Seroi's hands in an instant.

But I had missed my chance. I heard voices shouting; it was too late to jump without being seen. I huddled down under the cloak, below the edge of the wagon's gate, trying to think of what I might say to them when they lowered it and discovered me. I kept waiting for the rattle of the latch and the chains, but all I heard was the creaking of the wagon as the driver climbed down, and then more voices.

"Here you go" That was the driver's voice. "The whole load is to go straight to the mustering ground, to General Roichal's camp. And I mean the whole load. The barrels have been counted."

"What do you take me for, a thief?" came the affronted answer. "Don't be ridiculous."

"Just telling you. The whole castle's astir and the king is not happy."

"Oh? What could possibly be upsetting him besides famine, war, pestilence...?"

"You think your tongue is so sharp. Get up there, go on."

The wagon shifted again and I could hear the sound of the horses being changed, too. I dared a look over the top of the gate as we pulled away, but there was little to see other than the small light of a lantern in someone's hand as he walked the opposite direction. I could make out what might have been the edge of a building, a stable perhaps? It didn't matter. A few moments later I could not see it at all.

The new driver liked to sing and whistle to himself as the horses went along. I began to doze off as the sky lightened and I could see gray trees now hanging over the road. Gray trees? As the light strengthened, the color returned, verdant and vibrant, and I understood that in the predawn light I had been unable to see the color of the leaves.

Just as from inside the castle I had been unable to see past its walls. Now Jorin was out here somewhere and I had to find him. That was my last thought before I finally fell asleep.

I woke with a start as the gate banged open and a surprised voice cried out, "Oho! Jort, you've got a stowaway here!"

I scrambled up, but the man grabbed me. He was nearly as big as Bear, his arms as muscular, and wriggle as I might I could not get loose.

The driver, still whistling, came around the wagon to look at me. "What's this?"

"He was in the back, hiding there." The man twisted me until he could hold me by one arm behind my back. Now if I struggled, it hurt, so I stood still, my heart pounding, trying to think of what to say.

The driver, Jort, sauntered forward. He was wearing a military jacket, but it was loose, unbuttoned, hanging from his shoulders. I flinched back as he reached for my face, but all he did was fluff my hair. "So fair. And barefoot and barechested. Must be an escaped

Frangi boywhore, hm? What twisted noble's dungeon did you escape from, eh boy?"

I said nothing. They had no idea who I was. If they thought I was a Frangi, maybe I could feign misunderstanding, too.

"Let go of him, Bettin. If he runs, we'll have some sport bringing him down and spearing him, eh?" Jort chuckled and something in the tone of his chuckle made me think it wouldn't be knives of metal they'd spear me with. The big one let go my arm and I cradled it to my chest. "No no no," Jort said. "Let's have a look at you." He gestured to the cloak.

I couldn't very well pretend to be too stupid to understand that, could I? My fingers trembled as I undid the clasp and Bettin took the cloak from me and handed it to Jort.

Jort ran his fingers along the seams and then sniffed the cloth. "Definitely some noble's plaything. Feel the weave on this cloth..." He shook out the cloak and folded it then started to stuff it into a rucksack.

I made a distressed noise and reached for it. I'm not even sure why. Because it was Jorin's, and because without it I was far too exposed to their eyes. He just looked up at me with raised eyebrows. "Oh, you think this is yours? But we're going to feed you and keep you warm and dry when the rains come tonight. You owe us for that."

I pretended not to understand and reached for the cloak again.

"No," he said, as if I were a grabby child. "Bettin, count the barrels. I need to think about this. You, come." He gestured for me to follow him.

Not knowing what else to do, I did. He led me to a tent by the mouth of a cave in the hillside. I looked around for the first time and saw we were in a camp of sorts, with one or two wooden buildings and tents in the clearing between the edge of the woods and the start of the rocky hills.

He pushed me through the tent flap and I stumbled and fell onto a surprisingly soft carpet. Another man was there, and he looked up from the paper he was marking something on. "Jort? What's this?"

"I'm not sure," Jort said. He opened a chest and took out a bottle of something and drank deeply from it, then corked it and put it back. The other man handed me a metal flask of water and I drank greedily. Jort pulled out a piece of cheese from the chest and the crust end of a loaf of bread, and handed them to me where I was on the carpet. I gnawed on them like a mouse, trying to pretend I wasn't listening to every word they said.

"What do you mean he was in the wagon?"

"I mean, Bettin opened the back and there he was. The way I see it, there's two possibilities. He's an escaped boywhore, or he's supposed to be a secret gift for General Roichal. But Pelter didn't say anything specifically about it, only that the 'whole load' was supposed to go straight to Roichal."

"Jort! You don't suppose he suspects us...?"

"No, he just doesn't like me and he doesn't like having his milksacks in a sling." Jort sat on a low stool and ran his fingers through his short, dark hair. "I mean, if he is a gift for Roichal, that isn't the sort of thing one would say out loud. But it just seems far-fetched, even given the General's reputation..."

"A far out-dated reputation, I might add," the other man said. "When I was with him on campaign last year, I swear he never even spilled once in the night. Never had a camp follower in his bed. Nothing. All the man thinks about is strategy. He's no milk-sucker. I think he's dry between the legs, honestly."

Jort gnawed one fingernail. "Our best bet is to make him Roichal's problem, though." He stood then. "Leave me alone with him for a while."

The other man chuckled. "Can't hurt to sample the goods, eh? Jort, you pervert."

"Shut your mouth. That's what he's used to, isn't it? Poor thing probably needs a good fucking if he's been on the run. Isn't that what they say about the Frangi? They train them to crave master's milk?"

The other man just made a disgusted noise and pushed the tentflap aside, carrying his papers with him as he went. Jort secured the flap with a tie and then turned to me.

"I'm not convinced, you know, that you're not a spy sent by Pelter to catch us smuggling," he said. I just stared at him like I had no idea what he was saying. "Though where he found such a fair-haired youth as you, I couldn't guess."

The canvas of the tent was a cream-colored fabric and in the sunlight the interior was plenty bright to see by. Jort took me by the forearm and bade me stand again, then pushed my leggings down to my ankles. I wanted to cover myself, but was caught between on the one hand thinking then he might be sure I was a spy of some kind and on the other hand wondering if I truly were a Frangi boywhore, how would I react? The result was I stood as still as a well-trained horse having its saddle changed while he ran his hands down my back and over the curve of my buttocks.

He made an appreciative noise. "Not a mark on you. You're more and more of a mystery, little Frangi." Then his hand cupped my balls, as if weighing them. "Or perhaps not so little after all."

I was hardening in his grip and he stroked me, hastening the process. Then he stepped back to look at me. "You can see why the Frangi are such corrupt, decadent men," he said, more to himself than to me. "You're hard to resist."

He bent me over the chest then, and ran his finger up and down the crack between my cheeks. Then I struggled, fighting him. No! I didn't escape from Seroi to just have some corrupt smuggler soldier stick his prick into me.

He laughed, wrestling me down to the carpet. He kicked his own trousers off at some point while we fought and I could feel the threat of his hard heat against my thigh as he pinned me down.

The only thing I could think of was if I could make him spill, he would be unable to spear me. I wasn't even completely sure that was true, but it seemed likely. Jorin would always go soft in my hand and sometimes he wouldn't even want his prick touched at all afterward.

I got one hand free and stroked my fingertips up the side of his shaft where it was trapped against my leg. He shuddered and I licked my lips, fluttering my tongue suggestively.

He ran a finger around the wet edge of my lips and then

plunged it slowly into my mouth. I sucked and felt his cock twitch against my leg.

"Are you offering me your mouth instead of your hind hole?" he asked.

I just swirled my tongue around the tip of his finger and then sucked harder.

"Thunder's roll," he swore, moving quickly then. He sat up on the stool and pulled me between his knees with his fist in my hair. I don't know where the dagger in his other hand came from. "If this is all a trick to use your teeth..." he warned, holding the point in the soft spot behind my ear.

I drew a trembling breath but pretended this was the sort of treatment I was used to. I began licking his balls and was rewarded with a groan. His cock was a dark color, not just suffused with blood but darker like all his skin when compared to the pallor of Seroi. It had a graceful curve to it, like the bone hilts of the Pellonese swords my father had received as a tribute gift once. The knob was tapered and salty, tasting much more like Jorin's than like Seroi's.

I licked him up and down, up and down, and was just working up the nerve to actually suck him into my mouth when he took the choice from me and shoved in, holding my head steady as he thrusted. I gagged but that only seemed to spur him to push deeper, again and again. I couldn't breathe but it didn't matter for long, as he spilled in my mouth and all over my face quite speedily.

"Lightning strike me if that wasn't the sweetest mouth I've ever had on man or woman," he swore, head lolling back.

He seemed not to care that I was wiping as much of his seed from my face as I could onto the carpet, nor that my own prick was still as hard and straining as it had been when he'd stroked it into that state.

I wondered if I should try to run. But I was naked and I didn't know how many men were around, and his earlier description of a "hunt" made me shiver.

"Jort, you finished? Bettin's done swapping the casks."

Jort motioned at me to get my leggings back on. I did while

he got dressed himself and untied the tent flap. "How many?"

"Just two. Let's not take too many chances if they already suspect something."

"I told you, they don't suspect anything. Pelter just doesn't like me."

"Here." The other man handed him some papers, then looked at me. "What did you do to him? No no, don't tell me. I don't want to hear it. The poor thing looks like he's about to burst into tears."

I did? Very well, I knew a sympathetic spirit when I saw one. I pointed frantically at Jort's rucksack.

The other man crossed his arms. "What did you take of his?"

"You can't be serious. Whether we consider him a whoreslave or a prisoner of war, he doesn't 'own' anything."

"Jort."

"Fine. Maybe he's just cold." He dug the cloak out again and threw it at me. I gathered it up greedily and pulled it around my shoulders.

"If you leave now, you can make the outpost by nightfall."

Jort stretched and yawned. "All right. The sooner we're rid of this load the better. Rations are scarce enough as it is. Hey whore, you'd better take a piss before we get going. I'm going to chain you in the wagon so you don't make trouble."

I blinked, pretending I didn't know what he said.

He took me to a small shed then, standing alone at the edge of the camp, and I wondered what it was until he opened the door and I could smell it. There was a barrel lid over a hole in a shelf, and he lifted it and pointed down into it, then pointed at my cock in my leggings, and then pointed into it again.

"Oh, lightning strike me if you get it wrong," he said, and took out his own cock and pissed in a long, pungent stream. "Got the idea? Okay. go on."

He actually left me alone then, although I could hear him standing outside the door. I freed my cock from my leggings but I was still too hard to piss. My only real choice was to milk myself.

I tried to make it quick, but although I reached the point of spilling quickly, I could not seem to go over the edge. I tried until it became painful. Even imagining it was Jorin's hand milking me did not help. Neither did imagining it was Seroi's, and yes, I was desperate enough to try that. But no, I could not bring myself off.

I emerged from the shed near tears, on shaky legs, but Jort did not seem to notice. He led me back to the wagon which looked unchanged to my eye and urged me to take up my spot in the back. Good to his word, he looped a chain around my ankle and locked it tight, then locked it to the gate latch, slipping the key into his own pocket.

Within minutes we were on the road again, and I let myself cry at last, when the sound of the wheels and the horses would mask the sound. I cried myself to sleep and when I woke much later I found my cock had finally gone to sleep, too. I pissed off the back of the wagon, leaving a dark trail in the dust of the road. At least by tonight we would reach the army camp, wasn't that what they'd said? The outpost, at least. Maybe I would catch up to Jorin there. Surely once we were together we would figure out a way to get free and run away. Maybe we could run all the way to Pellon.

28: Jorin

In the morning a commander came, and he and two other officers supervised our march from the camp. They hadn't given us weapons yet, or orders, and I wondered how far we would be going. Not far on foot, it turned out, as they marched us down to the river and loaded us onto a barge. We were twenty four men in total, including the commander and his second, and two bowmen who took turns on top. From the way the other men eyed them I knew they were less there to protect us from the enemy than to shoot any of us that tried to flee.

We were on the barge all day, traveling on the river, and when night fell, the commander gathered us together to speak of our "mission" and of the pardon we would each be given for our crimes if we did this service to the crown.

If we survived, of course. He did not say that part, though I think every man there knew it well enough. I saw others casting their gazes about as if looking for escape, but there was none with the archers watching us from the barge roof. I overheard them talking about how most of the army was being mustered to the east, and lamenting that we were not joining them. In the morning we would draw near Tiger's Mouth, they told us, and we would be armed once we reached the encampment after sunrise.

We bedded down on the deck of the barge, and I found the motion of the boat and the rushing sound of the water enough to lull me to sleep.

I was wakened by the sound of a scream. I felt a jolt as if the barge had run around or struck something, and there were men running on the roof, shouting. In the darkness the lanterns cast very little light, but a sudden bright plume of fire lit the night just off to one side. I saw the silhouette of men being flung back from the blast in the split second before I closed my eyes and shielded my face. If I had been on my feet I would have been knocked down, surely.

I did not wait to see if the next ball of fire would explode on the deck itself. In the dark and with the archers all too busy with the chaos, I slipped over the side and into the river.

I had not expected the river to pull me away from the side so quickly but the barge was stuck where it was and once I was in the water, I was not. I paddled hard, trying to keep my head above the water, which was fortunately not very rough or that might have been the end of me. I kicked off the boots they had given me and then I could swim a little better, but it had never been a skill I'd cultivated. The rough uniform I wore weighed me down, but I didn't dare stop paddling long enough to try to shrug free of it. Luckily, my struggling in the water took me toward the bank and I was able to get myself up onto a pebble-lined shore without further danger. I could still hear the shouts and saw another gout of flame go up into the sky.

Was it the Night Riders? There were the rumors about them taming a dragon to do their bidding. Sergetten had said there was no such thing as dragons (at least, not any longer) and I believed him. If not for that fire I might have thought the commotion merely my fellow conscripts in revolt. But it seemed more likely that the transport was under attack.

All the more reason for me to get away as quickly as possible. If only I could catch my breath. My limbs felt leaden after how hard my blood had pumped as I'd swum. I forced myself to crawl out of the open and into the brush, so should the barge break loose and come downriver, no one would see me.

I lay there under the broad leaves of some bush in full summer bloom, listening in the dark, the scent of the flowers overwhelming the wet odor of my uniform. I could hear nothing conclusive. I decided to wring out what I was wearing, to have some hope of it drying. I took it off, wringing out the shirt and pants and then hanging them in the branches of the bush.

The scent from the blossoms I brushed as I moved was heady

and sweet. Not falla but some flower I didn't know. I lay back down
to rest and wait for my uniform to dry and for whatever might
happen next. Surely if it was the Night Riders taking the barge, it
would soon be moving again, toward Tiger's Mouth where their
stronghold was? Or would they just destroy it where it was?

These thoughts did not get far in my mind, as a great drowsi-
ness seemed to come over me. Swimming for my life must have
exhausted me more than I expected. I fell into a dream, then, and
in the dream Kenet came crawling under the hanging boughs of
the bush to join me. His hands examined my skin, tracing the
marks the final beating and the ropes had left there. "Leave it," I
said. "Kenet, kiss me."

He did, and his mouth was sweeter than the nectar of this
flower. Some part of me knew, though, that it was a dream, that I
was inventing this vision to comfort myself. When I opened my
eyes, he would not be there, but for the moment, I could dream.

When I tried to open my eyes, however, I found I could not.
They were bound with some kind of cloth, or so it felt like when
I tried to blink. I took stock of my situation quickly. My hands were
bound behind my back and I was seated on a chair. Or more likely
a stool, since I could feel nothing behind me.

"He's awake," came a low voice to my left.

"Ahhhh, good." The one on my right sounded like he was
smiling. "I was starting to worry he wouldn't, after all the tingle-
tingle in his system."

Oh. The bush I had been under. My knowledge of botany was
quite limited, after all, but I knew of the numbing medicine one
could make from the tinglebush's leaves and berries. Apparently
the flowers, too, could have such an effect. I wondered if I had
damaged my ability to feel, but I felt no tingling now. In fact, I
could feel the air moving against my bare skin. I wondered if they
had found my uniform when they'd found me, or if my nakedness
was evidence they had not.

"Gresh, leave us."

"If you're going to question 'im, I should stay."

"I'm not going to question him. Not yet anyway."

"Oh. Right. Suit yourself." I heard the footsteps as the man with the lower voice turned and walked away. Were we in the open? Outdoors?

I shivered suddenly as warm fingers ran across the back of my shoulders. I expected to feel the steel of a dagger next, but no, his fingers just made their way around to my throat, brushing up my chin and then over my lips. I pulled away at that, though the touch had not been painful.

"Who are you?" I demanded. "I've done nothing to harm you."

A soft huff of breath that might have been a laugh. "If you answer my questions, maybe I will answer yours," he said.

"I thought you said you weren't going to question me."

"What I told Gresh to get us some privacy, and why, is not your concern. Or perhaps it is, but... well, that is for us to discuss a bit later, perhaps." His voice had a kind lilt, and it sounded somewhat familiar.

"What are you talking about? Do I know you?"

His hand cupped my cheek, then my ear, and it didn't feel like an unfriendly touch. It felt warm and comforting, not at all like he was trying to threaten me. "Well, why don't we start there? What is your name?"

For the life of me, I couldn't remember the name I'd used at the camp. "I'm not a threat," I said, trying to buy time. "This isn't necessary."

"I'll be the judge of how much secrecy is necessary," he said. "Your name, please."

"Jorin," I said then, and my fake name came into my head the moment I said it. "Though the army has me listed as Crieg."

"Oh, how interesting. And why is that? Surely there must be a fascinating story there?" He moved away as he spoke and I heard him stoking up a fire. The cloth must have been thick on my eyes for me not to have seen the glow.

"I... the army... I was on a barge transporting conscripts to Tiger's Mouth." I realized I could not assume he knew anything about that. He might just be a traveling brigand who came across me asleep under the influence of tingle-tingle for all I knew. "About two dozen including me. It didn't matter if they knew who I was since they were sending us to die, I'm pretty sure."

"Oh? And wouldn't you have wanted word to be carried to your family of your death?"

"I was orphaned a long time ago," I said. For some reason admitting it now made my heart hurt in a way it had not in years. Perhaps because this time I was truly alone when I said it. I couldn't keep the sadness out of my voice.

He was silent a long time then, and the only thing I could hear was the hiss of the fire, a small pop coming from it from time to time. In the silence my pain seemed to grow and I wondered if the sudden onset of maudlin grief was a common effect of tingle-tingle.

I startled a bit as he spoke, now quite close though I hadn't heard him move. And I was even more surprised by his words. "I think I know who you are."

"I'm nobody," I insisted.

"Then does it matter if you die?" He spoke as if the question were an intellectual curiosity, running his fingers through my hair as he talked. "Sent on a suicide mission, then left to die on a sinking barge, and yet you are here, alive. What do you live for?"

Kenet, I thought. I live to see Kenet again.

Then I wondered if he could read my mind, as his fingers brushed over my balls so much like Kenet's used to. "There's someone," he said. "Not your mother, if you're an orphan. And you're too young for a wife..."

I growled as his hand slipped around my shaft then, and it must have been the aftereffect of the flowers and the dream I'd had, but it felt so very much like Kenet's hand.

The thought occurred to me, what if I was still dreaming? "This isn't real," I said to the phantom who was now bringing me to full hardness. "It's a tingle-fever dream."

"Perhaps it is," he admitted. "Perhaps I am just a figment of your imagination, of pleasures you can only dream of."

With that I felt the wetness of his tongue up and down my

cock, and I groaned. "Kenet," I whispered as he took me full into his mouth.

"Jorin," he whispered as he came up a few seconds later, nipping at my chest and then meeting my mouth with his.

He pulled the blindfold away then, and for a moment my eyes were dazzled by the fairness of his hair. Kenet! But then as he slipped his hand over my mouth to keep me from crying out, I could see, no, it was not him, though this man bore a strong resemblance to him, at least in the firelight and with the flower poison still running through me. He was bare to the waist, but it was not Kenet.

"No, I'm not he," he said. "But I have no doubt you are Jorin, now."

I nodded, not understanding any of this but trusting him without knowing why. I could see now, even in the firelight, that his skin was tanned by weather and wind and his hands were callused like Jaiks's. He let go my mouth and slid his hand over my hair. "You were right to keep your identity a secret, or to try to," he said, "but you talked while you dreamed."

"Ah." My heart sank. What else had I given away about myself? Or about the prince? My cock throbbed where it stood between my legs and I still did not know what this man's intentions were.

He studied my face, then my cock. "The others will have my milksacks if they think I let your hands loose. Tingle-tingle, well, it's not unheard of for a man to have a reaction like yours, but I can't very well let you take care of it yourself..."

I just looked at him. I would not beg.

"They think I'm going to do this anyway," he said with a shrug and a chuckle. "After all, the Night Arts require certain perversions." He unbuckled his belt and set it aside, knife and all, and then doffed black boots and trousers.

He straddled my lap, now as naked as I was, and wriggled until our two cocks were together. He stroked them in a single grip and I moaned.

"You're going to have a terrible headache tomorrow," he said, then spat into his palms and slicked us both up and down. "No way around it. But this, this I can take care of."

For a moment he became Kenet again, but when my senses cleared, I asked, "But who are you?"

"You can call me Kan," he said, as he sped up his stroke. "That is, if the others don't overrule me and decide to kill you anyway."

"The others?"

"You poor thing, this whole situation must be confusing. I'm sorry, Jorin, you're probably going to pass out when you come. If you don't wake, it'll be because the others did away with you. If you do, it'll be because I convinced them that you can help us. Maybe even that you... want to join us."

"Join you? But who are you?"

"Hm, yes, that would be best. You'll probably have to convince the others that your desire to join us is quite sincere. That may take some doing on your part... are you loyal to Kenet, still?"

"What? Of course!" I gasped as his hand twisted slickly around the head of my cock. "I-If you are loyal to Kenet, too, I would gladly join you. But who are you?"

He chuckled. "I assure you we mean the princeling no harm if he is as innocent as we deem. But haven't you figured it out by now? Or is your head still so muddled from the flower? I'm the leader of the Night Riders."

And with that revelation, both our cocks began to spurt and I cried out, overwhelmed by sensation and information at once. And as I would later learn, Kan was usually right when it came to predictions. I passed out immediately, before I could even frame another question for him in my mind, slumping into his arms like an unstrung puppet and wholly at his mercy.

29: Kenet

We passed a check point of some kind around dawn, the guards bantering with Jort before letting us pass, and the wagon rolled on and on. I wondered why I didn't feel hungry at all, but my stomach was in such knots from fear and worry I couldn't have eaten anything now even if my hands had been free and a banquet were in front of me.

I had plenty of time to try to free myself from the chains if it could be done. It could not. If they were truly delivering me to General Roichal, I might find myself headed straight back to Seroi and my father if he were to recognize me. I tried to remember when the last time he had banqueted at the royal table had been. Ten years ago? When he had been made commander of the whole army. I was fairly sure he had not returned since, and even then, I don't know that he ever got much of a look at me. I remembered him as a broad-shouldered man, with his hair in need of cutting and a perpetual frown creasing his brow.

We changed horses again at midday and no one opened the back of the wagon to find me there. A few miles later, Jort made me drink some water but I really could not eat. I finally slept fitfully through the heat of the afternoon, and then woke as the wagon went through another check point. The sun was setting as we came into a camp, a circle of tents visible all around in the fading light. I could hear many voices.

And then suddenly the back of the wagon was flung open and Jort was standing there grinning, gesturing at me. "Here you are."

The man standing next to him was in some sort of uniform, but not like a soldier's. He had an apron on as well. A cook? He wore a disdainful expression. "This? This is what our king sends to boost morale? Whiskey instead of grain? And what between sky and sea are we supposed to do with a whoreslave?"

Jort clapped him on the shoulder. "You said it yourself. He's a morale booster. Surely if you just leave him in a tent by himself at night, it'll ease tensions, eh? Word'll spread quickly enough among those with a taste for that sort of thing."

The cook rubbed his chin. "True. Not a tent, though. We'll have to keep him chained like the spy we caught a couple of months ago."

I bowed my head, trying to appear docile, but the knowing laugh that Jort gave sent shivers down my back. The only way I was going to get free was if they decided I was no threat.

"All right. Well, let's get him out of the way of unloading."

Jort unlocked the chain from the bolt in the wagon and then nudged me with his elbow. I climbed carefully down, my wrists still bound together. The cook and he marched me toward a rough hewn building.

"The stables?" Jort asked.

"Yes," the cook said. "Then the muckboy can clean up after him and feed him, too. I don't have time to deal with a whoreslave or prisoner with a hundred new soldiers arriving every day now."

I looked back and could see a line of men taking the barrels off the wagon. Ahead of us the stable looked like it had stalls for ten or twelve horses, though as we went through the wide door I could only hear two. It smelled just like the stables at the castle and I wondered if that would matter to the men who would come to relieve themselves in secret with me. The roof was made of canvas, but the walls were solidly constructed, and of course each stall had a place where a horse could be tethered. Jort locked the chain to an iron ring in the far wall of one stall. He took the cloak from my shoulders, but before I could protest, had made a sort of bed for me by gathering it around clean hay. He handed the key to the cook and the two of them left me like that.

There were no more tears left for me to cry now. I pulled at the chain, but if a horse couldn't dislodge the ring, where was I going to find the strength to?

This is what you have reduced me to, Seroi, I thought. You have made me nothing more than an animal. He had trained me like a hunting dog, and now I wasn't even that, not even a prized pet, but just a beast waiting to be slaughtered. Only it would not be knives the men would cut me open with, but their cocks.

Jorin, where are you? Was he here somewhere with the army? Was there any hope he might hear the rumor of my arrival and deduce what had happened? In my mind's eye I could see Seroi beating him and hear him screaming. I shook my head, trying to rid myself of the image, but it was as if I could not stop thinking about what had happened. I could hear my father accusing him of wanting to bed me, my own father slashing open my tunic in front of him as Jorin's cock strained toward me.

I had no doubt at all that Jorin desired me, that had we been able to steal an hour together before that fateful banquet I would have begged him to bed me as a man does a maid.

Now my vision changed, and I imagined him breaking the chains that held him taut, and stealing me out of the arms of my father. Yes. Straight into one of the castle's secret passages, with Bear blocking the way... I whimpered as I imagined him taking me against the rough stone of the passage, pushing his way into me. What would being fucked be like? All I knew is it would feel a hundred times better than Jorin's finger had, and a thousand times better than the slick thing Seroi had put into me...

I was asleep and dreaming of Jorin's cock inside me.

I woke at the sound of someone unlatching the stable door. Night had fallen and I realized with a start that I was erect and throbbing.

A fact I could not hide as a soldier slipped into my stall and uncovered a small lantern. He hung it over a peg by the door and then turned to look, his breath catching as he saw me. "Thunder's roll," he swore. "It's true."

He was an older man, and by the markings on his jacket I could see he was an officer. He stared at me for a few moments longer. I had only one strategy and so I employed it before he could think of what he wanted to do next. I beckoned him to come closer and I started to work his belt open with my bound hands.

He seemed too shocked to protest, and in short order his pants were down around his knees and his musky cock was in my mouth. He smelled nearly as strong as the horses and yet it wasn't an unpleasant smell in its way. Each stroke of my mouth up and down his shaft made my own cock throb.

He spilled quickly, his cry sounding as much surprised as anything, and then he hurried away, taking the lantern. He had not touched my cock, or anything but the back of my head as he'd spilled, as if afraid I might pull away too soon. His seed was acrid down my throat, but not bitter. I wondered how long it would be before the next one.

It wasn't long. Another officer, this one heavyset and carrying what looked like the identical lantern. I heard the stamp of a horse a few stalls over and worried that if we were too noisy, we might spook them. Perhaps war horses were not so easily spooked.

He, too, let me suck him as I wished until he spilled, and then he fled. My jaw ached and I rubbed it against my shoulder, hoping for a longer break between this one and the next.

Instead, it seemed this one had been waiting right outside for his turn. He had dark hair and eyes, his hair pulled back in a tai. He slipped his jacket off. I couldn't make out his rank either, but it must have been fairly high given the glimpse I caught of the markings.

"Lightning strike me if I've ever seen a sight as beautiful as you," this one said, and before I could do what I had to the others, he had knelt down beside me and stroked a hand up my shaft. I quivered under the touch. "Will you stay like this all night, to keep your hole tight? You've been well-trained. Where between land and sky did they find you, I wonder?"

I pretended I hadn't understood him, but what he'd said suddenly made me wonder if Seroi's training me for the ceremony had actually been something else. Was that why I couldn't come? Had I been made into the whoreslave these men assumed I was? Had it all been a charade to make me Seroi's whoreslave? That had to be Night Magic of the darkest kind! Difficult to believe, and yet given the situation I was in, I could believe such evil of him.

"Let me see how tight you are," the soldier went on, and pulled a crumpled bit of paper from his pocket. He was a handsome man, his hair black and straight like an inkstroke. In the paper was a whitish blob of grease, and he took a dab of it up on his finger and then pushed at me with his hands until I was on my knees, legs spread, holding onto the iron ring for support. He pushed his slick finger into me and I cried out at the sudden intrusion.

"Thunderclouds," he swore. "Any man's cock would tear you open, you're so tight," he said, pushing the finger in and out.

It felt good. The grease and the slickness and even the intrusion itself, now that I was getting used to it, felt good. I could not hold back a groan.

It seemed, though, that it would not be Jorin who would be the first to breach me with his cock. I was out of tricks for how to stop it from happening. I could not worry over Night magic I did not understand, all I knew was that my heart ached in my chest to think that it would not be him. The most I could do now was imagine that it was his hands pulling at my cheeks, his fingers that were spreading me open.

"Good as you'd feel on my prick like that, little whore," he said then, "I don't have it in me to hurt you like that. Let's have you come first to loosen you up, and then I'll take you."

I cried out softly as he wrapped his slick hand around my cock, resting his own against my tailbone. Jorin, yes, I could imagine Jorin doing exactly this. Tying my hands to the headboard behind our bed so that I could not cheat and touch myself, and then teasing me like this.

My hips rocked into his grip and I could feel the hardness of him sliding up and down against my spine. How would it feel when it was inside me?

"You don't have to hold back," he whispered into my ear. "It's all right."

But I knew when I came—if I could come—he'd spear me, and I didn't want that. So I tried to hold back, and I hoped that whatever it was that had kept me from coming so far would keep working, at least for a little longer. It was the only way I could fight. But it was a fight I knew I could not win.

The strain was too much and I began to cry.

"Oh, sky above." He slowed down and then stopped his motion, though his hand stayed around my cock, his chest pressed against my back. "Listen, I'm not one of those who like it when you cry. I know there are the ones that like to hurt, that like it when you play at it like that. But I'm not like that. I'm not... Don't cry. Please. No no no, I can't do this if you're crying." And on he went like that, eventually letting me go and kissing away my tears and wiping them with his thumbs, trying to get me to stop any way he could, and failing. The tenderness, if anything, only made me cry harder.

And then there was a gruff voice at the door. "Marksin."

"Yes, Sir," he answered, though he did not get up from where he was cradling me in his lap. He had gone soft. I felt a bit bad about that.

The door opened and through my tears I recognized the man standing there. His hair had silvered a little at the temples, but he was largely the same frowning, broad-shouldered figure he had been ten years earlier at the banquet in his honor.

Marksin urged me to get off of him, then stood and put his uniform back on, all while General Roichal watched. Only when he was fully clothed did the general speak again. "You should have told me the moment you heard about this."

"I had to come see for myself, Sir."

Roichal made a harrumphing noise. "How long has he been here?"

"I am fairly certain not more than a day. He's in remarkably good condition. Far better than the last one."

The last one? I curled up as much as I could with my hands chained as they were.

Roichal shook his head. "You know I turn a blind eye to the men taking certain liberties with prisoners of war, but where did this one come from?"

"I will find that out, Sir. You can be certain of that. I will get to the bottom of this."

"Good. Now shield him." A moment later Marksin was using

my cloak and his arm to shield me. The general himself struck at the chain with something, once, twice, thrice, and suddenly my arms were free. The manacles that held my wrists together were still in place, but I said nothing about that. "Does he have shoes? No? Carry him then, Marksin. Take him to my tent."

"Sir? Are you sure you want that rumor spreading?"

"Rumors be damned."

"But Sir..."

"You have your orders."

"Yes Sir."

Marksin picked me up, cloak and all, and carried me as far as a horse tethered some distance away. He helped me up into the saddle and then walked, leading the horse.

Even in the dark I could tell the camp was far larger than I had thought. The small part of it I had seen before was only the station for provisioning. I drowsed a little as the horse walked, but we passed tent after tent, and I could smell the smoke of many different fires.

Eventually he stopped and helped me down, leading me into a large tent. He lit the lantern and then bade me sit on the low sleeping pallet. "Might as well put you there, little whore," he said. "I thought he'd long ago given up the appetites of the flesh, but you apparently tempt him beyond reason." He reached down and stroked my hair gently. "Don't be afraid. He's like me. No crying, all right? He's a good man and he will be good to you. He won't hurt you. He's... he's not like that."

As he spoke, I had the sudden feeling he was telling me far more than he'd intended. Perhaps because he believed I didn't really understand him. His voice grew soft with longing, and then he drew away suddenly as we heard someone outside the tent.

The general entered. "Thank you, Marksin," he said.

"Sir..." Marksin said, with a slight bow. "Will you be needing anything else?"

"No no, go get some sleep."

But I could see Marksin hesitate. "Sir..."

Their gazes met. Roichal was the first too look away. At me.

"That will be all, Marksin. Tomorrow we'll need to start inspection of all the newly arrived companies."

"Of course, Sir."

"And yes, I will forgive your lapse."

"Thank you, Sir." Marksin swallowed, apparently feeling he had pushed his luck far enough. Two strides to the tent's flap and then he was gone.

That left me alone with my next would-be conqueror. He regarded me, then pulled a ring heavy with keys from his belt. "Come here," he said.

I knelt at his feet and lifted my hands. He clucked his tongue, but said nothing, trying key after key until he found one that opened the manacles. He took them away and then rubbed my wrists. "All right, boy. I don't know how much of what I say you understand, but I have a feeling it's much more than you let on, eh? Just shake your head if you don't like what I say, all right? Now dig in that chest there and find something that fits you."

I must have looked startled because he chuckled at me and pointed to the chest. Inside there were shirts and trousers, all too large for me, but he dressed me with the cuffs rolled up and a belt to keep the pants from falling off my hips. "Better," he said and then sat down with a groan on the pallet, rubbing his thigh as if it were in pain. "Now, I know this isn't probably what you're used to, and it certainly isn't the kind of serving the men think is going on inside this tent. But get my boots off, boy. I can't bend as I used to."

Oh. When he'd put clothes on me, I'd had an inkling he wasn't going to bed me, at least not right away, and now I think I must have broken into a dazed grin. He chuckled as I worked to get his riding boots off. When his feet were bare, he wiggled his toes and sighed. "Work the knots out of my feet, boy. Go on."

I had never done anything like that before, but I rubbed the heel of my hand against the bottom of his foot and he seemed to like that quite a lot. He undid his jacket and tossed it aside, and undid his belt and let it fall as well, but it did not feel at all threatening to me. That was as much disrobing as he did.

Eventually he lay back on the bed and I kept rubbing at his feet.

I found I could dig my thumbs in and that seemed to please him greatly.

"I need a boy like you to assist me," he murmured, his hands folded across his chest. "I have not had a page in years. The old wound in my leg pains me. Especially when it gets cold. The summer heat has been good for it. But I can feel a cold fog coming off the coast. By morning, there will be a chill."

I said nothing.

"I don't suppose you have a name? Or is it one of those Frangi names I'll never be able to pronounce right? Ah, yes, right there. Page. I suppose you will answer to that well enough until you decide to tell me. Eh, Page?"

I gave a small nod at that.

"Don't get any ideas about running off, unless you want to end up fucked raw by every milksucking pervert in the ranks," he went on. "I'm not threatening you, Page. Just saying it's all too likely to happen. You'll never get out of the encampment without being caught, and well, the last spy they turned into a fucktoy... that was a very dismal business. War is not good for men's souls, Page."

He had said that tomorrow they would begin some kind of inspection, didn't he? Was that my best chance to find Jorin, then? I was sure if Jorin caught sight of me, he'd find a way to reach me. And it seemed I was safe with Roichal, at least for now.

"Enough for tonight, Page. Your fingers must be getting tired. All of you must be tired. Lie down here next to me." His words were slowing as he got sleepier and sleepier. But I decided I must not try to sneak off. Not until I knew more about where we were and the lay of the camp at the very least, and even then, staying with him might be my best chance to reach my goal.

Roichal patted the pallet next to him. I lay down tentatively.

He snorted. "You are the most skittish whore I've ever seen. I won't hurt you. But I told you, a chill is coming tonight and these tents are not made to keep out much cold." He pulled a light blanket over us both, and then curled me, spoonwise. His frame was larger than mine, and it was surprisingly comfortable. I half expected to feel an erection poking me in the back, but there was nothing. It seemed the general did not desire me, despite what Marksin had said. At least, not in that way.

And he was right about the change in the weather. I felt the chill on my nose as the night deepened, and I was grateful for his warmth. He seemed to sleep soundly.

Now that I felt safe and comfortable, I thought I would start to feel hungry, but I didn't. Maybe I was just so happy to be out of imminent danger that it would be a while before I felt hunger again? I wondered about such things until I fell asleep, too.

30: Jorin

When I came to, I was still bound, but this time my hands were in front of me and I was not blindfolded. I was lying on a blanket that smelled of horse and I appeared to be in a small tent.

My head felt like metalsmiths with hammers were shaping it from the inside and my mouth was as dry as if they had gagged me with cloth. I winced as someone pulled aside the flap of the tent and the brightness felt like needles in my eyes.

"Ah, poor thing. Here you go."

Kan. He crouched to enter the low tent and knelt by my head. I heard the sound of a flask being unscrewed. He tipped my mouth upward and poured a mouthful of something intensely bitter onto my tongue, but I swallowed it. He let go and already the pain had eased slightly. "I told you you'd feel like this. The tingle-tingle bush in full bloom? I'm not sure if you were lucky or unlucky there, my friend."

"Kan," I tried to say but it just came out a croak.

"One thing at a time," he said, putting a finger to my lips to quiet me. He gave me water next, then went back out of the tent. I did not hear his footsteps, but when he came back in, I had the impression he had circled the tent. "All right. Quietly now. I say lucky because if you'd been awake like the other soldiers you probably would have ended with an arrow in your back. And if you hadn't been hallucinating and talking aloud, I wouldn't have realized who you were before I slit your throat, either, Jorin Weltskin."

He knew who I was! I lay quiet and still for a few moments, thinking over how close I had come to being killed but nonetheless amused by his new name for me. Perhaps the part of the dream where Kenet had been checking over my scars wasn't completely a dream after all. The water eased the burning in my throat and I tried again to speak. "You say you won't harm the prince." Yes, I could speak. "But how can I join you if you fight the crown? Kenet has my loyalty and my goal is to return to him. You must... you must let me go."

He sat cross-legged next to me. "And where would you go? Weren't you exiled from the castle?"

Well, yes. What else did he know? My cheeks burned hot, but I was stubborn. "I will find a way to get him a message."

"And then what? Spirit him away? Actually, Weltskin, that is an excellent plan. We would have long ago kidnapped him if we had thought we had any hope of being successful." He shook his head slowly. "There's no getting through the defenses of that bastard Seroi."

I could not help it. I jerked upright at the sound of that name and made myself dizzy and had to lie down again, waiting for the nausea and vertigo to pass. But once they did, I said, "It was Seroi who separated me from the prince. Who had me banished."

Kan's hand was warm and solid on my upper arm as he helped me to sit up again. "Is that so? You may have to tell that tale to the others to convince them of the trueness of your heart."

"And are you convinced, Kan?" I asked.

He grinned. "You will have your opportunity to prove it to me. Joining our band is not a trivial step. Your loyalty and resolve will be put to the test. I cannot predict, though, how exactly the others will want to test you..."

I shook my head. "No one should doubt the lengths I will go to for Kenet."

Kan's hand slid over my bare back. "Indeed, if these marks are the testimony of it."

"You seem to know about me," I said then. "If so, you know I have been by his side, and receiving these welts on his behalf, since he was a very young child."

"As were you," Kan said, standing then. "If you are who you say you are, of course. As I said, you'll have to convince the others." He threw open the tentflap then and whistled. Gresh and a man I hadn't seen before lifted me from the blanket and carried me out into the summer sun, then into the trees. They stopped in a small dell, and Gresh held me still while the other lashed my bound wrists above my head to a long rope suspended between two trees.

I sighed in resignation. "Let me guess. You have a pulley somewhere so if you like, you can lift me in the air to hang like a puppet."

Kan took a swallow from a bottle that Gresh handed him. "Just so."

"Been strung up like this before?" Gresh asked, his frown making his brow protrude like a cliff. "How many times did you desert the army?"

"What are you talking about? Only the once, when you found me."

He snorted. "The looks of the marks on your back say you've been whipped plenty of times."

As he spoke I was aware of others coming into the clearing, though they were standing behind me. "Of course I have," I said. "I'm Prince Kenet's ladra'an. The king himself put those marks on my skin."

Laughter. I tried to turn my head to see the men behind me, but Gresh seized my chin. "Tut tut. Can't have you looking at them who don't wish to be seen." He wrapped a cloth around my eyes and tied it with a snug knot.

"Listen, it's true. Kenet picked me out of an orphanage when I was small. When we were both small. The only reason I'm not with him now is because the Lord High Mage wanted to get rid of me."

A hand pulled at my hair, forcing my head back. "Can you prove it?"

"What, that I lived in the palace until just a few days ago? Have any of you ever been there?"

"No," came the reply from more than one of them.

"Then what can I tell you that would prove so?" I sighed again. "This whole conversation will be more satisfying to you all, I can see, after you've beaten me. So why not just get on with that?"

The hand holding me disappeared as if the man couldn't stand to touch me, then, and he hissed as if burned.

I pulled at the rope. "Go on. You wouldn't bother to truss me up like this if you didn't intend to. Which of you is a bigger sadist than the king himself? Go on. I would like to find out. Perhaps there is one among you who hits even harder than Seroi. You can re-open the bleeding wounds he left."

"Kan," one of them said, as if asking their leader for help in shutting me up.

There was no reply. "Please, gentlemen," I went on. "I hate boredom more than I despise pain, and every minute we waste, Kenet is in danger, in the clutches of that mage. I can smell the horses even if I have not seen one. Who among you has a riding whip? My skin is not so tough as a horse's hide. I will scream."

I do not know where this bravado came from, honestly. But the more I said, the more unnerved they became, that much I could feel in the air. Just because I was the one tied and blindfolded did not mean I had no power at all.

"What about you, Gresh? You seem more like the barehanded type. Give me a good jaw-rattling slap. Will I spit blood? Or use your knuckles. It can't be worse than fight practice with the castle guard, or the bruises King Korl himself left me with..."

Then I heard Kan chuckling. "Well, men? Ah, I see. I'm sorry Weltskin, they are waiting for me to go first."

I shivered as his hand ran down my back. "I told you. I don't care what you do to me if you help me return to Kenet's side."

One of the others spoke. "I won't be goaded into dealing pain. If that's what the prisoner wants, we shouldn't give it to him. How do we know he isn't a spy of Seroi's anyway, who might have some spell on him that would bring us harm if we harm him?"

Kan chuckled again. "Good thinking, Merrl, but if you're going to be thinking, why not consider this? Look at him. I'd say there are only three possibilities here. One, as Gresh thinks, he's a soldier who has been beaten within an inch of his life each time he's tried to desert the army, two, he's an escaped slave who either had a true pain-dealer for a master or he was so uppity and rebellious he deserved every one of the scars..."

"Or both," someone chimed in.

"Or both," Kan allowed. "Or three, he really is the prince's whipping boy, in which case he could be an ally more powerful than any we've encountered yet since crossing the Serde."

I heard Gresh growl. "I say it's still too great a risk. We are still not in a position to attack Seroi. He won't be of any use to us until then."

I growled back. "I want to join you, you milksucking bastard. If your aim is bringing down Seroi, we have a common enemy. And I can fight! Do you think I'm some court-raised tiptoe dancer?"

I heard the sound of the blade going through the rope before I felt my hands come free, but before I could get the blindfold loose, someone was tackling me to the ground. Whoever it was couldn't have made a worse mistake. I couldn't see, but with him trying to wrestle me, I didn't have to. His clothes also hindered him while my nudity made me hard to grab onto. I had him pinned in under a minute, and pressed my forearm against his throat.

"Do you yield?" I insisted. "Or do the Night Riders not honor such concepts?"

I could hear Gresh's heavy footfalls as he charged toward me, but he stopped before reaching us. My guess was that Kan held him back.

"We have our own kind of honor," Kan said. "Men, if he lets Derget go, will you accept what he says?"

Gresh grunted. "I still say it's too dangerous to just trust him."

Kan laughed. "All the more reason to bind him as a Night Rider."

Gresh didn't sound happy, but he agreed. "Fine. If that's what it'll take, I'm sure I can muster the milk."

Kan came closer to me and the man who was now wheezing some in my grip, Derget. "All right, Jorin Weltskin. If you truly want to join the Night Riders, this will make you one of us truly."

"I told you," I said. "For Kenet, I would do anything. You may flay the skin from my body if that's what it takes. And if you fight Seroi, I will fight with you."

"Your promises will not be necessary because our intention is to bind you using Night Magic. Your loyalty will be ensured. But it is not our way to force such a bond, which is why I ask. If you are willing, let go of Derget, and we will begin the ritual immediately."

"I will be compelled to be loyal, you say," I asked, easing up on Derget a little but not letting him free yet. "But are you compelled to be loyal to me in return?"

Kan laughed. "A very good question. Yes, yes there is a mutual component to the binding."

"Keep him blindfolded and don't let him know which of us holds his leash," Gresh said. "That way there can't be any accidents."

"But how could I harm you if I'm loyal to you?"

"Magic is a tricky thing," Kan answered. "Usually this spell binds slave to master, but we have modified it to ensure mutual loyalty through the group. Without a single man holding your leash, we won't leave you the temptation of trying to engineer your freedom subconsciously, or, for that matter, the temptation of fixating on any of us."

Fixating? I still didn't know what they were talking about exactly, but I let Derget free and reached for the blindfold.

Kan's hands stopped mine. "I thought we just agreed to leave that. We really are going to start right now."

I thought I heard a distant roll of thunder. "All right," I said. "What should I do?"

"I want him tied," Gresh said.

"You can't go first," Derget complained. "You're too enormous."

Kan laughed. "Smallest to largest, then? Derget, does that mean you are first?"

Derget stammered at the insult and I suddenly understood what they were going to do and what they were speaking of. They were going to fuck me.

Kan must have felt the ripple of comprehension moving through me. His fingers held my wrists, but loosely. "You did say 'anything.'"

"I am not objecting," I answered, though my heart was beating wildly and I felt like the ground was moving beneath my feet.

And then they were lifting me, settling me on my back on a blanket. I half-expected them to tie me down, limbs spread, but then I remembered he had used the word willing. My hands and voice shook, though, as I reached up blindly, saying, "Who is first? Come come."

A man's mouth met mine roughly, teeth knocking against my lips as his eagerness bore him down. I could feel his cock against my belly, already hard.

Kan was chanting in a quiet voice, but not so quiet I couldn't make out that the words were in the old tongue. The pungent scent of incense reached me then, while the man between my legs slid his hand down between my cheeks. His fingers were greased and I wondered if one of the others held a pot of it close by?

Then he sank a finger into me and I let out a groan, fragments of my dream of Kenet dancing in front of my closed eyes. The man began to pump and I met each push of his finger with a motion of my hips, suddenly needy for more, and making his cock rub against my belly with each thrust.

He cried out suddenly, his voice young-sounding in his dismay as hot milk spurted across my stomach.

There was quite a bit of chuckling, though they were careful as they ribbed him not to say his name. I had no trouble telling who took his place though: Kan himself.

He slipped a finger into me. "This will be your first time?"

"Yes," I admitted.

"And yet you agreed to take all of us, if necessary? Weltskin, as you may have gathered by now, we have to each take a turn."

"I am no more at your mercy now than I was when I was strung up and expecting you to flay me," I pointed out. "Isn't that part of the point? I'm willing no matter what you do."

"We need to each spill some milk inside you. Inside," he repeated, and the others laughed good-naturedly at the one who had spilled too soon. "That means, well, it means not just a ritual penetration."

"I told you, I'm willing," I repeated.

"I know that, I'm merely *apologizing*," he replied. "I dislike dealing pain *unintentionally*."

Gresh snorted. "Is it all right if I intend to?"

"Later, Gresh," Kan said. "I, at least, don't." And with that, he added another finger to the first, and they made a squelching sound as he pressed them into me.

I soon found my breaths coming and going in time with the motion of his hand, and then he shifted to lie between my legs and I felt the hot, blunt end of him rubbing between my cheeks.

His mouth was at my ear though, nibbling and breathing warm, moist pleasure down my neck. "Think of Kenet," he whispered, as his cock pushed into me.

My cry caught in my throat, the pain completely unlike anything I'd felt before. I struggled reflexively, trying to push him out, anything to ease the sharp, sudden discomfort, but he only pushed further in, making it worse.

Then his hand wrapped around my cock and stroked, and miraculously, it took only a few strokes before everything eased. His whispers continued and they were like what you say to a spooked horse, murmurs of encouragement that I didn't have to understand the words of to be calmed by.

He moved faster as I relaxed more and as the motion of him inside me felt better and better. Then he let go my cock and just concentrated on fucking me.

When he was drawing close to his release, he spoke again. "I will leave you as you are," he said, "so that the ease you felt from your cock being touched will still be possible with the others. I know, you might be more relaxed and looser after you spill, but... you won't thank me if I do that to you now. Trust me."

"All right." I squeezed tight as if trying to hold my own release in and succeeded in gripping his cock with my body so well that he began to spill then. His kiss was surprisingly sweet and eager as he rode out his release into my body.

All too quickly, he was gone, replaced by another. Derget? Whoever he was, he was of similar size to Kan, both in his body and his cock. He fucked with a ferocity that felt like revenge, though, and so I guessed it was Derget, who hadn't enjoyed being bested. He did not touch my cock—in fact he shifted my position onto all fours so that my cock swung untouched under me while he ploughed me from behind. When he came, he howled.

The next also came from behind, and this time I reached under myself to stroke as he worked himself into me. Larger. This cock was larger and it took much longer for him to come. I couldn't touch myself for very long without coming dangerously close to spilling. When he came at last, he pulled out so quickly I felt droplets of his milk all over my back, as well, but as long as some had gone inside, I supposed it was all right.

There were six all told, and the last of them all was Gresh. Somehow I had known it would be. I felt the tug on my wrist as he brought my hands behind my back and tied them together. Then I felt his finger probing at my now well-fucked hole, and it felt nearly like it might be too big to fit. He was almost as big as Bear, I thought.

Then he rubbed his cock up and down in the slick crack and I trembled. Definitely too large. I tried to relax but it was impossible.

I felt Gresh's meaty hands on my hips, pulling me into place as his impossibly large cock pushed at my hole but did not actually make it through the opening. Then some other hand stroked my cock.

Kan. "Come on, Weltskin. You can do it. And if you can't... well, I have some healing potions you can take."

At that Gresh gave a mighty push and it felt like he tore me open. I know now that he hadn't, but at the time I didn't know whether that was possible or not, and it felt like he had. That would mean that the hot liquid running down my legs was blood?

But no, it was milk. Apparently all it took was one stroke inside me to get Gresh to spill. He smacked me hard on the arsecheek as he pumped his hips back and forth a few times, then pulled out.

"There, we're almost done," Kan said, rolling me onto my side and then taking me in his arms, my wrists still bound behind my back. "Well, technically the spell is done. But I should like to see you spill now."

"You're kind," I said, as he stroked my cock for me.

"And cruel, too," he said in reply. "Night Magic requires it. Night Magic requires both pleasure and pain. Something tells me you've seen too much of one lately and not enough of the other. Come for me now, Jorin Weltskin. And be one of us."

I do not know if it was merely that I was ready to spill, or if there was something in the spell that made it happen, but as he commanded me to come, milk fountained out of me in heavy spurts. Each stroke of his hand brought forth more.

And then he kissed me again. A sob caught in my chest then, and I stifled it. He did still remind me of Kenet, enough to sharpen the longing I felt. Or maybe it was the other way around, that I longed for Kenet so much, that I could almost imagine that this was him in my desperation.

They freed me of bonds and blindfold then, and I learned there were actually twenty Night Riders in all, twelve present at the camp at the time. Each of the twelve came and kissed me on the cheeks and welcomed me to the group, and they all seemed sincere, even Gresh, whose hand lingered a moment on my cheek. And then Kan took me back to the tent and made me drink a healing tincture of some kind which made me sleepy.

"When can we go to save Kenet?" I asked, as my eyes were trying to close of their own accord.

"Sleep now, strategy later," Kan said. "I was going to put some clothes on you first, but I don't think you can lift your head."

"Of course I can," I said, but I failed to prove it, falling asleep a moment later.

31: Kenet

The next day dawned damp and chill, but the fog burned off by midmorning. From the rise where Roichal's tent was pitched I could see a large portion of the camp. How many men were here? Thousands, certainly. Finding Jorin was going to be quite a task.

Again I felt no urge to eat. After he had breakfasted himself, though, Roichal taught me to shine his boots and how to oil the leather of his armor. There were many buckles to be shined also, and to be kept from rust. He watched over me for a while, and then left me alone with the tent flaps up to let in light to work by. A soldier sat outside, whistling as he repaired something leather with a long needle. He wasn't obviously a guard, but I wondered if he were there to keep an eye on me.

Roichal and Marksin came in at midday and Roichal gave me some bread and meat, but still I could not bring myself to eat it. They looked at me curiously and gave me plenty of fresh water. Roichal himself checked me for signs of fever, but I seemed well, just not hungry.

"He'll eat when he's ready to," Marksin said. "Just like a stray cat."

That made the general chuckle and pat my head affectionately, which felt better than it had any right to.

Then they prepared to make their round of inspections, and I tugged at Roichal's sleeve, wanting to go along. He put his hands on my shoulders. He was not that much taller than me in truth, but his presence was much more imposing. "I think it's best you stay here and stay out of trouble."

I put a hand on my chest and said, "Page."

He laughed. "Can you ride a horse?"

I nodded emphatically.

He looked me up and down, then called for one of the men.

"You'll ride with me tomorrow, then," he said, "all right?" And he gave instructions to the man as to what sort of uniform I should be fitted with.

He and Marksin went off, then, and the other soldier, whose name I hadn't learned, outfitted me in a blue uniform with silver trim, sewing the crest of a thornflower onto the shoulder—Roichal's crest.

I was wearing it when he returned after the evening meal. He tried again to feed me and again I did not eat. I tried to swallow a little bread, but it only made me feel ill.

He closed all the flaps of the tent as evening came on, and the chill returned. He examined the job I had done with all his leather and buckles and was pleased. Then he took my hands in his and examined them in the lantern light.

"Well, you weren't a fighter," he said, his fingers rubbing over my palm. "And if you were a slave it was the kind who works on his back, hm? Will you tell me the mystery of who you are?"

I shook my head and put my hand on my chest again. "Page."

He sighed. "Yes, I suppose that is what matters now, isn't it. Very well, my page. Tomorrow I shall teach you a bit more about what a page does for the soldier he serves." He clucked his tongue. "And no, my boy, I don't mean like that."

The next day he kept his promise and I rode with him and Marksin to visit several different companies of soldiers. They were arriving from all over Trest. I was constantly looking for Jorin, but by halfway through the day my heart was no longer leaping each time I saw a windblown shock of shorn black hair. They bade me carry the pouch with various papers and records in it, which Marksin would shuffle through and note things upon at each stop.

Some of the time Roichal would hear a plea from a soldier who needed to return home. Some of the time he would grant leave. Marksin made notes.

Partway through the trip, Marksin commented quietly, but not so quietly that I could not hear, that he noticed a pattern in the general's grants of leave. "You haven't let any of the men from southern provinces go."

"Indeed. The last thing I need is for a man to go home to check that his family is safe from the pestilence, only to have him bring it back here and hand victory to our enemies in one awful blow."

Marksin merely nodded at this.

I eventually gleaned that some of these companies were only lately rejoining the main army, while others were being called to duty for the first time. We were clearly in the midst of preparing some sort of mass campaign. I'd no idea that the army was so large. No wonder there were ministers who often complained of how difficult they were to supply and feed.

Speaking of feeding, again I did not eat. Now I felt perhaps slightly lightheaded, but no hunger. Roichal pinched some of my skin as we sat in front of his tent that evening. The next nearest tent was at the bottom of the rise, and although I could see the light from their lanterns, they were far enough I could not hear the men's voices. Marksin sat with us, as he and Roichal shared some of the whiskey that had come from my father. The two of them were on folding seats of some kind, while I sat crossed-legged on the tramped grass.

"When was the last time you ate?" Marksin asked me. "Something other than a man's milk, I mean."

I merely shrugged. The last time... had been that bread and cheese that Jort had given me, and even that had been only a small taste.

Roichal was looking at me curiously then, his back straight. "They say there are Frangi boywhores who can live on nothing but that. I always took it for legend, but..."

Marksin sipped from a tin cup. "But you think this one is playing at it being true?"

"Possibly." Roichal tapped his chin thoughtfully. "I dislike puzzles I cannot solve."

That, for some reason, made Marksin bark, one short bitter laugh. They both drank in silence for a while after that, until Marksin said, "If it's milk he needs, have you been feeding him, Sir? He's your pet, after all."

Roichal made a noise. "You sound a bit jealous. Did you want his mouth then, Marksin? His arse wasn't enough for you?"

Marksin drained his cup and stood as if to leave. "I didn't. He was crying and you know I cannot abide any hint of..."

"Sit, Marksin, sit," the general said then, and although his voice was light, it was no less a command. Marksin sat.

"You taught me too well, Sir," Marksin said. "I'll never be able to... to force anyone."

"No one expects you to," Roichal said, shaking his head. "If they do, the Night has sickened their hearts. That is not what we are fighting for, is it?"

"No, Sir." Marksin hung his head now and I could not see his face the way his straight, dark hair hung.

They were both silent for a moment. "Do you have no one?" Roichal asked him in a low voice.

"No, Sir," Marksin answered, now almost a whisper.

I could see the expression on the general's face was pained. He looked at me. "Page," he asked softly, "would you be willing to help Field Marshal Marksin?"

"Don't," Marksin said, but I was nodding. "Sir, I don't need..."

Roichal made a skeptical noise. "Page," he said. "You don't have to if you don't want to. But I think of the field marshal here quite fondly, and as you can see he has no capacity to ask for himself."

I nodded again, and slipped my hand into Marksin's, squeezing it encouragingly. I rubbed my cheek along the back of his hand then. "Kind," I said. "Very kind."

Marksin's shoulders seemed to slump. "Yes, I was kind to you. I... tried, anyway."

"Go on," Roichal said. "He's your type."

"You don't know what my type is," Marksin said, but his resistance was gone.

I pulled him by the hand toward the opening of the tent, wondering if the general was going to follow or if he would leave us alone.

He did not follow. Marksin undid his belt and slipped his trousers down as he sat on the edge of the sleeping pallet. I urged him to at least get one leg free so I could kneel between his legs.

For all his protesting, his prick showed itself to be quite eager for attention.

I licked up the already-hard shaft and moaned myself at the flavor of him. The hunger I had not felt in days suddenly seemed to flare to life and I licked all around the head, lapping at the dewy, salty drops oozing up at the tip. Then I took him deep into my mouth, suckling.

His fingers swept through my hair and he groaned, too. "Thunder, but I've needed this."

It didn't take him long, and once he had spilled deep into my throat and I had licked him clean of every drop, he pulled me up into a kiss. Then he pushed me away, as if that had been too much. I kissed him on the forehead as if to say it was all right, and then I helped him to stand and right his clothes.

His hand reached toward my groin but I pulled away, shaking my head.

"You're sure? I'd be happy to oblige you," he said.

I just gestured for him to join the general sitting outside again.

Roichal had poured himself another measure and was sipping it and looking up at the stars. He had moved so that he was sitting on a fallen log. Once upon a time this rise must have been crowned by a tree, but a lightning strike must have brought it down. He beckoned for me to come sit beside him.

"Hungry now?" he asked.

I shook my head.

The two of them looked at each other. Marksin shrugged. "Either it's a charade and he'll eventually show the effects of not eating, or you'll catch him at it, or he really is a prize escaped from the Frangi court, and Night Magic really is as twisted as you've always told me."

"We shall see," is all Roichal said.

"Good night, Sir." Marksin sketched a brief bow, and then went down the hill in the dark.

I sat there feeling more chilled then than the night warranted. Seroi had truly tried to make me into a whoreslave; this seemed irrefutable proof of it.

Roichal slipped his arm around my shoulders. "And does my Page need anything?" he asked gently.

I shook my head, but leaned into him. He was solid and reassuring and just held me that way without trying to touch me or goad me into touching him. After a while, though, I wondered if maybe he had something in common with his second-in-command, which was that he too would not ask for what he needed. I slipped my hand to his belt buckle and looked up, questioning.

He just shook his head. "No need for that, Page."

I tugged on his belt somewhat insistently.

"Are you hungry?" he asked. "The truth, now."

I shook my head. I only wanted to please him.

"Then now is not the time," he said, removing my hand gently. "Come, let's to bed. Dawn comes early."

We got onto the sleeping pallet in our now accustomed position, facing the tent flap with him spooning me, one arm draped over me protectively. One of the positions Jorin had always loved.

I fell asleep wondering where he was. Was he near or far? There was no way I could ask about him without giving myself away. I could only wait and see what fate would bring next.

32: Jorin

When next I woke, I found Kan lying next to me, propped up on one elbow, as if he had been watching me sleep.

Much like Kenet used to. And will again! I told myself, but at that moment he felt very far away. And who knew if Seroi had somehow changed him by now?

These thoughts must have shown on my face. Kan stroked my hair in sympathy. "You're not alone anymore," he said. "You're a Night Rider now."

"Kenet is alone," I said. "His only ally is his childhood guard, but even he cannot keep him safe from the Lord High Mage. I fear for him." Judging by the light coming through the tent's canvas, the sun would soon be rising. "Seroi was training him for his coming of age ceremony. I fear he has dark designs on the prince."

Kan's eyebrows knitted. "Tell me what you know."

I told him what I could. That Kenet was under some kind of magical compulsion not to tell anyone, but that he was able to confirm or deny my guesses. That I knew Seroi milked him and that after their practice, Kenet was... different. "I think it was making him ill. His skin looked ashen and his milk..." Could I say it?

"Did you taste his milk, Jorin?"

I nodded. "And he mine. But we never... yesterday was my first time."

"So you said," Kan reminded me. "What did his milk taste like?"

"Normally, sweet. But after he had been to see Seroi, bitter. Almost burnt."

Kan's expression darkened. "And when was this coming of age ceremony to be?"

"Midsummer," I said. "Tell me what you know about it."

Kan shook his head. "For me to tell you what I know about the Night Arts will take considerably longer than the time we have available," he said.

"Is Kenet in danger?"

"Yes, but you already knew that. And I do not know enough to do more than guess at exactly what Seroi had in mind. But even you, with what little you know of the Night Arts yourself now, can make a guess."

Yesterday six Night Riders had planted their seed in me. I was bound to them now. "He means to bind the prince to him."

"I believe so, yes. By being the first to plant his flag in fertile ground, so to speak, Seroi can make a claim that subsequent invaders cannot." He shook his head. "I want to stop it happening as much as you do. With Kenet in his control, Seroi would be even more of a force to reckon with than he is now."

"He already has the king wrapped around his finger," I said.

But Kan shook his head. "But he does not control him the way he would if Kenet were bound to him with Night Magic. He manipulates Korl the King other ways, the usual ways, with fearmongering and deceit and flattery and shows of might at the proper times."

I looked up at him. "Kan."

"Yes, Weltskin?"

"Does the first... always have..." What were the words I was searching for? My voice shook a little. "Can you... control me?"

His face softened. "Ah, I see what you are thinking." He ran his thumb gently over my lips. "The first... always has a special bond, yes. But no, Weltskin, I cannot control you. Not with magic, anyway." He leaned down and kissed me and I felt a warmth and tenderness I had never felt before, except with Kenet. But this was different, too. "I didn't intend to be the first," he reminded me. "I thought you'd bond like a brother to Pietri and be good for each other... Ah, damn, I wasn't supposed to tell you who it was. Oh, you'd have figured it out soon enough, I'm sure. After he got overeager, though, I thought it best to do it myself, rather than it be one of the men who were less charitably inclined toward you."

"But if they don't control me...?"

"Jorin," he said. "Forgive me if I'm wrong, but I was under the impression you found me likable."

"I do," I admitted.

"And I thought you'd prefer to be more strongly bonded with someone you liked." He slipped his breeches down to his knees and revealed a ruddy erection, curved back toward his belly, his balls dusted with light-colored hair.

I did not hesitate to slip my hand around it. "All well and good," I said. "But don't tell me it was all altruism."

"I have no reason to lie to you," he said, thrusting into my hand. "I wanted you for a lover. It seemed likely I would have you anyway, regardless who went first, but I cannot deny being your first... makes me hard every time I think of it."

As he said it and I felt the hard flesh in my hand twitch, I felt an answering tug inside me. Magic? Or just arousal? I needed to know who was in control, though. "And are we lovers now, Kan?"

"If you agree to it and only if you agree to it," he said, face sober despite my stroking him. "Willingly. And not just willingly, but wholeheartedly."

I slid his breeches off him completely and then straddled him, so that our cocks touched. "I will willingly be your lover, Kan," I said. "But you cannot have my whole heart. Kenet has that." I found my fists balled with determination. "I... I will be Kenet's first. Not Seroi. I must."

He just nodded. "I figured as much. Very well, Jorin Weltskin. Your heart belongs to another, but at this moment, your body is yearning for no one other than me. I would gladly satisfy that need."

"You're my lover now," I said, rolling onto my back and pulling him with me like a wrestling partner. "It's your responsibility to do so."

"Indeed, I agree," he said, reaching for something I could not see. He slipped a hand between us then, between my legs, and the grease felt cool on my hole. "It's to be expected, but... you're a bit inflamed from yesterday."

"Will it hurt again?" I could not help but ask, even as the desire to have him in me flared inside me.

He kissed me before answering. "No, not like that again, and I apologize for that. If the circumstances had been different, I might've prepared you longer, perhaps lessening the pain. Today, I imagine it's mostly just that you're sore from all the penetration."

The grease he used felt as if it cooled the sore flesh, though, and by the time he pressed his cock inward, the only thing I felt was desire. I groaned deeply as he filled me, pulling him in close. His mouth went to my neck, drawing another groan out as he suckled while he pushed into me. He took his time, moving more slowly than any of them had the day before.

It felt good. Lightning strike me if I lie; I felt a desire like none I had known before, and it was to take him deeper and deeper. I made sounds I had never before made.

"Is this... is this what it feels like for a maid?" I asked as he settled into a steady rhythm.

"I've never been a maid," he said, "so I couldn't say. The maids tell me it feels very, very good, though."

I nodded. "Yes, yes it does."

"You come first this time." He stroked me until I spilled, then followed me a few seconds later, fucking me so hard the sound of our bodies slapping together might have easily woken the others. No one complained however, and within moments I felt myself drifting back to sleep, Kan still buried deep inside me.

33: Kenet

I played the part of Roichal's page for a few more days, as he and the field marshal checked over the growing army. One morning, though, Roichal's leg was so stiff, he could not mount his horse, and no amount of cursing and railing (and it was quite an amount, let me assure you) would change that. Marksin eventually forced him to lie back down and then went away, returning quickly with a jar which he thrust into my hands. "Go on. This will help him," was all he said, and then he hurried off, to make the inspections himself, I supposed.

Roichal actually uttered a moan then, the first sound of discomfort I could recall him making. He must have been in great pain. I hurried to kneel next to the pallet and show him the jar.

He clucked his tongue. "This salve is strong stuff, Page, but there is nothing else for it. Give it here."

He took the jar from me and I surrendered it, but part of me wanted to hold onto it. Hadn't the general said when I'd first arrived that he would teach me to rub his leg or some such? It wasn't his 'third leg' he'd been referring to, that much I was sure. He still had not made any move toward me sexually, unless one counted him putting me and Marksin together.

He seemed neither the type to condemn a man for desiring a man, given his charity toward his field marshal, nor sickened by the thought, as I knew some men were. Perhaps he simply did not desire me? He slept with me held close every night, though.

Under the blanket, so I could not see what he did, he shifted out of his trousers and his hands moved. His brow was damp with sweat from the effort of trying to get into the saddle, and the pain. I decided to insist he let me help.

I put a hand atop the blanket, his knee. What could I say? What words would a slave from another land have learned? "Help," I said then, and reached for the jar. "Page help."

"I can do this myself, Page. No need for you to involve yourself."

"Page help," I repeated, knitting my eyebrows together. "Strong hands." Not as strong as Jorin's but...

He caught one of my hands in his, and for a moment I thought I caught a flash of something eager in his eye. But then he was shaking his head. "I will be fine."

I just shook my head slowly, as if I didn't believe him. I rubbed his knee through the blanket.

That broke his resolve and he sighed. He swung his legs over the side of the cot and then draped the blanket so that only his bad leg was exposed. He could barely bend his knee at all and yet I could not see anything obvious. I expected to see scars or some kind of visible sign of the stiffness.

He put the jar back into my hands. "Start at the ankle and work your way up," he said, gesturing.

The stuff in the jar smelled strongly of mint and cinnamon and odd medicines, reminding me only a little of Seroi's concoctions. It was brown and seemed to melt a little under my fingers. I started rubbing in circles around his ankle and gradually worked my way upward.

Now that I could feel his muscles, I could feel that they were like stones, with no way for him to relax them. I worked slowly, only moving upward when I felt the flesh under my fingers start to feel supple and normal. By the time I was halfway up his thigh, a quarter of the jar was gone and my eyes were watering from the pungent scent of the salve.

"That's enough, you can stop there," he said, but I fixed him with a glare.

"Leg only," I assured him. He had rebuffed my advances to his breeches more than once, I didn't need to be told again and he seemed to know that. He nodded and I continued all the way up to the join of his hip.

He sighed again, this time with real relief, and it was easy to urge him to lie back down and cover his legs with the blanket again. He was asleep within a minute, a sure sign of how much the suffering had taken out of him.

I went to wash my hands of the salve. When I returned, Marksin was standing at the entrance to the tent, peeking sidelong through the flap.

"Ah, here you are. Well, I've gathered the reports of a few of the commanders we had been due to visit today." He handed them to me.

I did not have the carrying pouch I usually bore on these visits. Perhaps that was why I made the mistake I did. I looked down at the top sheaf, and read it.

I caught myself after a moment, but the redness of my cheeks surely gave me away as much as the obvious lingering of my eyes had. Marksin merely crossed his arms, regarding me.

"You're not fooling either of us, you know," he said. "You may as well drop the charade. It's obvious you understand us perfectly and it isn't as if we're going to forget and speak military secrets in front of you."

I just shook my head and shouldered past him into the tent, putting the reports beside the pallet where the general could see them when he woke. Marksin did not follow me.

I went back out and sat on the fallen tree. If I spoke, if I revealed that I could speak, there would be one advantage, and that would be I could ask questions. But would Marksin answer?

Oddly I found that days on end saying only a few words here and there had suited me. I wondered suddenly if that was part of the transformation Seroi had wanted for me? Did whoreslaves only use their mouths to suck milk?

That made up my mind for me. "I can speak," I said, though it came out a whisper. "I just... don't want to."

He let out a wry huff and sat next to me. "It's suited your purposes well enough, you mean."

"A mage..." Quite suddenly though, I could not speak. A choking sound came from my mouth, and then I doubled over, as my breath seemed to disappear inside me. I had forgotten the promise!

Seroi had bound me to silence on the subject of what he had done to me. I tried to think of something else to say and the moment I did, the choking sensation eased. "The sky is blue," I said, since that was what I had thought of, and then gasped, trying to suck in as much air at once as I could.

To my surprise, Marksin's hand was steadying me. "Careful, careful," he said. Then, "When was the last time you ate solid food?"

I shrugged. " The days run together... before you met me, though."

"This is the work of a Night Mage, that much is clear. But how did you escape from the Frangi court to end up all the way here? Can you tell me, or does the spell compel your silence?"

I shook my head.

"What can you tell me? If you care for him at all, you must tell me all you can," he said with a jerk of his head toward the tent, meaning if I cared for Roichal. "You do realize that just as you can be magically compelled not to speak, you could be compelled to do things as well. How do I know you are not an assassin sent to do away with him when the right moment comes?"

"Lightning strike me if I am," I said. "I'm no assassin. I'm... I'm not sure what I am now." And that was the truth without me saying anything about what Seroi had done. "You seem... you seem to know something about Night Magic."

"Only a little," he said in a resigned voice. "Roichal knows a bit more, but even he..." He stroked a hand over my hair. "Even he was surprised to find that you seem to be living on my milk alone. I wonder, how long can you go before you need more?"

I put a hand over my mouth; I was suddenly nearly drooling. "I don't know." It came out a whisper.

He sat back as if trying to put some distance between us.

"Go," I said gesturing toward his tent at the bottom of the hill. "I... I won't. Not without his permission."

He stood, backing away, as he said, "Neither would I, Page. Send for me when he wakes."

"I... I will." My stomach grumbled and I clutched at it. "Go."

He hurried down the hill, but his gait was stiff and I wondered how hard and throbbing his prick must have been. I went back into the tent and watched Roichal sleep for long minutes while trying to decide what to do. Why had I said that I wouldn't suck Marksin's milk without the general's permission? It seemed right. And Marksin had agreed with me. Even he accepted what had never been spoken aloud by any of us. I belonged to Roichal. I was his.

I crawled under the blanket with him then, shivering a little with the strength of the hunger in me. I wondered if I should try to eat some actual food, but a part of me knew it would do nothing for me. And what about... my own milk? Would it slake my thirst? But I had been unable to spill. Was this why?

I eventually passed into a fitful sleep, and woke some time later when the general stirred. He rolled onto his back and I tucked myself into the crook of his arm. He did not raise his head but stroked my side and said, "Thank you, Page."

"Is your leg feeling much better, Sir?" I asked.

If he was surprised to hear me utter a full sentence, he showed none of it. "Much better, yes, thank you. And how about you?"

I hesitated a moment before answering. "I'm... I'm hungry, Sir."

"Ah. Hungry for what, though?"

"I... Not for bread, Sir." I hid my face against his side then, as if admitting it aloud were shameful. Oh Seroi, what did you do to me?

Roichal hushed me. "I am sure the field marshal would be pleased to provide for you if you are in need," he said in a gentle voice.

"I... I know, Sir." Why did I feel so miserable? I was trembling. "I wouldn't... that is... neither of us would, without your permission."

His thumb traced my cheek as he shifted to face me, and then my trembling ceased when he placed one very soft but very deliberate kiss on my forehead, claiming me for his own in a way that spoke to me without any need for words.

"Go to him," he whispered then. "Go and have your fill, and then come back to me."

I didn't want to leave him. I wanted to stay there in his arms, even as hunger gnawed at me. I could remember the salty taste of Marksin's cock, the tang of his milk, but I did not want to leave Roichal's side. I also knew better than to argue with an order, though. I nodded and slipped from his bed without a word.

Marksin was more adventurous with me this time, touching more of me and letting me touch more of him. But no matter what caresses he gave to my body, none came close to surpassing that one kiss of Roichal's.

34: Jorin

There was a moment, one morning, when I was half-asleep still, when I believed that everything that had happened had been an awful nightmare, and that the man in my arms was Kenet. I could taste the back of his neck where my nose was buried, and hear the frits on the balcony, and I thought, what a terrible dream that had been and thank the sky above that all was well.

I slid my hand down his body to seek his cock, to bring him to full hardness before he could wake. As I did, though, I felt a sudden ache inside me, a sudden need for him. I gasped and jerked and that woke him.

Kan. He chuckled. "Good morning, lover."

"G-good morning..."

He turned to look at me, his brows knit with concern. "Are you well, Jorin?"

"I'm not sure." I slipped my hand off him but the throbbing need inside me stayed the same. "I... is it always like this?"

He reached for my cheek, just a caress, but it calmed me to feel that he cared. "You'll need to be more specific. Is what always like what?"

He knew Night Magic. He probably knew better words for it than I did, but I tried. "It's like a hunger in me, a painful one, whenever..." I hadn't quite made the connection until now. "Whenever you get hard."

Kan just looked at me for a moment, his expression changeless. Was he trying to see if I was lying? I didn't know. Then he spoke. "It's the bond's magic. It wasn't meant to be quite so strong, but perhaps something about you has strengthened it."

"Something about me?"

He pushed me gently onto my back and kissed me, then suckled at one of my nipples until I mewled like a kitten. Then he stroked me with one hand while he propped his head up on his bent arm and answered my question. "Yes, something about you. Maybe having been owned all your life made you more receptive to the submissive role. It could be your longing for your prince meant the spell settled more deeply because of how vulnerable your heart is. Or perhaps it's purely your inherent sensuality that is causing this reaction." He reached for the pot of grease he always kept within arms reach of where he slept, specifically for this purpose. As the first finger breached me, the ache eased a little, but I knew it would soon return in greater force if he did not fuck me.

It had been several days since my initiation and binding, but only on hearing him say the words did the pattern become clear to me. "So, I will ache with need until you spill. Must you spill inside me? Or will my lust abate if you are satisfied some other way?"

"Given that I did not anticipate you would have this reaction to the spell, I cannot say for sure. Perhaps we should experiment? Would you like to do that?"

I pulled at him. "I would like you to fuck me."

"I know. But seriously, Jorin, the purpose of the spell was not to make you my—our—whoreslave, but merely to secure your loyalty. Yes, some of the binding elements are the same, but... lightning strike me if I lie, but I did not intend it to go this far. Are you sure it isn't merely that you're attracted to me, and now that you have had my cock, you simply want it again?"

"Speculate later," I growled. "Fuck me now."

"All right, if you insist." He mounted me then despite the fact he'd barely stretched me, but the intense sensation that swept through me as he rammed in could hardly be called pain. It was bliss.

He worked himself to the edge of coming, then backed off. "It isn't good for you to be too closely tied to me alone," he said. "We must let one of the others have a turn."

"What would happen if the bond between us... tightened?" I imagined it like a set of ropes connecting us together, drawing tighter and tighter.

"You've already told me your heart belongs to Kenet. If you're going to be with him, someday the bond between us will need to be severed. If we make it too strong, the only way to break it will be to do severe damage to one or both of us." He had slowed the thrusts into my body then, and I savored the feeling of him going in and out.

"You're right, that would be bad," I said. "But how can I be sure you're not merely feeding me a story to justify making me the fucktoy of every man here? After my experiences with Seroi, I do not trust Night Magic any more than I can see my hand in total darkness."

"Rightly so," he nodded. "In fact, you cannot be sure. But I will tell you this. Our intent, if you will remember, was for you not to know whom your many masters are. The way the spell has taken you, though, I have no doubt you will be able to tell who they are easily enough. Unless we allow things to solidify on me alone, you may find you have the talent to know when any of those who took you in the woods that day are hard and in need of release. That was definitely not our intent."

"All right." That made sense.

"I would like to test it, if you're willing."

"How?"

"I must spill first, and your aching will subside, will it not? And then I will go wake one of the others, and make him hard, and we shall see if you sense it."

"And what then?" I could not keep an edge of anger out of my voice. "Will you let him fuck me while your milk is still hot inside me?"

Kan kissed me then. "Only if you wish it. If you prefer, I will let him find his release with me, and that way we shall also test if the feeling subsides when he is satisfied, or if you are only sated when it is your body that is taken."

"And... if I am not sated?"

He kissed me again, to placate me. "Jorin. I will take care of you. Trust me. If it's cock you need, that I have." And with that he began fucking me too hard and fast for either of us to speak further. When he spilled, I felt something inside me release as well, even though I did not come. He waited until he had gone completely soft and slipped from me before he wriggled down my body and placed a kiss on the head of my still-hard cock.

"I will be back to take care of you," he said, as if speaking directly to my prick. I laughed in spite of myself and he slipped from the tent.

I lay there in the morning glow, listening to the frits and other birds, stroking myself idly but feeling largely content to wait for his return. We had waited three days at the camp at Tiger's Mouth for his ranging band to return, and then set out ourselves toward the castle. Three days we had traveled, and it was slow going, staying off the well-traveled roads and uphill all the way.

Then suddenly I felt the ache flare to life in me again and I moaned without meaning to. I stroked myself harder but it did nothing to alleviate the pangs of need rippling through me. I slid a finger inside my slick hole but it was not enough.

Thunderclouds roll, was this what Kenet was going through at the hands of Seroi? The realization hit me like a flash of lightning. Was this what he was fighting? He had told me that Seroi hadn't fucked him, but it was suddenly painfully clear to me that this was what Kenet would be reduced to on midsummer night. I saw red as I imagined him begging Seroi to spear him, anything to ease the ache, the intense need. And Seroi granting him his wish, since after all, how could he refuse a royal decree?

And how could Korl have let it happen right under his nose? Sergetten used to mutter, when he thought we couldn't hear, that the king was blind, but not to see that his own son was being twisted into not just a whoreslave but a Night-bound one?

These thoughts, or perhaps it was the desperation caused by the ache inside me, had me near tears by the time Korl returned. The ache abated when the man he had gone to see had come, but the thoughts did not.

This time when Kan made love to me, I think it was to comfort me. Although I felt Kenet was farther from me than ever, at least for a few moments of pleasure I was not alone.

35: Kenet

The next day, the general was still not recovered enough to ride. The leg, which had been stiff to the point of agony, was now too weak to support his weight. He instead moved to sitting on the fallen tree and various commanders came to report to him. Now that my charade of ignorance was over, I took on the duties of an actual page, and recorded names and made notes as I was bade to. The only thing he did not let me see was an envoy's package with the royal seal on it. I noted he did not let Marksin see it either. In the afternoon, when I was not looking, he limped into the tent and read it, and then, I assume either hid it or burned it as I did not see it anywhere.

That evening, the cook's men filled a large half-barrel with steaming water from kettle after kettle. After they left, Roichal eased his leg into the water. He looked supremely uncomfortable to be just sitting still, though. Restless.

I put my hands onto his shoulders. He still wore his breeches and a loose white shirt. I kneaded his shoulders like the kitchen maids in the castle did bread and he grunted in approval.

It was only enough to stave off his impatience for a few minutes, and he pulled his leg from the water while still hot and dried it off with a cloth.

"Page," he said then, and there was a curious tone in his voice. "Come here."

"Sir?"

He gestured in front of him. He was seated on a folding stool with the barrel just to one side of him.

"I would like to look at you."

"Of course, Sir." I bowed my head. So, I thought, the time had come at last? I began to undo the uniform jacket. It felt like it took me a long time to remove all of my clothes, and unless he said to stop, I assumed I should remove everything. Soon I was standing on the canvas in nothing at all.

He gestured me closer and dipped the cloth into the warm water. I stood close enough to touch, and he reached up and scrubbed gently at my chest. He proceeded to work over every inch of me, including my face and all the way down my legs, turning me around and doing my back and the globes of my arse.

"Lean forward and pull them apart," he said, but there was nothing wanton in his voice, only a kind of fondness. He scrubbed the tender pucker I exposed, and my balls, then turned me one last time to wash my prick.

The blood which had rushed to my cheeks at stripping in front of him, now rushed somewhere else.

"You are still a mystery to me, Page," he said, "though I know you better and better."

I could only nod.

"There is not a mark on you at all. You can't have been a whoreslave unless you had an unusually lenient master. Marksin believes you may be under a compulsion not to speak of your master? All I can say is, if a Night Mage was your master... well, you would bear the scars of his practice, except you have none. But who else could have bespelled you to live off a man's milk and nothing else? As I say, a mystery."

"Yes, Sir," I said, as he rubbed the wet cloth up and down my shaft as if washing it still, but his purpose was clearly different. He pulled me down to sit on his good knee.

"You haven't come in how long?" he asked. "That cannot be healthy, even for a whoreslave who needn't eat. I plan to see if you can come tonight, though, if we are patient." He tossed the cloth aside. "I'll use an unguent to be sure you do not get sore. You'll need to retrieve it from the small chest inside the larger one there." He pointed across the tent.

The top of the large chest was being used as a kind of table, and I moved the sheafs of reports aside, then opened the lid. A smaller and much more ornate chest was nestled there and I lifted it out. There was no key, just a fancy-looking latch. I popped the latch and the lid sprang open.

Inside was a single feather, a gold coin, and a strip of leather. Nothing that looked like a jar or bottle of unguent. "Sir? I don't see it." I carried the chest to him to show it.

"Ah, I must have misplaced it," he muttered, looking around as if it might appear in his sight. "Well, no matter, put the chest away. Perhaps it's just at the bottom of the larger one."

Something about the way he said it made me think he had known the jar wasn't there. For some reason he had wanted me to see what was in the chest? As I shut it and latched it, I wondered if I should have taken a closer look at the contents. I found the jar and returned to him.

He had shifted to the pallet and sat back with his legs wide, gesturing for me to come sit between them. There was no bulge in his breeches and I again wondered why he did not desire me, when it seemed every other man under the sky did.

He nestled my back against his chest, and then greased his palms, taking hold of me firmly and stroking upwards. Up and up and up, each hand following the other, always in the same direction. It was beyond arousing and I was soon writhing against him, on edge but unable to spill over.

He slowed then, and teased me the way Jorin used to, touching me so lightly I thought I might go mad, giving just enough pressure to move my foreskin up and down. Then the firm upward stroke returned.

Just when I was about to beg him to stop, though, he whispered into my ear. "Come for me, Page. Spill into my fingers."

And as if his order could not be disobeyed, I found myself doing just that. That and crying out with relief. Spurt after spurt after spurt shot from my prick, eventually settling to a steady ooze. I took a long time to go soft. When I did, he held me cupped in the warmth of his hand, his other around my chest, holding me close.

"How..." I could barely speak, not from any compulsion this time, but merely from being out of breath and my throat raw. "How did you know?"

"I didn't," he said, kissing me on the temple. "I made a guess. I was either correct, or that was entirely coincidental."

"But... but the field marshal told me to come, that night... that night in the stable. But I still could not."

Roichal chuckled. "Then perhaps I am better at it than he? More likely, Page, it is that I made it an order. I feel sure the field marshal did not."

Perhaps he hadn't. Most of what I remembered of that night now was that Marksin had tried to soothe my tears.

"Perhaps," I allowed.

"You sound unsure. Is there more I should know, that you are able to tell?"

I turned in his arms, putting mine around his neck. I expected again to feel his eager cock poking me in the belly, but I did not. His face was close to mine and in the lanterns his eyes looked like tiny fires burned in them. "Maybe... maybe not everyone can grant that permission. Maybe only you can."

He stroked my hair. "Is that the way it feels?"

I nodded.

"Then you must tell me when you feel the need to spill, Page. Just as you must tell me when you are hungry, or if you have other needs."

I nodded again, wondering if I dared to ask. He seemed to be waiting for me to say something, though, so I did. "Will you... will you kiss me like you did last night?" I wasn't even sure if saying so would explain how I felt.

But I think he knew. He caressed one of my cheeks with his thumb, and then tilted my head with his fingers at the back of my neck. "You are a mystery," he said in a low voice. "But Fate has sent you to me. That I believe." And with that he leaned in and pressed a soft but lingering kiss against my forehead, every bit as searing as the previous one, marking me as his in my soul.

36: Jorin

We drew ever nearer the castle, and one day we climbed a ridge and could just make it out, partway up a mountain on the horizon, like one small white tooth in a great jaw of grey teeth. With it seemingly so near, all I wanted to do was ride all night until we reached the walls, but Kan called for us to set up camp.

"We'll wait here until a sentry can go and return with news," he said as he dismounted.

"And how long will that be?" I was still on my horse.

"Two days, at least. We can go no nearer without knowing more. Seroi's magic—"

"Save your explanations," I said bitterly as I swung down out of the saddle. What I would have given at that moment just to have caught a glimpse of Kenet on a balcony, just to know that he was well. If he was well, that is.

Kan ruffled my hair. "I have something that will distract you today," he said.

"Oh? And is that something about as long as a dagger but with a much blunter end?"

"Tcha. That, too, but no, I was thinking of fight practice."

We grinned at each other. "I would enjoy that very much."

"I knew you would," he said, as we led our horses to tether and began removing their tack.

The Night Riders each had a task in setting up the camp. We were eight on this journey, and each man seemed to know just what was expected of him, and quickly shelters were erected, the horses tended and groomed, food prepared... I was the only one who had no role.

Or did I? Fight practice, Kan had said. I set to preparing a fight-ing ring, then, in a small dell. The trees here were tall and thickly leaved, and very little underbrush grew other than moss and ferns, making it easy to clear the space. Rocks and branches I flung aside, and then tramped down the ferns and other greenery.

No one ate heavily, but the fact that we ate before the fighting indicated to me that fight practice might go on for quite some time.

They already knew I could fight after the way I had bested Derget. The first few bouts were almost friendly. I exchanged falls with Pietri and everyone seemed pleased with that. I then got to watch Kan fight Gresh to a standstill, at which point they both conceded the ring to the next pair. I fought Derget a bit later, and this time he knew not to let me get hold of him, and we exchanged stinging blows. Kan was right, I greatly enjoyed the practice, and it was good for all of us to hone our skills.

A piercing bird call suddenly caught our ears and every man fell silent. That was Willim, who had taken care of the horses and who hadn't fought, calling for caution.

Kan made a gesture with his hand and closed his eyes. Everyone held their breath but I could not guess what sign they were waiting for.

Then Kan made an answering bird call, the all-clear signal, and Willim confirmed it. I let out a sigh. I didn't know how they knew it was safe, but I assumed it had to be Night Magic.

The sun was setting now; soon it would be too dark under the trees to practice more. Kan whistled to Willim more conventionally. "You ought to take a turn. Derget, you take watch."

Willim limped reluctantly forward and I wondered what injury he had suffered that gave him such a limp. "There's only one kind of fight I can do that could be at all fair," he said with a smirk. "Anyone care to?"

Gresh spat in disgust. "I'd split you open like a lightning-struck tree," he said.

Willim had chestnut brown hair hanging over one eye. He brushed it back with a hand. "What about you, Kan?"

Kan's grin was wolfish. "If you insist. But do you really think you can take me?"

Willim pulled his tunic over his head to reveal a tanned chest and began to unlace his breeches. "I have before," he said.

"Mm, don't know which I'd like better sometimes," Kan answered. He stripped down to nothing and I was interested to see two of the others return to the circle with a large piece of hide of some sort. By its size it must have been two hides stitched together. They pegged it down to make a smooth surface, padded underneath by the flattened bracken. Kan and Willim stepped barefoot onto it, then began greasing each other's skin with something from a jar.

The greasing was arousing enough to watch, but as Willim wrapped one hand around Kan's cock, one around his own, I felt the bond flare inside me. I stifled a small sound. The ache was sudden and intense, like the ice-chill of the lake in winter. I kept my mouth shut, though, hugging myself with crossed arms.

It was, as I had guessed from Gresh's reaction, a fuck fight. Fuck or be fucked. But with each man slippery with grease, the wrestling was like none I'd ever seen before. I expected them to laugh from time to time, but each was giving it his full concentration, and that included the spectators. Willim, for all his difficulty walking, was a picture of perfect grace when on a horse, and was slippery as a snake on the ground. They fought like weasels, twisting over and over each other, each trying to gain the advantage.

The ache intensified as they went on, their cocks rubbing against each other and against the leather under them. It was the strongest I'd felt it, I realized. Was the bond strengthening still further? Or was it that both Kan and Willim were among my masters?

My breath caught as I realized what was happening. Every man there, even Gresh, was aroused by the sight, by the slick slip of skin over skin, and by the whimpering sound Willim made as Kan thrust between his legs, not able to get inside him, but fucking the tight space between his thighs. Then suddenly Willim wriggled in some perfect way to push Kan over, and nearly did push into him, ending up rutting against his tailbone.

Every thrust, every throb of blood in each of the cocks of the men there, beat inside me like a drum. I hadn't been aware of standing, only of falling to my knees with one hand outstretched toward them, beseeching.

Both combatants looked up, then focused on me. "Thunder's roll," Kan swore. "Quick, get his clothes off him."

Hands were stripping me, then, and I could barely see, because of the tears the intense need and pain had brought to my eyes. I could hear Gresh, though, demanding to know what was going on.

Kan's explanation was short and incomplete, but his band did not question his orders once given. Willim was the first to get his cock in me and although I felt a wave of relief for a few seconds, the aching returned nearly as strong as before after a few minutes. Kan barked to Pietri to take my mouth, and quite suddenly it was filled with a sweet young cock. They had moved me now so that I was riding Willim's cock, and sucking Pietri's, but it still wasn't enough. Kan knew. Somehow, he knew. I felt him behind me then, lifting me off of Willim's prick and ploughing into me himself, for five, ten, fifteen strokes, then pulling out and pushing me back down onto Willim.

"Closer," I heard him insist, and I had the feeling the others had moved in, even those I could not see. Each man was stroking himself. I could tell this without even having to look. I could sense where every cock in the dell was. Kan repeated his trick a few more times, pulling my hole free of Willim and fucking it himself quickly at intervals. But it wasn't enough. It still wasn't enough.

Then Kan pushed his way into me while Willim's prick was still inside. And that was not only enough, it was very nearly too much. My cry was muffled by Pietri's cock, but even to my ears it sounded more like a cry of ecstasy than of desperation.

And then, incredibly, Kan was ordering Willim to find my cock with his hand and to make me spill. Now it was too much, just too much sensation and too much magic and my body could not hold it all, and my milk shot from me with as much force as my scream. A scream that was quickly cut off by Pietri's own spill into my mouth. I felt the hot rain of those close by, painting me with their seed, and deep in me, two cocks twitching against each other as they pumped me full.

I had never felt a release like it; a lightning strike could not have been so searing. I fell limp into their arms as if I had been struck, but there was at least a grin upon my face.

37: Kenet

The next morning the general met with a bevy of his top commanders. I was bade to wait in the field marshal's tent with two other pages while they conferred. The pages served the two largest battalion commanders, and knew one another, it seemed. They were probably the same age as me, yet they were so much more knowledgeable than I was. I listened to them go on about all things military for some time without saying a word, but eventually their attention turned to me.

"So, you're Roichal's new boy," one of them said. He had a shock of dark hair like Jorin's but he was far more rangy, his arms too long for the uniform jacket he wore.

"Yes," I said, not sure how else to answer.

He and the other one exchanged looks, and then he pressed on. "So where were you the night they made that spy into a fuck-slave? Did you get a turn?"

For a moment I was too shocked by the question to realize what he was asking. "I-I... Wh-what?" I sputtered.

They looked at each other and nodded, as if my lack of answer confirmed something for them. The shorter one sidled toward the tent entrance. "He's all yours, Jorl. I haven't the stomach for it."

Jorl removed his too-short jacket and made a beckoning motion toward me. "Come on, now. We can do this nice or we can do this rough. I like it both ways. My commander promised me a turn the next time we captured a spy. It's a crime for Roichal to be keeping you to himself."

"He hasn't touched me!" I cried, taking a step back, but my protest was a bit weak. Perhaps because just last night he truly had touched me, just not in the manner I—and everyone—expected. "You... you don't know of what you speak."

"Don't play stupid. Come on, Misk," he then said to his friend. "At least hold him down for me. No one has to get hurt that way."

I took another step back, turning to the side in a defensive stance better suited to a sword than my bare hands, but I had to show them I would not allow them to take me without a fight.

Misk lingered by the tent flap, looking unhappy. "Leave it, Jorl. He's not going to play."

"Tcha. You really have no stomach for it. Fine, sit outside and listen to me make him squeal." Jorl took a step toward me and Misk went out.

I glanced around for something I could use as a weapon. The lantern was hung out of my reach. The field marshal was wearing his sword. His extra boots were sitting next to his chest. His folding camp stool, though, would it make a good club? It was three sturdy pieces of wood, hinged together. I snatched it up and brandished it.

Jorl laughed. "Think you're a rough and tumble little thing, don't you? You can't have been a spy. Cook was right. You had to be an escaped whoreslave to begin with."

It hit me then that it was true. That was exactly what I was. I had escaped, barefoot and nearly naked, from my master. "And what if I was?" I spat at him. "That doesn't make me your hole to fuck."

He snorted and took another step toward me. "Doesn't it?"

I hissed like a cornered snake.

"Come on, now. Don't be that way. Wouldn't you rather be with a healthy young soldier like me than crushed under that fat old man?"

"He's not fat!" The general, as I had seen, was quite muscled and fit, even his lame leg. "And I told you, he hasn't fucked me. I'm a page now. Go suck your friend's milk if you're so hungry for it."

But then there was a sharp hiss from outside the tent, and a moment later Misk stuck his head back in. "Best get your uniform on. They're coming."

Jorl made a disgusted noise and then pulled his jacket on. A few moments later the voice of his commander calling him could be heard, and he piped up quickly and exited.

Marksin stuck his head in a moment later. "Why are you holding that stool?"

I hadn't realized it was still in my hand. "Oh, just... talking about fencing with the other pages."

"Fencing." He eyed me skeptically.

"Yes." I put the stool down and then walked, stiff with bruised dignity, back up the hill to the general's tent. Marksin followed.

There were still the remnants of the meal the commanders had eaten during their long conference. I sat quietly while Marksin and Roichal talked about nothing consequential and two of the cook's boys came and cleared everything away. Once they were gone, though, Marksin made one check of the tent's perimeter and then drew the flap closed.

"Tell the general what happened today," he said.

I looked up with a start. "Nothing happened today."

Marksin sat on the chest while the general himself sat on the sleeping pallet. "Sir," Marksin said, "I believe there was some kind of incident with the pages."

Roichal made a small gesture toward his leg and I slipped to my knees at his feet to pull his boots free. "Is that so."

"Your page was holding a stool when I found them."

I began rubbing his ankle, looking at it instead of at his face. "Is that so, Page?" he asked me.

"Yes, Sir," I said.

"Sir," Marksin continued. "I worry that it may not be safe to leave him alone with other men."

Roichal grunted as I worked out a knot behind his heel. "Page," he said softly. "I believe it would be best if you told me what happened today."

I looked up in surprise. I had been girding for an order, as if he could make words spill out of me the way he did my milk. But no, there was just this gentle, reasonable request. "Um, I don't wish to make trouble."

"You make trouble by your very presence," Marksin said under his breath.

"One of the other pages asked if I was... if I was the one that

Cook captured. He said he... he had been promised a turn. I told him it didn't matter where I came from, I wasn't his... his... to do with what he liked." I could not bring myself to use the words that Jorl had used. "So then he said I should like to have a go with a soldier like him and not you, Sir. I told him you hadn't done anything of the sort, but I don't think he believed me."

Roichal lifted my face to his with two fingers under my chin and placed a kiss on my forehead. "That is because you are terrible at lying," he said affectionately. "At least when it comes to some things."

I went back to working my way up his leg. "Well, Marksin," he said, "you may be right. It may not be safe for Page to be alone with other men. I have been wondering about it, and I have to wonder if there is more to it than his mere beauty." He stroked my hair as he said this and I blushed deeply under the praise of my looks.

"Sir?" Marksin asked.

"He's under some kind of spell that has him living healthy off nothing but your milk," Roichal pointed out. "Don't you wonder if he's a bit like a hind in season? The hart, they say, can smell her for miles."

"Is that possible?" Marksin looked alarmed.

Roichal shrugged. "What do you think, Page? Has nearly every man you've met since your escape tried to put his prick in you?"

"Well, not *every* man..." I said.

Marksin hung his head. "I don't know how we're going to keep him safe, then."

Roichal's voice was suddenly grave. "But we must. I will keep him at my side at all times, and if I must speak in confidence to someone else, then you must keep him close by you."

"And then for conferences like today? You cannot seriously be thinking he can sit beside you while strategy is planned? What if he truly is under a compulsion to spy?"

"It cannot be helped," the general said. "You will have to absent yourself to keep him safe, and then return him to me." He grunted again as I made my way up his thigh. "Marksin, you are the only man I can trust."

"And if he is truly giving off some magical scent that makes men wild, what makes you think I will be able to resist much longer?"

Roichal chuckled. "I have no doubt that Page would not let you try without protesting and your aversion to taking a boy against his will is strong. Else you would have taken him when you had the chance."

"True." Marksin looked slightly relieved by this thought. "I would... it would destroy me to betray you, Sir."

"I know," Roichal said softly, caressing my hair. "And as usual I must ask something unfair of you. At least there are some benefits to you, though, to the protection you provide our young charge."

Marksin colored deeply. "Yes, Sir."

"Page," the general said to me in a gentle voice. "Would you drink a little of the field marshal's milk now?"

"Oh yes, Sir," I said. "Though I would prefer to drink all of it."

He chuckled. "Just a figure of speech," he assured me. "Of course you may drink all of it. Come up on my lap so I may stroke you while you do as I ask."

"Yes, Sir." I got to my feet and stripped down to bare, then straddled his legs so that we were both facing Marksin. Roichal's hand was warm as he cupped my balls.

Marksin took off his boots and stepped out of his trousers, then came to stand facing us, one leg on either side of the general's feet. This put his prick very close to my mouth, but I reached up and stroked and teased him with my hands first, which drew approving noises from both of them. Roichal began to stroke me at the same time, and then I took Marksin into my mouth.

For a while, one of the general's hands stroked up and down while the other toyed with my balls. But then he left my balls alone and I felt Marksin thrust a bit harder than before. My eyes flickered open to see the general had one hand on Marksin's hip, pulling him in and encouraging him to fuck my mouth rather than simply stand there and let me do as I would.

I moaned. It felt, well, it felt as if the general were the one fucking my mouth, even if it wasn't with his own prick. Marksin's hands were on my shoulders, but then they moved to the general's, and I heard the general say something approving.

The next thing I heard him say was the quiet but firm order to spill. To my surprise, Marksin cried out and spilled at the same moment, and the general's chest bumped against my back as all three of us twitched and jerked and spasmed.

Yes, all three. Marksin blinked in surprise as Roichal seemed to swoon behind me. "Sir!" he said in alarm, steadying him. I reached behind me to do the same.

"It's all right," Roichal growled, voice low and hoarse. "Sky above..." Now he leaned against me for support, his forehead against the back of my shoulder. "That... I had forgotten..."

"Forgotten?" I asked, too stunned to stop myself.

"The last time I actually experienced release... more than ten years ago."

"Ten years!" Marksin's voice was just as alarmed as before.

"Yes, ten years." He lifted his head and turned mine enough that he could kiss me, his mouth on my mouth. Then he seized Marksin by the collar and pulled him into a kiss, too. Marksin made a sound of surprise and for half a second tried to pull back, then made a needy groan and surrendered his mouth to being plundered by Roichal's tongue.

38: Jorin

Kan sounded as exhausted as I felt when he said, "This is not good."

I could not move, I was so spent. But someone was lifting me off of Willim, and someone else was washing my chest with a wet cloth... and it felt like they all still wanted to touch me. We were still in the dell where fight practice had happened, and where we had just spilled our milk simultaneously. "I'm sorry," I said, when I finally could speak, though I kept my eyes closed. "I didn't mean to interrupt."

"Shush, you," Kan said. "I didn't think. It was stupid of us to have aroused you so."

Willim was still wrapped partway around me, or so it felt like. "Will someone please explain to me what just happened? Not that it wasn't quite enjoyable."

Gresh grumbled, but I could feel his hand stroking my thigh as if he were patting down a horse after a race. "Weltskin here got bound to us. Seems though he got a bit too strongly bound, eh Kan?"

"Yes," Kan admitted. "Is your reaction getting stronger each time, Jorin?"

"I think so. This might have been a special case, though, given that it was all of you aroused at once."

"Hm, possible, but I worry that by trying to give you six masters, rather than diluting the spell, we've increased its power sixfold." Kan kissed me. Many hands were cleaning me up, then, and I just stayed limp and let them do what they would. "Normally, that isn't what would happen, but as I am learning, you are a singular individual, Jorin Weltskin."

Pietri piped up next. "How do we fix it, then? Will it fade after a while?"

"And will it be an orgy every day until then?" Derget asked. "Not that I would mind that, but, it's somewhat inconvenient in the midst of us trying to spirit the prince away."

"All too true," Kan said with a sigh. "All right, up up. Let's get set for the night and I will ponder the solution." He assigned watches as he helped me to my feet.

When we were bedded down in the tent, he spoke to me quietly. "I think we will need the expertise of someone who knows more Night Magic than I do to unravel the mystery of you," he said. "But reaching him is not always easy. In fact, Night Magic itself is the only way I know to draw him to us."

"Would that not draw the attention of Seroi, though, too?" I asked. "Given that we are so near to him?"

He clucked his tongue. "Distances will not matter if we perform the spell correctly."

"We?"

"I did say it would be Night Magic, didn't I?" There was a hint of mischief in his voice.

I chuckled. "Are you sure this isn't just another excuse for an orgy?" I pretended to complain. "My arse is sore from being fucked so much."

"Mm, is it now? I'll have to take your mouth in the morning then," he said, kissing me suddenly in the dark. "And the spell will have to wait until tomorrow night."

"Wait, this is a spell we could do tonight?"

"Well, actually, I wouldn't recommend it, given how spent you are. And yes, it's best performed at night. Did you think the name Night Magic was entirely metaphorical?"

"I never thought about it before," I said. "So, what is Night Magic, exactly?"

"I could tell you," he said, spooning me close, "but then I would need to swear you to secrecy."

"Tcha. You already have me bound in spirit and body," I said.

"I'm only joking, Weltskin."

"It's hard to tell sometimes."

We lay still and quiet for a while, but I did not feel sleepy. I listened to the rustle of the forest outside, the warm wind through the trees. Midsummer could not be more than a few days away, could it? I had lost track.

"Night Magic," Kan said softly, as if we had continued talking, "is the forbidden magic because it draws on the lust of male for male. One hardly bothers to call Day Magic by that name, because it is seen as right and natural. The desire between men and women creates life, the most magical act of all."

"But... but surely my desire for Kenet is the most natural thing in the world?" I asked, wonderingly. "We were only boys when we discovered..."

"Hush," he said. "I am not condemning you or the prince. Far from it. I, too, believe, that the lust of a man for a man is nothing evil. But that is still the key that unlocks the door to the kind of magic that could turn your Kenet into a whoreslave whose pain can only be assuaged by Seroi's hand."

"I see."

"The Frangi long ago embraced the power found in the Night Arts and made their nation strong with it. That made all other nations nervous, but it was fine so long as that power was not abused. Do you know what started the current war between Trest and Frangit?"

"No," I admitted. "And wait just a moment. I thought the Night Riders came from Frangit."

"Do we sound like Frangi to you, Weltskin?"

"Well, no. Although you are somewhat blond..." I teased.

He laughed. "True. But it would probably shock you to find that there are dark-haired Frangi, too. The most prized boys for slaves, though, are always blond and fair-skinned."

"Why?"

"Because they believe that the welts show most beautifully on fair skin." He kissed the back of my neck. "Obviously, the forbears who set that standard had never seen one as beautiful as you."

"I..." The thought that he found me beautiful stole my voice for a moment as I knew not how to respond to such a compliment.

"Make no mistake, Jorin," he said. "You are very pleasing to the eye. Growing up in Kenet's shadow, you might not have taken your measure."

"The guards used to remark I was too pretty when we had fight practice," I said. "But I thought they merely meant I needed my nose broken a few times."

He chuckled and his breath was warm against my spine.

"You were going to tell me how the war started," I reminded him.

"Was I? No, I merely asked if you knew, but if you insist..."

I elbowed him playfully, and soon we had a small wrestling match of our own going on in the low shelter. He pinned me beneath him, though, easily enough, having started out in such a position of advantage. "The Night Mages, it is said, began kidnapping boys from Trest and making them into whoreslaves," he whispered into my ear. "There is great power to be had in evil acts, but it is short-lived and difficult to maintain without continuous fodder. A single Mage, bound to a single willing lover, can increase his power threefold."

He began to rut against me slowly, with just a subtle roll of his hips.

"But if that same Mage were to bind a dozen unwilling boys to him, perhaps fucking them to ruin and replacing them with fresh bodies when needed? Well." He went on. "Three-hundred-fold is not out of the question, though, as I said, it would be difficult to maintain."

I could feel him hardening gradually, both from the bulge pressing into my leg and through the bond. I understood suddenly, he was making the arousal slow for my sake, trying prevent the sudden ache of need that would spear me through. "And Seroi...?"

"I believe he is trying to shape a willing pet of the princeling, whose blood holds such power that to have him in thrall... indeed, it is unfathomable just how powerful that would make him."

"Would?"

"Aye. I must believe he has not succeeded at it yet. I must believe we are fated to stop him." He still held me pinned where I was. "Some lucky cloud must be hanging over your head, Jorin

Weltskin, for you to have survived all that you have and to be here, a day's ride from rescuing him."

I could not speak as his cock nosed close to my entrance.

"Enough lessons for one night," he whispered. I spasmed in his arms as the sudden flare of desire gripped me, and he ploughed into me with one unerring thrust. We fucked just like that, him never letting go, his panting breaths hot against my neck, until we both came. Then we were truly spent and I was asleep before his cock could even slip from me. Perhaps it never did. I woke some hours later with him pumping inside me again, only this time he was murmuring words I could not make out. The spell for summoning help? The chant was low and rhythmic, matched to his thrusts, and I dared not move or make a sound lest I disturb the workings of the magic. That is, until I found myself on the verge of spilling. I opened my mouth to say so but before I could utter a peep, his hand covered my mouth and nose. I struggled for air out of reflex, only to find myself thrusting back into his penetration even harder, as if my body would accept lust in place of breath...

I blacked out when I spilled, but oh, how good it felt! Or perhaps it was the first breath I drew afterward that felt so very wonderful. I could not tell. I was dizzy and about to fall unconscious again when I heard an unfamiliar boot step in the bracken outside the tent. I crouched defensively almost without realizing it.

"Calm, Weltskin, calm," Kan said, his hand on my shoulder. "If the spell has worked, then that is the sound of a friend." He tossed open the flap and laughed. "Indeed!"

A man with dark hair, overgrown to his shoulders, stepped forward. In the moonlight I could only make out his profile but it was his voice, as deep and bitter as ever, that I recognized without fail. "This is outrageous! Explain yourself, Kan. I see no threat to you here inside your warding circle."

"Sergetten!" I cried.

"Indeed," Kan repeated as he stood. He made no effort to hide his nakedness, either. "Indeed. I see no introductions are necessary as you two are well acquainted."

Our old tutor and the king's top advisor rushed forward, a white ball of light flaring in his hand. I could see his face clearly now, the hawk-like expression I knew so well. "Jorin!"

I found myself backing away, heedless of my own nakedness. Kan turned to look at me. "What's wrong, Jorin?"

"Seroi taught him," I said. "Everything he knows of Night Magic, he knows from that beast."

The two of them exchanged a wordless look. Then Kan said to me, "And I learned from Sergetten."

I felt ill. "You can't... you can't seriously think Seroi would let his apprentice run around without binding him in some way? You cannot trust him!"

Sergetten chuckled. "I see someone thinks he knows everything about Night Magic. What nonsense have you been filling his head with, Kan? I can sense you've been stuffing his arse but good."

"Ah, but therein lies the problem," Kan said. "We bound him as a Night Rider, but he hasn't taken to it like the others..."

"If the glistening trail down his thighs is any indication, he seems to have taken to it just fine," Sergetten sneered.

Kan shook his head. "Jorin, put a shirt on and go wake the others. It's nearly dawn. I'll... explain things here."

I didn't move.

Kan sighed. "Jorin, please. Begging you as my lover to trust me, please go and wake the others, before I am forced to test if the bond will compel you to obey me."

I grabbed my shirt and a pair of trousers and put them on, as well as my boots, never taking my eyes off Sergetten except for a moment here and there when I had to. For his part, he stared back at me with a cool expression. As I finally turned to go, he and Kan began to whisper sharply at each other.

The sun was rising, but my heart was sinking.

39: Kenet

The general let Marksin free of the kiss, patted me once more on the shoulder, then fell backwards onto the sleeping pallet, already unconscious. Marksin and I stared at one another for a moment, then by some silent mutual agreement we set about getting Roichal out of his jacket and into a better sleeping position.

I looked with some dismay at the sleeping pallet. "There is only room for two..."

He waved a hand at me, and I could see the mask of diffidence he normally wore trying to descend.

"Please stay," I said, before he could mutter something, and I saw his eyes widen. "Please, Marksin."

"But..."

"I don't know what the history is between you, and you don't have to tell me." I struggled for the proper words to speak truthfully without offending him. "I don't know why he... he needs me in between in order to... to acknowledge you. But... but I think he would want you to stay."

He nodded then, as if it pained him to agree and yet he clearly did not want to leave. "Take your place," he said softly, as if he did not want to wake the general. "Go on."

I watched him carefully as I lifted the general's arm and settled myself against him. Roichal pulled me close without waking, snuffling a bit until he settled again. Marksin made a headroll of his trousers and lay down facing me on the canvas beside the pallet, his jacket over one shoulder as a blanket. "That's... that was the first time he's kissed me since..." He shook his head as if finding the right words was difficult for him, too. "In over ten years."

"That's more than half my life ago!" I blurted.

He allowed himself a small smile. "I was a page, too, once.

When he was a cavalry commander. We were ambushed by the Frangi; it was total chaos. When I finally found him, he had been fighting a Night Mage, hand to hand. He was... on the ground, on all fours, struggling to get to his feet again. Who knows how many times the Mage had knocked him down? Then he screamed—thunder, what a scream. I charged the Mage with another man's sword then, and drove him off.... He disappeared in a puff of smoke."

I tried to imagine Marksin as my own age, swinging a sword with his hair short and his sleeves too small. "What happened to the general?"

"There was no blood, no nothing, but he was shaking all over, as if he couldn't control his limbs. His eyes were rolling up in his head. I screamed for help but no one came."

"No one?"

"We were the only two who survived the ambush."

"What did you do?" My eyes must have been as wide as a curious cat's.

"I... I don't know what came over me. The spasms stopped and I was holding him and... I thought he was dying in my arms. I..." He broke off, and fought for a moment. When he went on, there were no tears, not even a tremor in his voice, though it was gentle. "I kissed him."

I might have let out a sob myself then, though.

After a few moments, Marksin went on. "He came to shortly after that. He had no memory of the ambush beyond the first few moments. None at all."

"Even...?" I could not say it and neither could the field marshal. Roichal either did not remember the kiss, or was choosing to pretend it had never happened.

"He taught me everything I needed to know to survive as a soldier. I don't mean how to fight. I mean... he taught me where to spill my milk, how to... to find willing or at least allowable sources of relief," Marksin said quietly. "But he... he never hinted that we could be that for each other, nor even just I for him. And after that attack... everything changed."

I tried to remember Roichal's visit to the castle, when he was honored. I had been just a boy. "But, wait, didn't he win some important battle against the Frangi? Single-handedly? Well, with the help of some farmers or something?"

Marksin's smile was genuine. "We were able to save six horses, and the two of us managed to recruit four young men from a nearby village, and yes, we routed and drove off an entire incursion battalion. We were both promoted after that, but that separated us. It took me a few years to get back to working under his direct command again."

His single-minded loyalty made me feel unworthy. For even as I found safety and pleasure and even a kind of peace in Roichal's arms, Jorin was never far from my mind. I felt even worse to realize with no doubt now, having heard the story, that Marksin envied me my place, and probably by all rights belonged in it.

That only brought me back to the eternal question, why was Roichal the only man who hadn't tried to fuck me? Did his refusal to do it extend all the way back to the days before the attack, or was there some other reason why he wouldn't have taken Marksin when he was a page? And how did I fit in now? My presence had clearly changed the balance somehow, but I didn't understand how.

"Thank you," I said then, as my eyes started to close. "Thank you for telling me that."

"Thank *you*," he answered with a sleepy chuckle. "You have opened a door for me I thought long since closed in my face. I... I had no idea he had not found release in ten years. I had assumed he took his pleasures elsewhere. Tomorrow... hmm. Tomorrow maybe he will pretend not to remember. But I will remember. I will."

There was still a smile on his face as he fell asleep. So I did not feel completely worthless then.

40: Jorin

I went to Gresh. Somehow, I knew if I was to find an ally among the Night Riders against Sergetten, he would be the most likely candidate.

I was correct. I shared some cold bread with him as dawn broke and Kan and Sergetten were still in hushed, vehement conference. We sat on fallen logs and broke out the rations, waiting for the others to join us. There would be no cooking fire this morning while we hid from detection. "So," I said, carefully at first, "Sergetten is Kan's mentor in Night Magic?"

"Aye." Gresh gnawed the rough crust of the bread, his eyes never straying far from the tent where our leader and my old tutor were speaking.

"He used to teach me the history of Trest," I said, "and every time I, or the prince, named something wrong, he would rap me on the back of the knuckles with a stick. I would get that same stick applied to my arse if Kenet drew frits in the margins of a book or daydreamed instead of reading his assigned chapter. But."

"But?"

"But that isn't why I don't trust him." I chewed slowly, choosing my words. "He is Seroi's apprentice."

Gresh grunted agreement.

"And if there's one thing I know, it's that Night Magic can twist a man's desires."

Now he chuckled, low in his throat. "Are you saying you wouldn't have taken on the lot of us without it? Don't fool yourself, Weltskin. You love the thorn of the man as much as the rose of the maid."

"True. But the mage put a spell on the prince to keep him from speaking to me of certain things. Who knows what lies or omissions Sergetten might be subject to?" I shook my head. "Understand me, Gresh. I am bound to obey Kan, by my own honor as much as by magic. But if Sergetten should prove to be our enemy? We must be careful."

Gresh nodded. "He has always aided us in our cause. But I will keep watch should the snake coil to strike."

The rest of the band knew who our visitor was by then, but none dared disturb his discussion with Kan. Willim in particular seemed agitated, limping toward the tent more than once as if to see whether they were finished yet.

I was shocked by what I witnessed next. Sergetten at last emerged from the tent, his face a mask of anger and trouble. When he saw Willim nearby he stalked over to the young man and I feared Willim would receive some reproach for eavesdropping.

Instead, Sergetten pulled Willim close against him and bent him backwards in a heated kiss. When the kiss ended, their mouths only moved apart far enough to allow speech, their foreheads still touching.

I had never heard such a tender voice from Sergetten, though compared to someone else he might have sounded brusque as he asked, "How is your leg?"

"I haven't needed the crutch since your last visit," Willim answered, a bit breathless, "though the pain has been worse of late."

"I shall see what I can do about that, my frit," Sergetten said, holding him by the chin.

"Now?" Willim asked, on the verge of begging.

Sergetten looked up then, his black gaze falling on me. "There are matters I must attend to, but... yes, lad, you first."

They went to the tent Willim and Pietri had shared the night before, and Pietri came to sit with us, looking a bit put out.

No one had to tell me what it was Sergetten and Willim had gone to the tent to do. The Night Magic cure for everything seemed to be a good arse-coring.

Kan was chuckling when he came up to us. "I need to make the circle safe again. I won't be long." And he went off into the trees.

As soon as he was out of sight, I asked what he had meant by that. Pietri explained. "He sets a magical perimeter each night, but sunrise obliterates it and he must do it anew."

"Have to wait here for the sentry to return anyway," Gresh said, and then clapped me on the shoulder. "You'd best be ready for Kan to come back thorny as a bramble bush, though."

"Oh." Of course. He was using some kind of Night Magic to make a safe circle, of course he was going to be...

Oh. The moment he brought himself to full hardness, I sensed it. I excused myself to the tent we shared, stripped out of my clothes, and lay down. I tugged on my own prick and closed my eyes and I could see him moving through the trees, his own hand milking a droplet of dew to the tip.

If he made a magical perimeter, though, I wondered, why did we need to assign watches? Perhaps it would not keep intruders out, but merely give us earlier warning of their arrival? There was much I needed to know.

He returned after making the way all the way around. He made a dismayed sound when he realized the state I was in, sweat breaking out across my brow as I tried to bite down on the painful need.

"Your mouth," he said, as he pulled me to him. "Your arse has been treated roughly enough, and may yet be again, soon."

I took him in gladly then, and he carried the scent of evergreen trees, and sechal bark, and other scents of the forest. He was sizable, with more girth than Kenet, but he moaned with appreciation as I suckled. I continued to tug at my cock with my other hand, and it was not long before we both spilled.

We had not yet covered ourselves when Sergetten threw back the flap. "I must speak with Jorin."

Kan yawned, unconcerned at his cock hanging limp from his trousers, as usual. "Very well. Alone, or would you like me here?"

"It matters not. But you have yet to eat this morning," Sergetten pointed out with a raised eyebrow at Kan.

"Point taken. I shall get some bread in my belly and come back in a while." He pressed a kiss to my forehead, closed up his clothes, and went off.

I was just starting to sit up, one hand reaching for my shirt, when Sergetten's hand on my chest pressed me down, his dark eyes glittering. "He has told me much," he said, and I knew he meant that Kan and he had spoken of my condition. But had they spoken of the prince and the danger he was in?

"Have you seen Kenet?" I asked, ignoring the fact that he was holding me down. I would not give him the satisfaction of making me squirm with struggle. "Have you been to the castle?"

"I ask the questions," he said, voice quiet with menace. "When you have answered them, perhaps I will answer yours in turn."

"I'm not..."

"How long ago did you leave the castle?"

I had lost count. "Two weeks? Three? Seroi arranged it. He..."

"I heard you were banished after Kenet escaped your attempt to rape him."

"That's not true!" Now I couldn't help but struggle, trying to sit up and face him like a man, not on my back like a whoreslave. My anger surged, but the more I pushed, the heavier his hand felt. I was reduced to snarling at him.

"I did not say it was true," he said, calm as a frozen lake. "Merely that I had heard that."

"It's Seroi who plans to fuck him," I blurted, finally. "On mid-summer night!"

He snorted skeptically. "And how do you know that?"

"After you left the castle, Seroi began tutoring the prince. Up in his tower. Kenet was bespelled not to speak to me of what they did, but he didn't need to speak to hint to me what manner of 'tutoring' he was receiving. It was all preparation for his coming of age ceremony, or so Kenet and the king were told, but..."

Sergetten's eyes were black and cold. "What was Kenet able to tell you? Or communicate to you?"

"That Seroi milked him and performed spells that turned Kenet's milk sour. Well, not sour. Bitter. To the flavor of ash."

A hint of a cruel smile crept onto Sergetten's face. "How long have you been drinking Kenet's milk? How many years, ladra'an?"

I tried to wriggle out from under his hand again, but he not only held me fast, he moved so that his other hand took hold of my balls.

"How many years," he repeated.

"Not years," I said, wondering when Kan would return. "We only just recently discovered that."

"We? Be clear with me as to how reciprocal the prince was to you."

"He tasted my milk as well, if that is what you are asking."

"It is. And? What else? Who has fucked whom?"

"Since my banishment, half the men west of the Serde have had me," I spat back, "but there will be no shelter from the storm for any man who has touched Kenet!"

"Save your romantic proclamations for someone who cares," he said, giving my balls a light slap.

"Seroi is making the prince into a night-bound whoreslave," I insisted, ignoring the sparks I saw before my vision.

"You lie," he growled, and slapped my balls again, harder.

I had to catch my breath before I could protest. "I don't. Didn't Kan tell you all this?"

"Kan knows more of Night Magic than most, but barely more than you, you ignorant little dirt-eater." Now I gasped, for as he spoke, instead of striking me again, as his magic held me down he produced a jar from somewhere on his person and in a flash pushed cold, slick finger into me. It was cold enough to make me gasp and he crooked his finger inside me. He lifted the heavy hand but now I found if I squirmed or struggled, I only caused myself discomfort as I was hooked more deeply than any fish. "Tell me again, everything you know. Every detail. Every word or gesture or secret you and the prince exchanged."

I tried to fight. Everything in me said that I should not answer, that every word spoken was a betrayal of Kenet, that every word heard by Sergetten would flow into the ears of Seroi. And Kenet would be the one to bear the punishment meted out by the mage, not me. Kenet would be the one pricked and bloodied by Seroi's thorn.

But Sergetten was relentless, and I could not help but tell him many fragments of the story. He seemed relieved to hear that we never had drawn any of the serving maids into our beds, but at times it seemed to me he was more alarmed or more angry about what Kenet and I had done with each other than what Seroi had subjected Kenet to.

But then Kan did return. He knelt beside me with some alarm. By then Sergetten had one of my knees pressed to my chest and one of his long fingers still deep in me. "Is this necessary?" Kan asked.

"I assure you, it is," Sergetten said. "You'd left him quite sore and the balm on my finger will restore him. However, he is resisting my interrogation. You must compel him to the truth, Kan."

"I'm not entirely sure that is within my powers," Kan said. "I hadn't intended to bond him as a slave at all, you know, merely to loyalty."

Sergetten laughed. "You asked me before, Kan, what could cause a man to react the way Jorin has to your Night Magic. Listen well, for this key unlocks more than one door."

I groaned. I knew Sergetten's lecturing voice all too well and wondered how much longer I would be forced to listen to him while trapped in such an uncomfortable position. Kan just nodded.

"You have drawn part of a circle," Sergetten said, wiggling his finger in me for emphasis, "inside Jorin. The partial circle is like a hole you have dug. Water will keep flowing into the hole to fill it, unless you fill the hole with something else, or complete the circle so that it is sealed."

Kan frowned. "Can you never speak plainly?"

"The hole is not merely a metaphor," Sergetten said, stabbing his finger into me and making me yelp. "Poor Jorin feels that with every inch of his skin, every beat of his heart. He needs to be filled."

"We know that."

"And you also know it is worsening. Where will you find enough men to sate him when it took seven of you the last time? The circle must be closed. Only after that can we contemplate undoing the bond which is trying so very hard to close on its own."

"So, close the circle," I gritted out.

Kan put a hand on my shoulder, squeezing with gentle affection. "Closing the circle means completing the master-slave bond. Doesn't it, Sergetten?"

"Just so," Sergetten said.

"Fine." I squirmed, even though it sent painful shocks through me. "Let Kan bond me as his own. And then we can set about undoing it."

Sergetten spoke to Kan as if I had said nothing. "You do not have the skill to do it in such a way that the bond can be undone later. You want him too much, Kan. You cannot be the one."

Now Kan's eyes flashed with defiance. "Can't I? Perhaps you need to teach me more."

"You know far too much for your own good, as this mess proves."

"I suppose you are the only one with the knowledge and skill to do it?"

"Of course I am the only one," Sergetten said, sounding surprised. "Be reasonable, Kan. This man is not yours to hold in bond for life."

"Nor yours!" Kan's hand was on my shoulder.

"And I will not make him mine for life!" Sergetten's shout shook the tent. "You idiot, there is only one man he belongs to, and he has belonged to him, body, heart, and soul, since he was barely old enough to walk! He belongs to the prince and none other!"

I was thunderstruck. To hear him say it that way, to hear him say aloud that which I had felt in my heart since the day Kenet had plucked me from the dirt, left me stunned speechless.

Sergetten went on in a quieter voice then. "You know this to be true, Kan. You have played at games with this boy, but that is all they can be. I must bond with him so that the braid can be undone later, without destroying him."

Kan's caress on my shoulder brought me back to the present. "I'm sorry, Jorin. He's right. Sergetten must be your master now."

"No," I said, looking from Kan to Sergetten. "I won't agree to that."

Sergetten pinched one of my nipples and I cried out. "You have no choice. Not if you wish to be sane much longer."

I growled at him. "I won't negotiate my own enslavement with a man whose is finger-raping me while we speak."

Sergetten let out a huff, withdrew from me not at all gently, and said, "Ungrateful wretch. Very well. Put some clothes on, as well, if it will make you feel better. It will not change the facts of the situation, nor my urgency to see this done."

I sat up and put a shirt on but did not bother with the rest. "While we are here debating points of magic, Kenet is in danger," I said.

"Jorin," Kan began, but Sergetten silenced him with a gesture.

"Do you think you will just ride up to the gates and ask the guard to send him down?" Sergetten asked with a laugh. "Soon the only saddle you'll be able to stay on is one with a phallus affixed to its middle. Is that what you want, ladra'an? You will be reduced to begging these men to fuck you, not just every day, but every few hours, then perhaps every hour. Kan tells me you already needed three at once..."

"Enough. I understand. If I do not take a master, I will be reduced to a drooling hulk of need. Tell me what happens when I do take a master, though."

"Your master needs to be someone who is skilled in Night Magic, first of all to be able to control you without allowing you to come to harm, secondly to actually be able to fulfill the needs you exhibit, both those triggered by the spell and your own twisted, internal lusts, and third, to train you for your eventual lifelong bond."

Sergetten had called me an idiot often enough. But perhaps he was right, for I found myself having to ask, "What do you mean? Eventual lifelong bond with whom?"

"With Kenet, you idiot!"

Oh. I was thunderstruck again.

Perhaps if I had been given a few more minutes, I would have wrapped my head around all that Sergetten had said and understood all he was trying to say, or maybe I would have finally exposed the flaw in his plan that would show him to be full of lies. It sounded as if he had come to the conclusion that Kenet and I needed to be bonded, and that he would help this to come about, and yet there was still so much I did not know and did not understand. But I did not have a few minutes to think it through. From somewhere nearby a birdcall sounded that sent them all into action as Kan whispered to me, "Man approaching on horseback!"

I got into my pants and boots as quickly and quietly as I could, then. If we were about to face soldiers or guards, it would be a battle best fought with clothes on and knives in our hands.

41: Kenet

The next morning I opened my eyes expecting to find Marksin lying next to the pallet, but he was already up and about. The general stirred the moment I moved, and seemed much revived, claiming it had been the best night's sleep he'd had since before the war had begun. His leg was stronger, and in the afternoon he and three commanders rode up onto a nearby ridge to survey the army from there. I stayed behind with Marksin. Neither he, nor the general, said a word about what had happened the night before, but Marksin and I acknowledged each other with a shared glance from time to time.

While the surveying was going on, Marksin enlisted my aid in paperwork, for I could read, write, and figure sums. "Each battalion will eat two bullocks a day, right down to the hooves," he told me, "so figure for me how many head of cattle we shall need to feed the entire encampment for two more weeks."

The missing part of the equation, of course, was how many battalions we were, with more arriving every few days, but it was easy enough to estimate based on expectations. The number I arrived at, though, seemed impossibly high. I did it again to be sure.

"Why so quiet, Page?" he asked, from where he was figuring something else, feed for the horses, perhaps.

"This does not seem like the right number," I said, not wishing to admit any mistake. "When I know this number equals half the entirety of the southern herds, at the size of the herds before the blight."

Marksin looked at the number on the parchment. "No, Page, I would say that looks about right."

"But if we take all the meat in the country, what will the rest of the people eat?"

"Oh they will get by on what fruit they can pull off the trees, and wild deer," he said mildly, but I looked up and saw the expression on his face. He was joking, but in the most serious way. "You see how high the cost of war is, yes?"

"And this is not even for war, just for a standing army," I said.

"This is one of the reasons we may be ordered into action soon," he said. "For while we are doing nothing but waiting, we are eating our way through the stores of the nation. And what goodwife would not give up her share of beef to ensure that her sons in the army are fed? None. But if the harvest is poor, and the animals continue to sicken? That goodwife may have nothing left to give."

"But..." I was speaking aloud my thoughts without censoring them. "If she falls ill and her garden fallow and her village comes to nothing... then what is the army fighting to protect?"

He looked at me curiously, as if he had not expected this kind of philosophy from an escaped whoreslave. "Well, but can the army fight the blight? It cannot be beaten with swords or cannon."

"But if the soldiers were home to work their crops, the pestilence might be slowed," I said. "I have heard it takes two men ten days to burn the pestilence out of an orchard, from first tree to last. But in ten days the first tree purged may begin to show the signs again. Ten men, though, could clear the same orchard in two days, isn't that right?"

"That may be so," he said. "But this raises another question in my mind."

"Which is?"

He raised an eyebrow. "How do you know so much about the southern herds and the eastern orchards?"

I just blinked at him for a few moments. I couldn't tell him I was the prince, no matter how much I trusted him. "I, my master..." What was a plausible explanation, that my master liked to discuss the economy while I suckled his milk?

Marksin cuffed me gently on the shoulder. "Don't look so stricken. I know you cannot speak of him. Let us look at the farm yield reports that came in the last packet from the castle, and see what we may yet requisition."

He set me to tallying grain yields, which quieted my curiosity for a time, but eventually I had to ask how much longer he thought we would remain here before the battle was to begin.

"That is the question on everyone's minds, is it not?" he said, lighting a lamp over our heads. I had not even realized that the sun was already setting. "An army of this size does not amass without a plan of attack. I do not think it is my place to tell you anything more, Page, though I have little doubt the general might, should you ask him."

He pulled his hair back in a tail and set his jacket hanging on a peg, rolling up his sleeves to bare whipcord strong arms. He sat and took up the ink again, as if to begin a new ledger, but his gaze remained on me.

"You think I should not ask him," I said.

"You exert an influence on him unlike any I have ever seen," Marksin said. "That is the plain truth."

"And you think I could be a threat."

"Night Magic has a hold on you, that much also is a plain truth." He gestured in my direction. "Need I say more?"

"No, I suppose not. Yet if I am such a threat, why keep me so close?"

Marksin raised his eyebrow again. "You are surprised that he wants to keep you in his bed?"

"No," I said again, but my mind was turning things over again and again. Was this merely that the general had taken a liking to me? But if it was, then again I had to ask why had he kept me pure? Even to the extent of protecting me from others. Perhaps it was best not to go delving into it too much; so long as the state of affairs remained as it was, I was safe.

We said no more about it, and prepared reports and requisitions to go by messenger at first light. Marksin had a man bring some bread and meat; it was enough for two, the man not knowing that I would touch none of it. The general came in some time later, and finished what Marksin had not. The distant sound of some men singing down in the camp reached us as the general tied the tentflap closed.

"I take it all three of us are not yet fed," he said, removing his jacket and laying it across the chest.

"No, Sir," I answered.

"And are you hungry, Page?" he asked, as he lowered himself slowly to the pallet. I hurried over to pull his boots free.

"Not especially, Sir, but I would not say no to a meal, either." I began to rub his leg, a hopeful tone in my voice that I could not erase, for I hoped perhaps tonight it might finally be the general's turn to spill into my mouth.

"Good boy," he said, but he stopped my hands on his thigh. "I have been thinking about it, and think we should treat this condition with precision. What man does not need to eat every day? And surely your master, if he kept so fine a whoreslave as you, would never have skipped a day without the pleasure of filling you up?" He gestured for Marksin to come closer. "They say, also, that a man's milk flows best if spilled with regularity, sweet and creamy if kept fresh, rather than souring in his ballocks. Though you, Page, would know that better than I."

His words had set up a fine edge of anticipation in all of us, yet Marksin was still too much a soldier to do anything without an order to spur him. He was standing beside us, nearly at attention he was so stiff. So I took the initiative. "May I suckle the field marshal now, Sir?"

"Yes, Page," he said, stroking my hair. "But don't make him spill until I say. For now enjoy the appetizer that is the salt that comes before the cream."

"Yes, Sir." I stayed on my knees, undoing Marksin's belt and baring his cock, the rest of his uniform rucked down around his thighs. A salty dewdrop was already awaiting me, and I took my time taking it up with the very tip of my tongue and exploring the tiny slit from which it had issued. The head was different from the shaft in both texture and flavor. The head was softer, and muskier from hiding all day in the folds of his foreskin, while the shaft was stiffer flesh and tasted more of his sweat.

Marksin's hands were at his sides, while Roichal's roamed over my back and hair. I barely noticed as he slipped me out of my jacket and shirt as I sucked and sucked. I opened my eyes, though, when he pulled me back gently from the prick in my mouth to kiss me, his own tongue taking the place of Marksin's cock and seeking out what new flavors it could.

"Stand up, Page," he said then, and "On your knees, Marksin."

Marksin did not hesitate to drop to his knees, but he found it somewhat difficult with his boots and trousers still on. He paused to shuck them, then knelt where he had been standing.

"If you would be so good as to reciprocate Page's attention," the general said.

Marksin nodded as if he didn't trust his voice, and his hands shook as he undid my uniform trousers and bared me. Roichal had one hand in the small of my back, one on Marksin's shoulder, and smiled indulgently as Marksin rubbed his cheek against my hip, savoring the moment before his lips brushed against my cock.

I had thought myself careful, slow, and seductive, but he made me out like a bull calf at a teat in comparison. He nibbled and kissed all along the shaft, until I was twitching with the desire for more, and only then did his tongue dart out to taste me. I knew beyond any doubt that this was how Marksin would have treated Roichal, had he been given the opportunity.

Roichal groaned in appreciation. "Beautiful."

Eventually things reached the state that they always must, though, and I was on the edge of spilling, though I did not fear that I would, not without a command from the general. It was difficult to keep silent, though, as Marksin continued to suckle and work.

"Switch places again," Roichal said softly.

I put my hand on Marksin's cheek as he eased his mouth from my prick. He stood, but before I could kneel, he pulled me into a kiss, letting me taste my own salt and musk on his lips. Roichal tugged at my hips then, and I sat in his lap like the night before, straddling his legs and facing Marksin, who fed his cock into my mouth eagerly.

We knew Roichal would be trying to recreate whatever it was that had triggered his release before. And we were both willing—more than willing, eager—to repeat it.

This time there was one change, though. This time instead of his hand pulling at Marksin's hip, driving him into my mouth, he reached further around. I felt the jolt go through Marksin as he found his entrance being dandled, then heard the liquid sound of Roichal wetting his fingers thoroughly before reaching around him again.

This time when the command to come issued from his lips, he must have penetrated Marksin with his finger, for Marksin's milk shot with intense force into my mouth, his cock thrumming madly. My own cock jerked in Roichal's hand, answering the call.

But we had no way to know if the general had come, too, until he told us he had when we both inquired. And then he pulled Marksin in for another kiss, growling when it was over, "Tomorrow, you will kiss me with Page's milk still on your lips."

"Yes, Sir," Marksin whispered, head bowed.

We lay down again in the same configuration as the night before, with Roichal spooning me and Marksin on the ground next to us, his face only a short distance from mine.

"Sir," he asked, for this time the general had not fallen unconscious immediately, "is it truly permissible for us to use Page like this?"

"How do you mean? He cannot live without a man's milk, and it is not healthy for him, or any man, to go too long without release. This is the only way for him."

"No, no. I mean, is it truly all right for me to drink his milk, even if he is touched by Night Magic?"

"Ah, I see. Marks, I do not think we have anything to fear from the magic that courses through Page's veins. Page is the only one who would be in jeopardy, were he not in our arms."

"Thank you, Sir."

"Stop worrying, Marks. He is a gift. A true gift of Fate. Some magic in him allows me the release I have sought for a decade. I shall not question that."

"Thank you, Sir," he repeated, then said, "Thank you, Page."

"And I you," I answered sleepily. Seroi was evil, of that I was sure, but perhaps some good would come of his spells.

42: Jorin

A man on horseback approached, more than that I did not know. We each stood at the ready, weapons drawn, and I wondered if we should be hiding behind trees. But then Kan raised his hand and Sergetten did the same, each whispering words in a language I did not recognize, and I looked around us in amazement as each man seemed to melt into shadow, myself included. No wonder the Night Riders had eluded their pursuers for so long.

We held our breath, for though we were invisible now, the camp was still easily discovered by anyone who came through this section of the woods. I could hear the steady tramp of a horse.

Then another bird call, and the sentry we had sent to spy on the castle rode into the glade.

Kan let out a breath and we all reappeared, Pietri running forward to grasp the bridle of the horse as Herge leapt down.

"All of Maldevar is in an uproar," he said, as everyone gathered around him. "The Lord High Mage and the king's guard have been seen all over the mountain, questioning villagers, searching, they say, for a spy. We cannot go there now."

Sergetten stopped him from saying more. "Get some water and take care of your mount. We have some business to finish here, and then we will hear your full report."

I was not pleased to see that Sergetten so easily took over the giving of orders from Kan, though I did notice that after the order was given, the others seemed to glance to Kan for confirmation. He waved them to it, then spoke to Sergetten in a low voice.

Sergetten's voice had none of the quiet discretion of Kan's in it as he retorted, "You cannot be serious."

"I am quite serious."

"You are far too ruled by your passions to ever be a true

leader." Sergetten's face was a mask of disdain.

"Is that so? Then you understand I will not give him up so easily. I cannot."

I understood then. "Him" was me. "Kan, be reasonable. I deserve none of your jealousy for taking this task upon myself."

"How about envy, then? Will you have both Willim and Jorin for your own?"

"I will leave you with permission to fuck Willim as often as you like, how is that?" Sergetten chuckled.

"Tcha. Don't patronize me. I will acquiesce to your plan. But even you are not so cold-hearted as to tear him out of my arms without so much as a good-bye."

"Did you not just have your fill of him moments before I discovered you? Perhaps your own insatiability ought be studied."

"He is mine, Sergetten. Already. And he will never be yours unless he is persuaded."

Sergetten's reply was merely a silent glare.

"You know it to be true. He will fight you every step otherwise." Kan did not back down. "And it would be the decent thing to do. He and I are lovers. Even were we not magically bonded we should insist on this for decency's sake. Can you not see that?"

"Very well. A farewell fuck, and then I must complete the bond. I do not think we should wait for nightfall. Try not to make him too sore again, or he will surely blame me when his bonding is painful."

Kan gave him a small salute and then came to me, grinning. "Come on, Weltskin, back to the tent."

I went without saying a word. Once we had closed the flap, I sat cross-legged upon the blanket. "You are going to give me to him," I said, not so much because I needed any further explanation, but just to hear him say it.

"Yes and no," he said, sitting across from me and taking my hand. "I am a selfish, piggish man, and I know this. I have the love of every man in the band, so I shall not be lonely. But I did want you so very much, Jorin Weltskin."

I felt my cheeks grow hot as he kissed my hand.

"But I know you belong to another. I know your heart is Kenet's. So I would be a fool to try to make you mine in any case. Sergetten is half-right. I know I have the skill to unbraid the bond. I probably would lack the will to, though." He pulled me to him then and kissed me hard, bruising my lip against my teeth.

"So what about now?" I asked. "What will you make of me this last time?"

"A memory," he said. "If you felt anything for me, if you are grateful for anything I have done for you, honor those feelings and mine by doing as I ask. I promise I shall ask only for pleasure."

Something told me I might have little enough of pleasure with Sergetten. "All right."

"Undress me, Jorin. Undress me and worship every inch of skin you uncover."

We grinned at each other, but I knew his order was quite serious. I got him out of his clothes piece by piece, kissing him as I went, at the crook of his elbow, and across the nipples, and up the inside of his thigh.

"Ah, you are so good," he said, as I spent a little extra worship on his prick, bringing him to full length with my mouth. As I expected, bringing him erect set off the hollow ache in my own gut. "So very good."

He was lying on his back now, having accepted all I had done passively. "Now, take the jar, and grease yourself well. Turn around so I may see you preparing your body for me."

I did as he asked, leaning my weight on two knees and one hand while I greased myself with the other. He reached up to spread my cheeks with his hands, then, and watched as I pushed fingerful after fingerful of grease into myself.

"It may be wise to keep yourself prepared so," he said.

"For Sergetten?" I asked.

"For your own sake," he said. He stroked himself then and caused the hunger to flare in me again.

I turned to face him, climbing over him then, until we were face to face. "He will be cruel to me."

"How do you know?"

"He has always been cruel to me," I said. "Why should that change? And you saw how..."

"Hush. No more talk of Sergetten," Kan said. "This memory is for me. But I will say, you may find his demeanor changed when you are bonded."

I shook my head in disbelief, but said nothing more. Instead I steadied his prick with one hand and pressed my arse back, trying to impale myself. The need flared hotter and higher as I came closer to having him, worsening with each failed attempt. The angle was wrong, it was too slippery, and Kan was somewhat softer than usual after having come so recently. I whimpered.

"Come on, Weltskin," Kan crooned, "put me inside you. Milk me for all I'm worth."

I stroked him then, with my slick hand, even though every stroke that made him harder made the burning need inside me more searing. At last I pushed myself onto him with a cry.

"Beautiful," he said, his hands caressing my ankles and the tops of my feet on either side of him. "Now milk me."

He would give me no help, not even a roll of his hips. I had to lift myself with my legs and slam myself down, trying to ease the ache and push him as deep into me as possible. I wanted more, needed more, but if I went too far, he slipped free, making me cry out in loss, and if I stayed too shallow, it wasn't what I needed.

It was hard work, milking him like that, but I heeded his words. He had rescued me, and treated me well, and comforted me, and loved me. I knew in my heart that if I did this for him, he would be my ally to the end.

And he would always be my first. "This cock..." I said, as I continued to move, "I shall never forget, was the first to breach me."

"Yes-s-s-s," he agreed, his breath growing ragged as he came close to spilling.

His hand took hold of me suddenly, stroking me too, and he said, "Spill with me one last time, Jorin."

It was his last command to me, and one my body obeyed without hesitation.

43: Kenet

I was accompanying the general the next day, on horse, as he greeted another battalion commander just arriving from an area near the Frangi border. The commander was a grizzled old soldier with one eye named Harman, and it was clear he and Roichal had known each other for many a year. I had barely dismounted from my horse when they were embracing, beating upon one another's backs.

"I have something to show you," Harman said. His voice was as rough as his face.

"Indeed?" Roichal beckoned me to follow.

Harman hesitated. "You might not..."

"My page is not so tender as he looks. What is it, Harman?"

"You'll see." He led us to where his own command tent had been pitched, in the shade of a large tree. He opened the flap and led us inside. It took my eyes a moment to adjust to the dimness but I had heard a cry when he had entered.

There were six boys there, huddled together, the smallest ones covering their eyes with their hands.

"It's all right," Harman crooned. "You can look."

At first I thought there must be something they feared about the general, but as they peered at him curiously that did not seem to be the problem.

Harman explained. "We took them from the hold of a Night Mage near the border. They have been held in the dark and their eyes cannot bear the light."

Roichal started. "Held for how long?"

The eldest of them, who couldn't have been more than a year or two younger than me, answered. "Four years, Sir."

"Four years!"

"That is our guess from what we could tell of the passing of the seasons," he said, voice clear, though his eyes slipped closed as if accustomed to being that way. "I was taken in summer. The others have been nearly as long."

One of them moaned, the smallest one, and the others moved around him, touching him instinctively in the near dark. He was lying on an improvised pallet and wore just a tunic over him, exposing his emaciated arms and legs.

"What is wrong with this one?" Roichal asked in a quiet voice.

"We don't know, Sir," the eldest boy said. "We have not seen our master for nearly two months, and he cannot seem to eat without him."

Roichal and I shared a glance. Roichal continued to question them in a gentle voice. It seemed this mage had kept up the pretense of the youngest being his favorite, and had always fed him fine fruits and tender meats before the boy would... suckle. They were all pale, having been kept in the dark for so long, but the weak one had a shock of black hair like Jorin's.

I felt ill. I could not move from Roichal's side, yet I did not want to hear another word about what uses these boys had been put to, in the name of Night Magic. It was one thing for Jorin and I to have explored one another as boys, at play, and something entirely different for them to have been kidnapped and forced.

"The others are recovering well enough, with gradual exposure to light," Harman was saying in a low voice, "except for Istin."

Roichal pulled Harman to the deepest corner of the tent and they continued speaking to each other in urgent whispers.

I went and knelt by the sick boy. The others all looked up at me hopefully. "Are you a healer?" one of them asked.

I shook my head. "No. I... I am also escaped from a Night Mage," I said. Their eyes only widened. "I... I think I may know what your friend needs." I brushed the boy's hair from his forehead. He was too weak to do anything more than smile at me.

"If what you mean is more Night Magic, we shan't," the eldest said. "We would rather die than let another man touch us ever again."

I shook my head. "Not Night Magic, not exactly. I will never go back to the mage who made me what I am. Not willingly. But... though food will not sustain him, there is one thing that will. It need not come from the mage. It can come from any man."

One of them clutched at his stomach as if he were ill. The eldest covered his eyes again. Then he uncovered them and looked at me. "You suffer from this as well?"

I nodded. "There is a soldier who accommodates me," I said. "A good, kind man. But we do not speak of it and only he and the general know my story."

"Of course not," one of the others said.

The eldest shook his head. "I think Istin would rather die than suckle another man's pisshole."

At that pronouncement, though, the other one who looked quite young threw his arms around his comrade and burst into tears. "Istin, Istin, don't die! You can have my milk, every drop, served to you in a golden cup from a silver spoon if you want."

Istin's weak arm folded over his friend, patting him on the back. He croaked a few words that only the other boy could hear.

Roichal and Harman returned to us just as the eldest was asking me, "Is this a curse that cannot be broken?"

"I do not know," I said. "Will I be like this all my life? Would killing the mage who bound me like this release me? Or will the effect fade over time as I continue to be separated from him? I do not know."

"I will never leave you," Istin's friend swore to him, then looked around at us. "Leave us. Leave us, please!"

Harman said to Roichal, "Well, it would appear your page has settled the matter among them. Let us go, then."

Three of the boys tied scarves over their eyes and followed the eldest to the tent flap. They followed us outside, into the shade of the tree. Their leader squinted and shaded his eyes, but withstood the brightness.

Roichal spoke to him. "For now I must leave you in the care of Commander Harman who will report to me of your welfare. Come, Page, we have much to discuss."

When we were mounted and riding once again, where none could eavesdrop, he told me what a quandary the boys presented for him. "We are fortunate that they are not all afflicted as you are, but even one, and so young..." He shook his head. "They will allow no man to touch them, and I do not blame them in the slightest for that, but any man who would oblige the suckling of such a boy... I would want to run through with a sword myself and then leave to die of a gut wound on a buzzard-covered field."

I said nothing, just feeling ill thinking on it.

"We are fortunate that you coaxed them to a solution," Roichal continued. "If, indeed, we are correct about the boy's troubles. But it seems likely, does it not? It also increases my resolve that you must be provided for."

I looked at him in surprise. "You are not thinking of... of telling anyone else?"

He chuckled at my alarm. "Fear not, Page. You know I will not turn you into a whore for the camp."

"I... of course not... I..." My cheeks must have burned crimson. "I mean, the field marshal is plenty for me. I don't w—That is, there is only one..." Curse my tongue for having led me into a field of brambles again. I had no choice now but to plough through. "There is only one man I would... I would consider in addition to him."

"Oh?"

"You, Sir." I could not meet his eyes. I could barely look at the reins in my hand. All I could do was repeat myself in a whisper. "You, Sir."

Both horses pulled up short and I found his hand rubbing my knee affectionately. He looked back and forth, ensuring we were alone, before answering. "Knowing you desire it so keenly makes me wish your wish could be granted, Page," he said. "But it cannot."

"Yes, Sir," I said, feeling the disappointment as keenly as the desire.

He patted my knee again. "You must tell me, though, what desires you have, no matter what they are. You will do this for me as a service, if you are both loyal and obedient."

"Yes, Sir," I said again. "May I wait until nightfall, though, Sir?"

He laughed, heartily and loudly. "Yes, Page, yes you may." He spurred his horse into a trot and mine followed eagerly.

Nightfall and time for my evening "meal" came soon enough. Roichal insisted we vary our routine somewhat, and he and the field marshal played a game of cards with two of the other officers outside Marksin's tent while I sat quietly by, watching. After a while, the other two left, and Roichal and Marksin went into the tent. Only then did Roichal tell him about the boys who had been rescued.

"I hope this tale has not sickened you so much that you cannot perform well for our young page," he said. "For I would hate to see Page sicken and wither as that one did."

"Fear not," Marksin said, sitting on the edge of his own pallet and starting to remove his boots.

"May I?" I asked, sliding to my knees beside him. I looked back at Roichal, for I was asking for the general's permission as much as Marksin's.

They both assented, and I worked Marksin's boots off, then rubbed his bare feet. That produced louder—and more lascivious-sounding—groans than the times I had suckled him! Roichal laughed.

As I rubbed Marksin's feet I told him, "The general has asked me to demonstrate my loyalty and obedience by performing a service for him."

"Oh?"

"Yes. I have promised to tell him what I want."

Marksin was bemused by this. "And what have you told him?"

"So far, only that I wished I could suck his milk as well as yours, but he says that is a wish he cannot grant." I dared not look at the general as I said this. "Other than that, well, you two do not leave me wanting for much at all. Except, well..." I was rapidly realizing how silly what I was about to say would sound. But they both pressed me gently to go on. "Except... for wanting to perform more services, so that I might demonstrate my loyalty and obedience."

Marksin seized my wrist and pulled me up to look in his eyes. He and Roichal shared a glance. "And is it the spell that compels you to behave this way?"

I jerked in surprise and dismay. "No. No, I do not believe it is the spell that makes me feel this way."

"Are you sure?" he pressed.

I sighed unhappily. "No, I am not sure. But if my feelings are my own, then they are feelings of gratitude. You and the general have earned my loyalty and my respect. You have earned my affection, as well, and as for obedience, well, that is one of the only ways I can show my loyalty and my appreciation."

I felt the general move behind me and felt the warmth of his hands stroking my hair. "You are a good boy, Page," he said, in a whisper.

"Thank you, Sir." I bowed my head. Was it the spell? I remembered feeling this before, when Seroi praised me. But was it Night Magic, or was it just something about me?

I could count the times my father had praised me on my fingers, while Jorin bore countless marks of his disappointment. Sergetten had not been much freer with his praise.

Seroi had only praised me for surrendering to him. Bit by bit. How then, could I submit to these men, and feel so good about it, without it being Night Magic?

The difference was that these men had earned my loyalty, my obedience, my affection, and my love. I leaned into Roichal's touch. "I am not a gift from Fate," I said, my eyes closed. "You have earned me."

He chuckled then and pulled me into a kiss. "Get undressed. Both of you. Down to your bare skin."

The lanterns were all out in the next nearest tents and the night was warm enough for sleeping in nothing. Marksin and I both stood and we helped each other out of uniform, until we were both naked.

"On your back, Page," Roichal said. "Marks, atop him, feed him even as you taste him yourself."

Marksin climbed over me, straddling my face so that his prick hung down. I lapped at it like a ripe fruit hanging from a vine. Meanwhile, his own mouth sought out my prick, his dark hair tickling me as it hung down.

His prick felt all wrong like this, upside down in my mouth, and I worried that I would scrape him where he was sensitive with my top teeth, but if the enthusiastic way he began to pump his hips, fucking my mouth, was any indication, then it felt good enough.

He was more aggressive sucking me this time, and one of his hands tugged and played with my milksacks while he sucked. Roichal circled us, looking at different angles, but did not touch us.

"Pull out now," he told Marksin as he might have been getting close. He knelt by my feet. "Page, pump him with your fist and lick his head, but don't make him spill yet. Marks, I want you to make Page spill, though."

"Yes, Sir," Marksin said, then put his mouth back where it had been.

"Page, when you are ready, you will ask my permission to come. I may grant it right away, or I might not. Understand?"

"Yes, Sir," I said, then went back to licking. Salty droplets were oozing freely from Marksin and I lapped them greedily. At that point, I would have gladly swallowed his piss had he wished it, but that was an abasement they did not seem inclined to pursue. I thought again of the boys they had rescued from the dungeon of a mage and the many depravities they had been forced to suffer. I was lucky to have fallen into Roichal's and Marksin's hands.

I had to pull Marksin's prick aside to call out hoarsely, "Oh, please, Sir, may I spill now?"

Roichal chuckled. "Ten more thrusts, Page," he said, sinking his hands into Marksin's hair and holding him fast. "On the tenth you may spill. Ten thrusts hard, into this willing mouth."

Marksin's groan was muffled by my cock, but it did not sound like a protest. My hips were already pushing upward, so close, and his throat was so soft, hot, wet... I made it to the seventh thrust before I began to cry out, but I gave three cries of agony before my release finally came. Marksin swallowed just as greedily as I usually did, then suddenly my cock flopped wetly onto my belly as Roichal pulled him into a rough kiss.

While they kissed, I resumed pumping Marksin's shaft with my hand, licking the head all over. His groans into Roichal's mouth took on a desperate tone.

Roichal broke free, and traced Marksin's swollen lips with his fingers. "Up for a moment." He directed us to shift, so that now Marksin straddled me again, but with both of our heads pointing

the same direction. His cock fit better into my mouth this direction, and I wrapped my fist around it again, mouthing the head.

Roichal repositioned himself to play with Marksin's arse. He
was still fully clothed, but straddled my hips with his knees.

My mouth was busy now, waiting for Marksin's milk, but the
two of them could both speak. Marksin surprised me by doing so,
though. He was normally so stoic and quiet. "Sir," he said, jerking
as Roichal did something behind him. "Would you... you you consider it... a... a sign of my... my loyalty and obedience..." He gasped
as Roichal did something else. It felt like he was probably fucking
him with his finger.

Roichal finished the sentence for him. "Were you to tell me
what your desires are? Aye, Marks, I would be honored to know."

But then Marksin fell silent, and it felt like the general was
pumping his fingers in and out, driving Marksin's cock into my
mouth. There was another rhythm in his body, though, and I laid
a hand on his chest, realizing that he was weeping.

"Come for me, Marks," Roichal said. "Hold nothing back."

And then a flood of milk was pumping down my throat, and
Marksin's sobs broke.

When the seed and tears ceased to flow, Roichal urged Marksin
onto his side, and me into his arms. He put a cloak over us, there
on the floor of the tent. "Hold him for me, Page," he said quietly,
kissing me on the forehead. "Stay with him. You did well."

Then he kissed Marksin on the forehead, too. "Thank you,
Marks. You please me well, too."

Marksin was too overwhelmed to answer, just a few fresh tears
leaking from his eyes, which I kissed away. Roichal stood. "Stay
together," he said, and then withdrew.

I wondered where he could be going, but I had my orders and
would not stray from them. Marksin's tears were salty, and when
he kissed me again, his tongue tasted sweet in comparison. We
kissed each other deeply, and though each of us burned with a
passion for someone absent, it did not matter. The kisses were still
sweet.

44: Jorin

In the end, we waited until nightfall after all. Kan and I fell back to sleep in each other's arms, and when Sergetten woke us at midday he handled my cock and balls with brusque disgust. "I could take you now, but the ritual would be devoid of pleasure for you in this state," he said, letting my limp cock fall from his grip. "Remember this later when you think me a master without mercy. I was not the one who would have sent you flaccid and spent into a Night Magic bonding."

Kan said nothing to that, and so neither did I.

Sergetten harrumphed. "Wash. Wash yourself well, dirt-eater. And be ready at sundown." He left us, then, the tent flapping shut behind him.

"Shall I come with you?" Kan asked.

I shook my head. "And be tempted into taking me for the last time, again? No, Kan. Let me go."

He ran his fingers through my hair. "You are such a brave beast."

"I am not. I have no choice."

"You are. To accept the bond of a man you know will be cruel to you."

"He will not be half so cruel to me as Seroi is to Kenet."

Kan could think of nothing clever to say to that and he let me go.

I made my way to the creek where we watered the horses, and piled up rocks at the edge of one small dip, making a pool up to my knees. I washed as well as I could, scrubbing myself everywhere, including between my legs, even though that would rid me of the grease Kan had suggested I use.

I wondered if Kenet was doing something similar right now, preparing himself for Seroi's thorn to prick him. Anger burned in me, making my ears hot, as I imagined Kenet experiencing the kind of searing need I had. Kenet's desire had ever been mine and mine alone, from the first time it had flared in him, and I wanted nothing more than to cut out Seroi's heart for taking that from me.

I hurried back to the camp. I knew we would not be moving until after the ritual, but I was impatient to plan Kenet's rescue and to hear the rest of what the sentry had to say.

When I arrived back in the glade, though, I found the mood changed. Everyone was preparing to go as soon as the ritual was complete, but no one would meet my eyes. What had Sergetten told them?

I followed Gresh back to the watering hole, where he filled the small casks. "What did I miss?"

"We must away as soon as you are severed from us," he said with a shrug. "Back to Tiger's Mouth."

"What? What about the prince?"

"He's not there."

"Not where?"

"The castle. At least, that is what Sergetten says."

"What!"

"Go ask him yourself. Herge brought us a broadsheet with the picture of the missing spy on it. Herge had thought it was Kan, that this was how they would catch us at last... but Sergetten said no, it is a picture of the prince."

I ran back to the camp this time, but neither Kan nor Sergetten were in evidence. I asked after them, but no one seemed to know where they had gone. Finally Willim pointed up the hill, and I climbed up the gentle side of the slope that ended in a small bluff. They were at the top, where it was clear and grassy, gesturing at the ground and arguing.

They fell silent as they saw me approaching. "What is this about Kenet escaping?" I demanded.

"We do not know yet for certain," Kan said.

"Yes, we do," Sergetten countered. "It is plain that he has escaped the Lord High Mage's plans, and rather than let the populace know that their crown prince is on the run, they have told them that he is an escaped spy. So few know his face, it is an easily believed tale. His hair is as fair as a Frangi's."

"But where is he?" I cried.

"That, we have no idea of," Sergetten said coolly.

I do not know what came over me. I threw myself at his feet, on my knees. "Do what you will with me, but find him. Is there some form of Night Magic that can find him? I do not care what I must suffer, Sergetten, if it will save him from harm."

For a moment I saw something like sympathy flicker through those dark eyes, but then he just shook his head with disdain. "You know nothing of what you speak."

"Is there a spell, then? Whatever you must do, I will bear it. Please." I imagined that there must be something like what Kan had done in the night that drew Sergetten to us. Could we bring Kenet to us, too?

Sergetten slid his hand into my hair and chuckled darkly. "To think I did not dream you would ever actually beg."

"Don't toy with him, Sergetten," Kan warned.

"And why shouldn't I?" Sergetten asked. "He will shortly be mine to do with as I wish. In fact, he will need to be trained most rigorously. Well, Jorin, what is it Kan has dubbed you? Weltskin? You will do anything I ask of you?"

"Anything," I said.

He leaned over and pulled at my hair until we were nose to nose. "What I ask, then, is that you trust me."

My breath caught.

"I want the prince safe and out of the hands of danger as much as you do," he said. "But you must trust me. If what you have told me of Seroi is true..."

"It is! It is irrefutable!"

"Hush!" He shook me. "If indeed his lordship intended to turn the prince into a night-bound whoreslave, he must be stopped at all costs. For if he should succeed, the whole of Trest would enter an era of darkness the likes of which you cannot even imagine."

"Then we must find Kenet!"

"Yes, we must. But there are things that must happen first."

He loosened his grip some. "Like you must be trained. You cannot be trained until we are bound, and we cannot be bound until you are loosed by the others, and you cannot be loosed by the others until sundown." He let me go then as he stepped back. "And it will go so much better for you if you trust me."

"How? How can I trust you if Seroi has enchanted you with Night Magic of his own?"

"He has not."

"He waited until you were out of the way to start bespelling Kenet. How do you know you did not leave under some compulsion?"

"Because I know!" he roared. "I know much better than you the powers his lordship exerts. I know, too, the reasons your assertion about his intentions for the prince may be misinformed. I, however, cannot take the chance that you may be correct and must act as if you are, until proven otherwise. Kenet must be found."

"Swear to me you will never do him harm and I will obey your every word," I said.

He laughed, which was not the reaction I was expecting. "You are in no position to bargain, Jorin Weltskin. In a few hours, you will obey my every word, regardless."

I folded my arms. "And you wonder why I do not trust you?"

"Don't be daft. I know exactly why you do not trust me, which is why I know it is of no use to try to convince you otherwise." He took a few steps away from me, as if to return to the camp, but looked back when I called his name.

"Sergetten! I will have your promise, or I will not go through with this." I held Kan's gaze with mine and knew he would back me at least this far. "This is not about magic, but about honor."

Sergetten laughed bitterly. "A dirt-eater's honor?"

"Call me what you like. I am a ladra'an of the royal household..."

"I was given to understand you had been exiled from that post."

"Not by Kenet."

"Who could be said to have abdicated his claim to the throne by his flight."

"Sergetten," Kan said, voice low. "You will shut your mouth and listen to what Weltskin has to say or never mind the consequences, I will not let you lay a finger on him."

Sergetten folded his arms then, mimicking my pose. I held firm and spoke. "It is not my honor that matters here, in any case. It is yours, Sergetten. Swear to me that you will release me from the slave bond when Kenet and I are reunited and that you will never harm him or help him to come to harm."

Sergetten shook his head. "My first allegiance above all others is to the king, and passes only to his son upon his death."

"Very well. Then swear to me in such a way as not to compromise your first allegiance."

"I am trying to point out that this feeble attempt to wrest a measure of control when you have none, just to assuage your fears, is pointless. What if Korl has ordered me to bring you to him for punishment at any cost? I would be compelled to deceive you."

"And yet you just asked me to trust you!" I wanted to grab him by the edges of his collar and shake him.

He gave me a slight bow, as if I had scored a point. "Indeed. I ask you to trust that I will make the right decisions about my allegiances should they conflict with one another. Nothing is absolute, Jorin. If the king put a dagger into my hand and said 'kill the prince' I doubt that I could do so without hesitation. A lack of open defiance is not the same thing as acquiescence, and even perfect obedience is not the same thing as submission."

He looked at Kan. "Come, let's get out of the open. You, too, Weltskin."

I stood my ground. Perhaps it was childish, but part of me was arguing that I was not his slave yet and so should defy him now while I could.

"I understand you are frightened, and you should be," he said. "I understand you are trying to extract a piece of power from me, who will soon have all power over you. But that is exactly why I cannot give it to you. I don't expect a dirt-eater like you to grasp such logic, but I despair for you and your princeling if you do not

learn the lessons I have to teach you eventually." He glared at me
one last time and then stalked down the hill without looking back.
Kan looked from me to him back to me again, then finally turned
and followed him back to the camp.

I sat down in the grass and put my head in my hands.

I did not move from the spot. For a good while I was too angry
to think straight, and then when I felt calmer, I no longer wanted
to think through the tangles of logic that every argument with
Sergetten was. Instead, I let my mind go blank. I suppose one could
say I meditated, though it wasn't intentional. I watched the sun set
from up there, into a gorgeous summer sky of copper and orange.

And then I heard them coming. Kan and the men who had
bound me. I stayed as I was, and Kan knelt beside me and began
pulling me out of my clothes. Suddenly the others were helping,
and in a trice I was naked and being borne back down the hill on
their shoulders like a log.

They carried me to a clearing—it might have been the same
one we'd used for fight practice, only now they had torches burning. They laid me out upon the stitched hide, upon my stomach. I
wondered how elaborate the ritual would be.

Not very, as it turned out. To release me, each man spoke a few
ritual words as he spilled his milk onto me, painting my buttocks
with it. I wondered, was this why it was called "release"? Then,
after they had released me, Sergetten took me.

And yes, they call it taking. He bore me down with the weight
of his body, his cock seeking entrance even before our position
had settled, and unerringly spearing me. I could not tell if he had
slicked himself especially or if it was just that his prick was coated
with the seed of the others. There was enough grease that I felt not
the burn or discomfort of dry friction, just the intensity of pain
caused by his size. He was thick like Gresh, but long, too.

Once he had me pinned, he caught me around the throat
with a strap of leather. I could not help it. I fought, which only
drove his cock deeper into me, but I could not bear the thought
of him humiliating me so in front of the others, making me his
dog, his pet.

The moment the clasp closed though, I howled like a wounded animal, as the transfer became complete, and the aching need which had abated as each of my former holders had spilled returned full force. He fucked me hard and fast, then, and one might have called him merciless, except that the sooner he came, the sooner my pain would end.

He stroked me, too, in time with his thrusts, and I remembered what he had said earlier. Yes, his stroking of my cock did add pleasure to the experience; it did reverse some of the worst of my suffering. Had Kan not loved me so well, and so often, just a few short weeks ago I might have called that ecstasy.

Sergetten was chanting words in the old language they used, and for a moment I almost thought I could understand them. There was a word the others had repeated, too, that had to mean release. But what was Sergetten releasing this time?

It seemed to me I came as the world turned white, a sudden blast of cold but hot, dark but bright, everything shattering around me forever and ever and ever... And then suddenly time moved forward again and Sergetten slumped atop me, cock still buried deep.

I could feel carpet under my cheek, under my palms, and could sense we were indoors. The castle? I tried to raise my head.

"Down," he said.

I went still but not silent. "What happened?"

"I used the energy created by the bonding to send us back to the spot from which Kan plucked me."

"Where are we?"

"A safe place," he said, running a hand down my ribcage. "A small keep, easy to defend, difficult to find."

"But where?" I insisted.

"It would be better if you didn't know, but since you cannot run away from me now, I suppose there is little harm in assuaging your curiosity. We're near the border of Pellon, just north of there."

"So nearly to Frangit, as well."

"Glad to see some of those geography lessons sank in after all."

With that he jerked his cock free and left me gasping. He got to his feet. "You have something to say, Weltskin?" he challenged.

"Why, are you going to order me not to criticize my master?"

He laughed. "Oh, far from it. I encourage you to speak your mind. You will no doubt give me many more opportunities to correct you if you speak than if you sit quietly. Well, go on. Are you so eager for a round of punishment that you must start right away?"

"Will you punish me, even if I am right?"

He crouched beside me and ran a hand down my back. "Let me make a few things clear. You are not a whipping boy any more. Your punishment does not have to come as the result of an infraction. It does not have to be just, nor justified. It can be purely because I want to punish you. It can be purely because I want to teach you a lesson, and the lesson could be nothing more than 'I can do whatever I like to you.'"

"In that case, there really is no incentive for me to hold back anything I might say," I said.

"Just so. So what did you want to tell me, Jorin Weltskin?"

I sat up then so I could look into his face. I could see we were in a small room, a bed off to one side, on the other a long table covered with candles and lanterns, most of which were flickering. I put a hand to the collar around my neck. "Why this? Will you feed me from a dish on the floor and expect me to beg your table scraps, too?"

His eyes darkened. "You are truly an idiot."

"So you keep saying."

He reached out and ran a finger along the leather at my throat, then held up his arm so that his sleeve exposed a matching stripe of leather around his wrist. "This may act like a leash but I assure you turning you into a dog was not my intent. Our bond is meant to be temporary, remember?"

"Yes," I said, still not seeing what he was saying.

He stood, stiff with anger, but not too angry to say, "When the time comes to release you, it is much simpler both magically and symbolically for me to remove your collar than to try to unweave a set of spiritual bindings in your soul."

"Oh." I was too stunned for a moment to even consider apologizing. By the time I wondered if I should, he had already stalked to the door.

"You sleep there," he said, pointing to the low bed against the wall. "I am sick of seeing your face now." And with that, he slammed the door shut, and the flames that had been illuminating the room went out.

I crawled to the bed and climbed into it in the darkness, suddenly exhausted. It was done. I was bound to him. I wondered which of us was going to regret it more.

45: Kenet

Marksin and I were bent over requisitions and charts the next evening when the general came in.

Marksin set aside his ink. "Tell the general what you have concluded, Page."

I looked up in surprise. "Concluded?"

"Just a while ago, from your figures."

Roichal just looked at me expectantly, his hands clasped behind his back.

"Er, well, given the salaries of the officers and the price of feeding the ranks, including the horses and not included the provision of any weapons... Trest cannot afford to lose this war."

Marksin laughed. "That is not what you said."

"Isn't it?"

"No. You said 'Trest cannot afford this war.'"

I blushed, looking down at the parchment in front of me. "Oh. I... I suppose I've thought more about it since."

Roichal's expression was serious. "Aye, ugly isn't it? And yet if we invade Frangit, and take what we can, are we any better than brigands?"

My cheeks colored more deeply. "I... I was thinking more along the lines of reparations paid by their crown to ours after their defeat."

"Ah." Roichal and Marksin shared a glance. I half-expected one of them to comment on how this was perhaps higher political thinking than an escaped whoreslave could be expected to know, but neither of them said anything beyond that look. Roichal probed further. "But should their crown be allowed to stand after their surrender?"

I must have looked alarmed, for Marksin moved beside me and

put a hand on my arm. "Of course!" I stammered. "We are not seriously trying to annex Frangit, are we? I thought we were supposed to be defending against their incursions on our territory and sovereignty."

Marksin let out a breath. "They claim that we attacked first."

"Of course they do," I said. "Every aggressor will play victim in hopes of winning the fight and determining the historical record." This was something Sergetten had taught me.

Roichal chuckled. "Every aggressor, the armies of Trest included?"

"But we were attacked first, were we not?" I asked, my voice rising.

"That is a very good question," the general asked, then limped over to the sleeping pallet. Seeing him limp like that drove all thought of politics and justice from my head for a few moments and Marksin and I both hurried over to him. I was already on my knees when I looked up at Marksin, inviting him to help me with just a look. He hesitated only a moment, then joined me on the canvas, pulling the general's boots off, and rubbing his feet. I soon began to work my way up his bad leg, while Marksin continued to work the knots from the other foot.

I had made my way up to his knee when the general began to speak again. "Can you imagine, Page, a situation in which both nations might claim to have been attacked first?"

"But someone had to actually be first. Unless both attacked at the same time, in different places?"

"No no, it is not so tricky as that," he said. "Can you tell me what you knew of the war before you came to us?"

The war was not one of the subjects considered seemly at banquet in the castle. Sergetten had taught me much about the history of our neighbor nations, Pellon and Frangit, but had said little about the current war other than a few basics. "I heard that Frangi raiding parties on the orchard towns near the Northern Pass had begun the hostilities years ago. And that diplomacy had failed, and once rebuffed by their ruling council, we had no choice but to go to war."

"And so, we were the first to send an army to attack the other," Roichal said, "even if they were the first to do us harm. Both sides think they are in the right. In the end, though, might makes right."

He put his hand over mine, stilling it against his thigh, but he spoke to the field marshal. "There is something you must do."

"Sir?" Marksin looked up.

"You should lie with a camp follower in the next few days."

I was shocked to hear him say this. Marksin, though, was not, given the resigned look on his face.

"It has already been too long for you, Marks," he said. "And rumors, such as they are, must be quelled."

Marksin would not meet the general's eyes as he said, "Yes, Sir," his voice barely audible.

Roichal put a hand on his hair. "Is it so arduous a task I set before you?"

"No, Sir," he said, but he did not sound convincing. "If... if you like, I shall go tonight."

"That would suit me well," Roichal said. "But you must feed Page first."

I reached up and touched Marksin's cheek. "Sir? Could we not wait until after the field general is finished with his... errand?"

Marksin looked at me with pleading hope in his eyes. Roichal sifted my hair with his fingers. "Why do you suggest that, Page?"

"You said I should tell you what I want, isn't that right, Sir?"

"Yes, that's right, Page."

"I... I would like the field general to sleep in the tent with us. I-I want him here."

Roichal's other hand combed through the black silk of Marksin's hair. "And what does the field general want?"

Marksin's voice was hoarse, as if he could barely force out the words. "I will do as you ask, Sir."

Roichal pursed his lips, perhaps annoyed at having his question dodged. "Very well. Go seek out the prettiest and brassiest, the one most likely to burnish your reputation. When you are done, return here. Page, you do know that the field marshal will not have much to give you after having given the first seed to a female furrow?"

"I know, Sir," I said. Apparently there was still no chance of Roichal himself feeding me, but it also appeared that he was not sending Marksin away merely to get me alone.

Marksin kissed me and I felt his gratitude. He knew that I understood what he wanted, even if he could not voice it. Then he got to his feet and said, "Sir, would it be all right if Page would bring me to full length before I go?"

Roichal chuckled. "Nothing like going with sword drawn when looking for a duel," he said. "Go on, Page. Have a little taste of him."

I pushed down his trousers and breeches and sucked him until he was so long and hard I was choking on him. Then I did him up again, but the bulge was quite noticeable.

"Perfect," he declared, then gave a quick salute, and left.

Roichal then bade me order the cook's boys to bring him hot water for his leg again, and they again came and filled the wooden tub with pitcher after pitcher of heated water. He soaked his leg for a short time, then motioned for me to strip down. He repeated the washing of my skin he'd performed on me once before, going over every inch with a cloth, and saving my milksacks and prick for last.

Then he sat me across his lap, one hand in my hair as he kissed me, the other stroking my cock in a lazy, teasing rhythm. "The field marshal does have something of a reputation among the women," he said, talking softly to me while arousing me. "One would need to know him exceedingly well to realize that lying with them is a mere charade on his part."

I could only reply with a muffled moan, hiding my face against the cloth of his shirt as he brought me to the quivering edge of spilling and held me there with his thumb making slick circles around the head of my cock.

"Hm, and what about you, Page? Were you not bespelled, would you bury this I hold in my hand between a woman's thighs? Would you like to regardless of the spell?"

"But..." I panted. "But..."

"Ah, I know you cannot come without my command. You

would surely make a whore feel she failed you somehow if you did not spill. But if you wanted, my dear Page, we could have a girl brought here for you...?"

I shook my head, unable to speak to explain why I did not want to. And even if I could have spoken, I would not have been able to tell him the danger of creating a royal bastard.

"There, there, you know I won't ask you to do anything you don't wish to," he said in a low voice, slowing his stroking such that I could regain my breath. "Except, perhaps, tell me what you wish to hide."

"Sir?"

"Is there a reason you decided to suckle your nightly milk later, instead of first?"

I raised my head so I could look him in the eye. I thought I had answered that question already, but perhaps he didn't believe what I'd said. "I want him to spend the night with us," I said again. "If he goes off to the women after, you know he'll go back to his own tent rather than disturb us."

Roichal caught my mouth in a kiss, coaxing sounds from my throat and drinking them in greedily. When he pulled back, he said, "That is the truth, yet I sense that is not the whole truth."

I did not know if he was merely very good at reading me, or if the spell that made me a whoreslave allowed whoever I was submissive to the ability to know if I were hiding something. "Sir," I began, "I asked on the field marshal's behalf, as well."

"Did you, now?"

"Yes, Sir. He wants very much to spend the night, every night, alongside us, but he will not ask for himself."

"So you have taken it upon yourself to ask for him?"

"Yes, Sir. Is—" I paused as he ran a finger along my lips as if testing their plumpness. "Is that wrong?"

"He has told you this?"

"No, Sir. I just know it."

"Ah." He kissed me again. "No, Page, that is not wrong. But it is something for me to think on." He ran his finger over my then wet lips and I felt a slight tremor go through him. Was he thinking of allowing me to suckle his milk after all?

"Sir?" was all the question I could allow myself.

His voice was surprisingly soft for such a gruff man, much like his touch. "I see the doubts churning in you, through the windows of your eyes," he said. "Do you doubt I find you pleasing?"

"No, Sir." My voice was a whisper.

"Do you doubt I will protect you from any threat?"

I was surprised he would ask that, but I did not doubt it in the least. "No, Sir."

He pressed a soft kiss against my temple. "Then I will not concern myself over the other doubts swirling in you, Page. I know there are secrets you cannot divulge. And if you doubt yourself, well... I do not."

I was emboldened by his words and climbed astride his lap, my arms around his neck at first and my cock pressed between my own stomach and the cloth of his jacket. Then I undid the buttons and he did not object. Soon his only clothing was the swaddling he had wrapped around his waist, groin, and privates.

I rubbed the underside of my cock gently up and down the stripe of hair that ran from his bellybutton over the curve of his belly and disappeared below. My breath caught as I found the sensation far more arousing than I had expected to. Perhaps it was merely that it was his bare skin against mine and that alone was a thrill.

"Very good, Page," he whispered. "You are at your best, at your most perfect, when you are so ripe for the plucking."

"Does it please you to see me thus?" I asked, even though that was surely what he had just said.

"Aye. Balanced on the sword's edge of lust." He stole a quick kiss from my lips, then settled his hands on my hips, not to guide me but as if to feel the strain in my body as I teased myself. "When you spill tonight, Page," he said, "what would you like? Into Marksin's mouth again? Or something else? I was quite serious about a camp follower for you, you know, if you would like."

I shook my head, drawing a ragged breath. "N-no, Sir, please. I... I would prefer only you and..." My throat closed with emotion suddenly as I realized I was about to lie egregiously. I had been about to say "the field marshal" but of course my truest preference of all would have been Jorin. I swallowed the sudden tears that wanted to well up and choke me, turning them into a guttural moan as the general pulled me by my buttocks and trapped my throbbing cock between our bellies. "...and the company of men who can be trusted," I finished, for certainly that was true enough.

"How much do you trust me?" he asked then, nipping at my ear.

"Completely, Sir," I answered without hesitation.

I felt another tremor of lust go through him. "Marksin might be some time yet," he continued. "Would you feel it right for me to keep you on edge like this until he returned? Or should I allow you some relief now, and then tease you until you are begging for release again later?"

I sucked in a breath. "If by relief now you mean allowing me to spill, then, no, Sir, I feel it would be right to wait. But of course, what is right is determined by your orders. I would... I would gladly spill for you if you wished."

His chuckle was low. "What else might I have meant by relief?"

"Oh. Just, allowing me to subside for a bit."

His laugh brightened. "You sound positively disappointed by the prospect."

"Well..." I pressed my hot cheek against his shoulder. "Perhaps. After all, you have just told me you like me best when I am on the edge."

He took me by the chin so that he could look me in the eye. "It is also because you like it best when you are on edge that you are so beautiful, Page. Like a flower or fruit still dewy in the rising sun, caught forever in that moment, before falling from the bush."

"Yes, Sir," I agreed.

"Lie down, my Page," he said, shifting me from his lap. He stood and bade me lie on my back on the pallet and lift my arms above my head. He lay a cloth over my eyes, then bound my hands somehow, and then my ankles.

Then something very soft and slight ran up the inside of my thigh.

"It is my flywhisk," he murmured. A fine, long stalk of stiff, braided leather with several inches of horsehair at the end. He used it to brush the stinging flies from his horse's flanks when the horse's own tail was prepared for battle.

I felt the feathery touch up my legs several times, then the dewdrop that fell from my cock to my stomach as he applied it to my milksacks. Then suddenly—whisk—and the tails struck the inside of my thigh. I made a soft sound myself, of surprise. It did not hurt, only the very lightest of momentary stinging sensations, like a bit of sand in a gust of breeze, and then it was gone.

But then I felt it on my other thigh. Whisk whisk. And working ever closer to my milksacks. Whisk whisk whisk.

When he reached my milksacks I could not help but struggle as the stinging sensation intensified with each swat.

"Do you trust me, Page?" he asked again.

It took me a moment to find my voice. "Y-Yes, Sir."

"Then try to lie still. If you move too much I will miss my mark and cause you unwanted pain."

"Oh. Yes, Sir." I tried to take a deep breath, to still myself, and all I managed was to stiffen as he chose that moment to begin whipping my cock itself.

After that had gone on for quite a while, he asked me in a quiet voice. "And Page, may I trust you to keep from screaming? Or shall I gag you?"

"Um..." I wasn't sure how to answer. I wanted to prove myself, but I also did not want to bring a sentry running at an inopportune moment. "I... I will try to be good, Sir."

"Oh, Page," he said, his voice much closer to my ear now. "You are very, very good." And then he caught my scream in his mouth as he kissed me and took a firm grip on my cock at the same moment. He was pumping his hand up and down furiously, making me see dark clouds roil behind my eyelids, but I could not come no matter how much he did, not until he gave the word.

When he pulled back, he let my cock go, and I found myself gasping, almost sobbing.

Perhaps no "almost" is necessary. He kissed away a few tears. "Very good." He slid the cloth over my eyes away, and then propped a pillow under my head, so I was looking down my outstretched body. My thighs were pink and my cock quite red—as usual.

"Watch this time," he said, and started again from just the caress of the horsehair up the insides of my thighs.

He had to admonish me to keep watching when he started whipping my cock and so I did, holding in a breath to make sure I held in the cry that wanted to escape.

This time he soothed me with his mouth and tongue, nearly everywhere the flywhisk had touched, if it can be called soothing when my cock twitched inside his mouth like a mad thing, trying and trying and trying to spill.

At last he let me free of my bonds, and held me close for a while, rocking me gently and murmuring praise. Then he put the flywhisk into my hand. "When the field general returns," he said, "you shall demonstrate what you've learned."

"Sir?"

"I will guide you," he said. "But let it be your hand that holds the whisk."

"Yes, Sir."

He chuckled. "If I am right, and if you do well, perhaps the field marshal shall give you quite a meal tonight in spite of his earlier exertions."

"I don't wish to hurt him."

"Did it hurt?"

"Well, no," I admitted. "The sensation is too soft, too slight to feel like pain. It only hurts if you count the pain of not being able to come."

"Would you have come from just the whisk without the magic that holds you back?"

"Oh, yes, Sir. Undoubtedly," I said, and I felt that tremor run through him a third time, rendering him speechless.

We both looked toward the entry flap as we heard Marksin call out his approach. He entered to find us both staring at him like hungry cats.

He said not a word as he doffed his boots and jacket and then sank gracefully to his knees in front of us.

46: Jorin

I spent the night restless, expecting at any moment Sergetten might come back and plough me. I tugged at the collar around my neck, quite sure that it was too tight by just a bit, not enough to be dangerous, just enough to annoy. I lay there wondering what kind of magic he would ply in the name of my "training" and what cruelties he might visit on me.

I remembered with sudden vividness the beating that Seroi had administered, while his phantom hand had stroked me. My cheeks burned thinking on it, which might seem odd, given the experiences I had lived through since. Yet there was nothing mortifying about being loved by the Night Riders, even when I was writhing helpless with lust before them. The only humiliating thing had been when Sergetten had collared me, but now that I understood it for what it was, I no longer felt mortified at all.

And yet the memory of being lifted on the chain like a criminal before the entire court, and of the way my cock strained toward Kenet as the king had slashed open his clothes... I had barely thought of it since I had been exiled from the castle, but now the scene consumed my thoughts utterly. I shivered, remembering how Korl had promised he would not stop beating me until Kenet begged him to.

There would be no Kenet here, though. Would Sergetten beat me until his arm tired? It was clear I could do nothing to please him and I had little desire to do so. Merely saving myself pain was not a good enough reason to bow before him. Was it? Perhaps it did not matter and he would just take his pleasure as he wished. I recalled Kan's admonition that I should keep my hole greased if I could. I wondered how often Sergetten would want to fuck me, and how much enthusiasm I would be required to show.

It must have been near dawn when I at last slept soundly, and then when I woke there was daylight coming through the narrow windows at the edges of the room. I was stiff, as if once I had fallen asleep, I had not moved. I sat up slowly to find a meal sitting on a low table next to the bed. A small amount of milk in a cup, and some boiled grains with bits of dried fruit, and a small piece of salt beef. I ate it greedily; no banquet had ever seemed more sumptuous after the traveling provisions and soldier's meals I had been living on. I half expected Sergetten to appear at any moment and correct me for eating too fast or using my hands instead of the spoon and dull knife provided, but he did not.

I assumed he was keeping watch over me, though. I would be a fool not to. I examined the limits of the room. The table had a stone bowl and a few other implements on it, but nothing much of interest. There were a few jars with large stoppers in them in a small cabinet to one side, and there was a shelf that looked as if it should hold books, but there were no books to be found. There were various lanterns and candleholders all around the place, none of which particularly matched, as if they had been collected over a long period of time. Through the tall, narrow slits of glassed-in windows I could see a wide green field and the edge of a forest.

When I had examined everything in the room three times over, and still there had been no sign of Sergetten, I tried the door. It opened, which surprised me. I looked out onto the landing of a dark staircase and decided not to venture further for now. I went back to sit on the bed. There were no clothes for me anywhere that I could discover, and I took stock of my physical health.

The balm Sergetten had used yesterday had left my arse feeling no ill effects of the rough usage. There were a few lingering bruises here and there from various things, but nothing worth devoting much attention to.

I wondered how long that would last.

Eventually I tired and lay down again, dozing off easily this time.

When I woke, there was a new meal on the low table, and some of the things on the table along the wall had moved, which made me wonder about how truly tired I was. I ate more slowly this time.

There was a generous portion of bread and one slim slice of salty ham, and some of the fruit of high summer. And a draught of clear, sweet water that had to have come from a deep well.

Again I saw no sign of Sergetten. I took another nap, wondering if dinner would appear in the same way, but when I woke again there was nothing. I could see the sun was setting and I wondered if I nightfall would bring the return of my Night Magic master or not.

It did not. I eventually began to move through the series of sword practice drills Bear had taught me, miming a non-existent sword in my hands, out of sheer boredom, though I had to stop when it became too dark to see. I had no means of lighting the lamps in the room. Did he expect me to go looking for him? Or to stay here? Or was it a waiting game to see what I would do?

I decided if that was so, I would stay put and make him come to me. I woke once during the night at the sound of the door closing, and found more food had been left for me. It wasn't until dawn I found that a number of books had been returned to the shelf, though.

The next day I took one from the shelf and examined it, but it was in the old tongue and I could not read it. I put it back, and walked through my sword drills again, and examined what was in the large jars. At least one of them appeared to be the same balm Sergetten had used on me, but it was hard to be sure by scent alone.

When the second night fell and still I had seen no sign of Sergetten, I began to worry. What if some accident had befallen him? But no, then who was leaving the food?

What was he waiting for? Was he busy with his mission for the crown? Or was this part of the power game he played with me?

It was the longest I had gone without sex, and without release, since I had left the castle. I had little to occupy my mind other than alternating between worry over my own fate and Kenet's, and soon Kenet was all I could think of.

On the third night I lay upon the sleeping pallet and stroked myself, imagining that it was my prince's hand rather than mine arousing me so.

Later, when I discovered I could not spill, no matter how I tried to coax or force my straining cock into it, the only release I could find was in tears.

It was not yet dawn when I was woken by the sound of voices, low enough, yet some part of me had been straining to hear his return. I stole out of the room and down the stairs until I could hear them clearly. I stood with one hand on the stone, one hand cupping my ear to catch the echoes from some parlor below I could not see.

The first voice sounded like an elderly woman. "Please, your lordship, we would not come to you in the dark of night if it were not urgent."

And then a man's voice I did not know, a younger man, from the sound of it. "We saw your light burning. We have been looking for it every night."

"What you ask is not so simple," Sergetten said, and I could hear the exasperation in his voice. "I cannot just clap my hands and make the blight go away."

"But Sir," said the woman. "The boy upstairs, I've been feeding him as you asked. Surely—"

Sergetten interrupted her. "Do not make assumptions about him."

There was a short bark of laughter. "Your lordship, please," she said, but sharply this time. "What other purpose would you keep a naked boy like a pet for?"

"Grandmum!" the scandalized young man exclaimed.

"Well? The blight doubles in size every day, your lordship," she went on. "If you expect your boy, or yourself, to eat half so well as you have, it must be beaten back, and we do not have the hands to do it. In five or six more days, the entire crop could be lost."

"Thank you for informing me," Sergetten said, and I could hear resignation in his tone now, softer and more diplomatic. "I can make no promises. The boy is an untrained initiate and I will not endanger him."

"We wouldn't ask you to," the young man said. "Of course not."

"My travels have been wearying and if I am to undertake this task, I must rest," Sergetten said then. "I must ask you to go, now."

I hurried back up on my bare feet, and into bed again, under the thin blanket, wondering at all I had heard. Sergetten had used Night Magic to transport himself and me halfway across Trest. Could he really cure a crop of blight? How? And what would I have to do?

Spread your legs, surely, I told myself wryly, for my experiences thus far had always seemed to include such things. I was somewhat mortified to find myself growing erect at the thought. I did not desire Sergetten the way I had Kan, and my memory of him taking me for the binding was more one of painful intrusion than the loving penetrations I had suffered at the hands and cocks of the Night Riders, and yet here I was, quickening at the realization that inevitably, he would have me again.

Quite suddenly the lamps came ablaze, and a moment later he strode into the room, still in his riding trousers and a plain black shirt. "On your knees," he said, pointing to a spot on the worn rug that ran along the worktable.

If he was surprised to find me awake, or erect, he did not show it as I took my position on my knees, facing him, my palms on my thighs.

"Your education has ever been my task," he said, while rolling up his sleeves. "Unfortunately, we have little time for you to learn all you need to know. Do not make this harder than it already is."

I didn't know what to say to that, so I merely nodded.

"The magic that binds us gives me certain powers over you, though I may choose not to exercise them. For example, I can take your voice so that you may speak only to me and not others, or even not at all. Or nothing but the words, 'yes, Sir' or 'no, Sir.' You will note that I have not done this."

"Yes, Sir. I see that," I answered, just to prove it was true.

He folded his arms. "Now that we are properly bound, you

will no longer experience painful longing to be fucked every time I am aroused. That is, unless I wish you to." He ran his palm over the bulge of his cock and I could see it lengthening under the dark cloth. Then he pointed a finger at me and whispered a word in the old tongue.

I gasped as I was suddenly seized by that lustful ache, and I double over as if he had kicked me in the gut.

"The pain will stop if you show a proper obeisance to your master," he said.

"P-proper—?" I could barely get the word out. It felt like nothing short of his cock ramming into me would do.

"I am subtler and less of a wild beast than Kan," he said. He beckoned me to crawl to him. "Show me your obedience and your submission to what I am, and I will reward you by alleviating the pain. If you truly cannot divine an answer, of course, I could always just fuck you raw and leave you brimming with my milk, which would also answer for your condition. Prove to me you are a tameable beast, Jorin Weltskin."

He was some kind of a lord in this faraway fief, wasn't he? Did his supplicants kneel and kiss his ring? I was already on my knees.

I crawled to him, the pain already less as I did, and I took his fingers in mine, but it was not his ring I kissed, but the strap of leather around his wrist that matched the one around my neck. The moment my lips touched the leather, the ache subsided.

He tipped my chin upward with his fingers, searching my eyes. "Good," he said. "You inspire confidence that perhaps you can be tamed. Now, in addition to your voice, and your hunger to be fucked, I also control your release."

I felt my cheeks go hot as I recalled touching myself earlier.

"Yes," he said, as if he had read my mind, "I have already taken that from you. Every drop of your milk belongs to me, now. And if we are to accomplish all that we need to, we will need every drop, so you are not to waste any."

"Yes, Sir," I said, thinking on the conversation I had overheard. "Is my milk the key to curing the blight?"

It was the wrong thing to ask, apparently. He slapped me. "How dare you spy in your master's house!'"

"I wasn't spying, I just overheard—"

He slapped me again, and his teeth were gritted as he went on. "Another power your master holds. I know when you lie to me. And here is another. I control not only your ability to release, but your arousal itself." He snapped his fingers and my cock went limp, a cold sweat breaking out all over me as the fever of lust I had felt earlier left me completely.

"Hands and knees," he snapped, and I leaned forward so that I was on all fours. He retrieved something from the table, a tall and slender piece of earthenware with a wide mouth I had taken for a flower vase. He placed it on the rug under me so that my flaccid cock hung down into it, and then grabbed a fistful of my hair.

"You are correct that your milk is, indeed, one key to driving back the blight. You have also surmised by now that Night Magic always requires a certain amount of pain. But you, Weltskin, I know you can take more pain than the average boy, isn't that so? After all, you're a whipping boy of the royal household. Why, there might even be certain kinds of pain you barely mind at all."

I said nothing. After all, I had said too much already.

"I assure you, though, that his will not be one of those kinds," he said, voice low with menace. I wondered what he was going to do. Cut me? Burn me? But all I could do was wait to hear. "Do you recall I said that I control your release?" He shook my head a little as if to shake loose an answer from me.

"Yes," I said. "But I am not near to spilling now."

"No, you are not," he agreed. "You are not the slightest bit aroused. Which is why it will be a unique agony you suffer when I speak the word that will make you spill nonetheless."

"Oh." I swallowed. He seemed to be giving me time to either consider my plight, or perhaps build up dread. I would have bowed my head, but he held me fast. "I-I'm sorry," I said.

"You're not," he replied. "But you will be." And with that he spoke the word to force the milk from my sacks into the vessel. The painful force and searing agony in my cock was nearly matched by the scream that tore from my throat.

47: Kenet

Marksin could tell the moment he stepped into the tent that something had changed. I felt my own pulse pound in my ears as he sank to his knees with perfect grace in front of us. I felt like an unruly beast myself in comparison, but perhaps that was true. I was a barely broken-in yearling, while he was a prized war mount.

"Do you wish to see the rest of him?" the general asked me, as if I had not already seen all of him before. That was the thing, I suppose. Each time was a new time.

"Yes, Sir," I said.

"Go on and take his shirt," he urged in a low voice.

I circled around behind Marksin, who stayed perfectly still on his knees, and reached behind him to lift the garment over his head, baring his stomach first, and then the rest of his upper body, revealing him to the man who sat on the edge of the sleeping pallet.

The muscles of his bare shoulders and neck were beautiful to behold and I ran my lips along them, catching the scent worn by the camp whore he had just come from, pungent as incense.

"Tell me, Marks," Roichal said, as embraced him from behind, stroking his flat stomach and teasing the nubs of his nipples. "Did you please her well?"

"I did, Sir," he answered, and I could hear his answer vibrate through his chest as I had my cheek pressed against his back. "Two of them, in fact."

"Oh, indeed? Was there enough milk to go around?"

"Oh, yes, Sir," he said. "I ploughed them each in turn, and then they shared a drink from my fountain, tongues battling for every drop."

This image, I admit, made my own loins twitch. I imagined

myself and Jorin doing the licking, though. Or Marksin and Jorin licking me. Or me and Marksin licking the general...

"You'd best set his prick free, Page," Roichal said then. "I believe the field marshal's description has roused us all."

My hands worked at his uniform trousers, and he stood so that I could pull them down, helping him to step out of them before he knelt again. My own prick pressed against his back, while my hands reached around him to massage his sacks and ensure that his prick was as eager for us as it had been for the women.

Marksin moaned. "Did I do well, Sir?"

"Yes, field marshal, I would say you accomplished my orders beyond any reproach."

Marksin bowed his head. "I have found I enjoy having two bed partners," he said quietly, and Roichal chuckled in answer. Indeed.

"Page, do you remember what we talked about?"

"Yes, Sir."

"Let the field marshal come to me then, and I shall hold him for you." Roichal gestured to Marksin who hesitated a moment, then settled in the spot between Roichal's legs where I had sat before. Roichal urged him to press close, Marksin's back against his chest, and his legs spread wide, his cock stiff but so pendulous that it still hung downward.

"Lace your fingers behind your neck," Roichal said, then peered at me over Marksin's shoulder. "Pick up the flywhisk."

I took up the horsehair whisk, the braided leather handle warm in my hand. Marksin's eyes were wide for a moment, but then he shut them.

"I can feel him trembling," the general told me. "And you've yet to even let him feel it."

A ragged breath escaped Marksin at that.

"Quiet, now," Roichal murmured into his ear. "The next tent is not so very far away, you know."

I swung the whisk a few times, this way and that, then remembered that the general had let me feel its caress before its sting. I brushed it up and down Marksin's thighs, and the tremble increased enough that I could see it.

I began to whisk very lightly at his inner thighs, but kept catching the tip of his cock with it. Roichal then lifted his cock, holding it against Marksin's belly, leaving his plums hanging as a ripe target.

Roichal's other hand ended up over Marksin's mouth, holding him fast and silent, while the general egged me on with looks and sporadic words. And then quite suddenly the general moved from merely holding Marksin's cock to pumping it with his hand. "Page," he said, and needed say no more for me to drop to my knees and open my mouth, awaiting what milk might come.

"Come for me, now, Marks," the general said, into his ear. "Spill for Page, spill for me." And as commanded, the milk came forth, and I suckled the glistening head while the general pumped drop after drop. Marksin's hands had come loose and his arms hung at his sides, limp.

"Very good, Page." Roichal kissed Marksin on the neck in the same spot I had. "Now give as good as you got. I can see your prick would like some attention." He tapped on Marksin's lips and Marks opened his mouth without opening his eyes.

I fed him my cock slowly, and he made a muffled and hungry sound as he suckled.

I could not miss seeing the general's eyes, the look on his face, given that his chin rested upon Marksin's shoulder. "Sir?" I asked. "Would you... like a taste?"

"Aye, Page," he said. "Just a lick or two."

And so I withdrew my prick from Marksin's mouth, glistening with spittle, and pressed it between the general's lips. This time it was me who made the needy sound.

The general had a hand on my hip then, encouraging me to pump in and out, in and out, then pulling me out and nudging me back to Marksin's mouth. They shared me that way, five or ten pumps into one mouth, then into the other, then back again, and it was not long at all before I was on the edge off spilling once again.

"Sir?"

"I'm ready, Page," he said, holding tight to the man in his arms. "Push and push now, and I'll tell you when to spill down his throat."

I fucked Marksin's mouth then, with my hands in his hair, until Roichal gave the word, and then I had to bite my lip to keep from shouting as I came.

And I felt it this time, like a spasm in the air itself, as Roichal came, too. Marksin must've also, for his eyes flew open.

"Thunderclouds roll," he swore, then, sounding exhausted, but happy.

I encouraged the two of them to merely collapse on their sides, still pressed together like spoons, while I lay down alongside. I could not have told you which of the three of us was asleep first.

I awoke in the middle of the night—no, it was just pre-dawn, the hour that the camp first began to stir. And I could hear a whispered argument going on just outside the tent.

That's the thing about tents, isn't it? Nothing so solid as a door, and I could hear the whispers perfectly well, though no one down the hill could.

It was the one word, said with such urgency it bordered on fear, that woke me. "Sir!"

"You needn't worry, Marks."

"But Sir! This is no trivial matter!"

"Page has been entrusted to our care."

"By circumstance, not by royal decree! And even so! The penalty...! Striking the royal flesh is punishable by castration!"

At that Roichal chuckled, low and deep in his chest. "I would hardly call brushing his skin with a flywhisk 'striking' him."

"The crown may not see it that way!"

"Hush, Marks. Will you be the one to tell them?"

"Of course not! But the pr—"

"Hush, hush. Do you agree he is safer with us than anywhere else in Trest?"

"Yes."

"Then do not worry. He would no more betray me than you would."

"You seem so sure of that. Yet he is bound by night spells of some kind."

"That he is. Please, Marks, leave the worrying to me. It is none of your responsibility. Now please assure me that these concerns of yours are truly over the identity of our charge, and not that I have overstepped my bounds with you at last?"

There was silence for a moment, and I feared that perhaps we had been wrong and pushed Marksin too far, but the next thing I heard was the tent flap being pushed aside, and although I continued to feign sleep, I peered through slitted lashes just enough to see Marksin had knelt at Roichal's feet, his head bowed and accepting the stroking of the general's hand down the sleek blackness of his hair.

So, they knew I was the prince. I wondered how they knew, and for how long. But they did not know that I knew, and I was, as they said, safest playing the role of Roichal's page. Perhaps so long as I did not do anything but play my part, I would be able to stay as I was until I could find Jorin. There were still men arriving from the west; surely one of these battalions would be his.

48: *Jorin*

I dream of Kenet. I dream that I roll over in the night, and feel him there. I know it is him, by his scent, by the sound of his breath— so familiar it nearly makes my heart break like some half-remembered lullaby. My hand slides along his ribcage and he whimpers, pressing against me, nestling close in the crook of my arm.

I know what I will find when I slip my hand over his hip and then to his crotch. I will find him warm and moist, perhaps not fully hard yet. I hope I will find him half-flaccid so that the pleasure of him coming alive in my hand can be mine.

It is. I stroke him slowly, so slowly, that fresh whimpers issue from his throat as his hips jerk with impatience, nudging at my hand like a horse's head eager for a carrot.

"Shhh," I soothe. "Let us not rush."

"But..."

"Hush. Have I ever left you unsatisfied, my prince?"

He shakes his head and hides his face in the softness inside my upper arm, the lifts it once more, his breath mingling with mine as he speaks. "It's just been so long since you touched me this way."

I chuckle. "And have I lost my touch?"

"No! It's just..."

"Just what?"

He closes his eyes in shyness. "I am so very close already."

His cock feels like fine-polished wood enclosed with velvet as I tighten and loosen my grip, slowing the pace even more, then letting go completely, to cup his face with both hands and pull him to me for a kiss. His mouth is soft and yielding, his breath sweet.

My breath catches as his fingertips brush my own cock, which until that moment I had been able to ignore. Now, though, the throb of desire borders on painful. I feel a rush from groin to head as I realize the surest cure for this pain is to bury myself in him.

"Kenet," I breathe, kissing across his cheek, his ear. I know with all surety that what I am asking him is to take my pain for himself. I know now what it is to be breached by the urgent thrust of a lover, especially that first time. "May I?"

His fingers continue to tease, as does his voice, breathy with anticipation. "May you what?"

"Lie with you as a man does a maid. My thorn, your rose."

His laugh is shy and musical, like a frit's call in spring, but I can hear the note of fear in it.

"I must hear you say yes, my prince."

His answer startles me. "Never once were you asked whether you agreed to be beaten in my stead."

I shake my head, trying to find the words to explain. "You, or your father, never need ask, for what was I but yours to do with as you wished? You plucked me from the dirt for that purpose."

His fingers close around my cock with an urgent tug. "But you were never asked whether you considered that fair exchange."

"Tcha, don't be foolish, Kenet. I was yours as surely as your shoes. Do you ask their permission before you walk upon them?"

His stroking becomes more urgent still. "You understand, then."

"Understand what?"

His voice is a moist whisper in my ear. "Why you mustn't ask me for permission to prick me."

"Wh—"

"Because I am yours, Jorin. Yours as surely as anything is anyone's."

I cannot help myself. His hand has brought me to a fever pitch and I flatten him under me, crazed with need for him. But my mouth is still arguing. "But— but you are a prince. I am nothing. I own nothing."

"Nothing but me," he says, wrapping his legs around me. "Yours."

And there I am, still trying to slow everything down, trying to protect him from the pain, trying to protect him from the ravishing my own body wants to deliver to his. "Kenet. It will hurt like this," I try to explain.

But the word "yours" seems to echo in my ears, spilling again and again from his lips, an insistent spell that cannot be denied. His lips are sweeter than any fruit and I realize with a sudden bolt of heartbreak that this is only a dream. A moment later and my entire body is rudely awakened by a searing jolt of pain as a strap of leather catches me on the buttocks.

Sergetten pulls my head back by the hair. "You've slept long enough."

When I struggle to fight back tears, he must think himself so cruel to inspire them. Or perhaps he thinks me soft. I resolve to prove otherwise.

49: Kenet

The following day, Roichal was thrown as we were skirting the edges of the camp, along the eastern woodlands. I was riding beside him, the field marshal just ahead, and two regional commanders just behind, when something spooked the mare he was riding that day. She reared and then rolled. My own horse shied and bolted aside and I wondered if there had been a viper in the road, but by the time I turned the mare back toward him, the others were off their horses and helping him up. There was no sign of any snake that I could see. The mare was standing still and shivering, as if in fear, but also nuzzling at him as if in apology. The general spoke soothing words and remounted without much difficulty.

So, I thought, his leg is truly not bothering him. In fact, he had hardly mentioned it at all in several days. Marksin and I exchanged a glance and I wondered if he was thinking of sending the general back to the tent to rest, or to be examined. I shook my head slightly. He wouldn't take kindly to being babied and Marksin knew so.

We finished that day's rounds quickly, though, not seeing all the men, but collecting lists of their names from their commanders. The war had been going on for years, but the army had never gathered so many fighting men at once before. I made no pretense of taking the evening meal with the others, and retired to the tent with the lists as quickly as I could.

My heart leapt to see a "Jolan," wondering for a moment if that could be him, mispronounced? But no, the man was listed as having two brothers, and hailing from east of Maldevar; it could not be him. I went over the lists twice, then began looking through the older rosters.

I blinked suddenly as if blinded by lightning, as a thought seared me. What if...? Please, no. What if the reason his name did not appear was because he had already been killed?

I knelt and threw open the low, wooden chest that held some of the other records, an entirely different set of names, my heart pounding, even as another thought came to me—what if he dared not use his true name? Whether from the shame of his banishment from the castle, or fear of Seroi finding him and exacting revenge after I had fled? I might not find anything...

"Ho there, Page, are you in need of something?" Marksin stood in the tent entrance, one flap still lifted on the back of his arm, a lantern in his other hand. "I didn't mean to startle you."

I had been so deep in my thoughts that I hadn't even heard him approach, and now I must have looked every bit as guilty as I would have if he had caught me stealing cakes from the kitchen. (Jorin had received quite a beating the one time I had.) "I, um, just..." I shrugged and sat back on my heels with a sigh.

He came in and set the lantern down on the larger chest we used as a table, the one that had the wooden box inside it with the general's odd knickknacks. He regarded me, but in the end he said nothing, neither an accusation of spying nor a question about what I was doing, although I could almost see him yearning to ask it.

Instead he turned away and began to unfasten his jacket. He stripped out of it and everything else with a brusque efficiency that made me think, under it all, that perhaps he was angry with me.

He faced me again and I could see some kind of emotion clouded in his eyes, too well tamped down for me to discern what. I had not moved from where I was on the canvas floor.

"What are you waiting for?" he snapped. "The general will be here any moment."

Oh! I froze for another moment, as the realization sank in that Roichal had sent him here to await him. So that we could both await him!

I stripped out my things hurriedly, my heart racing. What if someone else came to the tent and found the two of us there, naked? The consequences could be dire... and yet I found myself only all the more thrilled, my blood surging. When I knelt beside him by the pallet, my prick stood up from my lap like a snake rearing to strike.

I could not help but look at Marksin's, lying quiet on the black mat of his curls like an obedient dog. I wondered which the general preferred, the rampant stallion barely held in check or the well trained pet?

Time went by and neither of us moved. I could not help but go over what Marksin had seen me doing, trying to come up with a plausible story I could tell him. Could I tell the partial truth... that one of my guards had gone into the army and I hoped to know of his fate? But wait, how could I tell them I had guards if I had decided not to speak of being prince? Bah.

I had come to no conclusion when the tent flap opened suddenly and the general stepped in, securing the flap behind him so that no one else could barge in. He had not even looked at us, so far as I could tell, and he acted as if he were alone, whistling to himself as he unbuckled his sword and hung it within reach of the pallet, then undoing his jacket and hanging that as well.

When he turned his attention to us, he was in breeches only, and I could see some silver hairs mixed with the darker ones in the well of his chest. He looked at us, standing a few feet away, and merely held out his hands, palms toward us, and cocked his head slightly.

I have no idea which of us moved first, Marksin or myself; perhaps we truly did move together. We crawled forward quickly, each kissing one of his palms and licking his fingers, salty and rough. His calluses rubbed over my cheek as I nuzzled at him. "Good boys," he said, as if to a pair of hunting dogs, moving to stroke us each on the hair. "Turn around. Shoulder to shoulder. Show me your tails."

We did as he bade us, and then I sucked in a breath as the light touch of one finger ghosted over the pucker of my hole. I think he did the same to Marksin. Then he reached under us both and his hands were taking hold of my prick and milksacks, not in a teasing way, but almost as if he were measuring their weight.

Then he let go and moved back from us, but neither Marksin nor I dared a look over-shoulder to see what he was doing.

Then the feather-light touch to my hole came again, and again, teasing and teasing.

Marksin was the first to let out a moan.

"How long has it been?" the general asked, from close behind. He must have been sitting or kneeling behind us.

"Sir?" Marksin asked, as if he hadn't understood the question.

The touch disappeared from my rear and he asked again. "How long, Marks, since you felt something... here?"

I heard the gasp as he did something to Marksin, but I dared not look.

"Yes, here," the general went on. And then I heard the sound of a cork coming out of a bottle, and smelled the scented oil.

Marksin groaned again, his arms shaking. He gave up trying to stay on all fours, and let his head sink to the canvas, not incidentally angling his arse upward.

I was looking without even realizing it, at him pressing one cheek to the ground while arching his back as the general did something that sounded quite wet. This prompted a higher pitched groan followed by another low one. Long strands of dark hair obscured part of his face.

"Defy me by failing to answer," the general said, his voice even more gentle in his threats than usual, "and I will have Page flog you until you cannot ride and then send you back to your tent alone and unsatisfied. Which will mean Page will go hungry, as well."

Marksin's gasp was closer to a sob this time. I think truly the threat to be sent away was more than sufficient to cow him. "I'm sorry, Sir, I don't mean to defy you. It's merely that it was long enough ago to be difficult to remember."

I stared openly over my shoulder, my self-imposed discipline forgotten, as Roichal's arm moved back and forth, fucking Marksin with his hand. There was no rebuke, so I kept watching, wondering how many fingers were in him.

"Surely," Roichal went on, "if it were such a rare event, you would recall it better. If you cannot recall how long ago it was, you can at least describe the circumstances to me."

Marksin colored deeply, as if choking for a moment. "Yes, Sir," he finally went on, a bit breathless. "It was at least four years ago, near the Pellon border. A... a tavern whore."

"Oh? And how, pray tell, did a tavern whore satisfy your needs? Surely just one finger was not enough for you?"

"No, Sir..." Marksin said, then grunted as he was pushed forward slightly. I surmised that Roichal had just added a second finger to the first. "Although she did begin that way, as she thought I had never... taken pleasure there before."

"But of course. What upstanding model of our citizenry would dare to?" He chuckled at his own sarcasm. "Continue."

"She said her mother was from Pellon and she had lived there for a time, so she knew things most of our women do not," he said. "She had a phallus made of steel. She said a swordsmith had made it as a joke for a Pellonese noble who had bragged too much about his prowess..."

"And men do tend to sometimes confuse their swords with their pricks. Go on."

"Yes, well. She... she bade me put it into her first, to warm it up and make it slick, and then... and then... ungh!" He grunted as the general added another finger, and then poured some oil from the bottle for good measure. I had half expected him to open his breeches and pull out his cock at last, but no, it was just his hand.

"Steel can be so unforgiving," Roichal said. "Could you really take pleasure from it, when what you crave pulses with lifeblood, hot and just yielding enough for your muscles to grip...?"

Marksin made a cry of dismay, muffled quickly by his arm.

"How long since you had a man's thorn?" Roichal asked, his voice soft yet merciless.

Marksin sobbed.

"How long, Marks?"

Neither of us could make out the answer the first time, but then he moved his arm aside and spoke it clearly. "Ten years, Sir."

Ten years! I thought of how it had been ten years since Roichal had come.

Ten years of war.

I shivered, wondering if Roichal would give in at last and grant Marksin what he so very clearly desired. Would I witness the moment, or should I excuse myself?

"Page," Roichal said, never taking his eyes off the place where his fingers were moving in and out of the field marshal, "Oil yourself." He held the bottle to me and I took it, breaking pose completely. "Your prick," he added, realizing that the command might have been unclear to me.

I did as he asked, my cock looking red and dark in the lantern light, but I could not help but ask a question of my own. "Sir? I... I've never done this before. That is, if what you're asking me to do is.... is fuck the field marshal."

He chuckled. "Yes, Page, I'm asking you to 'fuck the field marshal.'" He punctuated his sentence with a few extra hard thrusts of his hand. "He needs it so very much, don't you see?"

"Oh, Sir, I would never dream of denying him. Or you. I just... don't know if I can serve him well."

He grinned at me. "Oh, your part shall be easy and painless. After all, I have stretched him out fairly well, so your cock will not hurt him too much."

"Hurt him?" I blurted out the question before I could stop myself.

"If it has truly been as long as he says," the general went on a bit more soberly, "even with his adventure with the cold steel phallus, he will be nearly as tight as if he had never done this. The first time hurts the most, they say, but I am not so sure about that. I think when we are young perhaps our bodies have a certain natural elasticity that we lose as we age. A man tightens up more and more over the years if he does not keep in shape."

Marksin whimpered, which I took to mean he agreed with this assessment of himself.

"Not only that," Roichal said, as he patted Marksin's rump with his free hand, "but the field marshal here won't be able to relax in the slightest. Oh, the way would be easier, perhaps with no pain at all, if he could just relax. But he won't. Because of a few things. One, because it is hardly his nature to relax. Two, because I require that he not spill until you are able to catch it in your mouth. Three, because I wish to see the exquisite look of agony on his face when you breach him." With that, the general moved around to sit on the edge of the pallet, gesturing for me to take his place behind Marks. He leaned over and took a fistful of Marksin's hair, lifting him up onto all fours again. "Oh, and the fourth reason. Because he will be so disappointed if we go too easy on him, Page. This I know."

Marksin nodded.

"Look at me, Marks," Roichal whispered, cradling his chin. "Now, Page. As deep as you can go. *Now.*"

Marksin was silent, but I felt the tremor run through his entire body, even as the intense shock of being enveloped in squeezing heat ran through me. We held that pose, both quivering, for an eternal moment.

Then Roichal spoke, his eyes still locked with Marksin's, but the command was for me. "Deeper now."

I pulled on Marksin's hips, until my balls rested against him. My own cock throbbed inside him, twitching madly like a trapped thing, and I held my breath, knowing it would ruin all if I spilled now.

"Now pull out very slowly," Roichal said. "As slow as you can. All the way out."

I kept my hands on his hips as I eased myself backward, gasping as it felt like the grip of the tightest fist I had known slipping off the most sensitive part of my cock as we parted. I was a little amazed to see how his body closed up as if I had not just been in there. Marksin whimpered.

"Do you want more?" Roichal asked him.

"Yes, Sir, please."

"Then tell me what you want." He caught my eye for a moment and winked at me, as Marksin bowed his head for a moment. But Roichal would not let him get away with that, lifting his chin again. "Tell me."

"I want... I want you to fuck me, Sir," Marksin said, his chest shaking, and I realized that every word he spoke came forth with the force of a confession.

"And I am," Roichal said, gesturing me to press forward again. "Do you like my prick? It's a long one, isn't it? It stabs you deep."

"Yes, S——!" Marks did not finish what he was saying as my thrust went all the way in, making him suck in a sudden breath.

"Do it again like that, Page, a few more times. Let him catch his breath in between, and then give him the entire length to the hilt."

"Yes, Sir," I answered, watching again as that tiny, brown rose tightened anew. "Is each time like the first time if I do it this way?"

"He will get used to it eventually," Roichal said. "For those who like pain, it is one of the more sublime ones a man can experience. For those who do not, well, they are unlikely to seek out such pleasures as this. Do you know what the pepperroot is, Page?"

"I know it is quite spicy," I said, as I punctured my way back into the field marshal's body.

"In its raw form, when first dug up, it is about the size of my fist," he said. "Do you know what one of the punishments for desertion of one's post is in the military?"

"No, Sir." It was hard to pull slowly out. Now that my cock had accustomed itself to the task, the urge to thrust and thrust and thrust was building.

"We peel a pepperroot, and push it into the deserter, yes, right up his arse, and put his breeches on, and then put him on his horse with his hands tied to the saddle. One sharp crack of the whip and he's off on the ride of a lifetime."

I thrust in just then. "Does it kill them?"

"Oh goodness no. The horse always comes back, looking for food and his companions, but the dear soldier is, well, you know the burn of the pepperroot on your tongue? Now imagine that inside your guts. Not to mention the fact that it probably tore you a bit, as we insert it none too gently. And passing it back out again is the only way to alleviate the burning, which can go on for many days before the spice is exhausted."

"But... but does it always hurt?"

"Pepperroot?"

"Oh. No, I mean... this," I said, then corrected myself as he raised his eyebrow at me. "I mean fucking, Sir."

"No, Page, fucking does not always hurt. I daresay the next time I put your prick into Marks, he won't be quite so tight. Which is not to say he isn't gaining pleasure from this. You should see the trail of slime he is leaving, as if a great slug is hanging between his legs."

I shared a wicked grin with the general then and I reached around to feel the slime myself, running my hand up and down Marksin's hot prick. He shuddered and made a whining sound.

"That's enough of that, Page," Roichal said in another gentle voice. "Especially if you want that milk for yourself."

"Yes, Sir." He continued to direct me, how fast to thrust, how deep.

Eventually though he asked, "What do you think, Marks? Shall I spill in you or on you?"

"In me, Sir," Marksin answered without hesitation. "In me, and I shall lick your cock clean after, if you wish it."

Roichal laughed at that, but with joy, not scorn. "Oh, you are a dirty, dirty thing."

"Only because it is you," Marksin said, his tongue now as loose as his arsehole was becoming. "I would lick your boots clean, as well."

Roichal laughed again. "But then I would not want to do this," he said, pulling Marks up to him for a kiss. I shuffled forward, staying in him with some effort.

"Finish in him now, Page," Roichal said, between kisses. "I think if I hold him like this while you come, I may find release myself." Marks was up on his knees, his own crotch pressed close to the general's, and there was just enough space for me to keep my hips moving. Roichal pulled him tight, his tongue plundering and claiming Marksin's mouth.

I did as I was told, thrusting and thrusting without needing any more exhortation to finish what I had begun. When I spilled, the pleasure of moving in him only increased, slick and hot, and I slammed up into him more, the pleasure sparking all over me like rolling thunderclouds.

I slumped against Marksin's back, then slipped to the floor, utterly spent.

But not quite sated. I licked my lips as Marskin turned toward me then, his cock dripping with anticipation.

"Fuck his mouth until you spill," the general said simply, and Marksin leaped upon me, eager as ever to do his bidding.

50: Jorin

I awoke sore and stiff, my eyes still closed but my awareness of my skin, of my bruises, spreading through my body. Curiously enough, all Sergetten had done last night was beat me with a leather strap until I literally could not take another blow, and was on the verge of begging him for mercy even though I knew I would receive none. Just as I was ready to let the words spill forth, he stopped.

I did not know if the bond spell allowed him to see my thoughts or if it was mere luck.

He did not fuck me nor make me spill, and he had let me go back to sleep immediately.

But now I was awake, and I took stock of my aches. No, it hadn't been as brutal as Seroi or the king's last beating of me. And yet it had reduced me somehow.

"I know you're awake."

I rolled over carefully—hissing as welts were scraped by the rough blanket—until I could see him. He was seated on a stool at the table, his legs crossed, a sechal twig in his fingers which he chewed fastidiously. I wondered how long he had been sitting there, watching me.

I wondered if I should crawl from the bed to kneel at his feet.

He continued to regard me, but he did not seem to be expecting me to do anything. He stared at me, but seemed deep in thought, nibbling at the bark on the twig and sighing from time to time.

At last, he spoke. He uncrossed his legs and set the twig aside. "Do you wish to know what I did with the milk I forced from you?"

I pushed myself upright enough to get on my knees on the bed before answering, "Yes, Sir."

He stood, one eyebrow lifted in surprise. "I beat back the blight," he said crisply. "All of it. In one sweep."

I bowed my head. "That is good, Sir."

"I don't just mean in one orchard. I mean in this entire region." He stepped to the edge of the bed.

I didn't know what to say to that, so I said nothing.

"I want you to understand why I am making the decision I am," he went on, and reached toward me with his open hand.

I flinched away from him and he closed his eyes as if I were testing his patience. I forced myself to hold still and was rewarded by a gentle touch to my hair.

"Your milk is very potent," he said.

I could not keep silent. "And does that justify milking me in the most painful way possible?"

To my surprise, I did not earn a slap for that, nor even his ire. In fact, he agreed with me. "No," he said. "It does not. That is why I have decided to return the control of your release to you, at least, in some measure."

I looked up at him, caught off guard and uncomprehending. "Sir?"

"The evil Night mages of old drew great power from the helplessness of others," he said. "You have given yourself freely to me, and yet..." He shook his head. "I do not know that I can explain the nuance. Your milk was all the more potent for having been torn from you with pain, and yet, regardless of what good I might do with such power, it is not..." He shook his head. It wasn't often one saw Sergetten search for words and I wondered if that was because he thought me too stupid to understand the larger ones. "Suffice to say that I will only utilize the spell to force your milk from you should in either the direst of circumstances or if you earn the severest of punishments."

My head spun. "But... but I thought you said one of the lessons I must learn is that you can hurt me merely because you wish to."

"I believe you know that perfectly well, now."

"Um, yes," I agreed. But that hadn't been my point.

But now I was not sure what my point had been.

"What I mean when I say you now control your release in some measure is that I will no longer hold you in check with the bond magic, nor will I force you to spill when not aroused." His fingers brushed a bit of overlong hair from my eyes. "This is not completely a blessing for you, as I will still expect you to be obedient to me. In other words, you will still need my permission to spill, but you will not be magically prevented from doing so. Your own willpower will be the only thing that holds you back until I grant permission."

I nodded, but could not help but ask, "And what will the punishment be for spilling without permission?"

His fingers slid into my hair and he took a firm but not painful grip. "That will depend on the circumstance and on how disappointed I am. But your worst punishment will no doubt be knowing that whatever magical use I might have put your milk to is utterly wasted if you spill too soon."

"Oh." He was perhaps right. After all, a spanking or beating was something I knew how to shrug off. Guilt over ruined crops and the hunger of people? That I would not be so quick to ignore. "I shall do my best then."

He let out a huff of breath, Sergetten's idea of a laugh. Keeping one hand tight in my hair, he reached for my cock with the other, or so I thought. Instead he merely drew a line down my stomach with one finger. "Can you make your cock rise without my assistance?"

"You mean..." My hand twitched but I dared not reach for it. I knew too well the kind of traps Sergetten always laid in his lessons. "Untouched?"

He nodded and let go my hair, stepping back. "Stay on your knees. Hands behind your back."

I posed as he asked and then looked down at my prick. It was half-hard already, which made me wonder truly who was its master, me or Sergetten. Make it rise? I drew a deep breath, trying to think of something arousing.

But thoughts of Kenet quickly slipped from erotic ones to worry over where he might be and what peril he might be in.

I looked up at the sound of something heavy hitting the table. Sergetten had brought out an hourglass and set it running. "If your rod is not stiff by the time the sands wear down, you know that I shall punish you for disobeying me."

"Yes, Sir," I said.

"Perhaps I should make you choose what your punishment should be," he said, taking his seat on the stool again. "What would you deem fair?"

"I thought you said... well, that it would depend on how disappointed you are." I tried to imagine a hand stroking me, but that made me think of Seroi's invisible touch, and if anything my milksacks shriveled a bit. "Well... Given that you claim to expect almost nothing of me, as I am stupid and worthless, you cannot truly be very disappointed, can you? So the punishment should be mild."

Again that huff of a laugh. Apparently his fuse was slow to light today. "You are avoiding making an answer," he said. "And that, too, is a punishable offense." He leaned a piece of slate against the wall on the table and made a tally mark upon it. "So now I shall owe you, in any case. Perhaps it will help your answer if I outline for you some choices."

"Please," I said.

"There are many methods of punishment. Deprivation is one. It comes in many forms, such as the withholding of food or water, or even attention or affection. Similar but not quite the same is endurance, for example if I were to force you to sleep bound in an uncomfortable position, or to maintain a certain posture." He took up the sechal twig and stripped off a bit of bark, chewing it slowly as he talked. "Neither of those would require any effort on my part, unlike corporal punishment, with which you are already intimately familiar—striking, flogging, whipping, and so on. Another form that requires me to give some effort is, of course, sexual punishment, which could include anything from requiring you to perform sexual acts you would find distasteful, to fucking you with painful objects. Let us assume for now that those are the four main styles of punishment you should choose between, given that you are a novice at this."

I wondered what the other styles that weren't for novices were, then vowed I would never find out, because I would figure out how to please him before then... or would be bonded to Kenet by then. "Well, Sir, I would think deprivation wouldn't be the best, since maintaining my health is necessary for our—your—goals," I began.

He gave an approving nod. "Go on."

"And..." I hesitated for a moment, but his eyes darkened and I hastened on. "And if I had to guess, Sir, I would say that you derive more satisfaction yourself from the latter two, even though they require some effort on your part."

His grin was crooked. "Just so. Which leaves us with the familiar and the unfamiliar. You have had a rather strong first taste of sexual pain in the past few days. Would you choose it over being beaten?" he leaned forward slightly, hanging on my answer.

I found my eyes on my cock, which appeared to have gone to sleep. "In my estimation, the sexual element adds a level of severity."

He cocked his head. "Are you sure? For some slaves, the arousal and possibility of release makes it milder than the plain beating-for-beating's-sake."

I could only shake my head. "Perhaps it's merely my upbringing as a whipping boy," I said. "Beat me across the thighs with a switch, very well. But shove something into me first, and then switch me? Worse."

"Noted." He stood. "You still have not chosen."

"The punishment should match the crime," I said. "Switch me, then, for failing to answer quickly enough. And should my cock not respond? Then...? Then something more... intimate."

He pointed to the hourglass. I had not even noticed that the grains had long since run down. I bowed my head, waiting.

Sergetten tossed a pair of boots onto the bed next to me. "Put those on, and go cut your switches, then. For I have none handy, here. If you happen across any villagers in the woods, worry not. They are accustomed to bare-arsed boys haunting these grounds. They know not to lay a hand on you."

I returned a short while later, my legs scratched from the underbrush, with a handful of green switches. He was waiting in the same small room where I had been sleeping, though it looked to me as if he had done something with the jars and there was a slight smell of something burnt.

Sergetten directed me to bend over and grip the edge of the bed, leaving my back in a long, flat plane and my arse pointed toward him. The beating was not what I would have called severe, though the cutting blows left me with a few bloody welts.

But then came the "more intimate" portion. "Turn around," he said. "Sit on the edge of the bed. Spread your legs."

He looped a thin cord around the head of my cock, pulling it up to a stretched length, flaccid as it was, and then putting the other end of the cord in my teeth.

He stepped back and flexed the switch in his hand. "Close your eyes," he said. "And do not move."

I heard the switch cut the air half a moment before it struck me on the right milksack, and I let out a strangled cry through my clenched teeth. Another blow, the same as the first, but on the other side. Then four or five in quick succession, leaving me gasping around the cord. Fresh sweat broke out all over me.

But my ballocks were not the only thing to receive his attention. No. He proceeded to stripe my cock itself, all the way from the root to the head, with the thinnest of the switches, until I could not hold the cord any longer because I could not help but scream freely. But even that did not stop it, because, traitorous thing, it had stiffened and grown while being striped and now it stood up proudly to take its punishment.

When he stopped, I fell back limp on the bed, thinking it was over.

I was wrong. His hand closed around my sore but still straining prick. The bed creaked as he sat on the edge and milked me by tugging my loose foreskin up and down in his fist.

I thrashed in his grip, painful and pleasurable at the same time, my wits entirely scattered, and animal noises coming from my throat.

"I have not given you permission to spill," he warned, but he slowed his hand not at all.

I was near to exploding. "Sir..." I begged. "Sir, I cannot hold it back."

"But you must," he said. "I command that you do."

"But... but..." But there was no holding back. I screamed not in pain, but in helpless ecstasy, as milk shot in spurts up my stomach, one drop even hitting me in the cheek. I must have come with such force that I blacked out for a moment, for when I opened my eyes, he was already standing by the table, shaking his head at me. He then tossed a small jar and a flat wooden spoon to me. "Scrape up what you can, into that jar. I shall return for it later, and to collect on your next."

Next? Oh. He put another tally mark on the slate. For my coming without his permission.

I resisted the urge to fling the jar against the door after it closed behind him. Could I have actually held back without magical help? Or had this been just a different way to force me?

I had no answers, and a head full of questions. Like, where did humiliation fit in the scheme of punishment types?

Perhaps it was a given.

51: Kenet

Something was going to happen. Something soon, it seemed, given the number of strategy sessions Roichal held among his top commanders, and the duration of them. One night they continued far past sundown, and I fell asleep sitting on the floor of the tent, leaning against a chest.

When I woke, Marksin was pulling my boots off. We were in his tent. From here, closer to the main camp, I could hear men singing along while one played a drum and another bowed a string. I tried to sit up, but he just twisted the other boot off and tossed it aside, his firm hands on my ankle.

"He's given orders for me to feed you," he said quietly. "And then I shall remain here as your guard."

"Do you think that's necessary?" I asked. After all, who would bother me if no one knew I was in the field marshal's tent?

"It doesn't matter if it's necessary," he said, kneeling close. "Those are his orders. Would you contradict them?"

"No! No, of course I wouldn't..." I trailed off as he slid a hand into my hair. I could not meet his eyes.

"It's all right," he said. "I've lived a lifetime of discipline. You're still learning."

"I still—"

He cut me off with his words, as he unbuckled his sword belt. "How would you like it?"

His milk, he meant. "Er, um..." It felt distinctly odd not to have Roichal there directing us in what to do. It seemed neither of us quite knew who was in charge. "Well, it's best freshest from the source...?"

He laughed. "Of course. I meant, what position should we adopt."

I sat up then and moved from the cot, urging him to sit or lie down. "Please. Let me pleasure you as best I can."

He sat and opened his trousers but did not remove any of his uniform. We did not enjoy quite the same privacy here as we did in the general's own tent. I had forgotten that. I knelt between his spread knees and took his damp ballocks in the palm of my hand, easing them away from the bunched fabric, and then lowering my mouth to the pendulous cock that hung from them.

He tasted musky, of saddle and sweat, and the scent brought my own prick to quivering hard while I teased him with the tip of my tongue. I did not tease him for long, however, and quickly I was taking as much of his considerable length down my throat as I could manage. He whispered to me then, how fast, how much to squeeze his sacks, how hard to suck... the result of which was he spilled quickly and efficiently.

When I had swallowed all I could, though, he pulled me up into a deep kiss, his tongue searching after the taste of his own musk, it seemed. When he paused, we were both breathless. His lips moved against mine as he spoke. "Thank you, Page."

"Tcha. Thank you, for the gift of your milk, as always."

He shook his head slowly, his forehead against mine. "It always feels more like you doing a service to me than the other way around," he said. "May I—?"

He broke off, no doubt just remembering the thing I then voiced. "I cannot come without him."

"Of course," he said, pulling back. "I don't know what I was thinking."

I kissed him on the cheek to show I had no hard feelings, and then got to my feet. "You were thinking of me and my needs," I said. "That is admirable. But although at one time I think perhaps any man's command to spill would have released me, I suspect that now, Roichal's voice alone will do. And besides..." I shrugged, then, not quite sure how to express what I was thinking without it sounding like a rebuke to Marks.

But he finished the thought for me. "His orders were only to feed you, not give you release. Although I do not think he would begrudge it to you, I understand how loyal you feel, Page." He took off his jacket then, but adjusted his clothing so that he was covered up once again. "They may be at it all night. We should get some sleep if we can. Will you be able to?"

I sighed. My prick had gotten used to a nightly release and sat up straight like an expectant dog. I would have to ignore it. "I think so. You take the cot and I will lie alongside on the floor."

"No, you—" He stopped himself. "Well, all right. Except let us move so that the cot is between you and the flap."

We rearranged, and he placed his sword within his reach on one side of the cot, me on the other.

I found, though, that getting to sleep in my rampant state was somewhat difficult. Marksin, too, seemed restless. I asked him softly, "Marks?"

"Yes, Page?"

"Would you truly have fucked me? That night, I mean, the first night I was here? If I had not cried?"

He was silent a while and I wondered if he had drifted off, but then he spoke. "Word traveled to me quickly that you were there. A whoreslave sent from the castle? You had to be an escaped slave, I thought, who had just hidden in the wagon, but I had to see for myself."

"But how did you hear I was there? If no one suspects you of... of..."

"Hush. Most of the men know nothing of me, and then there are those who know of the exploits you have seen the general re-mind me to take part in, among the camp followers and the like. But you do realize by now, don't you, that the ranks are rife with the perverse who would openly condemn any man who admitted he lusted after other men or boys, yet who jump at the chance to ram their cocks into any hole of boy or man willing in secret?"

"I thought that was just something about me. Didn't the gen-eral say it might be magic?"

"It might be, Page, it might be, but there are those who have the urges, shall we say, and who only find outlet when something comes along like a spy to be punished. There is even a superstition among the ranks that spilling into a man will ensure they survive the next battle, while being the one to accept the milk ensures one's doom."

"Do you believe it?" I asked.

"Assuredly not," Marksin said. "In fact, I know it not to be true, but I can hardly tell the men that. At any rate, I have not answered your question. But yes, Page, had you not started to cry, I would have surely taken you."

"You would have been my first," I said then, rolling over so I could look at him.

He was looking down at me in the flickering lantern light. "So I gathered." Then he fell silent, studying me.

"I am not a whoreslave," I said, to which he nodded. "There is... there is someone I want for my first."

He nodded again, and I realized he must have thought I meant the general. I went on quickly. "Someone I've known for a long time, but we were separated. I had to flee danger and that was how I ended up here. He... I believe he is in the army."

Light dawned in Marksin's eyes. "That is why you have been sneaking looks at the names?"

I nodded. "But I owe so much to the general. For protecting me. I... I do not wish to betray the trust he has put in me. If... If I find the man I seek, I do not know what I shall do."

"Will you tell me his name?"

I shook my head and we both fell silent.

After a while, Marksin said, "So long as the search for your missing companion does not interefere with what duties you are assigned, you may continue. But if you find him, you must tell us before you act. Do you promise you will?"

"I promise I will tell you if I find him before I try to speak to him." I sighed as I felt the slight tingle that had to be the same magic that had bound me not to tell of Seroi.

We fell asleep soon after.

And I dreamed. I dreamed that Jorin was there, pulling me back against him, and then his hand reached down to stroke me. His cock was hot and insistent between my thighs, and I squeezed hard, trapping the length of him. You've gotten bigger, I tried to say, but the words wouldn't come. While we've been apart, your cock has grown.

His answer was to pump it back and forth in the tight clamp of my thighs, his breath warm in my ear. It was a dream, so I thought perhaps he could hear me even though I didn't speak aloud.

Oh, that feels good, I thought, hoping he could hear me. But I want you to spill inside me. As a man does a maid. I've been waiting so long for you, and it's been so hard sometimes.

But he did not make a move to push into me, just kept up his rhythmic rocking.

Then suddenly he was torn away and the sudden cold on my back woke me. I blinked, taking a moment to realize that I had been asleep and dreaming, and that Roichal had pulled Marksin off me by either the hair or the ear, I couldn't quite tell as I rolled over quickly and sat up, pulling my trousers up. Marksin must have rucked them down to my knees while we slept.

Roichal flung him down, perhaps too enraged to speak.

Marksin pressed his forehead to the canvas under us, his voice a hoarse whisper. "I'm sorry, Sir. I didn't realize. I was having a dream..."

"Tcha. You are the only one I trust and you cannot even trust yourself?" Roichal hissed back, but his demeanor was softening already. "Page, are you... hurt?"

"No, Sir," I said quickly. Then added, "And if by hurt you mean was I breached, no, Sir, it was between my legs only. And I too, was asleep."

Roichal shook his head. "We must protect you. Do you understand that?"

"Yes, Sir. I... I am quite willing to be protected in this matter." I exchanged a glance with Marksin, who then rehashed for the general the conversation that he and I had earlier.

To my surprise, Roichal chuckled. "That explains why you have been trying to push Marks to fulfil the role of bedwarmer for me, eh? You have nothing to fear from me in that regard, Page, no matter how seductive your arse's magic may be."

I found myself speaking even though I should have merely kissed his feet. "You are good men and I want you to be happy," I said, though I blushed as I did. "And I was not blind to how much care and regard you have each for the other."

Roichal chuckled again. "Well said. And this is a scroll which, once unrolled, cannot be put back into its case. Very well. But our more immediate problem is that both of you were trying to consummate an act which both of you wish to prevent. Page, you need to spill, too, and Marks, you have a debt to pay him. There's a simple enough solution to both conditions."

He seated himself on Marksin's cot before continuing. "Face down, arse up," he said to Marks. "And reach back and spread your cheeks so I can see you. Hm. You need grease…" Here he retrieved some and thrust two fingers into Marksin, laden with the thick, white stuff. Marksin grunted stoically.

Roichal wiped the excess onto my prick and then gestured. "Have at, my boy. And don't go easy. Your sweet prick isn't enough to harm him."

I was once again impressed by the field general's discipline. I did not go easy, and yet he made not a sound.

52: Jorin

If there was a lesson to be learned over the next few days of training under Sergetten, it was that my cock had a mind all its own. I could no more make it rise on command before him than I had been able to make it lie quiet the night the king had banished me. Sergetten snarled and snapped at me, as if he were more frustrated by my inability than I was myself.

He had me on all fours and was merely strapping me with full force across the buttocks when I thought to ask whether he truly expected me to be able to accomplish it, or whether it was merely a test—an excuse to lay into me. When his arm grew tired and I caught my breath, that is what I asked.

He threw down the strap and I saw it skitter across the wooden floor, coming to a stop just to the side of my hand. He reached under me, where he found, to my chagrin, that I had stiffened during the beating. "I need no excuse to stripe or flay you," he reminded me.

"That doesn't mean you would not use one, if you thought it instructional," I pointed out, then groaned as he tugged on my prick, ensuring its full engorgement.

"True. But yes, Jorin Weltskin, I expect you to master the ability to perform certain acts. One of them is readiness of this sort." He pulled me up onto my knees with a fist in my hair and slapped my cock.

I gritted my teeth, seeing stars. "If I could use my hand, it wouldn't be but a few—"

"Untouched," he growled. "If it were merely a matter of needing you to be hard, I could snap my own fingers and cause it to be, remember?"

"Then why—?"

"This is not a matter of your ability, Weltskin, but of your obedience."

I found I couldn't muster the words to refute that in that moment, and found myself struggling physically instead. His open hand slapped my face then, and I knew I should not fight, but I could not help myself, my own frustration boiling out of me as I pulled against his grip. He slapped me again, and then a third time, each blow heavier than the last, the third making me go still at last, with a kind of relief.

"You're crying."

Was I? I reached up to feel my wet cheek. "My apologies. I didn't mean to, Sir."

He swore softly, with a resigned air. In the brief struggle we had ended up half under the work table, my head in his lap. He loosened the hold on my hair. "I didn't strike you nearly hard enough for tears."

I tried to wipe at them hurriedly, but he trapped my hand, and reached up himself, tracing one wet track across my face.

"Tell me," he said.

I shook my head. "I've already said I was sorry."

"I don't want an apology. I want an explanation. Or at the very least a conjecture." His eyes were very black in the afternoon light that filtered through the narrow windows.

I took a breath. "Will you listen to what I say?"

"Are you under the impression I ask questions because I want something other than answers?"

"Well, actually, yes..." I flinched at the hardening of his eyes, but he did not strike, nor even move, so I went on. "It is easy to believe you merely want to torment me."

His voice was dangerous, a low growl. "You believe me that shallow."

"Er... well..."

"The truth, Weltskin. I promise you the punishment for lying will be far worse than that for telling me a truth I dislike."

"Sergetten," I said, trying to muster the right words, "I have no illusions about this. You have always despised me. You are cruel by nature and you enjoy hurting me. These things would be true were we bonded or not."

He said nothing to dispute this, which I took for agreement.

"You said I should learn that you can and will hurt me for no other reason than because I have no power to stop you," I went on. "I would say that is the first lesson I learned."

He shook his head slightly and looked for a moment as if he were going to say something. Instead, he ran his thumb over my cheek in a rough caress. Then, "It is the only lesson you've learned, it would seem," he said, "to the exclusion of all others. It was one I thought would take you much longer to accept."

"Why? You drove the point home clearly enough, and... and... and I'm a whipping boy to begin with. You think the king never took out his frustrations on me merely because he wished to? He never spoke of it so bluntly as you, but I did not doubt the reality of my station."

His tongue moved behind his teeth, as if he were tasting the veracity of what I said. "You never tried to escape taking Kenet's lashes? You never railed against it as unjust?"

I paused before answering, trying to make sure I spoke true. "I cannot think of a time when I did," I said. "After all, how could I allow anything like that to befall my prince? What loyal subject would not be honored to stand in his place and take his pain? Kenet is my protector, and I am his."

He pronounced my sentiments "Noble, if simplistic" with a nod. "Very well. I believe you. But you must believe something about me, as well. Something other than that my sole motive is to cause you pain."

"I believed Kan when he said you were my best hope of helping Kenet," I said, looking up into his eyes, which did not waver. "When he said only you could trammel the runaway spell the Night Riders had laid on me, and that you would stand with us against Seroi."

He was silent, searching my face, or maybe his own mind for an answer, for a long moment. "You still doubt I will stand against Seroi, though."

I nodded. To my surprise he ran a soothing hand through my hair and I was reminded that my cock had finally taken an interest in what was going on.

He seemed to come to some decision. "The situation with the Lord High Mage is quite delicate," he explained. "I have tried to stay as close to him as I could in order to root out his deepest plans. He thinks me loyal to him rather than the crown and I have done things in the court of Frangit that could, indeed, appear treacherous. But what I have done is train the Night Riders, not to bring down Korl and his line or to destroy Trest, though there are those among the Frangi who believe it so, but to purge the castle of the corrupt influence."

"Night Magic," I said.

"No," he said, eyes narrowed in frustration. "Night Magic is not inherently evil. But the way Seroi has used it most certainly is. If what you told Kan is true."

"You know I would not lie about Kenet."

He nodded this time. "You must understand, though, Jorin, that I will yet need to play the part of Seroi loyalist, for Kan and his band to succeed. There is no avoiding that. And I will need to swear you to silence on this matter, now that we have spoken of it."

"I—"

"Hush, have a little patience, please. There are correct ways to go about it." He let out a long breath. "You asked me once if I would swear my fealty in front of you, and I refused. I am... reconsidering my position on that topic. Do you know why?"

I shook my head.

"Guess," he said, with a hint of a smile. "At the least you will amuse me, at best, enlighten me as to your thought process, even if utterly wrong."

My mind raced. Why would Sergetten think differently now than he had the day he had bound me? He raised an eyebrow impatiently and I began to think aloud. "Since then... you have had more time to think about the things you learned from Kan?"

He shook his head. "My opinions on prior knowledge have not changed."

"All right, then, you learned something new. Like, you heard about something more that Seroi has done."

He shook his head again. "My opinions of the Lord High Mage and the situation in the castle have not changed."

"Well, then..." What had he learned since then? Perhaps my cock's impatient twitch led me to my next guess. "You've learned my milk is stronger than you expected. That your power from having me as a slave is increased!"

He did not deny this, but appeared to be waiting for me to continue.

"And... and so you... feel more confident that Seroi can be defeated?" I guessed.

"Tcha. You can be quick-witted at times, but thick as a stone others." He held me gently by the chin. "You. You have held up to every lashing and never shrunk from it or shirked your punishment. You have presented yourself as obediently as I could expect any man to... No, moreso, especially given our enmity. You appear to be truly trying to please me, Jorin Weltskin. Even when your mind and spirit are trying to rebel, and your tongue gets loose, you still earnestly present your body to me without fail."

As he spoke, I felt my pulse race and I was unsure why. My breath was short, but I moistened my lips and did not look away from his hawk-like gaze.

"You have earned my respect," he said finally. "I know you now far better than I did when we bonded. I feel confident, now, that I can allow you to earn a boon from me now and then. Do you still desire me to swear fealty?"

I answered as if he had presented me with a logic problem in an afternoon lesson with Kenet. "If I say no, and I find myself doubting you later, I will curse myself for a fool for not setting aside my doubts when I had the opportunity. If I say yes, though, am I failing to give you the loyalty a slave should?"

He chuckled. "Do not doubt yourself so much. To grant you this boon, I will demand a demonstration of your fealty to me. If you prove yourself, you will be rewarded. All will balance."

"Ah. All right. Then, yes, I am game to be tested."

He shifted then and bade me sit up. I settled onto my knees, my bare bottom on my feet, the welts from the strapping still quite hot and sore. He sat crosslegged facing me, close enough to touch, though we were not. My cock stood nearly upright and I did not dare look at it or touch it.

"You may recall we spoke of the types of punishment," he began. "Obviously, you have a high tolerance for the direct application of pain. Likewise, deprivation does not seem to have affected you unduly."

"Deprivation?" I burst out in surprise.

He clucked his tongue. "Had you not noticed that I have not fucked you since the bonding ritual?"

Oh. "I... I had, I just... I assumed there must be some Night Magic reason for it. Or maybe you were letting me recover after... after..."

His smile showed his amusement. "After you were the fucktoy of the Riders? Indeed, that is a high number of cocks to swallow in a short period of time. You are correct in that I am withholding myself from you for good reasons. But some slaves would have withered from the lack by now. Even were they, like you, not eager to couple with me."

"I never said I was... that is..." I closed my mouth before I could dig the hole any deeper.

"There is no need to lie to me, Jorin. You do not like me. You do not desire me for a lover. You do not lie awake dreaming of my cock. In fact, I am fairly sure you do not even remember what it looks like."

For some reason, his recitation of these facts only shamed me all the more. "I... I do not think I have ever seen it, Sir," I said. "The bonding was done in darkness and... and you have yet to spill into my mouth as well." Him remaining clothed each time he had beaten me or made me come had seemed a part of his power over me, as if my nakedness emphasized my vulnerability.

Or maybe there was another possibility that I had not thought of before then. "You do not like me, either," I said. "You do not want me for a lover. Else you would have done as Kan did, using me for pleasure and gratification, not just magic."

He shook his head at that. "You are wrong there, Jorin Weltskin. I would like very much to bury my prick in your body and leave you brimming with my milk. But I know we are not lovers and that our goals, magical and political, are more important than my personal pleasure."

"Ah."

"As I was saying. Deprivation and corporal punishment leave you laregly unmoved. You are sensitive to humilation, but perhaps so much so that it is counterproductive. I've little doubt that endurance will be met with the same earnest constitution that makes you near impervious to beaing beaten. That leaves us with what you yourself admitted is hardest for you, which is, admittedly, the sharpest of all the daggers Night Magic can bring to bear. Sexualized torture."

I merely swallowed, my heart hammering, waiting to hear what my fate would be.

"So I must devise a task for you that is difficult for you to accomplish or withstand, such that you will truly feel you have earned the boon I give." He leaned his chin on one hand, his dark hair falling over one eye, looking younger than I expected while he thought it over. "Perhaps it is high time I gave in. I have been emphasizing that we are a Night-bound master and slave, not bedmates. But I have already been surprised with how quickly you absorb the lessons I teach."

He got to his feet then. "Very well, a sexual challenge. Hm, how shall we make this difficult? Let's see." He walked around behind me. I felt him move close, and then wrap something around my wrists, cloth or leather by the feel of it, not rope. Whatever it was, it held my wrists together behind my back quite securely, though I could still move my fingers.

"Hm, and what else? Ah, I know." Now a cloth wrapped around my eyes, shutting out all light. "Now, stay still until I call you."

"Yes, Sir."

I heard him move away from me and the rustle of cloth. Was he getting undressed?

His voice came from across the small room. "I am on my back on your sleeping pallet," he said. "Your task is to take my cock up your arse, and milk it until I spill into you. You have one hour to accomplish this."

Oh. "Sir? Are you soft or hard?"

"Soft, Weltskin. I suggest you might want to do something about that. Your mouth, after all, is unencumbered."

And so it began.

53: Kenet

I gathered from the bits and pieces I heard that there was quite a bit of disagreement about how the military campaign was to be waged, and that this was the main reason we had not yet moved to attack. There were some towns refusing to send their men for fear of the Night Riders and the military leaders debated what to do about that. Then word came that a delegation from Pellon was at the castle and all planning ground to a halt. None of us could guess whether their ambassadors were there to sue for peace on Frangit's behalf, declare their alliance with us, or merely allow our army to pass through their lowlands to attack Frangit where the border was not mountainous.

Roichal and Marksin spent an hour after nightfall, after the news had come, drinking some of the whisky that had come from the castle on the same wagon as me. They were both a bit redfaced as they got ready for bed.

"Lightning strike me if we must sit here ten more days," Roichal swore as he sat heavily upon the pallet while Marksin and I, already naked and on our knees, pulled his boots free.

I could not help myself. "If not for the high cost to Trest's livestock and harvests," I said, "I would gladly spend another ten days like this."

Roichal chuckled, his voice slow and warm from the whisky. "Oh, would you? You are lucky that it is high summer and so parading about in nothing but your skin is comfortable. If we wage a winter campaign, or a mountain one, I doubt such an enticing sight as your two bare arses will greet me each night."

"We would if you wished it, Sir," I said as I rubbed his foot and worked my way up his leg. He had shed his own jacket and trousers, but was still swathed in the heavy breechclout he always wore. "Marks and I can come up with ways other than clothes to keep warm."

That even made Marksin snort with laughter.

He worked the right leg, me the left, even though Roichal had not complained of pain in some time. It was more a matter of the fact that we enjoyed touching him and serving him however we could, since he was adamant that when it came to intimate contact only certain things were allowed. He would touch us and kiss us, sometimes making us spill using his hands or on a rare occasion his mouth, sometimes penetrating Marksin with a finger or two, but never anything other than that. Never anything more than that.

He had no qualms about directing us to do what he would not, though. "Page," he said, then, "I would like to feel what it is like to be kissing the field general when you penetrate him."

"Indeed, Sir, with my finger, or my prick?"

"First one and then the other," Roichal replied smoothly, and the two of us shared a smile at the deeper shade of red Marksin had turned on being discussed in such a manner. The general wasted no time in pulling him into a kiss, Marksin on his knees between Roichal's. Roichal pulled him up until they were chest to chest, Marksin's bare cock against the wadded breechclout that must have hidden Roichal's own prick.

I could not allow myself to be distracted by the show they put on, however. I had my orders. I greased my fingers and slid them into Marksin, who made a gratifyingly high-pitched noise into Roichal's mouth. I fucked him with my fingers then for quite some time, trying to get him to make that sound again, but he didn't. Perhaps something bigger then, my own cock.

I greased myself up and positioned myself behind him, my hands against his hips.

"Marks's hole must be the same shape as your cock by now," Roichal joked, as he petted Marksin's hair and held him.

"I am not so sure about that, Sir," I said. "Even my fingers find him as tight as a fist."

"Very well, then, you may take it slow, but I want you to go as deep as you can on that first thrust, all the way in, if you can manage it."

"Yes, Sir, I am sure I can come close if not all the way."

"Good boy."

He never asked Marksin if he was ready, or anything like that, just pulled him back into a kiss, which Marksin joined with enthusiasm.

I pushed in to the hilt, not slowly at all, and the sound Marks made set all three of us to throbbing with desire. I could barely wait to pull back and thrust again, pushing into him with an urgency that had not been there until I'd breached him.

Each of my thrusts rubbed Marksin's own cock against cloth. I knew the general had come from pressing against us in the past—perhaps this was the most direct stimulation he'd allow himself?

While wrapped in such thoughts, I nearly missed the moment when Marksin began to struggle, trying to pull back from the kiss and Roichal not letting him, plundering deeply with his tongue. Marksin's cry was muffled and I realized as pulses rippled up and down my prick what must have happened.

Marksin had just spilled upon the general's belly and breechclout. The struggle had been him trying to speak, no doubt to ask permission. Now he wailed a bit as spurt after spurt shot from him.

"May I take what I can?" I asked the general.

"But of course," he answered. "I would not begrudge you your only meal of the day, Page."

I pulled out of Marksin, who moved to the other side of one of the general's legs and kept his head down as if in shame. I began licking all I could from the general's belly, working my way down his front.

Surely it was the whisky to blame for the fact that his usual defenses were down, I thought, as I sucked some from the breechclout itself. Or was his lack of resistance to what I was doing a sign that he would at last allow me to suckle from his prick directly?

Before he could stop me, I pulled the cloth down so my mouth could move down his skin, seeking it.

Roichal jerked then, realizing too late what I had done, and Marksin gave a cry of protest as the hand that had been sunk in his hair pulled free roughly in an attempt to cover what I had uncovered.

I, for my part, did not even quite realize what met my eyes, for one sees what one sees before one realizes what one does not see.

Roichal had no cock at all. No milksacks, either, nor even hair like Marksin's or mine. He sat up straight, pulling one futile moment at the cloth, and then sagging in defeat. "I knew... it was dangerous to let you get so close."

To which I blurted, "I would never speak your secret, s— ma'am!"

At which point, both of them burst out laughing. That was hardly the reaction I expected from such a shocking revelation, and it was only after Marksin mastered himself enough to speak that I gathered they were laughing at me.

"Oh, Page, can you truly be such an innocent? This is no maid's body you see before you."

"But—"

"Trust me, I know," Marks said, wiping mirthful tears from his eyes. He turned serious though, speaking to the general. "Sir, you were... you were not always like this."

Roichal shook his head. His eyes were soft. "No indeed, but I have been since that ambush that nearly took both our lives."

"But, but Sir, there is no scar," Marksin said, incredulous.

Roichal's voice was as quiet as a sword being drawn slowly from the scabbard. "The Mage who took my cock and balls did it with magic, not a blade," he said. But then he reached out and ruffled my hair. "You see, I told you your arse was safe with me."

Now that I realized the gravity of the situation, though, I found I could not joke. "A Night Mage... unmanned you? Just... just like that?"

"Well, there was a bit of fighting first, and he performed a complicated bit of spell. My memory of it is quite clouded," Roichal said. "I do remember him taunting me, though. He said he was going to fuck me with my own cock. Like he could add it to his own and then bugger me with it. He never got the chance, though. Some fool page tried to take his head off with a sword just then and that's all I do remember."

"Sir," Marksin said, but he couldn't say anything more, and after a long silence, Roichal pulled him into a one-armed hug. I moved aside and soon the two of them were holding each other quite tightly.

Marksin tried again, "I thought... It never occurred..."

"I know what you thought," Roichal said. "And I let you think it, thinking that I could never be what you wanted, what you needed, crippled as I am. Thinking that you would move on. That you would find someone else."

"There is no one else!" Marksin hissed, vehement.

Roichal chuckled and stroked his hair. "I appreciate the sentiment. However, you're mistaken. There is, in fact, someone else. Page?"

I had been trying to figure a way to withdraw. "Sir?"

"Come close and finish what you started. Don't think I do not see how eager your prick is to be inside him again. Hm. How many stripes do you think we should lay across his arsecheeks for spilling without my permission? Three? Five? Well, perhaps later. I want to feel you in him again."

I did as I was asked, and we resumed as before, only this time, without a stitch of cloth on any of the three of us.

54: Jorin

I have likely been remiss in relating what being beaten is like. There is quite a difference between being struck with a fist, as in a fight, and being strapped or whipped, as in the punishments I accepted, first as Kenet's ladra'an, then as Sergetten's bound slave.

There is no less violence in the whip, and indeed, far greater intensity of pain in the burn of leather across skin than in the mere crunch of knuckle or bone against flesh. A man is much more likely to scream upon a single touch of the strap than he would upon being kicked or punched.

I am not singular in this regard.

The punishment lash, though, does little damage when compared with a fighting blow. It raises a welt, perhaps draws blood, and it may leave a bruise, but the damage it does is largely to a man's pride rather than his flesh. That is, unless one's ability to withstand a beating is one's main source of pride.

As mine is.

This was why Sergetten could whip me until his arm was tired and yet leave me relatively unaffected.

I cannot say the same of sexual matters, though. Though Sergetten called me the fucktoy of the Night Riders, I am no whore. (Am I? I think back to the warmth of Pashal's hand around my prick as he held me steady to piss, and of him visiting my bed in the night. Of Kan finding me under the tinglebush, naked and seized with erotic dreams. Of me taunting the riders into taking action. Of desiring Kenet, and being ever ready to pleasure him, to bring him to peak after peak, night after night, in the secret confines of our bed...)

Perhaps, though, I could be said to have a sensual streak. If so, however, it did not feel like much help to me when I was faced with the task of mounting Sergetten with my eyes blindfolded and my hands bound behind my back.

I inched forward until my chest bumped the side of the sleeping pallet upon which I knew he lay. I got to my feet, and feeling with my toes, found the soft surface atop it and then climbed carefully over one of his legs, to settle between his knees.

He said nothing, made no sound but a pleased grunt as I brushed my lips against his inner thigh and kissed my way toward his prick.

His milksacks were damp and doughy, and I tugged them gently with my lips, feeling his shaft begin to fill. Oh yes, he liked that, and I took to licking the furred balls until another sound escaped him. I kept licking until I moved up the shaft itself, all the way to the leaking, salty tip. From there it was a simple matter of suction to pull the bulbous end into my mouth, and I was gratified to feel him quicken. I was the one who groaned as he came to full size in my mouth. I sucked and licked him, recalling that if he had wished it, I could be in an agony of need now, desperate to get him inside me. But he had kept his promises, so far, about not allowing the bond spell to rule my lusts that way.

I wondered if it might have been a blessing in disguise in this case, to want him that badly, rather than to be speeding clear-eyed toward an inexorable end in which I would take him into my body and milk him with my most intimate place, merely because that was the task set for me.

"There is a jar of unguent by my hip," he said, and I heard, or imagined, an edge of amusement in his voice. "When you have had enough of a taste of my flesh, you may wish to coat me with the stuff."

I nodded, flicking my tongue against the most sensitive spot I could find and making his hips jerk. I might have been smiling just a little as I twisted to get the jar of cock grease in my hands and opened it behind my back. I dug my fingers into it and then moved so that I was kneeling astride his chest, my hands behind me grasping that hot flesh, sliding up and down with the grease.

I then pushed my fingers into myself as best I could, which

was not very deep or very well, but at least I too, was greased. I rubbed the pucker of my hole against his shaft and gasped as unexpectedly intense pleasure sent sparks across my skin.

I hesitated, though, when I seated the spongy head against my hole. This would be a pain neither like a punch nor the cut of a lash. I had never received a spear wound, but after the way Kan had taken me that very first time, and how Gresh had shown me no mercy either, I could only imagine that it might feel similar.

No, actually, a spear is probably less painful, because its sharp point makes it easy to breach you. The blunt end of a cock, however, is something else entirely.

"Steady," he said, his voice soft. Almost kind. I wondered what his face looked like just then.

"I'm trying," I heard myself say.

"I know." I felt a caress down my chest, a finger circling one nipple but not not pinching it or pulling it directly. His next words were a goad, but a gentle one. "I thought you feared nothing, Weltskin."

"When did I claim that?"

"You certainly do not fear pain," he continued.

At that I bit my lip. "Not all pain... is the same," I said, pressing down and then slipping off target, despite my fingers trying to guide him in.

"Indeed," he agreed, giving one of my nipples a short pinch. "This will be a worthwhile pain, though, will it not?"

I reminded myself that by doing this I would earn his promise to protect Kenet.

"And it will not all be pain," he added, and I felt a hand tug at my cock. I grunted, as desire only tightened everything in me. "I am large, but I am confident you can accomodate me without injury. Your insides will not tear. Merely hurt."

"Yes, Sir," I said, but he was distracting me with steady strokes of my cock now and I might have said that to anything. In fact, I could not concentrate enough to finish what I was doing. "Please, Sir, leave my cock alone... for a few moments... if you would? I... I don't mean to presume to tell you what to do with me, I just... please. I will do as you ask now."

His only answer was to leave my cock alone.

Very well. Nothing left to wait for then. I pressed and pressed and pressed, and then quite suddenly my weight sank down and I screamed at the sudden burn of intrusion.

But like the lash, it was only sharp for a mere moment, and then the pain ebbed to something more bearable.

He gave me only a moment to adjust before he said, quite sharp, "Fuck me."

I moved slowly, but I moved, lifting myself up and then lowering myself down, taking him deeper each time, the pain now a kind of bearable ache that made me tremble all over. A pain that I controlled by my slowness, never becoming harsh again, but instead a steadier sensation...

I groaned, beginning to doubt it was pain at all. A fine sheen of sweat had broken out across my skin, and he blew on my nipples, making my entire torso quiver. I began to rock forward and back more quickly then, seeking more of that sensation.

I was quite unprepared for him to yank the blindfold away, unprepared for the brightness of the light and for the expression in his eyes, which was some kind of awe. Although as our eyes met, the spell did something—or Sergetten did—and so I may well be confused. In that instant I saw my own face, eyes round with surprise, cheeks utterly flushed with passion and lust, my lip aquiver with emotions I could not name.

"Spill, Weltskin," he whispered. "If you can."

He reached for my cock, but it was already twitching with expelled milk as he did so, shooting up his chest, one ambitious streak reaching his lips. He licked what landed there with relish and then pulled me down into a kiss, his cock snapping upwards into me, as he emptied his milksacks inside me.

His hands stroked my sweaty back and down my rump, and I realized he had released the binding on my wrists when I had gone limp against his chest.

We lay like that for a long time, my face buried in his hair where it was overlong on his neck and shoulder, our hearts and breathing gradually slowing.

I felt a twitch; he was still inside me. He whispered into my ear, the oath no less formal for the intimacy of the way the words were spoken: "Lightning strike me if I lie, but my heart, my spirit, and my body entire are forever dedicated to the royal line and the rule of Maldevar."

"Thank you," I whispered back.

"No thanks are necessary, sura'an," he said, kissing my temple. "You earned it well."

I had never heard the word he addressed me by before, and yet I knew in my heart what it meant. Not just "slave" but "my slave."

I was not sure how to feel about the fact that I had seemingly earned his affection, too. It felt good, though, that much I cannot lie about. It felt good to have him kiss me and hum with praise.

I eventually levered myself up and was surprised to find him still quite erect inside me, though I could feel the slippery issue of his milk as well.

"You look surprised," he said, a small smile on his face.

"I am accustomed to men going limp after they spill," I explained.

"I am no ordinary man," he said, settling his hands on my hips and thrusting upward into me. "Someday Kan, too, may learn enough Night Magic to keep stiff, but for now I am one of the few men within Trest's borders who can do this. Lie back."

He eased me onto my back, never coming free of my body, and then fucked me slow and gentle, both of us savoring every thrust. I had no desire to spill again myself, but his ability to remain erect apparently allowed him to come again, too. As he drew close to his release he could no longer maintain the languid, controlled rhythm and fell to a sudden, savage hammering.

I savored that, too. It felt good and right to accept his lust that way, and there was no pain at all, only explosions of sensuality across my skin and in my center.

He pulled free rather abruptly upon finishing, though, cock still dripping, and for a moment I wondered what I had done to displease him. Then I realized he had leapt from the low bed to answer an urgent knocking on the door. A voice was calling for him, claiming to have a message from the king himself.

55: Kenet

I was aiding the General with a revised tally in the afternoon when a young soldier in a wide-brimmed hat came seeking him. I was surprised to learn that he was only looking for Roichal because he was hoping to find me. He introduced himself as Van, and as he swept off the hat once he was inside the tent I recognized him by his brown curls as one of the boys Harman had rescued from a Night Mage's keep. One of the eldest, and it appeared they had made a soldier of him, now that his eyes were adjusting to the light.

Roichal exchanged a glance with me, as if to tell me he would be right outside if my virtue needed defending, but that he would leave us to speak in private.

Indeed, Van wanted to speak in nearly a whisper. "I want to ask your help. We know not who to turn to."

I held one of his hands as we sat upon a chest. "What do you need? I am no mage."

"Not that sort of help," he said, glancing back and forth. The flaps were up to let the air through, and I could see no shadows of anyone nearby. Roichal was whistling as he set to polishing his sword while sitting on the fallen tree outside. "I hope... I hope you can gain the sympathy of the General for us."

"But you assuredly have that—!"

"Hear me out. We are mostly from a village called Pallin and the area east of the Serde. The men of that area used to fight raids from Pellon a hundred years ago and we still have a militia."

A militia too weak to keep a Night Mage from preying upon children, I thought, but I said nothing, waiting to find out what his trouble was.

"The militia is refusing to answer the General's call," Van said.

"They are refusing to fight on behalf of the crown."

I was dumbstruck for a moment, then blurted, "Why?"

Van glanced from side to side again. The wind was starting to whip up and I wondered if we might have a summer storm, as we often did on a hot day such as this. "What we have heard is that they refuse fealty and tribute to a king that could not protect them from the attack of the mage."

"That makes no sense," I said. "For if what they want is a strong army, they must send fighting men. And was it not the army that rescued you from the mage in the first place? Was that not adequate protection?"

The boy shook his head. "We do not know why the mage left the keep undefended when he did, though we were glad of the rescue. The soldiers at first made out as if they had driven him off, but I now doubt that was the reason."

"But still—"

"The General means to send a troop of cavalry to put down the uprising before it spreads. Please, you must convince him otherwise! My own father and my eldest brother are there." Van's voice rose in vehemence, if not pitch.

"How do you know all this?" I asked.

"I am acting as Harman's own page now. I have heard him speaking with his seconds about it. They want his mounted scouts to accompany the action, as they know the area so well. The horsemen will move out tomorrow unless you can stop them."

I sighed. "Do your fathers and brothers know that you have been rescued? Wouldn't they prefer to join you here than to risk you becoming hostages of our own army?"

He blinked, brought up short by my question. "Hostages?"

Yes, I had been paying attention in at least some of Sergetten's lessons in statecraft and the mistakes of previous military campaigns in history. "I cannot believe that Roichal would prefer bloodshed over some other way of bringing the militia to heel. Do your people know you are here?"

Van bit his lip. "Harman said word would be sent to our families."

"And have you heard directly from them? Have you received any letters or messages?"

"Well, no." His eyes were not focused on me, but on some distant place in his mind. "Perhaps... perhaps they were never told."

"Or perhaps the word of the rebellion arrived here first." I could feel the tension rising in him, as if he were preparing to bolt like a rabbit. "Do not even think of running away," I warned. "You are safe here, and even if you are held as bargaining chips, you will not be mistreated. You have the sworn word of the General on that, remember?"

He looked at me with a pained expression. The wind blew one of the flaps loose and it became suddenly dimmer in the tent.

"Roichal does not break promises. You need not fear for yourselves. But if you truly wish to prevent a fight between the army men and yours, you will go to Roichal yourself now and offer to write a letter to your father, asking him and the rest of them to join us."

Van shook his head. "I cannot write."

"Then you shall dictate and I shall write," I said. I stood to call for the General just as a thunderclap deafened us. When my ears stopped ringing I could hear horses in a panic and men shouting, and a moment later the General burst in, just before another roll of thunder shook the air overhead.

"Get down the hill!" he cried. "Get down there, now!"

We ran with his arms at our backs, as if he could shield us from a bolt of lightning, down to Marksin's tent, which was the next closest. We were soaked to the skin from just the brief run down the hill, and as we reached the flap to go in, I looked back at the rise we had just come down. Was that why the tree had fallen? Lightning like a sudden claw raked the land, and I saw the tent collapse. A moment later, a dark funnel of wind began to twist from the sky toward the hilltop.

"Down!" Roichal flattened me and the other boy, while the thunder felt as if it shook the ground. Or perhaps that was horses stampeding, I do not know. Van was screaming in terror, nearby trees creaked and groaned, the rain fell so hard as to be louder than my own harsh breath, and thunder rolled and rolled. The packed soil beneath me was turning to mud and I found my fingers sinking into it. Sergetten had told stories of the fierce storms of the plains, but this was the first I'd experienced that was so sudden and so destructive.

But I did not scream like the boy beside me. Perhaps because I believed Roichal truly would shield us from harm. It was easier to lie still and let the thunder vibrate through me. Fighting it would only lead to pain. I held onto the land below me, as the wind threatened to uproot us. The land. My land. My kingdom someday.

In the flash of lightning that followed, though my eyes were closed, I could see the castle, a dark silhouette against the sky of Maldevar, the towers as sharp as the teeth of a wolf. Or the points on a crown.

And then the wind ceased, suddenly lifting, though a final sheet of rain slapped us before I raised my head.

Roichal got up cautiously, then helped Van to his feet. Marksin's tent was still standing, but many others were not. The sounds of distraught men and horses were loud, even as the raincloud, looking like a mountain, moved to the west, weakening.

There was no time then to speak to the General of Van's plight, as we were pressed into immediate service, helping the wounded, freeing men from collapsed tents, and so on.

It was nearly midnight before I collapsed, exhausted, onto the canvas floor of Marksin's tent. Marksin and Roichal came in not long after and Marksin lay down next to me, while the general sat upon the pallet. We were both still fully clothed, too tired to even remove our own muddy boots, but after a moment I nudged Marksin toward him. We each took hold of one of his boots and pulled them free.

"How bad is it, Sir?" I asked, as I set the boots aside.

"Bad, Page, very bad," Roichal said, lying back on the pallet. "Two hundred armored men on horse couldn't have done as much damage as that twister did."

"I am as tired as if I fought them myself, too," Marksin added, cushioning his head on his bent arm.

"Are the storms always like that?"

"I've seen some strong enough to tear the roof from a barn and throw a horse to the next village, but none that swept up quite so suddenly," he said.

Roichal nodded in agreement. "It was as if it came to attack us."

I took a deep breath. "Can Night Mages call upon the weather?"

The general looked at me as I settled crosslegged next to Marks. "I am not sure of all their powers, but it certainly seems possible. Why do you ask, Page?"

I closed my eyes for a moment, recalling perfectly the image that seemed burned into my eyelids, of the castle. "I think a Night Mage sent that storm. I think it was Seroi."

Now Roichal and Marksin exchanged a look. Marksin sat back up. "The Lord High Mage? Why do you think that?"

I could not explain the vision, though. I decided to take the conversation in another direction, the way my father would have done when he was not ready to explain something to a nobleman at his elbow. "Did you know that the boys in Harman's care are the sons and cousins of the Pallin militia who are refusing to report?"

Marksin looked surprised, more by the change of subject than by the news, I guessed, but Roichal nodded. "I learned so today."

"Then you know there is no reason to use force to bring them to cooperate," I said. "Bloodshed will only weaken us further."

Marksin frowned. "What are you proposing?"

"We have them as defacto hostages. Though perhaps it need not even go so far, if their families are unaware of their rescue and their militia fights on thinking the cause hopeless in the face of Night magic." I began to take off my still damp uniform. The night was becoming chill in the wake of the storm, but staying damp would only make it worse. "I can see no benefit at all to using force."

"Other than to send a message to other areas that might be thinking the same thing?" Marksin asked.

I shook my head. "By the time the word of the action spreads, the story may be further twisted," I said. "And if Seroi is spreading these rumors and stirring up this unrest himself, we only play into his hands by fighting amongst ourselves."

Marksin looked unsettled, but did not argue further. The general spoke next. "Well, perhaps, but perhaps the militiamen are actually in thrall of a mage themselves? Should we not send a force to the area then?"

"And end up ambushed as you were a decade ago?" I said, my voice rising. Indeed, perhaps it was the exhaustion, combined with the peak of my emotion that caused me to say what I said next. "I cannot let that happen."

Marksin looked back and forth between me and Roichal. Roichal merely gazed steadily at me, a quiet challenge.

I was down to only my trousers, but I got to my feet. "You do see the sense in what I am saying?" I essayed, giving him one last chance to capitulate.

His gaze never wavered, a hint of amusement at the corner of his mouth. "And if I do not?"

I had no choice. "You know who I am. Though I owe you for my safety and feel a compulsion of loyalty beyond measure to you, Sir, I am nonetheless, not to be denied."

Roichal chuckled. "I've never allowed your father to force a strategy I disagreed with upon me," he said. "I do not plan to start with his son."

I folded my arms. "But you don't disagree with me."

"Are you sure of that?"

"Yes." I moved closer, so that my shadow cast by the lantern was not across his face. "Am I wrong?"

"You are not wrong," he said with a laugh. "Very well, my prince. I would not choose bloodshed unless we were forced to defend ourselves. What would you have us do instead?"

I outlined for him the letters I thought the boys should write. When I was finished, he nodded thoughtfully. "A sound next step. But the letters will have to wait for daybreak, which will come far sooner than any of us might wish."

Marksin groaned tiredly. Roichal gave him a hard pat on the

shoulder. "Too tired to feed our royal guest?"

The field marshal lay his head on Roichal's knee. "Well, Sir, if the boy has the skill to rouse my prick, he is welcome to whatever he can suckle from it."

"Very well. No games tonight then, but Page, you should take some sustenance if you can." Roichal nudged Marksin toward me, then began to undress himself.

Marks gave me a small amount of help getting him out of his damp things and then lay flat while I wasted no time taking him into my mouth. Then I slurped on my own fingers for a moment, getting them wet enough to slide inside him while I worked. Despite his tiredness, he was soon firming up in my mouth, and I used all I knew of him to bring him to a peak quickly.

He was just beginning to twitch in my mouth, his skin breaking out in a sudden sweat so I knew he was close, when the sound of alarmed shouting reached us. I broke off, Marks and I both making hungry gasps, but there was no time to finish. I was still pulling my damp shirt back on when he raced out of the tent, the general right behind him.

Outside I could smell the smoke and ash in the air, then turned and saw the glow of the wildfire from behind the rise. Men and horses were screaming. Roichal and Marksin were having a brief argument, won by Marks when he said, "He isn't safe with me, no matter what you order!"

Roichal's answer was a growl, and then to pull me up onto a horse with him, and the next thing I knew, we were racing away from the growing glow in the sky, my arms around him and my cheek pressed against his sturdy, bowed back.

56: Jorin

Sergetten spoke to the royal messenger alone and returned to me in a foul temper.

"Eyes down. No, close them. Don't you dare look at me. Peek and I shall know, and your punishment shall be severe. On the floor. Hands and knees. Do not move. Don't even tremble."

I did as he asked, but I could not stop the sudden hammering of my heart. I tried to draw deep breaths, reassuring myself I had done nothing to draw this ire. I was burning with curiosity over what the messenger must have said, but either he would tell me when he wanted to, or he would not. This was certainly not the time to ask.

I heard him moving back and forth at the work table, opening and closing things, and ruffling the pages of a book. A sulfrous, burnt scent came to me as he set to doing something. Burning the message? Brewing something?

Don't look, I told myself, though my head had cocked a little at the smell. Don't look, don't look.

He clucked his tongue as if disappointed. "Head down. Forehead on the floor."

I bent and waited long moments, anticipating something more, whether a word or a blow I could not determine.

A word. "Reach back. Spread yourself. And then hold still."

I did as he asked, but I felt my face flood with heat, something akin to humiliation there, twisted with a thread of lust only made my cheeks burn hotter. He made a pleased sort of grunt, and that sent another wave of feeling through me, half humiliated and half gratified.

I stayed that way for a long time while he worked at whatever he was doing, but the burn of my emotions did not subside, and they flared two-fold again as I felt his attention return to me, as I heard the sound of his booted feet walking in a slow circle around me.

He came to a stop behind me and quite suddenly there was something cold and slick and smooth pressing against my hole, too large, too wide, too rigid... I cried out as he forced whatever it was inside, but the pain was momentary. For half a moment I thought he had withdrawn the object again, but then I felt its cold weight inside me.

His voice came to me from one side and I wished he would touch me, just lay a hand on me to steady me and let me know all was well. But he was circling again. "They must presume you dead," he said. "As far as the military knows, survivors of the attack that freed you were few, and many bodies were lost to the river. They know not, of course, that Kan and his men do not kill soldiers of Trest; they think you dead for certain. None would guess in a thousand-thousand years that you would be the boy serving me. However we cannot take the risk that you might be recognized. We will lighten your hair. You will wear a hood, you will not speak, and you will do whatever I say without hesitation, no matter how unpleasant or questionable the order may be. To do any less jeopardizes us both. Do you understand?"

I was surprised by the question, then realized that my answer was required in some ritual fashion. What had he put in me? "Yes, Sir," I said. "But if I will be wearing a hood, why lighten my hair?"

"I did not say it would be the hair on your head," he answered.

He bade me stand then, and bound my eyes with strips of cloth, and then led me to the low bed, and bound me hand and foot to the posts. He painted me then, brushing the hairs at my crotch and under my arms, and yes, on my head, with a vile-smelling concoction. And then he left me for some time.

I admit I dozed a little while he was gone. I was still tired from having been beaten and used earlier and I knew not how soon we would be leaving for the castle.

When he returned, it was with soap and water and cloths, but he did not set me free or let me see while he wiped and washed away the stuff, pouring scented water over me with no heed for the bedclothes.

Then he pushed one finger into me and I gasped. He probed around and I wondered if he could feel whatever it was he had put into me earlier. "We must make haste," he said, in a softer voice than I had heard since the messenger had come. "Eyes closed." And then there was one soft touch to my thigh.

I decided to grasp at it as if it were a kindness, though perhaps it was only incidental. Because what came next was as harsh as anything he had done to me before. He removed the bindings from my eyes and limbs, and fitted something close over my head. From the feel of it, the hood was akin to those they sometimes put on war horses, laced leather and shaped to cover my eyes, but leave my mouth free. So I could breathe? Or so he could hear me scream? Or so I had more than one accessible place to be fucked? Probably all three, I thought, as he pushed me up against the wall.

"Palms to the stone," he ordered, "legs spread. Back." He had me leaning foreward as if I were trying to push the wall down.

The next thing I felt was a searing pinch on one nipple. And then another to match on the other side. I was barely keeping in a cry when the pain intensified, and then was matched by another like it, but this one at my milksacks. Being bitten by rabid rodents couldn't have been more painful. I broke out in a sweat and fought to keep breathing. Another and another and another, and this time I heard the metallic sound like a buckle as he set whatever it was that was biting into my skin and then let it go.

The pain was sudden enough, and strange enough, and intense enough that I felt my hands starting to shake and I wondered how long I would be able to hold position—or if panic might come first. The word was out of my mouth before I even thought about it. "Please, oh please, no m—"

He seized me then from behind and my word was cut off by a cry that stuck in my throat as he forced his cock into me. One of his hands was around my throat, one around my waist, and there was no escape from the sudden intrusion. I bucked against him, unable to help myself, and everywhere one of the things was attached jolted simultaneously. And in the next moment he was plucking them off me, even as he drove into me and his other hand sought out my cock. My cock which was treacherously hard, or so I thought, until I realized how thankful I should be, as he spoke the word that made me come and made all my senses go white with intensity.

When I returned to awareness, it was on all fours on something soft. A bearskin? I hissed as Sergetten jerked free of me and then cried out as he plucked the last thing from my milksacks with a harrumph.

"Sky above, Sergetten! Cover that boy!"

All thought of pain left me as I recognized that voice, none other than Kenet's father, Korl, the king of Trest.

To my surprise, Sergetten laughed. "Don't pretend you're surprised. When you summoned me with such urgency, did you think I'd come overland? I have a faster horse than that." With that he slapped me lightly on the flank and I heard him get to his feet and adjust his own clothes. "My horse needs water, and if you want him covered you'll have to..."

"Here. Here."

I heard the sound of cloth rustling, as if the king had just shrugged off his own robe. Indeed, it was still warm from his body and familiarly scented as Sergetten laid it over my shoulders, and then pressed a goblet to my lips. I drank, and pulled the robe around me. It had the same flowery scent as the sheets Kenet and I had used to sleep on, and this more than anything proved to me that we were in Maldevar, in the castle.

I huddled against something large and wooden—a chest or armoire, I guessed—and then tried to pretend I wasn't there.

"Honestly, Sergetten, is it necessary for you to flout the perversions of your art? Even Seroi—"

"Spare me, Korl. Your messenger spent four days to reach me, and you did specify haste."

"But could you not have appeared in the mage's tower?"

"And potentially disturbed some workings of his with the energies of my spell? Don't be ridiculous. Besides, I would not normally expect to find you in your bedchamber at this time of day. Are you ill? Is this what required my return?"

"Don't bait me, Sergetten."

"As you wish."

I could hear Sergetten bowing low.

There was silence and then the sound of a resigned sigh as the king took a seat. "The plain truth is that I have not been well since shortly after Kenet's disappearance."

I heard the scrape of a chair, and then water or wine being poured. I presume Sergetten sat as well. "There has still been no sign of him?"

"None." In that one word, Korl sounded as miserable as I felt.

Sergetten swore under his breath. "We must delay military action until we have some idea as to his whereabouts."

"We cannot delay much longer."

"I will visit Roichal and his men tomorrow," Sergetten said. "If my horse is up to another ride."

I whimpered before I could stop myself.

The king slammed his cup down. "Is the cruelty necessary?"

"In point of fact, it is. The spell to carry us that far requires extremes of it. Fear not, Korl. I will not break the boy. He serves me willingly. And when he leaves my service he will be equipped to marry and father children if he wishes it. His fear and reluctance add potency to his submission, and thereby to the spell. Is this not something you grasp intrinsically in all power you wield?"

"Tcha. We have more pressing things to speak of than philosophy," Korl said, and then set to coughing. When the fit passed he took a drink and I heard his breathing laboring.

"Let me help you to bed," Sergetten said. "I will sit beside you and we can speak there."

"Very well."

There was rustling and movement, and when they spoke again, I could hear they were across the room. I could still hear their voices clearly enough, as the king began to tell Sergetten of the Pellonese diplomats and the spreading blight and the reports of potential rebellion. But all I could think of was that tomorrow

Sergetten would "ride" me again. His words to Korl were for me, I realized, his explanation of why he had treated me so harshly. But I knew, now, that it was a mixed blessing. For now that I knew this, would he not have to push me to further extremes to achieve the same effect? I dreaded what tortures and humiliations tomorrow would bring.

And Kenet, where was Kenet? I hoped that wherever he was, he was safe from the pain and fear that were my lot.

Can our heroes reunite to defeat evil?
The Prince's Boy is
Concluded in Volume Two!

About the Author

Cecilia Tan is "simply one of the most important writers, editors, and innovators in contemporary American erotic literature," according to Susie Bright. She is the author of many novels and short stories, editor of dozens of erotic short story anthologies, and the founder of Circlet Press. She was inducted into the Saints and Sinners Hall of Fame for GLBT writers in 2010 and has won the RT Reviewers Choice Award, the Romantic Times Pioneer Award, and Career Achievement Award in Erotica.

Also by Cecilia Tan:
Black Feathers
Daron's Guitar Chronicles
Edge Plays
Mind Games
Royal Treatment
Slow Surrender
Slow Seduction
Slow Satisfaction
Taking the Lead
Telepaths Don't Need Safewords
The Hot Streak
The Incubus and the Angel
The Siren and the Sword
The Tower and the Tears
The Velderet
White Flames

More Gay SF/Fantasy and Erotic Romance

Faewolf by D.M. Atkins and Chris Taylor
Faewolves, like werewolves, can walk among men. What happens when Kiya White Cloud, a young gay college student in Santa Cruz, wants one of these men enough to risk his heart—and his life? An m/m erotic romance from Circlet Press, Inc. [Warning: explicit sex, dubious consent, and rough scenes.]

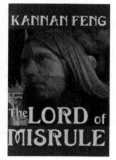

The Lord of Misrule by Kannan Feng
Verity Fen is the most promising young sorcerer to attend the Atia Selene university in generations. Wealthy, privileged, attractive, he seduces his fellow students and breaks their hearts. Until he falls for his own servant, Iskander, whose leather belt is a match for Verity's attitude.

Mate by Lauren P. Burka
Three short stories of erotic science fiction with a BDSM edge. Terry Montiero and d'Schane Grey are techies whose relationship is fueled by their chess game--a power game. Originally published in 1992 as a chapbook, the stories have been unavailable for years until this eBook revival.

Wired Hard 4 anthology, $6.99 ebook
The fourth volume of gay male sexuality and erotica, viewed through the lens of erotic science fiction and fantasy. Masculine tales of kings and castles, futuristic rentboys, phallic magic, and sexual technology. Includes Tom Cardamone, Jamie Maguire, Kal Cobalt, Zachary Jernigan, Gavin Atlas, Helen E. H. Madden, and more. Eight stories in all.

 www.circlet.com

Made in the USA
Charleston, SC
01 May 2016